Friedrich Schiller, Edgar Alfred Bowring

The Poems Of Schiller

Friedrich Schiller, Edgar Alfred Bowring

The Poems Of Schiller

ISBN/EAN: 9783741134234

Manufactured in Europe, USA, Canada, Australia, Japa

Cover: Foto ©Andreas Hilbeck / pixelio.de

Manufactured and distributed by brebook publishing software (www.brebook.com)

Friedrich Schiller, Edgar Alfred Bowring

The Poems Of Schiller

THE
POEMS OF SCHILLER.

TRANSLATED BY

EDGAR A. BOWRING, C.B., M.P.

SECOND EDITION, REVISED.

LONDON: GEORGE BELL AND SONS,
YORK STREET, COVENT GARDEN.
1874.

LONDON:

PRINTED BY WILLIAM CLOWES AND SONS,

STAMFORD STREET AND CHARING CROSS.

ORIGINAL PREFACE.

In venturing to submit to the public this attempt to render into English the poetical works of the great German lyric bard, the Translator feels it necessary to say one or two words respecting the motives which have induced him to undertake the somewhat daring task of appearing in a field that has been already partially occupied by others.

These translations were originally made by the Translator for his own amusement; but as he proceeded in what has been to him a labour of love, he was induced gradually to extend his original idea of making a mere selection, until he at length found himself drawn on to attempt the whole—and accordingly the following pages will be found to contain a version of *every piece, without exception*, that is contained in the authorized editions of Schiller's *Poems* (including the fine dramatic sketch of *Semele*, which is now given amongst his other poems)—and even all the minor pieces, which it has been usual to omit, as being without interest to the English reader. But the Translator has thought that, in order fully to appreciate the poetic genius of Schiller, his poems should be viewed as a *whole*.

With the same object, the metre of the original has

been adhered to as closely as possible, and in only a few unimportant instances has this rule been departed from. With regard to the Elegiacs in particular, in which metre some of the finest productions of Schiller are written (as, for instance, *The Walk*), the Translator has preserved the hexameter and pentameter of the German, not only because they admit of a more faithful rendering of the original, but also because he conceives that a metre which has been employed with such singular success by the German poet, cannot be entirely unsuited to a language so closely allied in origin and construction to the German as our own. He believes, moreover, that there is a growing taste in this country for the classical metres, which, it cannot be denied, have until very recently been far from popular. It is with respect to this class of poems, and also to several of Schiller's earlier pieces, the meaning of which is often mystical, and the metre very peculiar, that he especially hopes for the indulgence of the reader.

With regard to the translation itself, the Translator has invariably kept in view the necessity of preserving the strictest fidelity to the original, his desire having been to render Schiller's *Poems* into English, but nothing more. He feels that it would have been both absurd and presumptuous in him to have attempted to make any alterations in the productions of the great bard. Whatever may be the language into which Schiller is translated, whatever may be the nation where he is read, he has a giant-voice of his own, wherewith to make himself heard and understood.

The addition of an appendix, containing translations of all the various minor poems, &c., found in Schiller's dramatic works, completes the list of his recognised pieces.

It will now be necessary to say a few words respecting the *Suppressed Poems*, which are given in this collection.

Shortly after the publication of Schiller's celebrated *Robbers*, appeared a work entitled *Anthology for the Year* 1782, containing a collection of poems, evidently the work of several hands. It soon became known that it was edited by Schiller, and that he was the author of most of the pieces. This was subsequently fully proved, when he published the complete collection of his works, where the whole of the *Poems of the First Period*, together with two or three of the *Second*, are taken from the *Anthology*. But it was also known that, for various reasons, he had suppressed a large proportion of the pieces there published, and indisputably written by him.

The *Anthology* has for a long time been a literary rarity, known only to a few connoisseurs; and is probably entirely unknown to the English reader. It has been reprinted in Germany very recently, and advantage has been taken of its republication to introduce translations of the whole of the poems in it which critics have pronounced to be Schiller's and which are, notwithstanding, excluded from the collected editions of his poems. The original wild and fantastic dedication and preface are also added.

The total number of poems comprised in the *Anthology* is ninety, of which thirty are given elsewhere, under either the *First* or the *Second Period* of the recognised poems. Of the others, thirty-two are universally pronounced not to be Schiller's, and they certainly contain sufficient internal evidence of this fact, as nothing can be more vapid and talentless than they are. The following friends of the poet are believed to have been amongst their contributors—Petersen, Pfeiffer, Zuccato, Von Hoven, Haug, and Scharffenstein.

The remaining twenty-eight pieces, comprising nearly twelve hundred verses, are assigned by the almost unanimous voice of the commentators, Hoffmeister, Boas, Döring, Schwab, and Bülow to Schiller, and there are very few concerning which there is any question. They are accordingly all given here. As respects the thirty admitted into the collected poems, the later versions, as given by Schiller himself, have been invariably adhered to, rather than those found in the *Anthology*, whenever any difference exists between them.

Many of these early pieces are either inscribed to, or relate to, the Laura whose image first enslaved his mind, and whose influence over him, as evinced by many of his most impassioned poems, appears to have been unbounded.* The suppressed *Reproach—To Laura*, and the ode *To the Fates*, here given, may be added to the long list found in the *Poems of the First Period*.

Six pieces among the *Suppressed Poems*, of a humorous character, viz. *The Journalists and Minos, Bacchus in the Pillory, the Muses' Revenge, the Parallel, the Hypochondriacal Pluto*, and *the Satyr and my Muse*, combined with the *Wallenstein's Camp*, and the well-known *Celebrated Woman*, admitted into the published editions, go far to refute the opinion expressed by the most eminent of living critics, that Schiller was totally deficient in

---

* A case, presenting some curious points of resemblance to that of Schiller and his Laura, is recorded of himself by the greatest of modern Italian poets, Alfieri, in his *Autobiography.*

humour. It is certain, however, that he did not wield this power in the manner that he might have done, and the only poem of his mature years where we find any traces of it is his *Pegasus in Harness*.

The sublimity of the *Hymn to the Eternal*, and the terrific power of the sketch of the *Plague*, stand in strong contrast to the gentle but deep poetic feeling that breathes in every line of the poem entitled *Thoughts on the 1st October*, 1781, and to the pleasing mixture of repose and playfulness in *The Winter Night;* and the bitterness apparent throughout *The Bad Monarchs* is no bad evidence of the natural strength of Schiller's passions, before he obtained that complete control over them which his later works evince.

The Epigrams, &c. are, for the most part, quite insignificant, and only worth preserving as having been written by Schiller.

The poems in this volume are arranged in the precise order of the latest authorized German editions, both for convenience of reference, and because it does not appear that anything would be gained by a deviation from that arrangement.

The Translator is glad to avail himself of this opportunity to express his thanks to Lord Hobart and another friend,* for the many valuable suggestions with which they have favoured him during the progress of this work through the press.

London, April, 1851.

---

* The late Mr. Albany Fonblanque.

PREFACE TO THE SECOND EDITION.

In this Edition the Translator has corrected various minor mistakes and inaccuracies which had crept into the Original Edition, published by him upwards of twenty years ago; but substantially it differs but little from it. His excuse for its many imperfections is only to be found in his youth and inexperience at the time when he made the translations. He has, unfortunately for himself, now surmounted the first of these faults, whilst his kind readers will benefit but little from the cure of the second.

London, November, 1873.

TRANSLATOR'S APOLOGY TO THE READER.

In days of old, while Grecian bards yet sang,
  And, at Olympia vying, swept the chord,
Throughout the world the victor's praises rang,
  And great, exceeding great, was his reward.
The story of his prowess echoing sprang
  From land to land, and e'en to heaven upsoar'd;
And when his ashes slumber'd in the tomb,
His memory long surviv'd in pristine bloom.

And is it not so still?—yes! SCHILLER, thou
  Hast earn'd a glorious, an immortal name;
The universal voice hath wreath'd thy brow
  With laurels fair, in token of thy fame;
The poet's mantle bright thou wearest now
  Upon thy shoulders placed with one acclaim—
Thy native country holds thy memory dear,
It still hath bloom'd through many a changing year.

Yet thou hast liv'd not for *one* land alone,
  For the whole world are surely meant thy lays.
He, then, who seeks to make thy numbers known
  To those whose hearts their spell may upwards
    raise,

If in the language cloth'd, they call their own,—
    He who to others' ears perchance conveys
E'en a faint echo of thy minstrelsy,
He who dares *this*, may haply pardon'd be.

If, then, these feeble numbers have but power
    E'en on one bosom pleasure to bestow,
If they can help to cheer one heavy hour,
    Soothe e'en one sorrow, lighten e'en one woe,—
If to life's garland they can add one flower,
    Although unseen, forgotten, it may blow—
Then will the prize I covet be obtain'd,
I ask no more,—my utmost wish is gain'd.

CONTENTS.

Poems of the Third Period.

Suppressed Poems.

Appendix.

POEMS OF THE FIRST PERIOD.

HECTOR'S FAREWELL.

ANDROMACHE.

Art thou, Hector, hence for ever going
Where Achilles, with fierce vengeance glowing,
　To Patroclus piles a hecatomb?
Who, alas! will teach thine Infant truly
Spears to hurl, the Gods to honour duly,
　When thou'rt buried in dark Orcus' womb?

HECTOR.

Dearest wife, restrain thy tearful sadness!
For the fray my bosom pants with madness,
　This stout arm must Pergamus defend;
For my household Gods all dangers braving,
Should I fall, my Fatherland in saving,
　To the Stygian flood I'll glad descend.

ANDROMACHE.

For thy clashing arms I vain shall listen,
In thy halls thy glaive will idly glisten,
　Priam's hero-race in dust will lie;
Thou wilt go, where day can enter never,
Where Cocytus wails 'mid deserts ever,
　And thy Love in Lethe's stream will die.

HECTOR.

Though the ardent hopes, the thoughts I cherish,
All in Lethe's silent stream may perish,
　Yet my Love shall never die!
Hark! I hear the foe the walls assailing!
Gird my sword around me,—cease thy wailing!
　Hector's Love in Lethe cannot die! *

* In the original, the same word is repeated, as it is here, instead
of a rhyme being employed.

AMALIA.

Angel-fair, Walhalla's charms displaying,
  Fairer than all mortal youths was he;
Mild his look, as May-day sunbeams straying
  Gently o'er the blue and glassy sea.

And his kisses!—what ecstatic feeling!
  Like two flames that lovingly entwine,
Like the harp's soft tones together stealing
  Into one sweet harmony divine,—

Soul and soul embraced, commingled, blended,
  Lips and cheeks with trembling passion burn'd!
Heav'n and Earth, in pristine chaos ended,
  Round the blissful Lovers madly turn'd.

He is gone—and, ah! with bitter anguish
  Vainly now I breathe my mournful sighs;
He is gone—in hopeless grief I languish,
  Earthly joys I ne'er again can prize!

A FUNERAL PHANTASY.

Lo! on high the moon, her lustre dead,
O'er the death-like grove uplifts her head,
  Sighing flits the spectre through the gloom—
    Misty clouds are shivering,
    Pallid stars are quivering,
  Looking down, like lamps within a tomb.
Spirit-like, all silent, pale, and wan,
  Marshall'd in procession dark and sad,
To the sepulchre a crowd moves on,
  In the grave-night's dismal emblems clad.

Who is he, who, trembling on his crutch,
  Walks with gloomy and averted eye,
And bow'd down by Destiny's harsh touch,
    Vents his sorrow in a mournful sigh
    O'er the coffin borne in silence by ?
Was it " Father ! " from the youth's lips came ?
  Soon a damp and fearful shudder flies
Through his grief-emaciated frame,
  And his silv'ry hairs on end uprise.

All his fiery wounds now bleed anew !
  Through his soul, hell's bitter torments run !
" Father ! " 'twas that from the youth's lips flew,
  And the Father's heart hath whisper'd, " Son ! "
Ice-cold, ice-cold, in his shroud he lies,—
    By thy dream, so sweet and golden erst,
    Sweet and golden, Father, thou art curst !
Ice-cold, ice-cold, in his shroud he lies,
Who was once thy joy, thy Paradise !

Mild, as when, fann'd by Elysian gale,
  Flora's son over the verdant plain skips,
Girded with roses that fragrance exhale,
  When from the arms of Aurora he slips,—
Onward he sped o'er the sweet-smelling field,
  Mirror'd below in the silvery flood ;
Rapturous flames in his kiss were conceal'd,
  Chasing the maidens in amorous mood.

Boldly he sprang 'mid the stir of mankind,
  As o'er the mountains a youthful roe springs ;
Heav'nward ascended his wish unconfin'd,
  High as the eagle his daring flight wings.
Proud as the steeds that in passion their manes,
  Foaming and champing, toss round in wild waves,
Rearing in majesty under the reins,
  Stood he alike before monarchs and slaves.

Bright as a spring-day, his life's joyous round
  Fleeted in Hesperus' glory away;
Sighs in the grape's juice all-golden he drown'd,
  Sorrow he still'd in the dance light and gay.
Worlds were asleep in the promising boy,
  Ha! when he once as a man shall be ripe,—
Father, rejoice—in thy promising boy,
  Soon as the slumbering germ shall be ripe!

Not so, Father—hark! the churchyard gates
  Groan, and lo, the iron hinges creak!—
See the dreaded tomb its prey awaits!—
  Not so—let the tears course down thy cheek!
Tow'rd Perfection, lov'd one, hasten on,
  In the sun's bright path with joy proceed!
Quench thy noble thirst for bliss alone
  In Walhalla's peace, from sorrow freed!

Ye will meet—oh, thought of rapture full!—
  Yonder, at the gate of Paradise!
Hark! the coffin sinks with echo dull;
  As it re-ascends the death-rope sighs!
Then, with sorrow drunk, we madly roll'd,
  Lips were silent, but the mute eye spoke—
Stay, oh, stay!—we grudg'd the tomb so cold;
  But soon warmer tears in torrents broke.

Lo! on high the moon, her lustre dead,
O'er the deathlike grove uplifts her head,
  Sighing flits the spectre through the gloom—
    Misty clouds are shivering,
    Pallid stars are quivering,
  Looking down, like lamps within a tomb.
Dully o'er the coffin earth-flakes rise,—
  All the wealth of earth for one look more!
Now the grave barr'd up for ever lies;
Duller, duller o'er the coffin earth-flakes rise:
  Never will the grave its prey restore!

PHANTASY—TO LAURA.

NAME, my Laura, name the whirl-compelling
    Bodies to unite in one blest whole—
Name, my Laura, name the wondrous magic
    By which Soul rejoins its kindred Soul!

See! it teaches yonder roving Planets
    Round the sun to fly in endless race;
And as children play around their mother,
    Checker'd circles round the orb to trace.

Every rolling star, by thirst tormented,
    Drinks with joy its bright and golden rain—
Drinks refreshment from its fiery chalice,
    As the limbs are nourish'd by the brain.

'Tis through Love that atom pairs with atom,
    In a harmony eternal, sure;
And 'tis Love that links the spheres together—
    Through her only, systems can endure.

Were she but effaced from Nature's clockwork,
    Into dust would fly the mighty world;
O'er thy systems thou wouldst weep, great Newton,
    When with giant force to Chaos hurl'd!

Blot the Goddess from the Spirit Order,
    It would sink in death, and ne'er arise.
Were Love absent, spring would glad us never;
    Were Love absent, none their God would prize!

What is that, which, when my Laura kisses,
    Dyes my cheek with flames of purple hue,
Bids my bosom bound with swifter motion,
    Like a fever wild my veins runs through?

Ev'ry nerve from out its barriers rises,
    O'er its banks the blood begins to flow;
Body seeks to join itself to Body,
    Spirits kindle in one blissful glow.

Powerful as in the dead creations
  That eternal impulses obey,
O'er the web Arachne-like of Nature,—
  Living Nature,—Love exerts her sway !

Laura, see how Joyousness embraces
  E'en the overflow of sorrows wild !
How e'en rigid desperation kindles
  On the loving breast of Hope so mild !

Sisterly and blissful rapture softens
  Gloomy Melancholy's fearful night,
And, deliver'd of its golden Children,
  Lo, the eye pours forth its radiance bright !

Does not awful Sympathy rule over
  E'en the realms that Evil calls its own ?
For 'tis Hell our crimes are ever wooing,
  While they bear a grudge 'gainst Heaven alone

Shame, Repentance, pair Eumenĭdēs-like,
  Weave round sin their fearful serpent-coils ;
While around the eagle-wings of Greatness
  Treach'rous danger winds its dreaded toils.

Ruin oft with Pride is wont to trifle,
  Envy upon Fortune loves to cling ;
On her brother, Death, with arms extended,
  Lust, his sister, oft is wont to spring.

On the wings of Love the Future hastens
  In the arms of ages past to lie ;
And Saturnus, as he onward speeds him,
  Long hath sought his bride—Eternity !

Soon Saturnus will his bride discover,—
  So the mighty Oracle hath said ;
Blazing Worlds will turn to marriage torches
  When Eternity with Time shall wed !

Then a fairer, far more beauteous morning,
 Laura, on *our* Love shall also shine,
Long as their blest bridal-night enduring :—
 So rejoice thee, Laura—Laura mine !

TO LAURA AT THE HARPSICHORD.

When o'er the chords thy fingers stray,
My spirit leaves its mortal clay,
 A statue there I stand ;
Thy spell controls e'en life and death,
As when the nerves a living breath
 Receive by Love's command ! *

More gently Zephyr sighs along
To listen to thy magic song :
The systems form'd by heav'nly love
To sing for ever as they move,
Pause in their endless-whirling round
To catch the rapture-teeming sound ;
'Tis for thy strains *they* worship thee,—
Thy look, Enchantress, fetters *me !*

From yonder chords fast-thronging come
 Soul-breathing notes with rapturous speed,
As when from out their heav'nly home
 The new-born Seraphim proceed ;
The strains pour forth their magic might,
As glitt'ring suns burst through the night,
When, by Creation's storm awoke,
From Chaos' giant-arm they broke.

* The allusion in the original is to the seemingly magical power
possessed by a Jew conjuror, named Philadelphia, which would not
be understood in English.

Now sweet, as when the silv'ry wave
Delights the pebbly beach to lave ;
And now majestic as the sound
Of rolling thunder gath'ring round ;
Now pealing more loudly, as when from yon height
Descends the mad mountain-stream, foaming and
   bright ;
Now in a song of love
Dying away,
As thro' the aspen grove
Soft zephyrs play ;
Now heavier and more mournful seems the strain,
As when across the desert, death-like plain,
Whence whispers dread and yells despairing rise,
Cocytus' sluggish, wailing current sighs.

Maiden fair, oh, answer me !
Are not spirits leagued with thee ?
Speak they in the realms of bliss
Other language e'er than this ?

RAPTURE—TO LAURA.

FROM earth I seem to wing my flight,
And sun myself in Heaven's pure light,
   When thy sweet gaze meets mine ;
I dream I quaff ethereal dew,
When mine own form I mirror'd view
   In those blue eyes divine !

Blest notes from Paradise afar,
Or strains from some benignant star
   Enchant my ravish'd ear ;
My Muse feels then the shepherd's hour
When silv'ry tones of magic power
   Escape those lips so dear !

Young Loves around thee fan their wings—
Behind, the madden'd fir-tree springs,
   As when by Orpheus fir'd ;
The poles whirl round with swifter motion,
When in the dance, like waves o'er Ocean, .
   Thy footsteps float untir'd !

Thy look, if it but beam with love,
Could make the lifeless marble move,
   And hearts in rocks enshrine ;
My visions to reality
Will turn, if, Laura, in thine eye
   I read—that thou art mine !

THE SECRET OF REMINISCENCE.

WHAT unveils to me the yearning glow
Fix'd for ever to thy lips to grow ?
What the longing wish thy breath to drink,—
In thy Being blest, in death to sink
         When thy look steals o'er me ?

As when Slaves without resistance yield
To the Victor in the battle-field,
So my Senses in the moment fly
O'er the bridge of Life tumultuously
         When thou stand'st before me !

Speak ! Why should they from their Master roam ?
Do my Senses yonder seek their home ?
Or do sever'd brethren meet again,
Casting off the Body's heavy chain,
         Where thy foot hath lighted ?

Were our Beings once together twin'd ?
Was it therefore that our bosoms pin'd ?

Were we in the light of suns now dead,
In the days of rapture long since fled,
          Into One united?

Aye! we were so! thou wert link'd with me,
In 'Æone that has ceas'd to be;
On the mournful page of vanish'd time,
By my Muse were read these words sublime:
          Nought thy love can sever!

And in Being closely twin'd and fair,
I too wondering saw it written there,—
We were then a Life, a Deity,—
And the world seem'd order'd then to lie
          'Neath our sway for ever.

And, to meet us, nectar-fountains still
Pour'd for ever forth their blissful rill;
Forcibly we broke the seal of Things,
And to Truth's bright sunny hill our wings
          Joyously were soaring.

Laura, weep!—this Deity hath flown,—
Thou and I his ruins are alone;
By a thirst unquenchable we're driven
Our lost Being to embrace;—tow'rd Heaven
          Turns our gaze imploring.

Therefore, Laura, is this yearning glow
Fix'd for ever to thy lips to grow,
And the longing wish thy breath to drink,
In thy Being blest, in death to sink
          When thy look steals o'er me!

And as Slaves without resistance yield,
To the Victor in the battle-field,
Therefore do my ravish'd Senses fly
O'er the bridge of Life tumultuously,
          When thou stand'st before me!

Therefore do they from their Master roam!
Therefore do my Senses seek their home!
Casting off the Body's heavy chain,
Those long-sever'd brethren kiss again,
   Hush'd is all their sighing!

And thou, too—when on me fell thine eye,
What disclos'd thy cheek's deep-purple dye?
Tow'rd each other, like relations dear,
As an exile to his home draws near,
   Were we not then flying?

MELANCHOLY — TO LAURA.

Laura,—in thy golden gaze
 Burns the morning sunbeam's glow,
In thy cheek the red blood plays,
 And thy tears, that pearl-like flow,
 Rapture as their Mother know—
He whom those fair drops bedew,
Who therein a God can view,
Ah, the youth who thus rewarded sighs,
 Sees new suns begin to rise!

And thy Spirit, bright and clear,
As the glassy waves appear,
 Turns to May the Autumn sad;
Deserts wild, inspiring fear,
 In thy genial rays are glad.
Distant Future, gloomy, cold,
In thy star is turn'd to gold;
Smil'st thou at the Graces' harmony?
 I must weep those charms to see!

Have not Night's all-dreaded Powers
 Undermin'd Earth's fastness long?
Yes! our proudly-soaring towers,
 And our cities, stately, strong,

All on mould'ring bones repose;
  From Decay their fragrant bloom
Drink thy flowers; thy current flows
  From the hollow of a—tomb!

Laura, yonder floating planets see!
Let them of their Worlds discourse to thee!
  'Neath their magic Circle's sway,
  Thousand springs have pass'd away,
  Thousand thrones the skies have sought,
  Thousand fearful fights been fought.
  Wouldst thou find their trace again,
  Seek it on the iron plain!
    Earlier, later, ripe to pass
    To the grave,—the wheels, alas,
  Of the Planets clogg'd remain!

Thrice look round,—and lo! the sun's bright rays
In the death-night's Ocean quench their blaze;
  Ask me how *thy* beams are fann'd to flame!
    Dost thou boast thy sparkling eye,
    Or thy cheek's fresh purple dye,
  That from crumbling Mould first came?
    For the hues he lent to thee,
    Maiden, Death with usury
Heavy interest soon will claim!

Maiden, do not scorn that mighty one!
  On the cheek a fairer, brighter dye
Is, alas! but Death's more beauteous throne;
  From behind that flow'ry tapestry
Marks his prey the Spoiler for his own.
Laura—in thy Worshipper confide!
  'Tis tow'rd Death alone thine eyes now strain;
  And thy beaming glances only drain
Life's frail lamp so niggardly supplied.
    "Yet my pulses," boastest thou,
    "Throb in joyous youthful play"—
  Ah! the Tyrant's creatures now
    Are but hast'ning tow'rds Decay.

And this smile the blast of Death
Scatters, as the zephyr's breath
   Scatters rainbow-colour'd foam.
Vain thou seek'st to find its trace,
E'en from Nature's spring-like grace,
   E'en from Life, as from his home,
Sallies the Destroyer base!

Stripp'd of leaves I see thy lifeless roses,
   Pale and dead thy mouth so sweet of yore,
And thy cheek, that dimples soft discloses,
   By the wintry tempest furrow'd o'er.
Gloomy years will, gathering blacker, stronger,
   Cloud the silver-spring of Infancy—
Then will Laura—Laura love no longer,
   Then will Laura lovely cease to be!

Maiden! as an oak thy Bard still rears his head;
   Blunt against my rock-like youthful might
Falls the death-spear's shaft, its vigour fled;
   And my glances,—burning as the light
Of yon Heaven,—my Soul more fiercely glowing
   Than the light of yon eternal Heaven,
   O'er its own World's heaving Ocean driven,
Piling rocks and overthrowing;
Boldly through the World my thoughts are steering,
Nothing save their barriers fearing!

Glow'st thou, Laura?—Swells thy haughty breast?
Learn then, Maiden, that this drink so blest,
    That this cup of god-like seeming,
    Laura, is with Poison teeming!
    Hapless they who ever trust
    Sparks divine to forge from dust!
    Ah! the boldest Harmony
      'Mongst the notes but discord breeds,—
    Genius, glowing Spark from high,
      On Life's glimm'ring lamp but feeds.

Lur'd from Life's bright throne away,
 Ev'ry Gaoler marks him as his prey!
Ah! e'en now, with shameless passion fir'd,
'Gainst me all my Spirits have conspir'd!
Let—I feel it—two short springs fleet by,
 Laura—and this tott'ring house of clay
Will with fearful ruin on me lie,
 Quenching me in my self-kindled ray!—

Weep'st thou, Laura?—Be that tear denied
Which as Age's penance is supplied!
 Hence! away! thou tear, thou sinner mean!
Wouldst thou, Laura, that my strength should sink?—
That I trembling from that Sun should shrink
 Who the stripling's eagle-course hath seen?
That my bosom's heav'nly flame so bright
 'Neath a frozen heart's cold touch should perish?—
That my Spirit should be reft of sight?—
 Must I curse the Sins that most I cherish?
 No! away! thou tear, thou sinner mean!
Break the flow'ret in its fairest bloom!
Quench, O Youth, with that deep look of gloom,
 Quench with bitter tears my torch's ray!
As when o'er the scene that most enthrals
On the tragic stage, the curtain falls
 Though each shadow flies,—the crowds all-breathless
  stay!

THE INFANTICIDE.

Hark!—the bells are tolling mournfully,
 And the dial's hand hath run its race.
In the name of God, so let it be!
 Grave-attendants,—to the fatal place!
Take, O World, this last departing kiss!
 Take, O World, these bitter tears away!
Yet thy Poison had a taste of bliss!—
 Bosom-poisoner, we are quit to-day!

Fare thee well, thou happiness of Earth,
　Now to be exchang'd for crumbling mould!
Fare ye well, ye days of rosy birth,
　That the maiden revell'd in of old!
Fare ye well, ye gold-embroider'd dreams,
　Heaven-descended Phantasies so bright!
Ah, they perish'd in their morning beams,
　Ne'er again to blossom to the light!

I was deck'd with rosy ribbons fair,
　Clad in Innocence's swan-like dress,
And my bright and loosely-flowing hair
　Rosebuds sweet then carelessly did press.
Woe, oh, woe! though garments white still grace
　Her who now is Hell's sad sacrifice,
Yet, alas, those rosy ribbons' place
　Now the fillet black of Death supplies!

Weep for me, oh, ye who never fell!
　Ye for whom the guileless lily blows,—
On whose gentle bosoms as they swell
　Nature her heroic strength bestows!
Woe!—this heart has felt frail passion's charms,
　Feeling now my judgment-sword must be!
Woe!—encircled in the False One's arms,
Slept my Virtue,—ah, too easily!

Ah, forgetting me, that serpent-heart
　Makes Another now perchance its prey,—
Overflows, when I to Death depart,
　At her toilet in some amorous play!—
Sports, it may be, with his Maiden's hair,
　Drinks the kiss that she responsive brings,
When upon the death-block spurting there,
　From my body, high the life-blood springs!

Joseph! Joseph! many a weary mile
　May Louisa's death-song follow thee!
And the belfry's hollow peal the while
　On thy startled ear strike fearfully!

When Love's soft and murmuring tones may swell
　　Tow'rd thee from some Maiden's tender lips,
Sudden let them plant a Wound from Hell,
　　Where Joy's rosy form its Being sips!

Traitor! heed'st thou not Louisa's smart?—
　　Not, thou Cruel one, a Woman's shame?—
Not the unborn Life beneath my heart?—
　　Not what e'en the tiger fierce would tame?
See! his sails now proudly leave this land,
　　Sadly after them is turn'd mine eye,
While around the Maids on Seine's far strand,
　　Breathes he forth his false and treach'rous sigh!

And my baby,—wrapp'd in soft repose—
　　Calmly lay it on its mother's breast;
In the beauty of the morning rose
　　Sweetly on me smil'd the infant blest.
Deadly-lovely was each feature fair
　　Of its blissful image tow'rd me bent;
While by Love and visions of Despair
　　Was its mother's tortured bosom rent.

" Woman, where's my Father?"—Thus it spoke
　　In its innocent mute thunder-tone;
" Woman, where's thy Spouse?"—responsive broke
　　From my inmost heart, with heavy groan.
Him who now may other children kiss,
　　Orphan, thou, alas, wilt seek in vain!
Thou wilt curse the moment of our bliss,
　　When the Bastard's name inflicts its stain.

And thy mother—in her heart is Hell!
　　Lonely sits she in wide Nature's All,
Thirsting ever at the blissful well,
　　Which thy sight converts to bitter gall.
Ah! with ev'ry sound from thee arise
　　Madden'd feelings of departed joy,
And Death's bitter arrow 'gainst me flies,
　　From the smiling glances of my Boy.

Hell surrounds me when thy form I miss;
　Hell, whene'er mine eyes thy form behold!
And the Furies' lash is now thy kiss,
　That from *his* lips ravish'd me of old!
From the Grave his Oath still thunders back,
　Ever does his Perjury kill on—
Here around me twined the Hydra black,
　And the work of Murder soon was done!

Joseph! Joseph! many a weary mile
　May the phantom dread thy steps pursue,
Catch thee in its ice-cold arms the while,
　From thy dream of rapture wake thee, too!
May thine infant's dying gaze so sad
　Glare down from the softly glimm'ring star,
Meet thee in its bloody vesture clad,
　Scourge thee back from Paradise afar!

See! there lay it lifeless at my feet,—
　Coldly staring, with a mind confus'd
Saw I then its Life-blood's current fleet,
　And my own Life with that current ooz'd;—
Fearfully the messengers of doom
　Knock e'en now,—more fearfully my heart!
Gladly haste I, in the chilly tomb
　Evermore to quench my burning smart.

Joseph! thou may'st pardon'd be by Heaven,
　Thou art pardon'd by the Sinner, too!
To the Earth my wrongs be henceforth given!
　Rake, ye Flames, the Death-pile thro' and thro'!
Joy! oh, Joy! His letters burn on high,
　And a conquering flame his oath devours,
While his kisses upwards blazing fly!—
　Yet was aught so dear in happier hours!

Sisters, trust your youthful roses ne'er,
　Trust them ne'er to false Man's treach'rous vow!
Beauty for my Virtue laid its snare,—
　On the Place of Death I curse it now!

Tears?—From stranglers' eyes can tears, then, gush
  Let my face the bandage quickly veil!
Hangman, canst not thou a lily crush?
  Do not tremble, Hangman pale!

THE GREATNESS OF THE WORLD.

THRO' the world which the Spirit creative and kind
First form'd out of Chaos, I fly like the wind,
    Until on the strand
    Of its billows I land,
My anchor cast forth where the breeze blows no more,
And Creation's last boundary stands on the shore.

I saw infant stars into Being arise,
For thousands of years to roll on through the skies;
    I saw them in play
    Seek their goal far away,—
For a moment my fugitive gaze wander'd on,—
I look'd round me, and lo!—all those bright stars had
    flown!

Madly yearning to reach the dark Kingdom of Night,
I boldly steer on with the speed of the light;
    All misty and drear
    The dim Heavens appear,
While embryo systems and seas at their source
Are whirling around the Sun-Wanderer's course.

When sudden a Pilgrim I see drawing near
Along the lone path,—" Stay!   What seekest thou
    here?"
    " My bark, tempest-tost,
    " Seeks the world's distant coast,
" I sail tow'rd the land where the breeze blows no
    more,
" And Creation's last boundary stands on the shore."

‘ Stay, thou sailest in vain! 'Tis INFINITY yonder ! ”—
‘ 'Tis INFINITY, too, where *thou*, Pilgrim, wouldst
        wander !
            “ Eagle-thoughts that aspire,
            “ Let your proud pinions tire !
‘ For 'tis here that sweet Phantasy, bold to the last,
‘ Her anchor in hopeless dejection must cast ! ”

ELEGY ON THE DEATH OF A YOUNG MAN.*

MOURNFUL groans, as when a Tempest lowers,
    Echo from the dreary house of Woe ;
Death-notes rise from yonder Minster's towers !
    Bearing out a youth, they slowly go ;
Yes ! a youth—unripe yet for the Bier,
    Gather'd in the spring-time of his days,
Thrilling yet with pulses strong and clear,
    With the flame that in his bright eye plays—
Yes ! a Son—the Idol of his Mother,
    (Oh, her mournful sigh shows that too well !)
Yes ! my Bosom-friend,—alas, my Brother !—
    Up ! each *Man*, the sad Procession swell !

Do ye boast, ye Pines, so grey and old,
    Storms to brave, with thunderbolts to sport ?
And, ye Hills, that ye the Heavens uphold ?
    And, ye Heavens, that ye the Suns support ?
Boasts the greybeard, who on haughty Deeds
    As on billows, seeks Perfection's height ?
Boasts the Hero, whom his Prowess leads
    Up to future Glory's Temple bright ?
If the gnawing worms the flow'ret blast,
    Who can madly think he'll ne'er decay ?
Who above, below, can hope to last,
    If the young man's life thus fleets away ?

* The youth's name was John Christian Weckherlin.

Joyously his days of youth so glad
Danced along, in rosy garb beclad,
   And the world, the world was then so sweet!
And how kindly, how enchantingly
Smiled the Future,—with what golden eye
   Did Life's Paradise his moments greet!
While the tear his Mother's eye escap'd,
Under him the Realm of Shadows gap'd,
   And the Fates his thread began to sever,—
Earth and Heaven then vanish'd from his sight,
From the Grave-Thought shrank he in affright—
   Sweet the World is to the Dying ever!

Dumb and deaf 'tis in that narrow place,
   Deep the Slumbers of the Buried One!
Brother! Ah, in ever-slack'ning race
   All thy hopes their circuit cease to run!
Sunbeams oft thy native hill still lave,
   But their glow thou never more canst feel;
O'er its flowers the Zephyr's pinions wave,
   O'er thine ear its murmur ne'er can steal;
Love will never tinge thine eye with gold,
   Ne'er wilt thou embrace thy blooming bride,
Not e'en though our tears in torrents roll'd—
   Death must now thine eye for ever hide!

Yet 'tis well!—for precious is thy Rest,
   In that narrow house the Sleep is calm;
There, with Rapture, Sorrow leaves the breast,—
   Man's afflictions there no longer harm.
Slander now may wildly rave o'er thee,
   And Temptation vomit Poison Fell,
O'er thee wrangle on the Pharisee,
   Murd'rous bigots banish thee to Hell!
Rogues beneath Apostle-masks may leer,
   And the Bastard Child of Justice play,
As it were with dice, with mankind here,
   And so on, until the Judgment Day!

O'er thee Fortune still may juggle on,
  For her minions blindly look around,—
Man now totter on his staggering throne,
  And in dreary puddles now be found!
Blest art thou, within thy narrow cell!
  To this stir of tragi-comedy,
To these Fortune-Waves that madly swell,
  To this vain and childish Lottery,
To this busy crowd effecting naught,
  To this rest with labour teeming o'er,
Brother!—to this Heaven with Devils fraught,
  Now thine eyes have closed for evermore.

Fare thee well, oh, thou to memory dear,
  By our blessings lull'd to slumbers sweet!
Sleep on calmly in thy prison drear,—
  Sleep on calmly till again we meet!
Till the loud Almighty trumpet sounds,
  Echoing through these corpse-encumber'd hills,—
Till God's storm-wind, bursting through the bounds
  Placed by Death, with Life those Corpses fills—
Till, impregnate with Jehovah's blast,
  Graves bring forth, and at His menace dread,
In the smoke of Planets melting fast,
  Once again the tombs give up their Dead!

Not in Worlds, as dreamt of by the Wise,
  Not in Heavens, as sung in Poets' song,
Not in e'en the People's Paradise—
  Yet we *shall* o'ertake thee, and ere long.
Is that true which cheer'd the Pilgrim's gloom?
  Is it true that Thoughts can yonder *be*?
True, that Virtue guides us o'er the tomb?
  That 'tis more than empty Phantasy?
All these riddles are to thee unveil'd!
  Truth thy Soul ecstatic now drinks up,
Truth in radiance thousandfold exhal'd
  From the Mighty Father's blissful cup.

Dark and silent Bearers draw, then, nigh!
  To the Slayer serve the Feast the while!
Cease, ye Mourners, cease your wailing cry!
  Dust on dust upon the Body pile!
Where's the Man who God to tempt presumes?
  Where the eye that through the Gulf can see?
Holy, holy, holy art thou, God of Tombs!
  We, with awful trembling, worship Thee!
Dust may back to native dust be ground,
  From its crumbling house the Spirit fly,
And the storm its ashes strew around,—
  But its Love, its Love shall never die!

THE BATTLE.

  With a dull, heavy tread,
    Like a storm-cloud o'erhead,
Moves the march through the wide plain so green;
    And the field for the strife,
    Where the stake is man's life,
In its boundless expanse is now seen.

Tow'rd the ground ev'ry eye is uneasily cast,
And each warrior's heart 'gainst his ribs beateth fast.

To the front now the Major with thundering pace
Gallops on past each pallid and death-lighted face—
            Halt!
And the regiments obey that stern word of command,
While in silence unbroken the front takes its stand.

    Glittering in the morning beam,
    See ye on yon hill the gleam?
    Is't the banner of the foe?
    Yes, their waving flag we know!

    Wife and children of my love,
    God protect ye from above!

Now merrily, merrily rise on the ear
The roll of the drum and the fife's note so clear;
Oh! hark to the wildly harmonious tone,
How it thrills through the marrow and thrills through
    the bone!

  God be with ye, comrades brave,—
  We shall meet beyond the grave!

  Soon the vivid lightning flashes,
  Soon the rolling thunder crashes
   From the fierce artillery;
  Eyelids quiver,—loud are heard
  Fearful sounds,—the signal word
   Through each rank runs rapidly.
  In God's name, so let it be!—
  Ev'ry breast now breathes more free.

  Death is loose, the din grows louder,—
   Sharper rings the musketry;
  Driven by the deadly powder
   Iron bullets fill the sky.

Almost touching each other the armies now stand,—
From platoon to platoon runs the word of command:
  "Make ready!" with thundering roar;
And sudden the foremost on knee sinking low,
Their death-laden weapons discharge on the foe,
  But many, alas! rise no more.
By the grapeshot resistless whole ranks are o'erthrown;
But as fast as the ranks in the front are mown down,
  O'er their bodies the hinder ranks pour.

  Devastation spreads around,
  Whole battalions bite the ground.

The sun now sinks to rest,—hot burns the fight,
While o'er the armies broods the murky night.

  God be with ye, comrades brave,—
  We shall meet beyond the grave!

The life-blood in torrents spurts high as the head,
The living confusedly mix with the dead;
The foot as it moves stumbles over the slain,
While the conflict 'gins raging more wildly again.
"What, Frank!　And thou, too?"—"Kiss my Charlotte
　　for me!
"Aye, Friend, that I will! .. Good God! Comrades, see,
　　see,
　"How the grapeshot bursts full on our rear!
". . . I will kiss her for thee!　Now in peace slumber
　　on,
"While I, left, alas! in the world all-alone,
　"Seek the fast-falling balls without fear."

Now hither, and now thither bends the fight,
Still murkier o'er the armies broods the night.

　　　God be with ye, comrades brave—
　　　We shall meet beyond the grave.

　　　What means this sudden trampling sound?
　　　The Adjutants are flying round,
　　　Dragoons are rattling 'gainst the foe,
　　　Whose thund'ring guns are lying low,
　　　While they in all directions fly,—
　　　Hurrah, my Comrades, Victory!
　　　Their coward limbs in terror shrink,
　　　And down their boasting banners sink!

　　　　Decided is the fearful fight,
　　　　The day gleams brightly through the night!
And hark, how triumphantly rise on the ear.
The roll of the drum and the fife's note so clear!

　　　Farewell, ye perish'd comrades brave—
　　　Oh, we shall meet beyond the grave!

ROUSSEAU.

Monument of our own Age's shame,
On thy Country casting endless blame,
   Rousseau's Grave, how dear thou art to me!
Calm repose be to thy ashes blest!
In thy life thou vainly sought'st for rest,
   But at length 'twas here obtain'd by thee!

When will ancient wounds be cover'd o'er?
Wise men died in heathen days of yore;
   Now 'tis lighter—yet they die again.
Socrates was kill'd by Sophists vile,
Rousseau meets his death through Christians' wile,—
   Rousseau—who would fain make Christians men!

FRIENDSHIP.

From the "Letters of Julius to Raphael;" an unpublished Romance.

Temperate is the Being-Ruler, Friend!—
On those Thinkers mean let Shame attend
   Who so anxiously seek Laws to solve!
Living-Worlds, and Regions of the Soul
On *one* Flywheel, tow'rd their limit roll;
   Here my Newton saw that Wheel revolve!

Spheres,—the slaves of but *one* rein,—it tells
Round the mighty World's heart, as it swells,
   Labyrinthine paths to cause to rise—
Spirits, in entwining Systems laced,
Tow'rd the mighty Spirit-Sun to haste,
   As the stream to join the ocean flies.

Was 't not this Machinery divine,
That compell'd *our* Bosoms to entwine
   In the blest and endless bonds of Love?
Raphael, on *thine* Arm—oh, ecstasy!
Tow'rd that mighty Spirit-Sun, e'en I
   On Perfection's path would gladly rove.

Joy, oh, Joy! Thou now art found by me!
I, of millions, have embraced but thee,
   And, of millions, mine art thou alone—
Let this World in Chaos still be lost,
Atoms in confusion wild be tost,
   Into one *our* Hearts for aye have flown!

Must not I, from out thy flaming gaze,
Of *my* Rapture seek the answering rays?
   'Tis in *thee* alone myself I view—
Fairer still appears the Earth so fair,
Brighter in the Loved One's features there
   Heaven is mirror'd,—of more dazzling hue.

Sweeter from the Passions' storm to rest,
Melancholy casts upon Love's breast
   All the burden of her tearful gloom;
Does not e'en tormenting Rapture seek,
In thine eyes that eloquently speak,
   Eagerly to find a blissful tomb?

Stood I in Creation all alone,
Spirits I would dream into each stone,
   And their forms with kisses then would greet,—
When my wailings echoed far and wide,
Would be happy, if the Rocks replied,
   Fool, enough! to Sympathy so sweet.

Lifeless groups are we, if hate we prove,
Gods—if we embrace in kindly love!
   While we languish for the Fetters blest—
Upwards through the thousand-varying scale
Of unnumber'd Souls that nought avail,
   Does this godlike impulse raise the breast.

Arm in arm, tow'rd some still higher sphere,
From the Mongol to the Grecian seer,
  Who is with the last of seraphs bound,
Roam we on, in dancing orbit bright,
Till in yonder Sea of endless light
  Time and Measure evermore are drown'd!

Friendless was the Mighty Lord of Earth,
Felt a *Want*—so gave the Spirit birth,
  Mirror blest where His own glories shine!—
Ne'er his Like has found that Being high,—
Nought e'er gushes—save Infinity—
  From the Spirit-Region's Cup Divine!

GROUP FROM TARTARUS.

HARK! Like the sea in wrath the Heav'ns assailing,
Or like a brook through rocky basin wailing,
Comes from below, in groaning agony,
A heavy, vacant, torment-breathing sigh!

Their faces marks of bitter torture wear,
While from their lips burst curses of despair;
  Their eyes are hollow, and full of woe,
    And their looks with heartfelt anguish
  Seek Cocytus' stream that runs wailing below,
    For the bridge o'er its waters they languish.

And they say to each other in accents of fear,
"Oh, when will the time of Fulfilment appear?"
High over them boundless Eternity quivers,
And the scythe of Saturnus all-ruthlessly shivers!

ELYSIUM.

THOSE groans of deep anguish no longer resound,
Each accent of sorrow, each sigh, is now drown'd
  In Elysium's banquets so bright;
In bliss never-ending, in rapturous song,
As when thro' the meadows a brook sings along,
  Elysium's days take their flight.

A May-day enduring, a ne'er changing spring
All gently its youthful and balm-laden wing
  Waves over the sweet smiling plain;
In visions ecstatic the days fleet apace,
The Spirit expands through the wide realms of space,
  And Truth rends the Cov'ring in twain.

'Tis here that the bosom is swelling alone,
  With rapture eternal and free from alloy;
The name of affliction is here e'er unknown,
  And sorrow means nought but a more tranquil joy.

The pilgrim beneath these cool shades lays to rest
His feverish limbs by long wand'ring opprest,
  His burden behind him for ever he leaves;
The sickle escapes from the hand of the reaper,
And, lull'd by the harp's strains seraphic, the sleeper
  Beholds in his vision the harvest's ripe sheaves.

He whose banner war's fierce thunder woke,
On whose ears the din of slaughter broke,
  'Neath whose foot the mountain quak'd in fear,
Slumbers calmly by the streamlet's side,
While its silv'ry waters onward glide,
  And forgets his wildly-clanging spear.

Here all faithful lovers meet again,
Kiss each other on the verdant plain,
   Scented by the balmy zephyr's breath;
Love here finds once more his crown of gold,
'Gins his endless marriage-feast to hold,
   Safe for ever from the stroke of Death!

THE FUGITIVE.

The air is perfum'd with the morning's fresh breeze,
From the bush peer the sunbeams all purple and
   bright,
While they gleam through the clefts of the dark-
   waving trees,
And the cloud-crested mountains are golden with
   light.

With joyful, melodious, ravishing strain,
   The lark, as he wakens, salutes the glad sun,
Who glows in the arms of Aurora again,
   And blissfully smiling, his race 'gins to run.

     All hail, light of day!
     Thy sweet gushing ray
Pours down its soft warmth over pasture and field;
     With hues silver-tinged
     The Meadows are fringed,
And numberless suns in the dewdrop reveal'd.

     Young Nature invades
     The whispering shades,
Displaying each ravishing charm;
     The soft zephyr blows,
     And kisses the rose,
The plain is sweet-scented with balm.

How high from yon city the smoke-clouds ascend!
Their neighing, and snorting, and bellowing blend

The horses and cattle ;
The chariot-wheels rattle
As down to the valley they take their mad way ;
    And even the forest with life seems to move,
    The eagle, and falcon, and hawk soar above,
And flutter their pinions in Heaven's bright ray.

        In search of repose
        From my heart-rending woes,
Oh, where shall my sad spirit flee ?
        The earth's smiling face,
        With its sweet youthful grace,
A tomb must, alas, be for me !

Arise, then, thou sunlight of morning, and fling
    O'er plain and o'er forest thy purple-dyed beams !
Thou twilight of evening, all noiselessly sing
    In melody soft to the world as it dreams !

Ah, sunlight of morning, to me thou but flingest
    Thy purple-dyed beams o'er the grave of the past !
Ah, twilight of evening, thy strains thou but singest
    To one whose deep slumbers for ever must last !

THE FLOWERS.

Ye offspring of the morning sun,
    Ye flowers that deck the smiling plain,
Your lives, in joy and bliss begun,
    In Nature's love unchanged remain.
With hues of bright and godlike splendour
Sweet Flora graced your forms so tender,
    And clothed ye in a garb of light ;
Spring's lovely children, weep for ever,
For living Souls she gave ye never,
    And ye must dwell in endless night !

The nightingale and lark still sing
  In your tranced ears the bliss of love ;
The toying sylphs, on airy wing,
  Around your fragrant bosoms rove.
Of yore, Dione's daughter* twining
In garlands sweet your cup so shining,
  A pillow form'd where Love might rest !
Spring's gentle children, mourn for ever,
The joys of Love she gave ye never,
  Ne'er let ye know that feeling blest !

But when ye're gather'd by my hand,
  A token of my love to be,
Now that her mother's harsh command
  From Nanny's † sight has banish'd me,—
E'en from that passing touch ye borrow
Those heralds mute of pleasing sorrow,
  Life, language, hearts, and souls divine ;
And to your silent leaves 'tis given,
By him who mightiest is in Heaven,
  His glorious Godhead to enshrine.

ODE TO SPRING.

Thou'rt welcome, lovely stripling !
  Thou Nature's fond delight !
With thy basket fill'd with flowers,
  Thou'rt welcome to my sight !

Huzza ! once more we greet thee !
  How fair and sweet thou art !
To usher in thy presence
  We haste with joyful heart !

* Venus.

† Originally *Laura*, this having been one of the " Laura-Poems,"
as the Germans call them, of which so many appeared in the
Anthology (see *preface*). English readers will probably not think
that the change is for the better.

Remember'st thou my Maiden?
  Thou never canst forget!
My Maiden lov'd me dearly,—
  My Maiden loves me yet!

For my Maiden many a flow'ret
  I begg'd of yore from thee—
Once more I make entreaty,
  And thou?—thou giv'st them me!

Thou'rt welcome, lovely stripling!
  Thou Nature's fond delight!
With thy basket fill'd with flowers,
Thou'rt welcome to my sight!

TO MINNA.

Am I dreaming? Is mine eye
  Dimm'd by some deceiving ray?
Is't my Minna passing by,
  Turning her cold look away?
She, who vain of each fair charm,
  Fans herself so haughtily,
Leaning on some fopling's arm,—
  Is't my Minna?—'Tis not she!

On her light hat, feathers proud,
  Once my gift, are waving yet;
While her breast-knots cry aloud,
  Saying: "Minna, ne'er forget!"
Flowers still grace her breast, her brow,
  Foster'd by my loving care;
Ah, that breast is faithless now,—
  Yet those flowers still blossom there!

Go!   Ador'd by empty wits,
    Go!   Without a thought of me!
Prey to venal hypocrites—
    Scorn is all I feel for thee!
Go! for thee once throbb'd a heart
    Fill'd with stainless purity,
Great enough to bear the smart
    That it throbb'd for such as thee!

'Tis by beauty thou'rt betray'd—
    By thy features, shameless one!
But their roses soon will fade,
    Soon their transient charms be gone!
Swallows that in spring-time play,
    Fly when north winds cold return;
Age will scare thy wooers gay,
    Yet a *friend* thou now canst spurn!

Ah! methinks I hear thee sigh,
    Wreck of what thou once hast been,
Looking back with streaming eye
    To thy May-day's flowery scene.
They who once thy kisses sought,
    On the wings of rapture borne,
Make thy vanish'd youth their sport,
    Laugh thy winter sad to scorn.

'Tis by beauty thou'rt betray'd—
    By thy features, shameless one!
But their roses soon will fade,
    Soon thy transient charms be gone!
How I then will scoff and jeer!—
    Scoff?   Great Heavens! oh, pardon me!
I will weep full many a tear—
    Tears of anguish weep for thee!

THE TRIUMPH OF LOVE.

A HYMN.

By Love are blest the Gods on high,
Frail man becomes a Deity
  When Love to him is given ;
'Tis Love that makes the Heavens shine
With hues more radiant, more divine,
  And turns dull Earth to Heaven !

In Pyrrha's rear (so poets sang
  In ages past and gone),
The world from rocky fragments sprang—
  Mankind from lifeless stone.

Their soul was but a thing of night,
  Like stone and rock their heart ;
The flaming torch of Heav'n so bright
  Its glow could ne'er impart.

Young Loves, all gently hov'ring round,
Their souls as yet had never bound
  In soft and rosy chains ;
No feeling Muse had sought to raise
Their bosoms with ennobling lays,
  Or sweet, harmonious strains.

Around each other lovingly
  No garlands then entwin'd ;
The sorrowing Springs fled tow'rd the sky,
  And left the Earth behind.

From out the sea Aurora rose
  With none to hail her then ;
The sun unhail'd, at daylight's close,
  In ocean sank again.

In forests wild, man went astray,
Misled by Luna's cloudy ray,—
   He bore an iron yoke;
He pin'd not for the stars on high,
With yearning for a Deity
   No tears in torrents broke.

   *   *   *   *   *

But see! from out the deep-blue Ocean
Fair Venus springs with gentle motion;
   The graceful Naiad's smiling band
   Conveys her to the gladden'd strand.

A May-like, youthful, Magic power
Entwines, like morning's twilight hour,
   Around that form of godlike birth,
   The charms of air, sea, heaven, and earth.

The day's sweet eye begins to bloom
Across the forest's midnight gloom;
   Narcissuses, their balm distilling,
   The path her footstep treads are filling.

A song of Love sweet Philomel
   Soon caroll'd through the grove;
The streamlet, as it murmuring fell,
   Discours'd of nought but Love.

Pygmalion! Happy one! Behold!
Life's glow pervades thy marble cold!
   Oh, Love, thou conqueror all-divine,
   Embrace each happy child of thine!

   *   *   *   *   *

By Love are blest the Gods on high,—
Frail man becomes a Deity
   When Love to him is given;
'Tis Love that makes the Heavens shine
With hues more radiant, more divine,
   And turns dull Earth to Heaven!

*   *   *   *   *

The Gods their days for ever spend
In banquets bright that have no end,—
    In one voluptuous morning-dream,
    And quaff the Nectar's golden stream.

Enthron'd in awful Majesty,
Kronïon wields the bolt on high:
    In abject fear Olympus rocks
    When wrathfully he shakes his locks.

To other Gods he leaves his throne,
And fills, disguis'd as Earth's frail son,
    The grove with mournful numbers;
The thunders rest beneath his feet,
And lull'd by Leda's kisses sweet,
    The Giant-Slayer slumbers.

Through the boundless realms of light
Phœbus' golden reins, so bright,
    Guide his horses white as snow,
    While his darts lay Nations low.
But when Love and Harmony
Fill his breast, how willingly
    Ceases Phœbus then to heed
    Rattling dart and snow-white steed!

See!   Before Kronïon's spouse
Every great Immortal bows;
Proudly soar the peacock pair
As her chariot throne they bear,
While she decks with crown of might
Her ambrosial tresses bright.

Beauteous Princess, ah! with fear
    Quakes, before thy splendour, Love,
Seeking, as he ventures near,
    With his power thy breast to move!

Soon from her immortal throne
  Heaven's great Queen must fain descend,
And in prayer for Beauty's zone,
  To the Heart-Enchainer bend!

   *   *   *   *   *

By Love are blest the Gods on high,
Frail man becomes a Deity
  When Love to him is given;
'Tis Love that makes the Heavens shine
With hues more radiant, more divine,
  And turns dull Earth to Heaven!

   *   *   *   *   *

'Tis Love illumes the realms of Night,
For Orcus dark obeys his might,
And bows before his magic spell:
All-kindly looks the King of Hell
At Ceres' daughter's smile so bright,—
Yes—Love illumes the realms of Night!

In Hell were heard, with heavenly sound,
Holding in chains its warder bound,
  Thy lays, O Thracian one!
A gentler doom dread Minos pass'd,
While down his cheeks the tears cours'd fast,
And e'en around Megæra's face
The serpents twin'd in fond embrace,
  The lashes' work seem'd done.
Driven by Orpheus' lyre away,
The Vulture left his Giant-prey; *
With gentler motion roll'd along
  Dark Lethe and Cocytus' River,
Enraptur'd, Thracian, by thy song,—
  And Love its burden was for ever!

   *   *   *   *   *

       * Tityus.

By Love are blest the Gods on high,
Frail man becomes a Deity
 When Love to him is given;
'Tis Love that makes the Heavens shine
With hues more radiant, more divine,
 And turns dull Earth to Heaven!

  * * * * *

Wherever Nature's sway extends,
The fragrant balm of Love descends,
 His golden pinions quiver;
If 'twere not Venus' eye that gleams
Upon me in the moon's soft beams,
 In sun-lit hill or river,—
If 'twere not Venus smiles on me
From yonder bright and starry sea,
Not stars, not sun, not moonbeams sweet
Could make my heart with rapture beat.
'Tis Love alone that smilingly
Peers forth from Nature's blissful eye,
 As from a mirror ever!

Love bids the silv'ry streamlet roll
 More gently as it sighs along,
And breathes a living, feeling Soul
 In Philomel's sweet plaintive song;
'Tis Love alone that fills the air
With strains from Nature's lute so fair.

Thou Wisdom with the glance of fire,
Thou mighty Goddess, now retire,
 Love's power thou now must feel!
To victor proud, to monarch high,
Thou ne'er hast knelt in slavery,—
 To Love thou now must kneel!

Who taught thee boldly how to climb
The steep, but starry path sublime,
 And reach the seats Immortal?

Who rent the mystic Veil in twain,
And showed thee the Elysian plain
   Beyond Death's gloomy portal?
If Love had beckon'd not from high,
Had we gain'd Immortality?
If Love had not inflam'd each thought,
Had we the Master Spirit sought?
'Tis Love that guides the Soul alone
To Nature's Father's heavenly throne!

By Love are blest the Gods on high,
Frail man becomes a Deity
   When Love to him is given;
'Tis Love that makes the Heavens shine
With hues more radiant, more divine,
   And turns dull Earth to Heaven!

FORTUNE AND WISDOM.

Enraged against a quondam friend,
   To Wisdom once proud Fortune said:
" I'll give thee treasures without end,
   " If thou wilt be my friend instead.

" My choicest gifts to him I gave,
   " And ever blest him with my smile;
" And yet he ceases not to crave,
   " And calls me niggard all the while.

" Come, Sister, let us friendship vow!
   " So take the money, nothing loth;
" Why always labour at the plough?
   " Here is enough, I'm sure, for both!"

Sage Wisdom laugh'd,—the prudent elf!—
    And wip'd her brow, with moisture hot:
" There runs thy friend to hang himself,—
    " Be reconcil'd—I need thee not!"

TO A MORALIST.

WHY teach that Love is nought but Trifling vain ?—
    Why cavil at our youthful joyous play ?
Thou art benumb'd in Winter's icy chain,
    And yet canst view with scorn the golden May!

When erst thou didst assail the Nymph's bright charms,
    A Hero of the Carnival,—didst trip
In German Waltz,—held'st Heaven within thine arms,
    And from the lips of Maidens balm didst sip,—

Ha, Seladon! if then Earth's pond'rous ball
    Had from its axis slipp'd with mighty groan,
Thine ears would not have heard the heavy fall,
    In Love-knot twin'd with Julia into one!

Oh, look back now upon thy rosy days!
    Learn that Philosophy degenerates,
E'en as the pulse with feebler motion plays;
    Thy knowledge, man Immortal ne'er creates.

'Tis well when, through the ice of Sense refin'd,
    The fervent blood more fiercely can expand!
What ne'er can be accomplish'd by mankind,
    Leave to the inmates of a better Land!

And yet in prison walls the Guide of Earth
    Confines the Soul whose life in Heaven began;
He will not let me rise to Angel-worth,—
    I fain would follow him, to be a Man!

COUNT EBERHARD, THE GROANER OF WÜRTEMBERG.

A WAR SONG.

Now hearken, ye who take delight
  In boasting of your worth!
To many a man, to many a knight,
Belov'd in peace and brave in fight,
  The Swabian land gives birth.

Of Charles and Edward, Louis, Guy,
  And Frederick, ye may boast;
Charles, Edward, Louis, Frederick, Guy,—
None with Sir Eberhard can vie—
  Himself a mighty host!

And then young Ulerick, his son,
  Ha! how he lov'd the fray!
Young Ulerick, the Count's bold son,
When once the battle had begun,
  No foot's-breadth e'er gave way.

The Reutlingers, with gnashing teeth,
  Saw our bright ranks reveal'd:
And, panting for the victor's wreath,
They drew the sword from out the sheath,
  And sought the battle-field.

He charged the foe,—but fruitlessly,—
  Then, mail-clad, homeward sped;
Stern anger fill'd his father's eye,
And made the youthful warrior fly,
  And tears of anguish shed.

Now, rascals, quake!—This grieved him sore,
  And rankled in his brain;
And by his father's beard he swore,
With many a craven townsman's gore
  To wash out this foul stain.

Ere long the feud raged fierce and loud,—
  Then hasten'd steed and man
To Döffingen in thronging crowd,
While joy inspir'd the youngster proud,—
  And soon the strife began.

Our army's signal-word that day
  Was the disastrous fight;
It spurr'd us on like lightning's ray,
And plunged us deep in bloody fray,
  And in the spears' black night.

The youthful Count his pond'rous mace
  With lion's rage swung round;
Destruction stalk'd before his face,
While groans and howlings fill'd the place,
  And hundreds bit the ground.

Woe! Woe!   A heavy sabre-stroke
  Upon his neck descended;
The sight each warrior's pity woke,—
In vain! In vain! No word he spoke—
  His course on earth was ended.

Loud wept both friend and foeman then,'
  Check'd was the victor's glow;
The Count cheer'd thus his Knights again—
" My Son is like all other men,—
  " March, children, 'gainst the Foe! "

With greater fury whizz'd each lance,
  Revenge inflam'd the blood;
O'er corpses mov'd the fearful dance—
The townsmen fled in random chance
  O'er mountain, vale, and flood.

Then back to camp, with trumpets' bray,
  We hied in joyful haste;
And wife and child, with roundelay,
With clanging cup and waltzes gay,
  Our glorious triumph graced.

And our old Count,—what now does he ?
  His son lies dead before him ;
Within his tent all woefully
He sits alone in agony,
  And drops *one* hot tear o'er him.

And so, with true affection warm,
  The Count our Lord we love ;
Himself a mighty hero-swarm—
'The thunders rest within his arm—
  He shines like star above !

Farewell, then, ye who take delight
  In boasting of your worth !
To many a man, to many a knight,
Belov'd in peace, and brave in fight,
  The Swabian land gives birth !

SEMELE:

IN TWO SCENES.

————

Dramatis Personæ.

Juno.

Semele, *Princess of Thebes.*

Jupiter.

Mercury.

Scene—*The Palace of Cadmus at Thebes.*

————

SCENE I.

Juno. (*Descending from her chariot, enveloped in a
cloud.*)   Away, ye Peacocks, with my wingèd car !
Upon Cithæron's cloud-capp'd summit wait !
       [*The chariot and cloud vanish.*
Hail, hail, thou House of my undying anger !
A fearful hail to thee, thou hostile roof,
Ye hated walls !—This, *this*, then, is the place
Where Jupiter pollutes his marriage bed
Even before the face of modest day !
'Tis *here*, then, that a woman, a frail mortal,
A dust-created being, dares to lure
The mighty Thunderer from out mine arms,
And hold him prisoner against her lips !

Juno ! Juno ! thought of madness !
Thou all lonely and in sadness,

Standest now on Heaven's bright throne !
Though the votive smoke ascendeth,
Though each knee in homage bendeth,
   What are *they* when Love has flown ?

To humble, alas, each too-haughty emotion
That swell'd my proud breast, from the foam of the
      ocean
  Fair Venus arose, to enchant Gods and men !
And the Fates my still-deeper abasement decreeing,
Her offspring Hermione brought into being,
   And the bliss once mine own can ne'er glad me
      again !

Amongst the Gods do I not reign the Queen ?
Am I not Sister of the Thunderer ?
Am I not wife of Zeus the Lord of All ?
Groans not the mighty axis of the Heav'ns
At my command ?   Gleams not Olympus' crown
Upon my head ?   Ha ! now I feel myself !
In my immortal veins is Kronos' blood, .
Right royally now swells my godlike heart.
Revenge ! revenge !
Shall she unpunish'd ridicule my might ?
Unpunish'd, discord roll amongst the Gods,
Inviting Eris to invade the courts,
The joyous courts of Heav'n ?   Vain, thoughtless one !
Perish, and learn upon the Stygian stream
The difference 'twixt divine and earthly dust !
Thy giant-armour, may it weigh thee down—
Thy passion for a God to atoms crush thee !
Arm'd with revenge, as with a coat of mail,
I have descended from Olympus' heights,
Devising sweet, ensnaring, flatt'ring words ;
But in those words, death and destruction lurk.
Hark ! 'tis her footstep ! she approaches now—
Approaches ruin and a certain death !
Veil thyself, Goddess, in a mortal form !   *[Exit.*

SEMELE.   (*Calling behind the scenes.*)
The sun is fast declining! Maidens, haste,
Scatter ambrosial fragrance through the hall,
Strew roses and narcissus-flowers around,
Forgetting not the gold-embroider'd pillow.
He comes not yet—the sun is fast declining —
     JUNO.   (*Hastily entering in the form of an old woman.*)
Prais'd be the Deities, my dearest daughter!
     SEMELE.   Ha! Do I dream?   Am I awake?   Gods!
         Beroë!
     JUNO.   Is't possible that Semele can e'er
Forget her nurse?
     SEMELE.   'Tis Beroë!   By Zeus!
·Oh, let thy daughter clasp thee to her heart!
Thou livest still?   What can have brought thee here
From Epidaurus?   Tell me all thy tale!
Thou'rt still my mother as of old?
     JUNO.   Thy mother!
·Time was, thou call'dst me so.
     SEMELE.   Thou art so still,
And wilt remain so, till I drink full deep
Of Lethe's madd'ning draught.
     JUNO.   Soon Beroë
Will drink oblivion from the waves of Lethe;
But Cadmus' daughter ne'er will taste that draught.
     SEMELE.   How, my good nurse?   Thy language ne'er
         was wont
To be mysterious or of hidden meaning;
The spirit of grey hairs 'tis speaks in thee;
Thou say'st I ne'er shall taste of Lethe's draught?
     JUNO.   I said so, Yes!   But wherefore ridicule
Grey hairs?   'Tis true that they, unlike fair tresses,
Have ne'er been able to ensnare a God!
     SEMELE.   Pardon poor thoughtless me!   What cause
         have I
To ridicule grey hairs?   Can I suppose
That mine for ever fair will grace my neck?
But what was that I heard thee muttering
Between thy teeth?—A God?

Juno.   Said I, a God?
The Deities in truth dwell ev'rywhere!
'Tis good for Earth's frail children to implore them.
The Gods are found where *thou* art——Semele!
What wouldst thou ask?
      Semele.   Malicious heart! But say:
What brings thee to this spot from Epidaurus?
'Tis not because the Gods delight to dwell
Near Semele?
      Juno.   By Jupiter, nought else!—
What fire was that which mounted to thy cheeks
When I pronounced the name of Jupiter?
Nought else, my daughter! Fearfully the plague
At Epidaurus rages; ev'ry blast
Is deadly poison, ev'ry breath destroys;
The son his mother burns, his bride the bridegroom;
The funeral piles rear up their flaming heads,
Converting even midnight to bright day,
While howls of anguish ceaseless rend the air;
Full to o'erflowing is the cup of woe!—
In anger, Zeus looks down on our poor nation;
In vain the victim's blood is shed, in vain
Before the altar bows the priest his knee;
Deaf is his ear to all our supplications—
Therefore, my sorrow-stricken country now
Has sent me here to Cadmus' regal daughter,
In hopes that I may move her to avert
His anger from us—" Beroë, the nurse,
" Has influence," thus they said, " with Semele,
" And Semele with Zeus "——I know no more,
And understand still less what means the saying,
That Semele such influence has with Zeus.
      Semele. (*Eagerly and thoughtlessly.*)
The plague shall cease to-morrow! Tell them so!
Zeus loves me! Say so! It shall cease to-day!
      Juno. (*Starting up in astonishment.*)
Ha! Is it true what Fame with thousand tongues
Has spread abroad from Ida to Mount Hæmus?
Zeus loves thee? Zeus salutes thee in the glory

Wherein the denizens of Heav'n regard him,
When in Saturnia's arms he sinks to rest?—
Let, O ye Gods, my grey hairs now descend
To Orcus' shades, for I have liv'd enough!
In god-like splendour Kronos' mighty Son
Comes down to her,—to her, who on this breast
Once suckled—yes! to her——
    SEMELE.   Oh, Beroë!
In youthful form he came, in lovelier guise
Than they who from Aurora's lap arise;
Fairer than Hesper, breathing incense dim,—
In floods of æther steep'd appear'd each limb;
He mov'd with graceful and majestic motion,
Like silv'ry billows heaving o'er the ocean,
Or as Hyperion, whose bright shoulders ever
His bow and arrows bear, and clanging quiver;
His robe of light behind him gracefully
Danced in the breeze, his voice breath'd melody,
Like crystal streams with silv'ry murmur falling,
More ravishing than Orpheus' strains enthralling.
    JUNO.   My daughter!—Inspiration spurs thee on,
Raising thy heart to flights of Helicon!
If thus in strains of Delphic ecstasy
Ascends the short-liv'd blissful memory
Of his bright charms,—Oh, how divine must be
His own sweet voice,—his look how heavenly!
But why of that great attribute
Kronîon joys in most, be mute,—
The majesty that hurls the thunder,
And tears the fleeting clouds asunder?
Wilt thou say nought of *that* alone?
Prometheus and Deucalion
May lend the fairest charms of love,
But none can wield the bolt save Jove!
The thunderbolt it is alone
Which he before thy feet laid down
That proves thy right to Beauty's crown.

SEMELE.   What say'st thou?   What are thunderbolts
  to me?
JUNO. (*Smiling.*)   Ah, Semele!   A jest becomes thee
  well!
SEMELE.   Deucalion has no offspring so divine
As is my Zeus—of thunder nought I know.
JUNO.   Mere envy!   Fie!
SEMELE.   No, Beroë!   By Zeus!
JUNO.   Thou swear'st?
SEMELE.   By Zeus!   By mine own Zeus!
JUNO. (*Shrieking.*)   Thou swear'st?
Unhappy one!
  SEMELE. (*In alarm.*)   What mean'st thou?   Beroë!
  JUNO.   Repeat the word that dooms thee to become
The wretchedest of all on Earth's wide face!—
Alas, lost creature!   'Twas not Zeus!
  SEMELE.   Not Zeus?
Oh, fearful thought!
  JUNO.   A cunning traitor 'twas
From Attica, who, 'neath a god-like form,
Robb'd thee of honour, shame, and innocence!—
                         [SEMELE *sinks to the ground.*
Well may'st thou fall!   Ne'er may'st thou rise again!
May endless night enshroud thine eyes in darkness,
May endless silence round thine ears encamp!
Remain for ever here a lifeless mass!
Oh, infamy!   Enough to hurl chaste day
Back into Hecate's gloomy arms once more!
Ye Gods!   And is it thus that Beroë
Finds Cadmus' daughter, after sixteen years
Of bitter separation!   Full of joy
I came from Epidaurus; but with shame
To Epidaurus must retrace my steps.—
Despair I take with me.   Alas, my people!
E'en to the second Deluge now the plague
May rage at will, may pile Mount Oeta high
With corpses upon corpses, and may turn
All Greece into one mighty charnel-house,

Ere Semele can bend the angry Gods.
I, thou, and Greece, and all, have been betray'd!
　　SEMELE. (*Trembling as she rises, and extending an arm
towards her.*)　Oh, Beroë!
　　JUNO.　　　　　　　　　　Take courage, my dear heart!
Perchance '*tis* Zeus! altho' it scarce can be!
Perchance 'tis really Zeus!　This we must learn!
He must disclose himself to thee, or thou
Must fly his sight for ever, and devote
The monster to the death-revenge of Thebes.
Look up, dear daughter—look upon the face
Of thine own Beroë, who looks on thee
With sympathizing eyes—my Semele,
Were it not well to try him?
　　SEMELE.　　　　　　　　No, by Heaven!
I should not find him then——
　　JUNO.　　　　　　　　What!　Wilt thou be
Perchance less wretched, if thou pinest on
In mournful doubt?—and if 'tis really he,—
　　SEMELE. (*Hiding her face in Juno's lap.*)　Ah! 'tis
　　　　not he!
　　JUNO.　　　　　And if he came to thee
Array'd in all the majesty wherein
Olympus sees him? Semele! What then?
Wouldst thou repent thee then of having tried him?
　　SEMELE. (*Springing up.*) Ha! be it so! He must unveil
　　　　himself!
　　JUNO. (*Hastily.*)　Thou must not let　him　sink into
　　　　thine arms
Till he unveils himself—so hearken, child,
To what thy faithful nurse now counsels thee,—
To what affection whispers in mine ear,
And will accomplish!—Say! will he soon come?
　　SEMELE.　Before Hyperion sinks in Thetis' bed,
He promis'd to appear.
　　JUNO. (*Forgetting herself, hastily.*)　Is't so, indeed?
He promis'd?　Ha!　To-day? (*Recovering herself.*)
　　　　　　　　　　　Let him approach,

And when he would attempt, inflam'd with love,
To clasp his arms around thee, then do thou,—
Observe me well,—as if by lightning struck,
Start back in haste.   Ha! picture his surprise!
Leave him not long in wonderment, my child;
Continue to repulse him with a look
As cold as ice—more wildly, with more ardour
He'll press thee then—the coyness of the fair
Is but a dam, that for awhile keeps back
The torrent, only to increase the flood
With greater fury.   Then begin to weep:
'Gainst giants he might stand,—look calmly on
When Typheus, hundred-arm'd, in fury hurl'd
Mount Ossa and Olympus 'gainst his throne:
But Zeus is soon subdued by beauty's tears.
Thou smilest?—Be it so!   Is, then, the scholar
Wiser, perchance, than she who teaches her?—
Then thou must pray the God one little, little
Most innocent request to grant to thee—
One that may seal his love and Godhead too.
He'll swear by Styx.   The Styx he must obey!
That oath he dares not break!   Then speak these words:
" Thou shalt not touch this body, till thou com'st
" To Cadmus' daughter cloth'd in all the might
" Wherein thou art embrac'd by Kronos' daughter! "
Be not thou terrified, my Semele,
If he, in order to escape thy wish,
As bugbears paints the horrors of his presence—
Describes the flames that round about him roar,
The thunder round him rolling when he comes:
These, Semele, are nought but empty fears—
The Gods dislike to show to us frail mortals
These the most glorious of their attributes;
Be thou but obstinate in thy request,
And Juno's self will gaze on thee with envy.

   Semele.   The frightful ox-eyed one!   How often he
Complains, in the blest moments of our love,
Of her tormenting him with her black gall—

Juno. (*Aside, furiously, but with embarrassment.*)
Ha! creature! Thou shalt die for this contempt!
Semele.   My Beroë!   What art thou murmuring
  there?
Juno.   (*In confusion.*)
Nothing, my Semele!   Black gall torments
Me also—Yes! a sharp, reproachful look
With lovers often passes as black gall—
Yet ox-eyes, after all, are not so ugly.
Semele.   Oh, Beroë, for shame! they're quite the
  worst
That any head can possibly contain!
And then her cheeks of green and yellow hues,
The obvious penalty of poisonous envy—
Zeus oft complains to me that that same shrew
Each night torments him with her nauseous love,
And with her jealous whims,—enough, I'm sure,
Into Ixion's wheel to turn all Heaven.
Juno.   (*Raving up and down in extreme confusion.*)
No more of this!
Semele.   What, Beroë! So angry?
Have I said more than what is true? Said more
Than what is wise?
Juno.   Thou hast said more, young woman,
Than what is true—said more than what is wise!
Deem thyself truly blest, if thy blue eyes
Smile thee not into Charon's bark too soon!
Saturnia has her altars and her temples,
And wanders amongst mortals—that great Goddess
Avenges nought so bitterly as scorn.
Semele.   Here let her wander, and give birth to
  scorn!
What is't to me?—My Jupiter protects
My ev'ry hair,—what harm can Juno do?
But now enough of this, my Beroë!
Zeus must appear to-day in all his glory;
And if Saturnia should on that account
Find out the path to Orcus—

Juno. (*Aside.*)　　　　　　　That same path
Another probably will find before her,
If but Kronīon's lightning hits the mark!—
　　　　　　　　　　　　(*To Semele.*)
Yes, Semele, she well may burst with envy
When Cadmus' daughter, in the sight of Greece,
Ascends in triumph to Olympus' heights!—

Semele. (*Smiling gently.*)
Think'st thou they'll hear in Greece of Cadmus'
　　　　daughter?

Juno. From Sidon to Athens the trumpet of
　　　　Fame
Shall ring with no other but Semele's name!
The Gods from the Heavens shall even descend,
And before thee their knees in deep homage shall bend,
While mortals in silent submission abide
The will of the Giant-Destroyer's lov'd bride;
And when distant years shall see
Thy last hour—

Semele. (*Springing up, and falling on her neck.*)
　　　　　　Oh Beroë!

Juno.　Then a tablet white shall bear
　　　　This inscription graven there:
　　　　Here is worshipp'd Semele!
　　　　Who on earth so fair as she?
　　　　She who from Olympus' throne
　　　　Lur'd the Thunder-hurler down!
　　　　She who, with her kisses sweet,
　　　　Laid him prostrate at her feet!
And when Fame on her thousand wings bears it
　　　　around,
The echo from valley and hill shall resound.

Semele. (*Beside herself.*)
　　　　　Pythia! Apollo! Hear!
　　　　　When, oh when will he appear?

Juno.　And on smoking altars they
　　　　Rites divine to thee shall pay—·

SEMELE.　(*Inspired.*)
　　　　I will hearken to their prayer,
　　　　And will drive away their care,—
Quench with my tears the lightning of great Jove,
His breast to pity with entreaty move!
　JUNO.　(*Aside.*)　Poor thing! *that* wilt thou ne'er have
　　　　power to do.　(*Meditating.*)
Ere long will melt . . . . . yet—yet—she call'd me
　　　　ugly!—
No! Pity only when in Tartarus!

　　　　　　　　　　　　　　　　(*To Semele.*)

Fly now, my love! Make haste to leave this spot,
That Zeus may not observe thee—Let him wait
Long for thy coming, that he with more fire
May languish for thee—
　SEMELE.　　　　　　　Beroë!　The Heavens
Have chosen thee their mouthpiece!　Happy I!
The Gods from Olympus shall even descend,
And before me their knees in deep homage shall bend,
While mortals in silent submission abide—
But hold!—'tis time for me to haste away!
　　　　　　　　　　　　　　　[*Exit hurriedly.*

　JUNO.　(*Looking after her with exultation.*)
Weak, proud, and easily-deluded woman!
His tender looks shall be consuming fire—
His kiss, annihilation—his embrace,
A raging tempest to thee!　Human frames
Are powerless to endure the dreaded presence
Of Him who wields the thunderbolt on high!
　　　　　　　　　　　　　(*With raving ecstasy.*)
Ha! when her waxen mortal body melts
Within the arms of Him, the Fire-distilling,
As melts the fleecy snow before the heat
Of the bright sun—and when the perjur'd one,
In place of his soft tender bride, embraces
A form of terror—with what ecstasy
Shall I gaze downwards from Cithæron's height,
Exclaiming, so that in his hand the bolt

Shall quake: "For shame, Saturnius! Fie, for shame!
" What need is there for thee to clasp so roughly?"
[Exit hastily.

(*A Symphony.*)

SCENE II.

The Hall as before.—Sudden brightness.

Zeus *in the shape of a Youth.*—Mercury *in the
distance.*

Zeus.   Thou Son of Maia!
Mercury.   (*Kneeling, with his head bowed reverentially.*)
Zeus!
Zeus.   Up! Hasten! Turn
Thy pinions' flight tow'rd far Scamander's bank!
A shepherd there is weeping o'er the grave
Of his lov'd shepherdess.   No one shall weep
When Zeus is loving: Call the dead to life!
Mercury.   (*Rising.*)   Let but thy head a nod almighty
      give,
And in an instant I am there,—am back
In the same instant—
Zeus.   Stay! As I o'er Argos
Was flying, from my temples curling rose
The sacrificial smoke: it gave me joy
That thus the people worship me—so fly
To Ceres, to my sister,—thus speaks Zeus:
" Ten-thousandfold for fifty years to come
" Let her reward the Argive husbandmen!"—
Mercury.   With trembling haste I execute thy
      wrath,—
With joyous speed thy messages of grace,
Father of All!   For to the Deities
'Tis bliss to make man happy; to destroy him
Is anguish to the Gods.   Thy will be done!

Where shall I pour into Thine ears their thanks,—
Below in dust, or at Thy throne on high?
   Zeus.   Here at my throne on earth—within the
     palace,
Of Semele! Away!

                                     [*Exit Mercury.*

                    Does she not come,
As is her wont, Olympus' mighty king
To clasp against her rapture-swelling breast?
Why hastens not my Semele to meet me?
A vacant, death-like, fearful silence reigns
On ev'ry side around the lonely palace,
So wont to ring with wild Bacchantic shouts—
No breath is stirring—on Cithæron's height
Exulting Juno stands. Will Semele
Never again make haste to meet her Zeus?
              (*A pause, after which he continues.*)
Ha! Can yon impious one perchance have dar'd
To set her foot in my love's sanctuary?—
Saturnia—Mount Cithæron—her rejoicings!
Fearful foreboding!—Semele—yet peace!—
Take courage!—I'm thy Zeus! the scatter'd Heav'ns
Shall learn, my Semele, that I'm thy Zeus!
Where is the breath of air that dares presume
Roughly to blow on her whom Zeus calls *His?*
I scoff at all her malice.—Where art thou,
Oh Semele? I long have pin'd to rest
My world-tormented head upon thy breast,—
To lull my wearied senses to repose
From the wild storm of earthly joys and woes,—
To dream away the emblems of my might,
My reins, my tiller, and my chariot bright,
And live for nought beyond the joys of love!
Oh heav'nly inspiration, that can move
Even the Gods divine! What is the blood
Of mighty Uranus—what all the flood
Of nectar and ambrosia—what the throne
Of high Olympus—what the pow'r I own,

The golden sceptre of the starry skies—
What the Omnipotence that never dies,
What Might eternal, Immortality—
What e'en a God, oh love, if reft of thee?
The shepherd who, beside the murmuring brook,
Leans on his true love's breast, nor cares to look
After his straying lambs, in that sweet hour
Envies me not my thunderbolt of power!
She comes—she hastens nigh!   Pearl of my works,
Woman!—the Artist who created thee
Should be ador'd.   'Twas I—myself I worship:
Zeus worships Zeus, for Zeus created thee.
Ha! Who will now, in all the Being-realm,
Condemn me?   How unseen, yes, how despis'd
Dwindle away my worlds, my constellations,
So ray-diffusing, all my dancing systems,
What wise men call the music of my spheres !—
How dead are all when weigh'd against a soul!
(Semele approaches, without looking up.)
My pride! my throne on earth!   Oh Semele!
(He rushes towards her; she seeks to fly.)
Thou fly'st?—Art mute?—Ha! Semele! thou fly'st?
  Semele. (Repulsing him.)   Away!
  Zeus.   (After a pause of astonishment.)
Is Jupiter asleep?   Will Nature
Rush to her fall?—Can Semele speak thus?—
What, not an answer?   Eagerly mine arms
Tow'rd thee are stretch'd—my bosom never throbb'd
Responsive to Agenor's daughter,—never
Throbb'd against Leda's breast,—my lips ne'er burn'd
For the sweet kiss of prison'd Danaë,
As now—
  Semele.   Peace, Traitor! Peace!
  Zeus.   (With displeasure, but tenderly.)   My Semele!
  Semele.   Out of my sight!
  Zeus.   (Looking at her with majesty.)
Know, I am Zeus!

SEMELE.   Thou Zeus?
Tremble, Salmoneus, for he fearfully
Will soon demand again the stolen charms
That thou hast robb'd him of—thou art not Zeus!
    ZEUS.   (*With dignity.*)
The mighty universe around me whirls,
And calls me so—
    SEMELE.   Ha!   Fearful blasphemy!
    ZEUS.   (*More gently.*)   How, my divine one?
       Wherefore such a tone?
What reptile dares to steal thine heart from me?
    SEMELE.   My heart was vow'd to Him whose ape
       thou art!
Men ofttimes come beneath a godlike form
To snare a woman.   Hence! thou art not Zeus!
    ZEUS.   Thou doubtest?   What!   Can Semele still
       doubt
My Godhead?
    SEMELE.   (*Mournfully.*)   Would that thou wert Zeus!
       No son
Of morrow-nothingness shall touch this mouth;
This heart is vow'd to Zeus!   Would thou wert He!
    ZEUS.   Thou weepest?   Zeus is here,—weeps Semele?
                     [*Falling down before her.*
Speak!   But command! and then shall slavish Nature
Lie trembling at the feet of Cadmus' daughter!
Command! and streams shall instantly make halt—
And Helicon, and Caucasus, and Cynthus,
And Athos, Mycale, and Rhodope, and Pindus,
Shall burst their bonds when I order it so,
And kiss the valleys and plains below,
And dance in the breeze like flakes of snow.
Command! and the Winds from the East and the
       North,
And the fierce Tornado shall sally forth,
While Poseidon's trident their power shall own,
When they shake to its base his watery throne;

The billows in angry fury shall rise,
And every sea-mark and dam despise;
The lightning shall gleam thro' the firmament black,
While the poles of Earth and of Heaven shall crack,
The Ocean the heights of Olympus explore,
From thousandfold jaws with wild deafening roar
The thunder shall howl, while with mad jubilee
The hurricane fierce sings in triumph to thee.
Command—
   SEMELE.   I'm but a woman, a frail woman!
How can the Potter bend before his pot?
How can the Artist kneel before his statue?
   ZEUS.   Pygmalion bow'd before his masterpiece-
And Zeus now worships his own Semele!
   SEMELE.   (*Weeping bitterly.*)
Arise—arise!   Alas, for us poor maidens!
Zeus has my heart, Gods only can I love.
The Gods deride me, Zeus despises me!
   ZEUS.   Zeus who is now before thy feet—
   SEMELE.   Arise!
Zeus reigns on high, above the thunderbolts,
And, clasp'd in Juno's arms, a reptile scorns.
   ZEUS.   (*Hastily.*)
Ha! Semele and Juno!—which the reptile?
   SEMELE.   How blest beyond all utterance would be
Cadmus's daughter—wert thou Zeus!   Alas!
Thou art not Zeus!   .
   ZEUS. (*Arises.*)   I am!
   (*He extends his hand, and a rainbow fills the hall; music
        accompanies its appearance*).
                    Know'st thou me now?
   SEMELE.   Strong is that mortal's arm, whom Gods
     protect,—
Saturnius loves thee—none can *I* e'er love
But Deities—
   ZEUS.   What! art thou doubting still
Whether my might is lent me by the Gods,
And not God-born?   The Gods, my Semele,

          .

In charity oft lend their strength to man;
Ne'er do the Deities their terrors lend—
Death and destruction is the Godhead's seal—
Bearer of death to thee were Zeus unveil'd!
(*He extends his hand. Thunder, fire, smoke, and earth-
    quake. Music accompanies the spell here and sub-
    sequently.*)

    SEMELE.   Withdraw, withdraw thy hand!—Oh, mercy,
    mercy
For the poor nation! Yes! thou art the Child
Of great Saturnius—

    ZEUS.   Ha! thou thoughtless one!
Shall Zeus, to please a woman's stubbornness,
Bid planets whirl, and bid the suns stand still?
Zeus *will* do so!—Oft has a God's descendant
Ripp'd up the fire-impregnate womb of rocks,
And yet his might's confined to Tellus' bounds;
Zeus only can do *this!*
    (*He extends his hand—the sun vanishes, and it becomes
                    suddenly night.*)

    SEMELE.   (*Falling down before him.*)   Almighty one!
Couldst thou but love!

                                  [*Day reappears.*

    ZEUS.   Ha! Cadmus' daughter asks
Kronïon if Kronïon e'er can love!
One word, and he throws off Divinity—
Is flesh and blood, and dies, and is belov'd!

    SEMELE.   Would Zeus do *that?*

    ZEUS.   Speak, Semele! What more?
Apollo's self confesses that 'tis bliss
To be a man 'mongst men—a sign from thee,
And I'm a man!

    SEMELE.   (*Falling on his neck.*)
Oh Jupiter, the Epidaurus women
Thy Semele a foolish maiden call,
Because, though by the Thunderer belov'd,
She can obtain nought from him—

Zeus. (*Eagerly.*)   They shall blush,
Those Epidaurus women!   Ask!—but ask!
And by the dreaded Styx—whose boundless might
Binds e'en the Gods like slaves—if Zeus deny thee,
Then shall the Gods, e'en in that self-same moment,
Hurl me despairing to annihilation!
Semele. (*Springing up joyfully.*)
By this I know that thou'rt my Jupiter!
Thou swearest—and the Styx has heard thine oath!
Let me embrace thee, then, in the same guise
In which—
Zeus. (*Shrieking with alarm.*)
                    Unhappy one!   Oh stay! oh stay!
Semele. Saturnia—
Zeus. (*Attempting to stop her mouth.*)
                    Be thou dumb!
Semele.   Embraces thee!
Zeus. (*Pale, and turning away.*)
Too late!   The sound escap'd!—The Styx!—'Tis death
Thou, Semele, hast gain'd!
Semele.   Ha! Loves Zeus thus?
Zeus.   All Heaven I would have given, had I only
Lov'd thee but less!
                    (*Gazing at her with cold horror.*)
                    Thou'rt lost—
Semele.   Oh, Jupiter!
Zeus. (*Speaking furiously to himself.*)
Ah! Now I mark thine exultation, Juno!
Accursed jealousy!   This rose must die!
Too fair—alas! too sweet for Acheron!
Semele.   Methinks thou'rt niggard of thy majesty!
Zeus.   Accursed be my majesty, that now
Has blinded thee!   Accursed be my greatness,
That must destroy thee!   Curs'd be I myself
For having built my bliss on crumbling dust!
Semele.   These are but empty terrors, Zeus!   In
    truth
I do not dread thy threats!

ZEUS.   Deluded child!
Go! take a last farewell for evermore
Of all thy friends belov'd—nought, nought has power
To save thee, Semele!   I am thy Zeus!
Yet *that* no more—Go—
    SEMELE.   Jealous one! the Styx!—
Think not that thou'lt be able to escape me.   [*Exit.*
    ZEUS. No!   Juno shall not triumph.—She shall
        tremble—
Aye, and by virtue of the deadly might
That makes the earth and makes the heavens my foot-
        stool,
Upon the sharpest rock in Thracia's land
With adamantine chains I'll bind her fast.
But, oh, this oath—
                    [*Mercury appears in the distance.*
                What means thy hasty flight?
    MERCURY. I bring the fiery, wing'd, and weeping
        thanks
Of those whom thou hast bless'd—
    ZEUS.   Again destroy them!
    MERCURY. (*In amazement.*) Zeus!
    ZEUS.   None shall now be bless'd!
She dies—

                    [*The Curtain falls.*

HYMN TO JOY.

Joy, thou Goddess, fair, immortal,
  Offspring of Elysium,
Mad with rapture, to the portal
  Of thy holy fane we come !
Fashion's laws, indeed, may sever,
  But thy magic joins again ;
All mankind are brethren ever
  'Neath thy mild and gentle reign.

CHORUS.

Welcome, all ye myriad creatures !
  Brethren, take the kiss of love !
  Yes, the starry realms above
Hide a father's smiling features !

He, that noble prize possessing—
  He that boasts a friend that's true,
He whom woman's love is blessing,
  Let him join the chorus too !
Aye, and he who but *one* spirit
  On this earth can call his own !—
He who no such bliss can merit,
  Let him mourn his fate alone !

CHORUS.

All who nature's tribes are swelling
  Homage pay to Sympathy ;
  For she guides us up on high,
Where THE UNKNOWN has his dwelling.

From the breasts of kindly Nature
  All of Joy imbibe the dew ;
Good and bad alike, each creature
  Would her roseate path pursue.

'Tis through *her* the wine-cup maddens,
  Love and friends to man she gives!
Bliss the meanest reptile gladdens,—
  Near God's throne the Cherub lives!

CHORUS.

Bow before him, all creation!
  Mortals, own the God of love!
  Seek him high the stars above,—
Yonder is his habitation!

Joy, in Nature's wide dominion,
  Mightiest cause of all is found;
And 'tis Joy that moves the pinion,
  When the wheel of time goes round;
From the bud she lures the flower—
  Suns from out their orbs of light;
Distant spheres obey her power,
  Far beyond all mortal sight.

CHORUS.

As through Heaven's expanse so glorious,
  In their orbits suns roll on,
  Brethren, thus your proud race run,
Glad as warriors all-victorious!

Joy from Truth's own glass of fire
  Sweetly on the Searcher smiles; ·
Lest on Virtue's steeps he tire,
  Joy the tedious path beguiles.
High on Faith's bright hill before us,
  See her banner proudly wave!
Joy, too, swells the Angels' chorus,—
  Bursts the bondage of the grave!

CHORUS.

Mortals, meekly wait for Heaven!
  Suffer on in patient love!
  In the starry realms above,
Bright rewards by God are given.

To the Gods we ne'er can render
  Praise for every good they grant;
Let us, with devotion tender,
  Minister to Grief and Want.
Quench'd be hate and wrath for ever,
  Pardon'd be our mortal foe—
May our tears upbraid him never,
  No repentance bring him low!

CHORUS.

Sense of wrongs forget to treasure—
  Brethren, live in perfect love!
  In the starry realms above,
God will mete as we may measure.

Joy within the goblet flushes,
  For the golden nectar, wine,
Ev'ry fierce emotion hushes,—
  Fills the breast with fire divine.
Brethren, thus in rapture meeting,
  Send ye round the brimming cup,—
Yonder kindly Spirit greeting,
  While the foam to Heaven mounts up!

CHORUS.

He whom Seraphs worship ever,
  Whom the stars praise as they roll,
  Yes—to Him now drain the bowl—
Mortal eye can see Him never!

Courage, ne'er by sorrow broken!
  Aid where tears of virtue flow;
Faith to keep each promise spoken!
  Truth alike to friend and foe!
'Neath kings' frowns a manly spirit!—
  Brethren, noble is the prize—
Honour due to ev'ry merit!
  Death to all the brood of lies!

CHORUS.

Draw the sacred circle closer!
　By this bright wine plight your troth
　To be faithful to your oath!
Swear it by the Star-Disposer!

Safety from the Tyrant's power! *
　Mercy e'en to traitors base!
Hope in death's last solemn hour!
　Pardon when before His face!
Lo, the dead shall rise to Heaven!
　Brethren hail the blest decree:
Ev'ry sin shall be forgiven,
　Hell for ever cease to be!

CHORUS.

When the golden bowl is broken,
　Gentle sleep within the tomb!
　Brethren, may a gracious doom
By the Judge of Man be spoken!

THE INVINCIBLE ARMADA.

She comes, she comes—Iberia's proud Armada—
　The waves beneath the heavy burden sigh;
Laden with bigotry and chains, the invader,
　Charged with a thousand thunders, now draws nigh;
And as she sweeps along in stately motion,
With trembling awe is fill'd the startled Ocean.
　　Each ship a floating citadel,
　　Men call her "The Invincible!"

* This concluding and fine strophe is omitted in the later editions
of Schiller's 'Poems.'

Why should she boast that haughty name?
The fear she spreads allows her claim.

With silent and majestic step advancing,
  Affrighted Neptune bears her on his breast;
From ev'ry port-hole fierce destruction glancing,
  She comes, and lo! the tempest sinks to rest.

And now at length the proud fleet stands before thee,
  Thrice-happy Island, Mistress of the Sea!
Mighty Britannia, danger hovers o'er thee,
  Those countless galleons threaten slavery!
    Woe to thy freedom-nurtur'd nation!
    Yon cloud is big with desolation!

How came that priceless gem in thy possession,
  Which raised thee high above each other State?
Thyself it was, who, struggling 'gainst oppression,
  Earn'd for thy sons that statute wise and great—
The MAGNA CHARTA—'neath whose shelt'ring wings
Monarchs but subjects are, and subjects kings!
To rule the waves, thy ships have prov'd their right,
Defeating each proud foe in ocean-fight.
All this thou ow'st,—ye nations, blush to hear it!—
To thy good sword alone, and dauntless spirit!

    See where the monster comes—unhappy one!
    Alas, thy glorious race is well-nigh run!
    Alarm and terror fill this earthly ball,
The hearts of all free men are beating madly,
And ev'ry virtuous soul is waiting sadly
    The hour when thy great name is doom'd to fall.

    God the Almighty look'd down from his throne,
And saw thy foe's proud "Lion-Banner" flying,
And saw the yawning grave before thee lying,—
    "What!" He exclaim'd, "shall my lov'd Albion,
    And all her race of heroes, now so free,
    Pine in the galling bonds of slavery?

Shall she, whose name with dread all tyrants hear,
Be swept for ever from this hemisphere ?"

"Never," He cried, " shall Freedom's Eden true,
That bulwark of all human rights, be shatter'd !"—
  God the Almighty blew,
And to the winds of heaven the fleet was scatter'd !*

THE CONFLICT.

No longer will I fight this conflict weary,
  The giant fight that Duty bids me wage ;
Why, Virtue, ask a sacrifice so dreary,
  If thou my bosom's pangs canst not assuage ?

I've sworn it,—yes ! I solemnly have sworn it,—
  Upon my passions to impose a rein ;
Behold thy garland !—yet, tho' long I've worn it,
  Take it back now, and let me sin again !

Dissolv'd be ev'ry vow between us spoken—
  She loves me !—What is now thy crown to me ?
Happy the man who, wrapp'd in bliss unbroken,
  His deep, deep fall can view so tranquilly !

She sees the worm my youthful bloom assailing,
  She sees my days in sorrow fleeting on ;
And my heroic efforts gently hailing,
  Awards the prize she deems me to have won.

Fair soul ! mistrust this virtue angel-seeming,
  For on to crime thy pity hurries me ;
In the unbounded realms where life is beaming,
  Is there another, fairer prize than *thee?*

* These last two lines refer to the medal struck by Queen
Elizabeth to commemorate the overthrow of the Armada, on which
was the inscription—*Afflavit Deus, et dissipati sunt.*

Or than that sin so dreaded by my spirit ?—
    Oh cruel, all-relentless tyranny !
The only prize my virtue e'er can merit
    Must, in the moment, see that virtue die !

RESIGNATION.

YES ! even I was in Arcadia born,
    And, in mine infant ears,
A vow of Rapture was by Nature sworn ;
Yes ! even I was in Arcadia born,
    And yet my short Spring gave me only—tears !

Once blooms, and only once, Life's youthful May ;
    For *me* its bloom hath gone.
The Silent God—O Brethren, weep to-day—
The Silent God hath quench'd my Torch's ray,
    And the vain dream hath flown.

Upon thy darksome bridge, Eternity,
    I stand e'en now, dread thought !
Take, then, these Joy-Credentials back from me !
Unopen'd I return them now to thee,
    Of Happiness, alas, know nought !

Before thy throne my mournful cries I vent,
    Thou Judge, conceal'd from view !
To yonder Star a joyous Saying went :
With Judgment's scales to rule us thou art sent,
    And call'st thyself REQUITER, too !

Here,—say they,—terrors on the Bad alight,
    And joys to greet the Virtuous spring.
The bosom's windings thou'lt expose to sight,
Riddle of Providence wilt solve aright,
    And reckon with the Suffering !

Here to the Exile be a home outspread,
    Here end the meek man's thorny path of strife!
A god-like child, whose name was Truth, they said,
Known but to few, from whom the many fled,
    Restrain'd the ardent bridle of my Life.

" It shall be thine another Life to live,—
    Thy youth to me surrender!
To thee this surety only can I give "—
I took the surety in that Life to live;
    And gave to her each youthful joy so tender.

" Give me the woman precious to thy heart,
    Give up to me thy Laura!
Beyond the grave will usury pay the smart."—
I wept aloud, and from my bleeding heart
    With resignation tore her.

" The obligation's drawn upon the Dead!"
    Thus laugh'd the World in scorn;
" The Lying One, in league with Despots dread,
For Truth, a Phantom palm'd on thee instead,
    Thou'lt be no more, when once this Dream
        has gone!"

Shamelessly scoff'd the Mockers' serpent-band:
    " A Dream that but Prescription can admit
Dost dread? Where now thy God's protecting hand,
(The sick world's Saviours with such cunning
        plann'd),
    Borrow'd by Human need of Human wit?

" What Future is't that graves to us reveal?
    What the Eternity of thy discourse?
Honour'd because dark veils its form conceal,
The giant-shadows of the awe we feel,
    View'd in the hollow mirror of Remorse!

“ An Image false of shapes of living mould,
    (Time’s very mummy, she !)
Whom only Hope’s sweet balm hath power to hold
Within the chambers of the grave so cold,—
    Thy fever calls *this* Immortality !

“ For empty hopes,—corruption gives the lie—
    Didst thou exchange what thou hadst *surely*
      done ?
Six thousand years sped Death in silence by,—
Has corpse from out the grave e’er mounted high,
    That mention made of the Requiting One ?”—

I saw Time fly to reach thy distant shore,
    I saw fair Nature lie
A shrivell’d corpse behind him evermore,—
No dead from out the grave then sought to soar
    Yet in that Oath divine still trusted I.

My ev’ry joy to thee I’ve sacrific’d,
    I throw me now before thy Judgment-throne !
The Many’s scorn with boldness I’ve despis’d,—
Only *thy* gifts by me were ever priz’d,—
    I ask my wages now, Requiting One !

“ With equal love I love each child of mine !”
    A Genius hid from sight exclaim’d.
“ Two flowers,” he cried, “ ye Mortals, mark the sign,—
Two flowers to greet the Searcher wise entwine,—
    Hope and Enjoyment they are nam’d.

“ Who of these flowers plucks one, let him ne’er yearn
    To touch the other sister’s bloom.
Let him enjoy, who has no faith ; eterne
As earth, this truth !—Abstain, who faith can learn !
    The World’s long story is the world’s own doom.

"Hope thou hast felt,—thy wages, then, are paid ;
    Thy Faith 'twas form'd the rapture pledg'd
        to thee.
Thou might'st have of the Wise inquiry made,—
The minutes thou neglectest, as they fade,
    Are given back by no Eternity !"

THE GODS OF GREECE.

Whilst the smiling Earth ye govern'd still,
    And with Rapture's soft and guiding hand
Let the happy Nations at your will,
    Beauteous Beings from the Fable-land !
Whilst your blissful worship smil'd around,
    Ah ! how diff'rent was it in that day !
When the people still thy temples crown'd,
    Venus Amathusia !

When the magic veil of Poesy
    Still round Truth entwin'd its loving chain—
Through creation pour'd Life's fulness free,
    Things then *felt*, which ne'er can feel again.
Then to press her 'gainst the breast of Love,
    They on Nature nobler power bestow'd,—
All, to eyes enlighten'd from above,
    Of a God the traces show'd.

There, where now, as we're by Sages told,
    Whirls on high a soulless fiery ball,
Helios guided then his car of gold,
    In his silent majesty, o'er all.
Oreads then these heights around us fill'd,
    Then a Dryad dwelt in yonder tree,
From the Urn of loving Naiads rill'd
    Silver streamlets foamingly.

Yonder Laurel once imploring wound,
  Tantal's daughter slumbers in this stone;
From yon rush rose Syrinx' mournful sound,
  From this thicket, Philomela's moan.
Yonder brook Demeter's tears receiv'd,
  That she wept for her Persephone,
From this hill, of her lov'd friend bereav'd,
  Cried Cythere, fruitlessly!

To Deucalion's race from realms of air
  Then the great Immortals still came down;
And to vanquish Pyrrha's daughter fair,
  Then a shepherd's staff took Leto's son.
Then 'tween Heroes, Deities, and Men,
  Was a beauteous bond by Eros twin'd,
And with Deities and Heroes then
  Knelt in Cyprus' Isle, mankind.

Gloomy sternness and denial sad
  Ne'er were in your service blest descried;
Each heart throbb'd then with emotions glad,
  For the Happy were with you allied.
Nothing then was Holy, save the Fair;
  Of no rapture was the God asham'd,
When the modest Muse was blushing there,—
  When their sway the Graces claim'd!

Palace-like, then smil'd your Temples all,
  Ye were honour'd in the hero-sport
At the Isthmus' crown-clad festival,
  And the goal the thund'ring chariots sought.
Beauteous dances that a Spirit breath'd
  Circled round your altars bright and fair;
Round your brows the crown of triumph wreath'd,
  Garlands graced your fragrant hair.

Thyrsus-swingers' loud Evoë then,
  And the panther-team that shone afar,
Welcom'd Him who Rapture brought to men;
  Fauns and Satyrs reel'd before his Car!

Round him sprang the Mænads' raving crew,
  While their dances show'd his wine's great worth,
And the Host's full cheeks of tawny hue
  Pointed to the cup with mirth.

In those days, before the bed of Death
  Stood no ghastly form.   Then took away
From the lips a kiss the parting breath,
  And a Genius quench'd his torch's ray.
Even Orcus' rigid judgment-scales
  By a Mortal's offspring once were held,
And the Thracian's spirit-breathing wails
  E'en the angry Furies quell'd.

Once again within Elysium's grove
  Met the happy Shade his joys so dear;
Lover faithful found his faithful Love,
  And his path regain'd the charioteer;
Linus' lute gave back each wonted strain,
  Admet clasp'd Alcestis to his heart,
And Orestes found his friend again,
  Philoctetes found his dart.

Nobler prizes then the wrestler crown'd,
  Who the arduous path of Virtue press'd;
Glorious workers then of deeds renown'd
  Clamber'd up to join the Spirits blest.
All the Band of Silent Gods the while
  Bow'd to Him who summon'd back the Dead;
From Olympus' height the twin-stars' smile
  O'er the waves the Pilot led.

Beauteous World, where art thou gone? Oh, thou,
  Nature's blooming youth, return once more!
Ah, but in Song's fairy region now
  Lives thy fabled trace so dear of yore!
Cold and perish'd, sorrow now the plains,
  Not one Godhead greets my longing sight;
Ah, the Shadow only now remains
  Of yon living Image bright!

All those lovely blossoms now are gone,
  Scatter'd by the North-wind's piercing breath;
To enrich, amongst the whole, but ONE,
  All this God-like world was doom'd to death.
Sadly turn I to the stars on high—
  Thou, Selene, canst not there be found!
Through the forest, through the waves I cry—
  Ah, they echo back no sound!

Feeling not the joy she bids me share,
  Ne'er entranced by her own majesty,
Knowing her own guiding spirit ne'er,
  Ne'er made happy by *my* ecstasy,
Senseless even to her Maker's praise,
  Like the pendule-clock's dead, hollow tone,
Nature Gravitation's law obeys
  Servilely,—her Godhead flown.

That to-morrow she herself may free,
  She prepares her sepulchre to-day;
And on spindle balanced equally,
  Up and down the Moons alternate play.
Idly homeward to the Poet-land
  Go the Gods—a world they'd serve in vain,
That's upheld by its own motive hand,
  Casting off the guiding-rein.

Aye! they homeward go,—and they have flown,
  All that's bright and fair they've taken too,
Ev'ry colour, ev'ry living tone,—
  And a soulless world is all we view.
Borne off by the Time-flood's current strong,
  They on Pindus' height have safety found:
All that is to live in endless song,
  Must in Life-time first be drown'd!

THE ARTISTS.

How gracefully, O Man, with thy palm-bough,
Upon the waning Century standest thou,
    In proud and noble manhood's prime,
With unlock'd Senses, with a Spirit freed,
Of Firmness mild,—though silent, rich in deed,
    The ripest son of Time,
Through meekness great, through precepts strong,
Through treasures rich, that time had long
    Hid in thy bosom, and through Reason free,—
Master of Nature, who thy fetters loves,
And who thy strength in thousand conflicts proves,
    And from the Desert soar'd in pride with thee!

    Flush'd with the glow of Victory,
Never forget to prize the hand
    That found the weeping Orphan child
Deserted on Life's barren strand,
    And left a prey to hazard wild,—
That, ere thy Spirit-honour saw the day,
    Thy youthful heart watch'd over silently,
And from thy tender bosom turn'd away
    Each thought that might have stain'd its
        purity;
That kind One ne'er forget who, as in sport,
    Thy youth to noble aspirations train'd,
And who to thee in easy riddles taught
    The secret how each Virtue might be gain'd;
Who, to receive him back more perfect still,
    E'en into strangers' arms her favourite gave—
Oh, may'st thou never with degenerate will,
    Humble thyself to be her abject slave!

In Industry, the Bee the palm may bear;
    In Skill, the Worm a lesson may impart;
With Spirits blest thy Knowledge thou dost share,
    But thou, O Man, alone hast Art!

Only through Beauty's morning gate
    Didst thou the land of Knowledge find.
To merit a more glorious fate,
    In Graces trains itself the Mind.
What thrill'd thee through with trembling blest,
    When erst the Muses swept the chord,
That Power created in thy breast,
    Which to the mighty Spirit soar'd.

What first was seen by doting Reason's ken,
    When many a thousand years had pass'd away,
A Symbol of the Fair and Great e'en then,
    Before the childlike Mind uncovered lay.
Its blest form bade us honour Virtue's cause,—
    The honest Sense 'gainst Vice put forth its
        powers,
Before a Solon had devis'd the Laws
    That slowly bring to light their languid flowers.
Before Eternity's vast Scheme
    Was to the Thinker's mind reveal'd,
Was't not foreshadow'd in *his* dream,
    Whose eyes explor'd yon starry field?

Urania,—the majestic dreaded One,
    Who wears a Glory of Orions twin'd
Around her brow, and who is seen by none
    Save purest Spirits, when, in splendour shrin'd,
She soars above the Stars in pride,
    Ascending to her sunny throne,—
Her fiery chaplet lays aside,
    And now, as Beauty, stands alone;

While, with the Graces' girdle round her cast,
    She seems a Child, by children understood;
For we shall recognise as TRUTH at last,
    What here as BEAUTY only we have view'd.

When the Creator banish'd from his sight
    Frail Man to dark Mortality's abode,
And granted him a late return to Light,
    Only by treading Reason's arduous road,—
When each Immortal turn'd his face away,
    She, the Compassionate, alone
Took up her dwelling in that house of clay,
    With the deserted, banish'd One.
With drooping wing she hovers here
    Around her darling, near the Senses' land,
And on his prison-walls so drear
    Elysium paints with fond deceptive hand.

While soft Humanity still lay at rest,
    Within her tender arms extended,
No flame was stirr'd by Bigots' murderous zest,
    No guiltless blood on high ascended.
The heart that she in gentle fetters binds,
    Views Duty's slavish escort scornfully;
Her path of Light, though fairer far it winds,
    Sinks in the Sun-track of Morality.
Those who in her chaste service still remain,
    No grovelling thought can tempt, no Fate
        affright;
The Spiritual Life, so free from stain,
Freedom's sweet birthright, they receive again,
    Under the mystic sway of holy Might.

The purest among millions, happy they
    Whom to her service she has sanctified,
Whose mouths the Mighty One's commands convey,
    Within whose breasts she deigneth to abide;
Whom she ordain'd to feed her holy fire
Upon her altar's ever-flaming pyre,—

Whose eyes alone her unveil'd Graces meet,
And whom she gathers round in union sweet
In the much-honour'd place be glad
    Where noble Order bade ye climb,
    For in the Spirit-world sublime,
Man's loftiest rank ye've ever had!

Ere to the world Proportion ye reveal'd,
    That ev'ry Being joyfully obeys,—
A boundless structure, in Night's veil conceal'd,
    Illum'd by nought but faint and languid rays,
A band of Phantoms, struggling ceaselessly,
    Holding his mind in slavish fetters bound,
Unsociable and rude as he,
    Assailing him on every side around,—
Thus seem'd to Man Creation in that day!
    United to surrounding forms alone
    By the blind chains the Passions had put on,
Whilst Nature's beauteous Spirit fled away,
    Unfelt, untasted, and unknown.

And, as it hover'd o'er with parting ray,
    Ye seiz'd the shades so neighbourly,
With silent hand, with feeling mind,
And taught how they might be combin'd
    In one firm bond of Harmony.
The gaze, light-soaring, felt uplifted then,
    When first the Cedar's slender trunk it view'd,
    And pleasingly the Ocean's crystal flood
Reflected back the dancing form again.
Could ye mistake the look, with beauty fraught,
    That Nature gave to help ye on your way?
The Image floating on the billows taught
    The art the fleeting shadow to portray.
From her own Being torn apart,
    Her Phantom, beauteous as a dream,
    She plunged into the silv'ry stream,
Surrendering to her spoiler's art.

Creative power soon in your breast unfolded;
　　Too noble far, not idly to conceive,
The Shadow's form in sand, in clay ye moulded,
　　And made it in the sketch its Being leave.
The longing thirst for Action then awoke,—
And from your breast the first Creation broke.

By Contemplation captive made,
　　Ensnar'd by your discerning eye,
The friendly Phantom's soon betray'd
　　The talisman that rous'd your ecstasy.
The laws of wonder-working might,
The stores by Beauty brought to light,
Inventive Reason in soft union plann'd
To blend together 'neath your forming hand.
The Obelisk, the Pyramid ascended,
　　The Hermes stood, the Column sprang on high,
　　The reed pour'd forth the woodland melody,
Immortal Song on Victor's deeds attended.

The fairest flowers that deck'd the Earth,
　　Into a nosegay with wise choice combin'd,—
Thus the first Art from Nature had its birth;
　　Into a garland then were nosegays twin'd,
And from the works that mortal hands had made,
A second, nobler Art was now display'd.
The Child of Beauty, self-sufficient now,
　　That issued from your hands to perfect day,
Loses the chaplet that adorn'd its brow,
　　Soon as Reality asserts its sway.
The Column, yielding to Proportion's chains,
　　Must with its sisters join in friendly link,
　　The Hero in the Hero-band must sink,
The Muses' harp peals forth its tuneful strains.

The wond'ring savages soon came
　　To view the new Creation's plan:
" Behold! "—the joyous crowds exclaim,—
　　" Behold, all this is done by Man ! "

With jocund and more social aim,
The minstrel's lyre their awe awoke,
    Telling of Titans, and of Giant's-frays,
And Lion-slayers, turning, as he spoke,
    E'en into Heroes those who heard his lays.
For the first time the soul feels joy,
    By raptures bless'd that calmer are,
    That only greet it from afar,
That passions wild can ne'er destroy,
And that, when tasted, do not cloy.

And now the Spirit, free and fair,
    Awoke from out its sensual sleep;
By you unchain'd, the Slave of Care
    Into the arms of Joy could leap.
Each brutish barrier soon was set at nought,
    Humanity first graced the cloudless brow,
And the majestic, noble stranger, THOUGHT,
    From out the wond'ring brain sprang boldly now.
Man in his glory stood upright,
    And show'd the stars his kingly face;
His speaking glance the Sun's bright light
    Bless'd in the realms sublime of space.
Upon the cheek now bloom'd the smile,
    The voice's soulful Harmony
Expanded into Song the while,
    And Feeling swam in the moist eye;
And from the mouth, with Spirit teeming o'er,
Jest, sweetly link'd with Grace, began to pour.

Sunk in the instincts of the worm,
    By nought but sensual lust possess'd,
    Ye recognis'd within his breast
Love-Spiritual's noble germ;
    And that this germ of Love so blest
Escaped the senses' abject load,
To the first pastoral song he ow'd.
Rais'd to the dignity of Thought,
Passions more calm to flow were taught

From the Bard's mouth with melody.
The cheeks with dewy softness burn'd;
The longing that, though quench'd, still yearn'd,
    Proclaim'd the Spirit-Harmony.

The Wisest's wisdom, and the Strongest's vigour,—
    The Meekest's meekness, and the Noblest's grace,
By you were knit together in *one* Figure,
    Wreathing a radiant Glory round the place.
Man at the Unknown's sight must tremble,
    Yet its refulgence needs must love;
That mighty Being to resemble,
    Each glorious Hero madly strove;
The prototype of Beauty's earliest strain
Ye made resound through Nature's wide domain.

The Passions' wild and headlong course,'
    The ever-varying plan of Fate,
Duty and Instinct's twofold force,
    With proving mind and guidance straight
Ye then conducted to their ends.
    What Nature, as she moves along,
Far from each other ever rends,
    Become upon the stage, in song,
Members of Order, firmly bound.
        Awed by the Furies' chorus dread,
        Murder draws down upon its head
The doom of Death from their wild sound.
Long ere the wise to give a verdict dar'd,
An Iliad had Fate's mysteries declar'd
    To early Ages from afar;
While Providence in silence far'd
    Into the world from Thespis' car.

Yet into that world's current so sublime
Your Symmetry was borne before its time.
When the dark hand of Destiny
    Fail'd in your sight to part by force

What it had fashion'd 'neath your eye,
In darkness Life made haste to die,
   Ere it fulfill'd its beauteous course.
Then ye with bold and self-sufficient might
Led the arch further thro' the Future's night :
Then, too, ye plung'd, without a fear,
   Into Avernus' ocean black,
And found the vanish'd life so dear
   Beyond the Urn, and brought it back.
A blooming Pollux-form appear'd now soon,
   On Castor leaning, and enshrined in light—
The shadow that is seen upon the moon,
   Ere she has fill'd her silv'ry circle bright!

Yet higher,—higher still above the Earth
   Inventive Genius never ceas'd to rise :
Creations from creations had their birth,
   And harmonies from harmonies.
What *here* alone enchants the ravish'd sight,
   A nobler Beauty yonder must obey ;
The graceful charms that in the Nymph unite,
   In the divine Athenè melt away ;
The strength with which the Wrestler is endow'd,
   In the God's beauty we no longer find :
The wonder of his time—Jove's image proud—
   In the Olympian temple is enshrin'd.

The world, transform'd by Industry's bold hand,
   The human heart, by newborn instincts mov'd,
   That have in burning fights been fully prov'd,
Your circle of Creation now expand.
Advancing Man bears on his soaring pinions,
   In gratitude, Art with him in his flight,
And out of Nature's now-enrich'd dominions
   New worlds of beauty issue forth to light.
The barriers upon knowledge are o'erthrown ;

The Spirit that, with pleasure soon-matur'd,
Has in your easy triumphs been inur'd
To hasten through an Artist-whole of graces,
Nature's more distant columns duly places.
And overtakes her on her pathway lone.
He weighs her now with weights that human are,
    Metes her with measures that *she* lent of old;
While in her beauty's rites more practis'd far,
    She now must let his eye her form behold.
With youthful and self-pleasing bliss,
    He lends the spheres his harmony,
And, if he praise earth's edifice,
    'Tis for its wondrous symmetry.

In all that now around him breathes,
    Proportion sweet is ever rife;
And beauty's golden girdle wreathes
    With mildness round his path through life;
Perfection blest, triumphantly,
Before him in your works soars high;
Wherever boisterous Rapture swells,
    Wherever silent Sorrow flees,
Where pensive Contemplation dwells,
    Where he the tears of Anguish sees,
Where thousand terrors on him glare,
    Harmonious streams are yet behind—
He sees the Graces sporting there,
    With feelings silent and refin'd.
Gentle as Beauty's lines together linking,
    As the Appearances that round him play,
In tender outline in each other sinking,
    The soft breath of his life thus fleets away.
His Spirit melts in the harmonious Sea,
    That, rich in rapture, round his senses flows,
And the dissolving Thought all silently
    To omnipresent Cytherea grows.

Joining in lofty union with the Fates,
　On Graces and on Muses calm relying,
With freely-offer'd bosom he awaits
　The shaft that soon against him will be flying
From the soft bow Necessity creates.

Fav'rites belov'd of blissful Harmony,
　Welcome attendants on Life's dreary road,
The noblest and the dearest far that she,
　Who gave us Life, to bless that life bestow'd!
That unyok'd Man his duties bears in mind,
And loves the fetters that his motions bind,
That Chance with brazen sceptre rules him not,—
For *this*, Eternity is now your lot,
Your heart has won a bright reward for *this*.
　That round the cup where Freedom flows,
Merrily sport the Gods of bliss,—
　The beauteous dream its fragrance throws,—
For *this*, receive a loving kiss!

The Spirit, glorious and serene,
　Who round Necessity the Graces trains,—
　Who bids his æther and his starry plains
Upon us wait with pleasing mien,—
Who, 'mid his terrors, by his majesty gives joy,
And who is beauteous e'en when seeking to destroy,—
Him imitate, the Artist good!
As o'er the streamlet's crystal flood
The banks with chequer'd dances hover,
　The flow'ry mead, the sunset's light,—
Thus gleams, life's barren pathway over,
　Poesy's shadowy world so bright.
In bridal dress ye led us on
Before the terrible Unknown,
　Before inexorable Fate.
As in your urns the bones are laid,
With beauteous Magic veil ye shade
　The chorus dread that cares create.

Thousands of years I hasten'd through
    The boundless realm of vanish'd time ;
How sad it seems when left by you—
    But where ye linger, how sublime !

She who, with fleeting wing, of yore
    From your creating hand arose in might,
Within your arms was found once more,
    When, vanquish'd by Time's silent flight,
Life's blossoms faded from the cheek,
    And from the limbs all vigour went,
And mournfully, with footstep weak,
    Upon his staff the greybeard leant.
Then gave ye to the languishing,
Life's waters from a new-born spring ;
Twice was the youth of Time renew'd,
Twice, from the seeds that ye had strew'd.

When chas'd by fierce barbarian hordes away,
    The last remaining votive brand ye tore
From Orient's altars, now pollution's prey,
    And to these Western lands in safety bore.
The fugitive from yonder Eastern shore,
    The youthful day, the West her dwelling made ;
And on Hesperia's plains sprang up once more
    Ionia's flowers, in pristine bloom array'd.
Over the Spirit fairer Nature shed,
    With soft refulgence, a reflection bright,
And through the graceful Soul with stately tread
    Advanced the mighty Deity of light.
Millions of chains were burst asunder then,
    And to the Slave then human laws applied,
And mildly rose the younger race of men,
    As brethren, gently wand'ring side by side.
With noble inward ecstasy,
    The bliss imparted ye receive,
And in the veil of modesty,
    With silent merit take your leave.

If on the paths of Thought, so freely given,
  The Searcher now with daring fortune stands,
And, by triumphant Pæans onward driven,
  Would seize upon the crown with dauntless hands—
If he with grovelling hireling's pay
  Thinks to dismiss his glorious guide—
Or, with the first slave's-place array
  Art near the throne his dream supplied—
Forgive him !—O'er your head to-day
  Hovers Perfection's crown in pride.
With you the earliest plant Spring had,
  Soul-forming Nature first began ;
With you, the harvest-chaplet glad,
  Perfected Nature ends her plan.

The Art Creative, that all-modestly arose
From clay and stone, with silent triumph throws
  Its arms around the Spirit's vast domain.
What in the land of knowledge the Discoverer knows,
  He knows, discovers, only for *your* gain !
The treasures that the Thinker has amass'd,
  He will enjoy within your arms alone,
Soon as his knowledge, beauty-ripe at last,
  To Art ennobled shall have grown,—
Soon as with you he scales a mountain-height,
  And there, illumin'd by the setting sun,
The smiling valley bursts upon his sight.
The richer ye reward the eager gaze—
  The higher, fairer orders that the mind
May traverse with its magic rays,
  Or compass with enjoyment unconfin'd—
The wider thoughts and feelings open lie
To more luxuriant floods of Harmony,
To Beauty's richer, more majestic stream,—
The fair members of the world's vast scheme,
That, maim'd, disgrace on his Creation bring,
He sees the lofty forms then perfecting—

The fairer riddles come from out the night—
    The richer is the world his arms enclose,
    The broader stream the sea with which he flows—
The weaker, too, is Destiny's blind might—
The nobler instincts does he prove—
The smaller he himself, the greater grows his love.
Thus is he led, in still and hidden race,
    By Poetry, who strews his path with flowers,
    Through ever-purer Forms, and purer Powers,
Through ever higher heights, and fairer grace.
At length, arrived at the ripe goal of Time,—
Yet one more inspiration all-sublime,
Poetic outburst of Man's latest youth,
And—he will glide into the arms of Truth!

Herself, the gentle Cypria,
        Illumin'd by her fiery crown,
        Then stands before her full-grown Son
Unveil'd—as great Urania;
The sooner only by him caught,
        The fairer he had fled away!
Thus stood, in wonder rapture-fraught,
        Ulysses' noble Son that day,
When the sage Mentor who his youth beguil'd,
Herself transfigur'd as Jove's glorious Child!

Man's honour is confided to your hand,—
        There let it well-protected be!
It sinks with you! with you it will expand!
        Poesy's sacred sorcery
Obeys a world-plan wise and good;
In silence let it swell the flood
        Of mighty-rolling Harmony!

By her own time view'd with disdain,
Let solemn Truth in song remain,
And let the Muses' band defend her!
In all the fulness of her splendour,

Let her survive in numbers glorious,
   More dread, when veil'd her charms appear,
And vengeance take, with strains victorious,
   On her tormentor's ear!

The freest Mother's Children free,
   With steadfast countenance then rise
To highest Beauty's radiancy,
   And ev'ry other crown despise!
The Sisters who escap'd you here,
   Within your Mother's arms ye'll meet;
What noble Spirits may revere,
   Must be deserving and complete.
High over your own course of time
   Exalt yourselves with pinion bold,
And dimly let your glass sublime
   The coming century unfold!
On thousand roads advancing fast
   Of ever-rich variety,
With fond embraces meet at last
   Before the throne of Harmony!
As into seven mild rays we view
   With softness break the glimmer white,
As rainbow-beams of sevenfold hue
   Dissolve again in that soft light,
In clearness thousandfold thus throw
   Your magic round the ravish'd gaze,—
Into one stream of light thus flow,—
   One bond of truth that ne'er decays!

THE CELEBRATED WOMAN.

A LETTER FROM ONE HUSBAND TO ANOTHER.

SHALL I lament thy lot?   Dost curse thy marriage
    vows,
  With tears of grief and rage combin'd?
And why?   Because thy faithless Spouse
  Seeks in another's arms to find
What she no more obtains from thee?—
  Friend, hearken to Another's cares,
And bear thine own more easily!

It pains thee that a Second shares
Thy rights?—How truly enviable thy case!
My wife belongs to the whole human race.
E'en from the Belt to the Moselle,
To Apennine's high walls as well,
  Even in fashion's native city,
She is exposed for sale in ev'ry shop,
  And may be handled (more's the pity!)
By ev'ry pedant, ev'ry silly fop
  On board the packet, on the coach's top,—
Beneath the cockney's stare must patient be,
  And, as each dirty critic may desire,
  Must walk on flowers or coals of fire
To the Pantheon or the pillory.
A Leipzig fellow—may the rascal meet his due!—
  As of a fortress, takes her topographic measure,
And parts for sale he offers to the public view,
  Which none but I should know about, had I my
    pleasure!

Thy wife,—thanks to the canon law, 'tis true,—
  The name of *consort* holds all-duly priz'd;
She knows its meaning and its practice too.
  As Ninon's husband I'm but recogniz'd.
Thou'rt grieved that at the Faro-table, in the Pit,
When thou appear'st, each tongue exerts its wit?

Oh, happy man!   How fortunate is he
Who can say that!   Good brother, as for me,
A whey-cure purchased me, at length, the honour
At her left side to humbly wait upon her.
Me no one sees, and ev'ry look is thrown
Upon my haughty spouse alone.

   The veil of night is scarcely rent,
When, lo! the staircase swarms with blue and yellow
    coats,
With unpaid letters, packages, and notes,
  To " The Illustrious Lady " sent.

How sweet her sleep!—to wake her though's my
    duty:
 " Madam, the last Berlin and Jena News ! "
Sudden her eyelids opes the sleeping Beauty;
  The first thing that they meet are—the Reviews.
Her fair blue eye for *me* has not one look,
A trump'ry Paper's all that it can brook.
Soon from the nursery comes a roaring cry,
And, asking for her little ones, she lays it by.

Her dressing-table now is set,
  But half-looks only on her glass she flings;
A grumbling and impatient threat
  To her affrighted Maid gives wings.
The Graces all have fled from her toilette,
And in the place of Cupids young and fair,
Furies upon her wait to dress her hair.

The sound of carriage-wheels has now begun,
  And nimble lacqueys from behind dismount,
To crave an audience with the Famous One:
  First for the scented Abbé, then the Count,
Or Englishman, who German scorns to know,
  Grossing and Son, or Messrs. So and So.
A thing that in the corner meekly takes its place,—
A Husband call'd,—is star'd at in the face.

Here may the dullest fool, the poorest wight,
    (And this *thy* rival surely would not do,)
Express his admiration at her sight,—
    Express it in my presence, too!
And I, for fear of being thought uncivil,
Must beg he'll stop to dine—(the devil!)

At table, Friend, begins my misery,
    Quickly each flask's contents are dried!
With Burgundy, that Doctors strictly keep from *me*,
    Her flatterers' throats I needs must keep supplied.
The meat that I so hardly earn'd at first
    Her hungry parasites' lean-paunches lines;
This fatal immortality accurs'd
    Has been the death of all my choicest wines—
    The plague take ev'ry hand that dares to print!
What, think'st thou, are my thanks?   A scornful
        hint,
A gesture or a rude and vulgar sneer.—
Dost guess the meaning?   Oh, 'tis very clear?
That any woman, who is such a jewel,
Should be possess'd by such a clown, seems cruel!

The spring-time comes.   O'er meadow and o'er plain
    Nature now throws her carpet, many-hued;
The flowers are clothed in smiling green again—
    Sweet sings the lark, with life teems ev'ry wood.
—To *her* no joy does spring impart,
The songstress of the feelings blest of love,
The witness of our sports—the beauteous grove,—
    Appeal no longer to her heart.
The nightingales have never learn'd to *read*—
    The lilies never to *admire*.
The joyous choruses all creatures lead,
    In her—an Epigram inspire!
But no!—The season's fine for travelling—
    How very crowded Pyrmont now must be!
    And all in Carlsbad's praises, too, agree.

Presto, she's there!—Amongst that honour'd ring,
　Where lords and sages are combining,—
All kinds of folk, in fact, of note,
Lovingly pair'd, as if in Charon's boat,
　All at one board together dining;
Where, from a distance thither lur'd,
The bleeding virtues of their wounds are cur'd,
And others—for temptation praying are,
That they may ward it off with more éclat.
There, Friend,—Oh, bless thy happier lot in life!
Leaving me seven young Orphans,—goes my
　　wife.

Oh, happy golden time of love's young day!
How soon,—alas, how soon thou'rt flown away!
A Woman who no equal has, or had—
A very Goddess, in her graces glad,
With radiant spirit, with a mind clear-sighted,
　And feelings soft, to pity open wide,—
I saw her thus, while each heart she delighted,
　Like a fair May-day sporting by my side;
Her beateous eyes appear'd to falter
　The blissful words: I love thee well!
And so I led her to the altar;
　My rapture then, oh, who could tell!
Of enviable years a blooming field
　From out this mirror sweetly on me smil'd;
A perfect heaven was then to me reveal'd.
　Soon round me sported many a lovely child;
Amongst them all, the fairest *She;*
　The happiest, *She,* amid the throng;
And *Mine* by spirit-harmony,
　By heart-alliance, firm and strong.
But now,—Oh, may he be accurs'd!—appear'd
　A Great Man, aye, a Shining Spirit, too.
　The Great Man did a deed!—and overthrew
The house of cards that I tow'rd heaven had rear'd.

What have I now ?—What sad exchange is this !—
Awaken'd from my madd'ning dream of bliss,
What of this Angel now remains to me ?
  A spirit strong within a body weak,
  Hermaphroditic, so to speak ;
Alike unfit for love or mystery—
A child, who with a giant's weapons rages,
A cross between baboons and sages !
One that has fled the *fairer* race,
To gain among the *stronger* a vain place,
  Hurl'd headlong from a throne eternal,
Flying the mysteries by Charm controll'd—
Eras'd from Cytherea's Book of Gold,*
  To gain a corner—in a Journal.

VERSES WRITTEN IN THE ALBUM OF A YOUNG LADY.

Sweet friend, the world, like some fair infant blest,
  Radiant with sportive grace, around thee plays ;
Yet 'tis not as depicted in thy breast—
  Not as within thy soul's fair glass, its rays
Are mirror'd.   The respectful fealty
That my heart's nobleness hath won for thee,
  The miracles thou workest ev'rywhere,
  The charms thy being to this life first lent,—
To *it*, mere charms to reckon thou'rt content,
  To *us*, they seem humanity so fair.
The witchery sweet of ne'er-polluted youth,
The talisman of innocence and truth—
  Him I would see, who *these* to scorn can dare !

* The Golden Book is the Roll in which, in some of the Italian
Republics, the names of noble Families were inscribed.

Thou revellest joyously in telling o'er
  The blooming flowers that round thy path are
    strown,—
The glad, whom thou hast made so evermore,—
  The souls that thou hast conquer'd for thine own.
In thy deceit so blissful be thou glad!
Ne'er let a waking disenchantment sad
  Hurl thee despairing from thy dream's proud flight!
Like the fair flow'rets that thy beds perfume,
Observe them, but ne'er touch them as they bloom,—
  Plant them, but only for the distant sight.
Created only to enchant the eye,
In faded beauty at thy feet they'll lie,
  The nearer thee, the nearer their long night!

POEMS OF THE THIRD PERIOD.

THE MEETING.

I SEE her still—by her fair train surrounded,
  The fairest of them all, she took her place;
Afar I stood, by her bright charms confounded,
  For, oh! they dazzled with their heavenly grace.
With awe my soul was fill'd—with bliss unbounded,
  While gazing on her softly radiant face;
But soon, as if up-borne on wings of fire,
My fingers 'gan to sweep the sounding lyre.

The thoughts that rush'd across me in that hour,
  The words I sang, I'd fain once more invoke;
Within, I felt a new-awakened power,
  That each emotion of my bosom spoke.
My soul, long time enchain'd in sloth's dull bower,
  Through all its fetters now triumphant broke,
And brought to light unknown, harmonious numbers,
Which, in its deepest depths, had liv'd in slumbers.

And when the chords had ceas'd their gentle sighing,
  And when my soul rejoin'd its mortal frame,
I look'd upon her face and saw love vieing,
  In ev'ry feature, with her maiden shame.
And soon my ravish'd heart seem'd heavenward flying,
  When her soft whisper o'er my senses came.
The blissful seraphs' choral strains alone
Can glad mine ear again with that sweet tone.

Of that fond heart, which, pining silently,
  Ne'er ventures to express its feelings lowly,
The real and modest worth is known to me—
  'Gainst cruel fate I'll guard its cause so holy.

H

Most blest of all, the meek one's lot shall be—
   Love's flowers by love's own hand are gather'd
      solely—
The fairest prize to that fond heart is due,
That feels it, and that beats responsive too!

TO EMMA.

FAR away, where darkness reigneth,
   All my dreams of bliss are flown;
Yet with love my gaze remaineth
   Fix'd on one fair star alone.
But, alas! that star so bright
Sheds no lustre save by night.

If in slumbers ending never,
   Gloomy death had seal'd thine eyes,
Thou hadst liv'd in memory ever—
   Thou hadst liv'd still in my sighs;
But, alas! in light thou livest—
To my love no answer givest!

Can the sweet hopes love once cherish'd—
   Emma, can they transient prove?
What has pass'd away and perish'd—
   Emma, say, can *that* be love?
That bright flame of heavenly birth—
Can it die like things of earth?

THE SECRET.

SHE sought to breathe one word, but vainly—
   Too many listeners were nigh;
And yet my timid glance read plainly
   The language of her speaking eye.

Thy silent glades my footstep presses,
  Thou fair and leaf-embosom'd grove!
Conceal within thy green recesses
  From mortal eye our sacred love!

Afar with strange discordant noises,
  The busy day is echoing;
And, 'mid the hollow hum of voices,
  I hear the heavy hammer ring.
'Tis thus that man, with toil ne'er-ending,
  Extorts from Heaven his daily bread;
Yet oft unseen the Gods are sending
  The gifts of fortune on his head!

Oh, let mankind discover never
  How true love fills with bliss our hearts!
They would but crush our joy for ever,
  For joy to *them* no glow imparts.
Thou ne'er wilt from the world obtain it—
  'Tis never captured save as prey;
Thou needs must strain each nerve to gain it,
  E'er Envy dark asserts her sway.

The hours of night and stillness loving,
  It comes upon us silently—
Away with hasty footstep moving
  Soon as it sees a treach'rous eye.
Thou gentle stream, soft circlets weaving,
  A wat'ry barrier cast around,
And, with thy waves in anger heaving,
  Guard from each foe this holy ground!

EXPECTATION.

Hear I the portal not flying?
Hear I the latchet not fall?
  No, 'tis but the Zephyr sighing
  Gently through the poplars tall!

Put on thy fairest dress, thou leafy grove,
  To welcome her sweet face its charms displaying!
Ye branches, weave a shady roof above,
  When she, at eve's soft hour, is hither straying!
And all ye balmy winds, that sportive rove,
  Awake, and round her blushing cheeks 'gin playing,
Soon as her foot, all-gently moving on,
Its beauteous burden bears to Love's own throne!

> Hark to yon sound that seems parting
> The bushes, and hastening near!—
> No, 'tis but the bird upstarting
> From the copse, in sudden fear!

Oh, quench thy torch, bright Day! And thou, pale
        Night,
  With thy propitious silence o'er us hover!
Around us spread a veil of purple light!
  Let mystic boughs our blissful meeting cover!
From listeners' ears, Love's raptures take their flight,
  They fly when Phœbus' beams the world rule over
For Hesperus alone, who silently
Casts down his rays, their confidant can be!

> Hear I not soft whispers cleaving
> The air as the echoes they wake?
> No, 'tis but the cygnet weaving
> Circlets in the silv'ry rake!

A flood of harmony mine ear assails,—
  The fountain's gush with murmur sweet is falling—
The west wind's balmy kiss the flow'ret hails,—
  And all creation smiles with joy enthralling;
The purple grape, the luscious peach that veils,
  'Neath shelt'ring leaves, its charms, seem softly
        calling;
The incense-bearing Zephyrs, as they blow,
Drink from my burning cheeks their fiery glow!

Down through yon laurel-walk rushing,
Hear not I footsteps resound?
   No, 'tis but the fruit all blushing,
   Falling ripen'd to the ground!

In gentle death now sinks day's flaming eye,
  And all his gorgeous hues are fast declining;
The flowers, that 'neath his fiery ardour sigh,
  Open their cups, when twilight soft 'gins shining;
The moon her silver beams sheds silently,—
  The world in shadows dim its form is shrining;
Each charm its circling girdle lays aside,
And Beauty stands disclos'd in modest pride!

   Is't not a white form advancing?
   Gleams not its soft-rustling train?
      No, 'tis but the yew-trees glancing
      Yon dim columns back again!

With sweet but airy dreams like these to play,
  No longer be content, thou bosom panting!
No shadowy bliss my heart's mad thirst can stay—
  She whom this arm would clasp, alas, is wanting!
Oh, guide her living, breathing charms this way!
  Oh, let me press her hand, with joy enchanting!
The very shadow of her mantle's seam—
But lo!—a form of life assumes my dream!

   And as, from the Heavens descending,
    Appears the sweet moment of bliss,
   In silence her steps thither bending,
    She waken'd her love with a kiss!

EVENING.

(AFTER A PICTURE.)

OH! thou bright-beaming God, the plains are
 thirsting,
Thirsting for freshening dew, and man is pining;
 Wearily move on thy horses—
 Let, then, thy chariot descend!

Seest thou her who, from Ocean's crystal billows,
Lovingly nods and smiles?—Thy heart must know
 her!
 Joyously speed on thy horses,—
 Tethys, the Goddess, 'tis nods!

Swiftly from out his flaming chariot leaping,
Into her arms he springs,—the reins takes Cupid,—
 Quietly stand the horses,
 Drinking the cooling flood.

Now, from the Heavens with gentle step descending,
Balmy Night appears, by sweet Love follow'd;
 Mortals, rest ye and love ye,—
 Phœbus, the loving one, rests!

LONGING.

COULD I from this valley drear,
 Where the mist hangs heavily,
Soar to some more blissful sphere,
 Ah! how happy should I be!
Distant hills enchant my sight,
 Ever young and ever fair;
To those hills I'd take my flight
 Had I wings to scale the air.

Harmonies mine ear assail,
  Tones that breathe a heavenly calm;
And the gently-sighing gale
  Greets me with its fragrant balm.
Peeping through the shady bowers,
  Golden fruits their charms display,
And those sweetly-blooming flowers
  Ne'er become cold winter's prey.

In yon endless sunshine bright,
  Oh! what bliss 'twould be to dwell!
How the breeze on yonder height
  Must the heart with rapture swell!
Yet the stream that hems my path
  Checks me with its angry frown,
While its waves, in rising wrath,
  Weigh my weary spirit down.

See—a bark is drawing near,
  But, alas, the pilot fails!
Enter boldly—wherefore fear?
  Inspiration fills its sails,
Faith and courage make thine own,—
  Gods ne'er lend a helping hand;
'Tis by magic power alone
  Thou canst reach the magic land!

THE PILGRIM.

Yes! 'twas in life's happy morning
  That I first began to roam,
And, Youth's transient pleasures scorning,
  Left for aye my native home.

All the wealth by fate imparted
  To the winds with joy I hurl'd;
Then with conscience single-hearted,
  Grasp'd my staff, and sought the world.

By a mighty impulse driven—
  By a voice of mystic strength—
" Go!" it cried, " to thee 'tis given
  Happiness to reach at length.

" When thou seest a golden portal
  Near thee lying, enter in ;
There, each thing that earth made mortal,
  Heavenly is, and free from sin."

Evening came, and morn succeeded,
  On I went unweariedly ;
But the rest my bosom needed
  Ever from me seem'd to fly.

In my path lay mountain ridges,
  Streams to hem my progress roll'd ;
Yet I spann'd their gulfs with bridges—
  Cross'd each flood with courage bold.

Till at length I reach'd a torrent—
  Eastward ran its waters clear ;
Trusting fondly to the current,
  In I plunged without à fear.

Soon into a mighty ocean
  I was carried by the stream ;
Vain now prov'd my self-devotion,—
  All was but an empty dream !

Nought, alas, can lead me thither !—
  Yon bright realms of Heaven so clear
Ne'er can send their brightness hither—
  And the There is never Here !

THE IDEALS.

AND wilt thou, Faithless one, then, leave me,
  With all thy magic phantasy,—
With all the thoughts that joy or grieve me,
  Wilt thou with all for ever fly?
Can nought delay thine onward motion,
  Thou golden time of life's young dream?
In vain! Eternity's wide ocean
  Ceaselessly drowns thy rolling stream.

The glorious suns my youth enchanting
  Have set in never-ending night;
Those blest Ideals now are wanting
  That swell'd my heart with mad delight.
The offspring of my dream hath perish'd,
  My faith in Being pass'd away;
The godlike hopes that once I cherish'd
  Are now Reality's sad prey.

As once Pygmalion, fondly yearning,
  Embrac'd the statue form'd by him,
Till the cold marble's cheeks were burning,
  And life diffus'd through ev'ry limb,—
So I, with youthful passion fired,
  My longing arms round Nature threw,
Till, clinging to my breast inspired,
  She 'gan to breathe, to kindle, too.

And all my fiery ardour proving,
  Though mute, her tale she soon could tell,
Return'd each kiss I gave her loving,
  The throbbings of my heart read well.
Then living seem'd each tree, each flower,
  Then sweetly sang the waterfall,
And e'en the soulless in that hour
  Shar'd in the heav'nly bliss of all.

For then a circling World was bursting
  My bosom's narrow prison-cell,
To enter into Being thirsting,
  In deed, word, shape, and sound as well.
This world, how wondrous great I deem'd it,
  Ere yet its blossoms could unfold !
When open, oh, how little seem'd it !
  That little, oh, how mean and cold !

How happy, wing'd by courage daring,
  The youth Life's mazy path first press'd—
No care his manly strength impairing,
  And in his dream's sweet vision blest !
The dimmest star in air's dominion
  Seem'd not too distant for his flight ;
His young and ever-eager pinion
  Soar'd far beyond all mortal sight.

Thus joyously tow'rd Heaven ascending,
  Was aught for his bright hopes too far ?
The airy guides his steps attending,
  How danced they round Life's radiant car !
Soft Love was there, her guerdon bearing,
  And Fortune, with her crown of gold,
And Fame, her starry chaplet wearing,
  And Truth, in majesty untold.

But while the goal was yet before them,
  The faithless guides began to stray ;
Impatience of their task came o'er them,
  Then one by one they dropp'd away.
Light-footed Fortune first retreating,
  Then Wisdom's thirst remain'd unstill'd,
While heavy storms of doubt were beating
  Upon the path Truth's radiance fill'd.

I saw Fame's sacred wreath adorning
    The brows of an unworthy crew ;
And, ah ! how soon Love's happy morning,
    When spring had vanish'd, vanish'd too !
More silent yet, and yet more weary,
    Became the desert path I trod ;
And even Hope a glimmer dreary
    Scarce cast upon the gloomy road.

Of all that train, so bright with gladness,
    Oh, who is faithful to the end ?
Who now will seek to cheer my sadness,
    And to the grave my steps attend ?
Thou, Friendship, of all guides the fairest,
    Who gently healest ev'ry wound ;
Who all Life's heavy burdens sharest,
    Thou, whom I early sought and found !

Employment too, thy loving neighbour,
    Who quells the bosom's rising storms ;
Who ne'er grows weary of her labour,
    And ne'er destroys, though slow she forms ;
Who, though but grains of sand she places
    To swell Eternity sublime,
Yet minutes, days, aye ! years effaces
    From the dread reckoning kept by Time !

––––––––––

THE MAIDEN'S LAMENT.

THE clouds fast gather,
    The forest-oaks roar,—
A maiden is sitting
    Beside the green shore,—
The billows are breaking with might, with might,
And she sighs aloud in the darkling night,
    Her eyelid heavy with weeping.

"My heart's dead within me,
　　The world is a void;
　To the wish, it gives nothing,
　　Each hope is destroy'd.
I have tasted the fulness of bliss below
I have liv'd, I have lov'd,—thy child, oh take now,
　Thou Holy One, into thy keeping!"

"In vain is thy sorrow,
　　In vain thy tears fall,
　For the Dead from their slumbers
　　They ne'er can recall;
Yet if aught can pour comfort and balm in thy heart,
Now that love its sweet pleasures no more can impart,
　Speak thy wish, and thou granted shalt find it!"

"Though in vain is my sorrow,
　　Though in vain my tears fall,—
　Though the Dead from their slumbers
　　They ne'er can recall,
Yet no balm is so sweet to the desolate heart,
When love its soft pleasures no more can impart,
　As the torments that love leaves behind it!"

THE YOUTH AT THE BROOK.

Near a brook a boy is sitting,
　　Twining many a garland gay;
But, alas! he sees them ever
　　Hurried by the stream away.
"Restless as those dancing waters,
　　My sad days are fleeting on;
Transient as those fragrant garlands,
　　Lo! my youth will soon be gone.

" Ask me not why I am sorrowing
  In the spring-time of my years!
Joy and hope fill every creature
  Soon as smiling Spring appears;
But the thousand voices hailing
  Nature wak'ning from her sleep,
In *my* bosom waken only
  Anguish bitter, torments deep.

" What avail to *me* the pleasures
  Spring is able to convey?
There is only *one* I sigh for,
  Yet, though near, 'tis far away.
Fain I'd seize the flattering vision,
  Fain I'd clasp it to my breast;
But, alas! it ever flies me,
  And my heart remains oppress'd.

" Leave thy castle proud behind thee
  Hither, maiden, wend thy way;
And I'll fill thy lap with flowers,
  Offspring of all-bounteous May.
Hark! the streamlet softly murmurs,
  Joyous carols fill the air;
E'en a cottage is a palace
  To a happy, loving pair!"

THE FAVOUR OF THE MOMENT.

So, at length, once more we meet
  In the Muses' glad domain!
Let us twine a garland sweet,
  Fit to grace their brows again!

To what God shall we now bring
　　Earliest tribute of our lays?
Let us first *His* glory sing,
　　Who with bliss our toil repays.

What avails it that a Soul
　　Ceres breathes into the shrine?
That great Bacchus brims the bowl
　　With the red blood of the vine?

If that spark which set on fire
　　Mortal hearths, comes not from high,
Joy will ne'er the soul inspire,
　　And the heart will vainly sigh.

From the clouds must fortune fall,
　　From the lap of Deities;
And the mightiest Lord of all
　　Is the moment as it flies.

'Mongst the things that have their birth
　　'Neath eternal Nature's sway,
Nought is god-like here on earth,
　　Save the thought's all-piercing ray.

Slowly stone and stone unite,
　　As the circling seasons roll;
But *our* work will see the light
　　Soon as fashion'd by the soul.

As the sunlight's radiant glow
　　Weaves a golden tapestry—
As upon her gorgeous bow
　　Iris quivers in the sky,

So each gift that joys the heart
　　Fleeteth as a gleam of light;
Soon for aye it must depart
　　To the darksome tomb of night.

MOUNTAIN SONG.

Yon bridge o'er the giddy abyss will conduct,
  From life unto death 'tis the portal;
But figures gigantic the lone way obstruct,
  And threaten to crush thee, frail mortal!
And, wouldst thou not waken the avalanche dread,
The terrible path thou must noiselessly tread.

High over the brink of the chasm profound
  An arch is in triumph suspended;
'Twas rais'd not by science of man from the ground,
  His thoughts to such height ne'er ascended,
Below, late and early, the fierce torrent boils—
Assails it in fury, but fruitlessly toils.

A dark and mysterious gate opens wide,
  Beyond seem the shadow-realms dreaded;
But sudden a region of bliss is descried,
  Where autumn and spring-time are wedded;
Oh, would I could fly to that vale of repose
From the labours of life, and its ne'er-ending woes!

Four streams to the plain with wild roar issue forth,
  Their source remains hidden for ever;
They flow to the East, to the West, South, and North,
  The world's four great highways they sever.
And fast as their mother with groans gives them birth,
They fly away swiftly and vanish from earth.

Two peaks, far above the weak gaze of mankind,
  From Ether's blue vault seem advancing;
Upon them, in vapour all-golden enshrin'd,
  The clouds, Heaven's daughters, are dancing.
Their course all alone they unceasing pursue,
The eye of no mortal their progress can view.

The Queen, on a throne that no time can e'er change,
  In glory and brightness is sitting ;—
She weareth a chaplet of diamonds strange
  To grace her fair forehead befitting.
The sun shoots his arrows of light at her ever—
They gild her, 'tis true, but their warmth they give never

THE ALPINE HUNTER.

WILT thou not the lambkins guard ?
  Oh, how soft and meek they look,
Feeding on the grassy sward,
  Sporting round the silv'ry brook !
" Mother, mother, let me go
On yon heights to chase the roe !"

Wilt thou not the flock compel
  With the horn's inspiring notes ?
Sweet the echo of yon bell,
  As across the wood it floats !
" Mother, mother, let me go
On yon heights to hunt the roe !"

Wilt thou not the flow'rets bind,
  Smiling gently in their bed ?
For no garden thou wilt find
  On yon heights so wild and dread.
" Leave the flow'rets,—let them blow !
Mother, mother, let me go !"

And the youth then sought the chase,
  Onward press'd with headlong speed
To the mountain's gloomiest place,—
  Nought his progress could impede ;
And before him, like the wind,
Swiftly flies the trembling hind.

Up the naked precipice
    Clambers she, with footstep light;
O'er the chasm's dark abyss
    Leaps with spring of daring might;
But behind, unweariedly,
With his death-bow follows he.

Now upon the rugged top
    Stands she,—on the loftiest height,
Where the cliffs abruptly stop,
    And the path is lost to sight.
There she views the steeps below,—
Close behind, her mortal foe.

She, with silent woeful gaze,
    Seeks the cruel boy to move;
But, alas! in vain she prays—
    To the string he fits the groove.
When from out the clefts, behold!
Steps the Mountain Genius old.

With his hand the Deity
    Shields the beast that trembling sighs;
" Must thou, even up to me,
    Death and anguish send ?" he cries,—
" Earth has room for all to dwell,—
Why pursue my lov'd gazelle ?"

DITHYRAMB.

NEVER,—believe me,—
See we the Deities—
    Never alone.
No sooner does Bacchus the Jovial greet me,
Than Love, smiling urchin, comes bounding to
        meet me,
    Phœbus the Radiant—he, too, is one!

I

See them advancing,
  Crowding the portal!
Soon in my dwelling
  Stands each immortal!

Say, ye Divine Ones,
How I, a frail creature,
  Due homage can pay?
Bright immortality send down from Heaven!
Yet what requital by me can be given?
    Oh, to Olympus guide upward my way!
Bliss dwelleth only
  In Jupiter's palace;
Brimming with nectar,
  Oh, give me the chalice!

Give him the chalice!
Brim for the Poet,
  Hebe, the bowl!
Moisten his eyes with the dew we quaff ever,
Let Styx, the dark torrent, be seen by him never,
    Let visions celestial brighten his soul!
The heavenly fountain
  Sparkles and bubbles,
Gladd'ning the bosom,
  And banishing troubles!

THE FOUR AGES OF THE WORLD.

THE goblet is sparkling with purple-tinged wine,
  Bright glistens the eye of each guest,
When into the hall comes the Minstrel divine,
  To the good he now brings what is best;
For when from Elysium is absent the lyre,
No joy can the banquets of nectar inspire.

He is blest by the Gods with an intellect clear,
  That mirrors the world as it glides;
He has seen all that ever has taken place here,
  And all that the future still hides.
He sat in the God's secret councils of old,
And heard the command for each thing to unfold.

He opens in splendour, with gladness and mirth,
  That life which was hid from our eyes;
Adorns as a temple the dwelling of earth,
  That the Muse has bestow'd as his prize.
No roof is so humble, no hut is so low,
But he with Divinities bids it o'erflow.

And as the inventive descendant of Zeus,
  On the unadorn'd round of the shield,
With knowledge divine could, reflected, produce
  Earth, sea, and the stars' shining field,—
So he, on the moments, as onward they roll,
The image can stamp of the infinite Whole.

From the earliest age of the world he has come,
  When nations rejoiced in their prime;
A wanderer glad, he has still found a home
  With every race through all time.
Four ages of man in his lifetime have died,
And the place they once held by the Fifth is supplied.

Saturnus first govern'd, with fatherly smile,
  Each day then resembled the last;
Then flourish'd the Shepherds, a race without guile—
  Their bliss by no care was o'ercast.
They lov'd,—and no other employment they had,
And Earth gave her treasures with willingness glad.

Then Labour came next, and the conflict began
  With monsters and beasts fam'd in song;
And heroes upstarted, as rulers of man,
  And the weak sought the aid of the strong.

And strife o'er the field of Scamander now reign'd,
But Beauty the God of the world still remain'd.

At length from the conflict bright Victory sprang,
  And gentleness blossom'd from might;
In heavenly chorus the Muses then sang,
  And figures divine saw the light;—
The Age that acknowledg'd sweet Phantasy's sway
Can never return, it has fleeted away.

The Gods from their seats in the Heavens were hurl'd,
  And their pillars of glory o'erthrown;
And the Son of the Virgin appear'd in the world
  For the sins of mankind to atone.
The fugitive lusts of the sense were suppress'd,
And man now first grappled with Thought in his breast.

Each vain and voluptuous charm vanish'd now,
  Wherein the young world took delight;
The monk and the nun made of penance a vow,
  And the tourney was sought by the knight.
Though the aspect of life was now dreary and wild,
Yet Love remain'd ever both lovely and mild.

An altar of holiness, free from all stain,
  The Muses in silence uprear'd;
And all that was noble and worthy, again
  In woman's chaste bosom appear'd;
The bright flame of song was soon kindled anew
By the minstrel's soft lays, and his love, pure and true.

And so, in a gentle and ne'er-changing band,
  Let woman and minstrel unite;
They weave and they fashion, with hand join'd to hand,
  The girdle of Beauty and Right.
When love blends with music, in unison sweet,
The lustre of life's youthful days ne'er can fleet.

PUNCH SONG.

Four elements, join'd in
  Harmonious strife,
Shadow the world forth,
  And typify life.

Into the goblet
  The lemon's juice pour;
Acid is ever
  Life's innermost core.

Now, with the sugar's
  All-softening juice,
The strength of the acid
  So burning reduce.

The bright sparkling water
  Now pour in the bowl;
Water all-gently
  Encircles the whole.

Let drops of the spirit
  To join them now flow;
Life to the living
  Nought else can bestow.

Drain it off quickly
  Before it exhales;
Save when 'tis glowing,
  The draught nought avails.

TO MY FRIENDS.

Yes, my friends!—that happier times have been
Than the present, none can contravene;
  That a race once liv'd of nobler worth;
And if ancient chronicles were dumb,
Countless stones in witness forth would come
  From the deepest entrails of the earth.
But this highly-favour'd race has gone,
  Gone for ever to the realms of night.
We, we *live!* The moments are our own,
  And the living judge the right.

Brighter zones, my friends, no doubt excel
This, the land wherein we're doom'd to dwell,
  As the hardy travellers proclaim;
But if *Nature* has denied us much,
Art is yet responsive to our touch,
  And our hearts can kindle at *her* flame.
If the laurel will not flourish here—
  If the myrtle is cold winter's prey,
Yet the vine, to crown us, year by year,
  Still puts forth its foliage gay.

Of a busier life 'tis well to speak,
Where four worlds their wealth to barter seek,
  On the world's great market, Thames' broad stream;
Ships in thousands go there and depart—
There are seen the costliest works of art,
  And the earth-god, Mammon, reigns supreme:
But the sun his image only graves
  On the silent streamlet's level plain,
Not upon the torrent's muddy waves,
  Swollen by the heavy rain.

Far more bless'd than we, in northern States,
Dwells the beggar at the Angel-gates,

For he sees the peerless city—Rome!
Beauty's glorious charms around him lie,
And a second Heaven up tow'rd the sky
    Mounts St. Peter's proud and wondrous dome.
But, with all the charms that splendour grants,
    Rome is but the tomb of ages past;
Life but smiles upon the blooming plants
    That the seasons round her cast.

Greater actions elsewhere may be rife
Than with us, in our contracted life—
    But beneath the sun there's nought that's new;
Yet we see the great of ev'ry age
Pass before us on the world's wide stage
    Thoughtfully and calmly in review:
All in Life repeats itself for ever,
    Young for aye is phantasy alone;
What has happen'd nowhere,—happen'd never,—
    That has never older grown!

PUNCH SONG.

(TO BE SUNG IN NORTHERN COUNTRIES.)

On the mountain's breezy summit,
    Where the Southern sunbeams shine,
Aided by their warming vigour,
    Nature yields the golden wine.

How the wondrous mother formeth,
    None have ever read aright;
Hid for ever is her working,
    And inscrutable her might.

Sparkling as a son of Phœbus,
    As the fiery source of light,
From the vat it bubbling springeth,
    Purple, and as crystal bright;

And rejoiceth all the senses,
　And in ev'ry sorrowing breast
Poureth Hope's refreshing balsam,
　And on life bestows new zest.

But their slanting rays all feebly
　On our zone the sunbeams shoot;
They can only tinge the foliage,
　But they ripen ne'er the fruit.

Yet the North insists on living,
　And what lives, will merry be;
So, although the grape is wanting,
　We invent wine cleverly.

Pale the drink we now are off'ring
　On the household altar here;
But what living Nature maketh,
　Sparkling is and ever clear.

Let us, from the brimming goblet,
　Drain the troubled flood with mirth;
Art is but a gift of Heaven,
　Borrowed from the glow of earth.

Even strength's dominions boundless
　'Neath her rule obedient lie;
From the old the new she fashions
　With creative energy.

She the elements' close union
　Severs with her sov'reign nod;
With the flame upon the altar,
　Emulates the great Sun-God.

For the distant, happy islands
　Now the vessel sallies forth,
And the Southern fruits, all-golden,
　Pours upon the eager North.

As a type, then,—as an image,
    Be to us this fiery juice,
Of the wonders that frail mortals
    Can with steadfast will produce!

NADOWESSIAN DEATH-LAMENT.

See, he sitteth on his mat,
    Sitteth there upright,
With the grace with which he sat
    While he saw the light.

Where is now the sturdy gripe,—
    Where the breath sedate,
That so lately whiff'd the pipe
    Tow'rd the Spirit Great?

Where the bright and falcon eye,
    That the reindeer's tread
On the waving grass could spy,
    Thick with dew-drops spread?

Where the limbs that used to dart
    Swifter through the snow
Than the twenty-member'd hart,
    Than the mountain roe?

Where the arm that sturdily
    Bent the deadly bow?
See, its life hath fleeted by,—
    See, it hangeth low!

Happy he!—He now has gone
    Where no snow is found:
Where with maize the fields are sown,
    Self-sprung from the ground;

Where with birds each bush is fill'd,
  Where with game the wood;
Where the fish, with joy unstill'd,
  Wanton in the flood.

With the spirits blest he feeds,—
  Leaves us here in gloom;
We can only praise his deeds,
  And his corpse entomb.

Farewell-gifts, then, hither bring,
  Sound the death-note sad!
Bury with him ev'rything
  That can make him glad!

'Neath his head the hatchet hide
  That he boldly swung;
And the bear's fat haunch beside,
  For the road is long;

And the knife, well sharpenèd,
  That, with slashes three,
Scalp and skin from foeman's head
  Tore off skilfully.

And to paint his body, place
  Dyes within his hand;
Let him shine with ruddy grace
  In the Spirit-Land!

THE FEAST OF VICTORY.

Priam's castle-walls had sunk,
  Troy in dust and ashes lay,
And each Greek, with triumph drunk,
  Richly laden with his prey,

Sat upon his ship's high prow,
  On the Hellespontic strand,
Starting on his journey now,
  Bound for Greece, his own fair land.
Raise the glad exulting shout!
  Tow'rd the land that gave them birth
Turn they now the ships about,
  As they seek their native earth.

And in rows, all mournfully,
  Sat the Trojan women there,—
Beat their breasts in agony,
  Pallid, with dishevell'd hair.
In the feast of joy so glad
  Mingled they the song of woe,
Weeping o'er their fortunes sad,
  In their country's overthrow.
"Land belov'd, oh, fare thee well!
  By our foreign masters led,
Far from home we're doom'd to dwell,—
  Ah, how happy are the dead!"

Soon the blood by Calchas spilt
  On the altar heav'nward smokes;
Pallas, by whom towns are built
  And destroy'd, the priest invokes;
Neptune, too, who all the earth
  With his billowy girdle laves,—
Zeus, who gives to Terror birth,
  Who the dreaded Ægis waves.
Now the weary fight is done,
  Ne'er again to be renew'd;
Time's wide circuit now is run,
  And the mighty town subdued!

Atreus' son, the army's head,
  Told the people's numbers o'er,
Whom he, as their captain, led
  To Scamander's vale of yore.

Sorrow's black and heavy clouds
   Pass'd across the monarch's brow:
Of those vast and valiant crowds,
   Oh, how few were left him now!
Joyful songs let each one raise,
   Who will see his home again,
In whose veins the life-blood plays,
   For, alas! not all remain!

" All who homeward wend their way,
   Will not there find peace of mind;
On their houschold altars, they
   Murder foul perchance may find.
Many fall by false friend's stroke,
   Who in fight immortal prov'd :"—
So Ulysses warning spoke,
   By Athene's spirit mov'd.
Happy he, whose faithful spouse
   Guards his home with honour true!
Woman ofttimes breaks her vows,
   Ever loves she what is new.

And Atrides glories there
   In the prize he won in fight,
And around her body fair
   Twines his arms with fond delight.
Evil works must punish'd be,
   Vengeance follows after crime,
For Kronion's just decree
   Rules the heav'nly courts sublime.
Evil must in evil end;
   Zeus will on the impious band
Woe for broken guest-rights send,
   Weighing with impartial hand.
" It may well the glad befit,"
   Cried Oïleus' valiant son,*
" To extol the Gods who sit
   On Olympus' lofty throne!

* Ajax the Less.

Fortune all her gifts supplies,
   Blindly, and no justice knows,
For Patroclus buried lies,
   And Thersites homeward goes!
Since she blindly throws away
   Each lot in her wheel contain'd,
Let him shout with joy to-day
   Who the prize of life has gain'd.

" Aye, the wars the best devour!
   Brother, we will think of thee,
In the fight a very tower,
   When we join in revelry!
When the Grecian ships were fir'd,
   By thine arm was safety brought;
Yet the man by craft inspir'd *
   Won the spoils thy valour sought.
Peace be to thine ashes blest!
   Thou wert vanquish'd not in fight:
Anger 'tis destroys the best,—
   Ajax fell by Ajax's might!"

Neoptolemus pour'd, then,
   To his sire renown'd † the wine—
" 'Mongst the lots of earthly men,
   Mighty father, prize I thine!
Of the goods that life supplies,
   Greatest far of all is fame;
Though to dust the body flies,
   Yet still lives a noble name.
Valiant one, thy glory's ray
   Will immortal be in song;
For, though life may pass away,
   To all time the dead belong!"

" Since the voice of minstrelsy
   Speaks not of the vanquish'd man,
I will Hector's witness be,"—
   Tydeus' noble son ‡ began:

* Ulysses.   † Achilles.   ‡ Diômed.

" Fighting bravely in defence
   Of his household-gods he fell.—
Great the victor's glory thence,
   He in purpose did excel !
   Battling for his altars dear,
   Sank that rock, no more to rise ;
E'en the foeman will revere
   One whose honour'd name ne'er dies."

Nestor, joyous reveller old,
   Who three generations saw,
Now the leaf-crown'd cup of gold
   Gave to weeping Hecuba.
" Drain the goblet's draught so cool,
   And forget each painful smart !
Bacchus' gifts are wonderful,—
   Balsam for a broken heart.
Drain the goblet's draught so cool,
   And forget each painful smart !
Bacchus' gifts are wonderful,—
   Balsam for a broken heart.

" E'en to Niobe, whom Heaven
   Lov'd in wrath to persecute,
Respite from her pangs was given,
   Tasting of the corn's ripe fruit.
Whilst the thirsty lip we lave
   In the foaming, living spring,
Buried deep in Lethe's wave
   Lies all grief, all sorrowing !
Whilst the thirsty lip we lave
   In the foaming, living spring,
Swallow'd up in Lethe's wave
   Is all grief, all sorrowing !"

And the Prophetess * inspir'd
   By her God, upstarted now,—
Tow'rd the smoke of homesteads fir'd,
   Looking from the lofty prow.

         * Cassandra.

"Smoke is each thing here below;
  Ev'ry worldly greatness dies,
As the vapoury columns go,—
  None are fix'd but Deities!
Cares behind the horseman sit—
  Round about the vessel play;
Lest the morrow hinder it,
  Let us, therefore, live to-day."

THE LAMENT OF CERES.

Is'T the beauteous spring I see?
  Has the earth grown young again?
Sun-lit hills glow verdantly,
  Bursting through their icy chain.
From the streamlet's mirror blue
  Smiles the now unclouded sky,
Zephyr's wings wave milder, too,—
  Youthful blossoms ope their eye.
In the grove, sweet songs resound,
  Speaks the Oread as of yore;
Once again thy flow'rs are found,
  But thy daughter comes no more.

Ah, how long 'tis since I went
  First in search o'er earth's wide face!
Titan!   All thy rays I sent
  Seeking for the lov'd one's trace;
Of that form so dear, no ray
  Hath as yet brought news to me,
And the all-discerning day
  Cannot yet the lost one see.
Hast thou, Zeus, her from me torn?
  Or to Orcus' gloomy streams,
Is she down by Pluto borne,
  Smitten by her charms' bright beams?

Who will to yon dreary strand
  Be the herald of my woe ?
Ever leaves the bark the land,
  Yet but shadows in it go.
To each bless'd eye evermore
  Clos'd the night-like fields remain ;
Styx no living form e'er bore,
  Since his stream first wash'd the plain.
Thousand paths lead downward there,
  None lead up again to light ;—
And her tears no witness e'er
  Brings to her sad mother's sight.

Mothers who, from Pyrrha sprung,
  From a mortal race descend,
May, the tomb's fierce flames among,
  On their children lov'd attend ;
Denizens of Heaven alone
  Draw not near the gloomy strand,—
Parcæ ! save Immortals, none
  E'er are spar'd by your harsh hand.
Plunge me in the night of nights,
  From the halls of heaven afar !
Honour not the Goddess' rights—
  They the mother's torments are !

Where she, with her consort stern,
  Joyless reigns, there went I down,—
With the silent shades, in turn,
  Silent stood before her throne.
Ah ! her eye, weigh'd down with tears,
  Seeks in vain the light so fair,
Wanders tow'rd far distant spheres,
  On her mother falling ne'er !
Till she wakes to ecstasy,
  Till with joy each bosom throbs,
And, arous'd to sympathy,
  Even rugged Orcus sobs.

Fruitless wish! Lamenting vain!
  In its smooth track peacefully
Ever rolls day's steady wain,
  Ever fix'd is Jove's decree.
He has turn'd his blissful head
  From the gloomy realms away;
She to me is ever dead,
  Now that she is Night's sad prey,—
Till the waves, that darkly swell,
  With Aurora's colours glow;
Till across the depths of Hell
  Iris draws her beauteous bow.

Is nought left me now to prove,
  Nought that as a pledge may stand,
That the absent still may love?
  Not a trace of that dear hand?
Can no loving bond, then, spread
  O'er a mother and her child?
Of the living and the dead
  Can there be no union mild?
No, she is not wholly flown!
  We're not wholly sever'd now!
For to speak *one* tongue alone
  The eternal Gods allow.

When Spring's children sink in death,
  When the leaf and flower decay,
Smitten by the Northwind's breath,
  Sadly stands the naked spray:
Then I take what best can live
  From Vertumnus' teeming horn,
Off'ring it to Styx, to give
  In return the golden corn,—
Into earth, then, mournfully
  Drop it on my daughter's heart,
That it may a language be
  Of my love, my bitter smart.

When the Hours' unchanging dance
  Brings with joy the Spring again,
Waken'd by the sun's bright glance,
  Will the dead fresh life obtain.
Germs that perish to the sight
  In the chilly womb of earth,
In the colour-realm so bright
  Free themselves again with mirth.
When the stalk shoots high in air,
  Shyly lurks the root in night;
Equal in their fost'ring care
  Are both Styx' and Æther's might.

Half they rule the living's sphere,
  Half the region of the dead;
Ah, to me they're heralds dear,
  Sweet tones from Cocytus dread!
Though herself be ever dumb
  In the terrible abyss,
From the Spring's young blossoms come
  To mine ears these words of bliss,—
That, e'en far from daylight blest,
  Where the sorrowing shadows go,
Lovingly may throb the breast,
  Tenderly the heart may glow!

Oh, be glad, then, evermore,
  Smiling meadows' children true!
For your chalice shall run o'er
  With the nectar's purest dew.
I will steep your forms in beams
  And with Iris' fairest light
Tinge your foliage, till it gleams
  Like Aurora's features bright.
In the Spring-time's radiance blest,
  In the Autumn's garland dead,
There may read each tender breast
  Of my griefs—my joys, now fled!

THE ELEUSINIAN FESTIVAL.

Wᴿᴇᴀᴛʜᴇ in a garland the corn's golden ear!
  With it, the Cyăne * blue intertwine!
Rapture must render each glance bright and clear,
  For the great Queen is approaching her shrine,—
She who compels lawless passions to cease,
  Who to link man with his fellow has come,
And into firm habitations of peace
  Chang'd the rude tents' ever-wandering home.

        Shyly in the mountain-cleft
          Was the Troglodyte conceal'd;
        And the roving Nomad left,
          Desert lying, each broad field.
        With the javelin, with the bow
          Strode the hunter through the land;
        To the hapless stranger, woe,
          Billow-cast on that wild strand!

        When, in her sad wanderings lost,
          Seeking traces of her child,
        Ceres hail'd the dreary coast,
          Ah, no verdant plain then smil'd!
        That she here with trust may stay,
          None vouchsafes a sheltering roof;
        Not a temple's columns gay
          Give of godlike worship proof.

        Fruit of no propitious ear
          Bids her to the pure feast fly;
        On the ghastly altars here
          Human bones alone e'er dry.
        Far as she might onward rove,
          Misery found she still in all,
        And within her soul of love,
          Sorrow'd she o'er man's deep fall.

* The corn-flower.

" Is it thus I find the man
  To whom we our Image lend,
Whose fair limbs of noble span
  Upward tow'rd the Heavens ascend ?
Laid we not before his feet
  Earth's unbounded godlike womb ?
Yet upon his kingly seat
  Wanders he without a home ?

" Does no God compassion feel ?
  Will none of the blissful race,
With an arm of miracle,
  Raise him from his deep disgrace ?
In the heights where rapture reigns
  Pangs of others ne'er can move ;
Yet man's anguish and man's pains
  My tormented heart must prove.

" So that a man a man may be,
  Let him make an endless bond
With the kind earth trustingly,
  Who is ever good and fond—
To revere the law of time,
  And the moon's melodious song,
Who, with silent step sublime,
  Move their sacred course along."

And she softly parts the cloud
  That conceals her from the sight ;
Sudden, in the savage crowd,
  Stands she, as a Goddess bright.
There she finds the concourse rude
  In their glad feast revelling,
And the chalice fill'd with blood
  As a sacrifice they bring.

But she turns her face away,
  Horror-struck, and speaks the while :
" Bloody tiger-feasts ne'er may
  Of a God the lips defile.

He needs victims free from stain,
    Fruits matur'd by Autumn's sun ;
With the pure gifts of the plain
    Honour'd is the Holy One ! "

And she takes the heavy shaft
    From the hunter's cruel hand ;
With the murd'rous weapon's haft
    Furrowing the light-strown sand,—
Takes from out her garland's crown,
    Fill'd with life, one single grain,—
Sinks it in the furrow down,
    And the germ soon swells amain.

And the green stalks gracefully
    Shoot, ere long, the ground above,
And, as far as eye can see,
    Waves it like a golden grove.
With her smile the earth she cheers,
    Binds the earliest sheaves so fair,
As her hearth the landmark rears,—
    And the Goddess breathes this prayer :

" Father Zeus, who reign'st o'er all
    That in Æther's mansions dwell,
Let a sign from thee now fall
    That thou lov'st this off'ring well !
And from the unhappy crowd
    That, as yet, has ne'er known thee,
Take away the eye's dark cloud,
    Showing them their Deity ! "

Zeus, upon his lofty throne,
    Hearkens to his sister's prayer ;
From the blue heights thund'ring down,
    Hurls his forkèd lightning there.

Crackling, it begins to blaze,
　From the altar whirling bounds,—
And his swift-wing'd eagle plays
　High above in circling rounds.

Soon at the feet of their mistress are kneeling,
　Fill'd with emotion, the rapturous throng ;
Into humanity's earliest feeling
　Melt their rude spirits, untutor'd and strong.
Each bloody weapon behind them they leave,
　Rays on their senses beclouded soon shine,
And from the mouth of the Queen they receive,
　Gladly and meekly, instruction divine.

All the Deities advance
　Downwards from their heav'nly seats ;
Themis' self 'tis leads the dance,
　And, with staff of justice, metes
Unto ev'ry one his rights,—
　Landmarks, too, 'tis hers to fix ;
And in witness she invites
　All the hidden powers of Styx.

And the Forge-God, too, is there,
　The inventive Son of Zeus ;
Fashioner of vessels fair
　Skill'd in clay and brass's use.
'Tis from him the art man knows
　Tongs and bellows how to wield ;
'Neath his hammer's heavy blows
　Was the ploughshare first reveal'd.

With projecting, weighty spear,
　Front of all, Minerva stands,
Lifts her voice so strong and clear,
　And the Godlike host commands.
Steadfast walls 'tis hers to found,
　Shield and screen for ev'ry one,
That the scatter'd world around
　Bind in loving unison.

The Immortals' steps she guides
  O'er the trackless plains so vast,
And where'er her foot abides
  Is the Boundary God held fast;
And her measuring chain is led
  Round the mountain's border green,—
E'en the raging torrent's bed
  In the holy ring is seen.

All the Nymphs and Oreads too
  Who, the mountain pathways o'er,
Swift-foot Artemis pursue,
  All, to swell the concourse, pour,
Brandishing the hunting-spear,—
  Set to work,—glad shouts uprise,—
'Neath their axes' blows so clear
  Crashing down the pine-wood flies.

E'en the sedge-crown'd God ascends
  From his verdant spring to light,
And his raft's direction bends
  At the Goddess' word of might,—
While the Hours, all-gently bound,
  Nimbly to their duty fly;
Rugged trunks are fashion'd round
  By her skill'd hand gracefully.

E'en the Sea-God thither fares;—
  Sudden, with his trident's blow,
He the granite columns tears
  From earth's entrails far below;—
In his mighty hands, on high,
  Waves he them, like some light ball,
And, with nimble Hermes by,
Raises up the rampart-wall.

But from out the golden strings
  Lures Apollo harmony,
Measur'd time's sweet murmurings,
  And the might of melody.

The Camenæ swell the strain
  With their song of ninefold tone;
Captive bound in music's chain,
  Softly stone unites to stone.

Cybĕlē, with skilful hand,
  Open throws the wide-wing'd door;
Locks and bolts by her are plann'd,
  Sure to last for evermore.
Soon complete the wondrous halls
  By the Gods' own hands are made,
And the temple's glowing walls
  Stand in festal pomp array'd.

With a crown of myrtle twin'd,
  Now the Goddess-Queen comes there,
And she leads the fairest hind
  To the shepherdess most fair.
Venus, with her beauteous boy,
  That first pair herself attires;
All the Gods bring gifts of joy,
  Blessing their love's sacred fires.

Guided by the Deities,
  Soon the new-born townsmen pour
Usher'd in with harmonies,
  Through the friendly open door.
Holding now the rites divine,
  Ceres at Zeus' altar stands,—
Blessing those around the shrine,
  Thus she speaks, with folded hands:—

" Freedom's love the beast inflames,
  And the God rules free in air,
While the law of Nature tames
  Each wild lust that lingers there.
Yet, when thus together thrown,
  Man with man must fain unite;
And by his own worth alone
  Can he freedom gain, and might."

Wreathe in a garland the corn's golden ear !
  With it, the Cyăne blue intertwine !
Rapture must render each glance bright and clear,
  For the great Queen is approaching her shrine,—
She who our homesteads so blissful has given,
  She who has man to his fellow-man bound.
Let our glad numbers extol, then, to Heaven
  Her who the Earth's kindly mother is found !

THE RING OF POLYCRATES.*

A BALLAD.

Upon his battlements he stood,
And downward gaz'd, in joyous mood,
    On Samos' Isle, that own'd his sway.
" All this is subject to my yoke,"
To Egypt's monarch thus he spoke,—
    " That I am truly blest, then, say ! "

" The Immortals' favour thou hast known !
Thy sceptre's might has overthrown
    All those who once were like to thee.
Yet to avenge them, *one* lives still ;
I cannot call thee blest, until
    That dreaded foe has ceas'd to be."

While to these words the King gave vent,
A herald, from Miletus sent,
    Appear'd before the Tyrant there :
" Lord, let thy incense rise to-day,
And with the laurel's branches gay
    Thou well may'st crown thy festive hair !

" Thy foe has sunk beneath the spear,—
I'm sent to bring the glad news here,

* For this story, see Herodotus, book iii. sections 40–43.

By thy true marshal, Polydore—"
Then from a basin black he takes—
The fearful sight their terror wakes—
A well-known head, besmear'd with gore.

The King with horror stepp'd aside,
And then, with anxious look, replied :
" Thy bliss to Fortune ne'er commit.
On faithless waves, bethink thee how
Thy fleet with doubtful fate swims now—
How soon the storm may scatter it !"

And ere he yet had spoke the word,
A shout of jubilee is heard
Resounding from the distant strand.
With foreign treasures teeming o'er,
The vessels' mast-rich wood once more
Returns home to its native land.

The guest then speaks with startled mind :
" Fortune to-day, in truth, seems kind ;
But thou her fickleness shouldst fear :
The Cretan hordes, well skill'd in arms,
Now threaten thee with war's alarms ;
E'en now they are approaching here."

And, ere the word has 'scap'd his lips,
A stir is seen amongst the ships,
And thousand voices " Victory !" cry :
" We are deliver'd from our foe,
The storm has laid the Cretan low,
The war is ended, is gone by !"

The shout with horror hears the guest :
" In truth, I must esteem thee blest !
Yet dread I the decrees of Heaven.
The envy of the Gods I fear ;
To taste of unmix'd rapture here
Is never to a mortal given.

" With me, too, everything succeeds ;
In all my sovereign acts and deeds
    The grace of Heaven is ever by ;
And yet I had a well-lov'd heir—
I paid my debt to fortune there,—
    God took him hence—I saw him die.

" Wouldst thou from sorrow, then, be free,
Pray to each unseen Deity,
    For thy well-being, grief to send ;
The man on whom the Gods bestow
Their gifts with hands that overflow,
    Comes never to a happy end.

" And if the Gods thy prayer resist,
Then to a friend's instruction list,—
    Invoke *thyself* adversity ;
And what, of all thy treasures bright,
Gives to thy heart the most delight—
    That take and cast thou in the sea ! "

Then speaks the other, mov'd by fear :
" This ring to me is far most dear
    Of all this Isle within it knows—
I to the Furies pledge it now,
If they will happiness allow "—
    And in the flood the gem he throws.

And with the morrow's earliest light
Appear'd before the monarch's sight
    A Fisherman, all joyously ;
" Lord, I this fish just now have caught,
No net before e'er hold the sort ;
    And as a gift I bring it thee."

The fish was opened by the cook,
Who suddenly, with wond'ring look,

Runs up, and utters these glad sounds:
" Within the fish's maw, behold,
I've found, great Lord, thy ring of gold!
    Thy fortune truly knows no bounds!"

The guest with terror turn'd away :
" I cannot here, then, longer stay,—
    My friend thou canst no longer be !
The Gods have will'd that thou shouldst die :
Lest I, too, perish, I must fly "—
    He spoke,—and sail'd thence hastily.

THE CRANES OF IBYCUS.

A BALLAD.

ONCE to the Song and Chariot-fight,
Where all the tribes of Greece unite
On Corinth's Isthmus joyously,
The God-lov'd Ibycus drew nigh.
On him Apollo had bestow'd
    The gift of song and strains inspir'd ;
So, with light staff, he took his road
    From Rhegium, by the Godhead fir'd.

Acrocorinth, on mountain high,
Now bursts upon the wanderer's eye,
And he begins, with pious dread,
Poseidon's grove of firs to tread.
Nought moves around him, save a swarm
    Of Cranes, who guide him on his way ;
Who from far southern regions warm
    Have hither come in squadron grey.

" Thou friendly band, all hail to thee !
Who ledst me safely o'er the sea !
I deem thee as a favouring sign,—
My destiny resembles thine.

Both come from a far distant coast,
  Both pray for some kind shelt'ring place;—
Propitious tow'rd us be the host
  Who from the stranger wards disgrace!"

And on he hastes, in joyous mood,
  And reaches soon the middle wood
When, on a narrow bridge, by force
Two murderers sudden bar his course.
He must prepare him for the fray,
  But soon his wearied hand sinks low;
Inur'd the gentle lyre to play,
  It ne'er has strung the deadly bow.

On Gods and men for aid he cries,—
No saviour to his prayer replies;
However far his voice he sends,
Nought living to his cry attends.
" And must I in a foreign land,
  Unwept, deserted perish here,
Falling beneath a murderous hand,
  Where no avenger can appear?"

Deep-wounded, down he sinks at last,
When, lo! the Cranes' wings rustle past.
He hears,—though he no more can see,—
Their voices screaming fearfully.
" By you, ye Cranes, that soar on high,
  If not another voice is heard,
Be borne to Heaven my murder-cry!"
  He speaks, and dies, too, with the word.

The naked corpse, ere long, is found,
And, though defac'd by many a wound,
His host in Corinth soon could tell
The features that he lov'd so well.
" And is it thus I find thee now,
  Who hop'd the pine's victorious crown
To place upon the Singer's brow,
  Illumin'd by his bright renown?"

The news is heard with grief by all
Met at Poseidon's festival;
All Greece is conscious of the smart,
He leaves a void in every heart;
And to the Prytanis * swift hie
    The people, and they urge him on
The dead man's manes to pacify,
    And with the murderer's blood atone.

But where's the trace that, from the throng,
The people's streaming crowds among,
Allur'd there by the sports so bright,
Can bring the villain black to light?
By craven robbers was he slain?
    Or by some envious hidden foe?
That Helios only can explain,
    Whose rays illume all things below.

Perchance, with shameless step and proud,
He threads e'en now the Grecian crowd,—
Whilst vengeance follows in pursuit,
Gloats over his transgression's fruit.
The very Gods perchance he braves
    Upon the threshold of their fane,—
Joins boldly in the human waves
    That haste yon theatre to gain.

For there the Grecian tribes appear,
Fast pouring in from far and near;
On close-pack'd benches sit they there,—
The stage the weight can scarcely bear.
Like ocean-billows' hollow roar,
    The teeming crowds of living man
Tow'rd the cerulean Heavens upsoar,
    In bow of ever-widening span.

---

    * President of the Council of Five Hundred.

Who knows the nation, who the name,
Of all who there together came?
From Theseus' town, from Aulis' strand,
From Phocis, from the Spartan land,
From Asia's distant coast, they wend,
  From ev'ry island of the sea,
And from the stage they hear ascend
  The Chorus's dread melody,

Who, sad and solemn, as of old,
With footstep measur'd and controll'd,
Advancing from the far back-ground,
Circle the theatre's wide round.
Thus, mortal women never move!
  No mortal home to them gave birth!
Their giant-bodies tower above,
  High o'er the puny sons of earth.

With loins in mantle black conceal'd,
Within their fleshless hands they wield
The torch, that with a dull red glows,—
While in their cheek no life-blood flows;
And where the hair is floating wide
  And loving, round a mortal brow,
Here, snakes and adders are descried,
  Whose bellies swell with poison now.

And, standing in a fearful ring,
The dread and solemn chant they sing,
That through the bosom thrilling goes,
And round the sinner fetters throws.
Sense-robbing, of heart-madd'ning power,
  The Furies' strains resound through air
The list'ner's marrow they devour,—
The lyre can yield such numbers ne'er.

" Happy the man who, blemish-free,
Preserves a soul of purity!
Near him we ne'er avenging come,
He freely o'er life's path may roam.

But woe to him who, hid from view,
  Hath done the deed of murder base!
Upon his heels we close pursue,—
  We, who belong to Night's dark race!

" And if he thinks to 'scape by flight,
Wing'd we appear, our snare of might
Around his flying feet to cast,
So that he needs must fall at last.
Thus we pursue him, tiring ne'er,—
  Our wrath repentance cannot quell,—
On to the shadows, and e'en there
  We leave him not in peace to dwell!"

Thus singing, they the dance resume,
And silence, like that of the tomb,
O'er the whole house lies heavily,
As if the Deity were nigh.
And, staid and solemn, as of old,
  Circling the theatre's wide round,
With footstep measur'd and controll'd,
  They vanish in the far back-ground.

Between deceit and truth each breast,
Now doubting hangs, by awe possess'd,
And homage pays to that dread might,
That judges what is hid from sight,—
That, fathomless, inscrutable,
  The gloomy skein of fate entwines,
That reads the bosom's depths full well,
  Yet flies away where sunlight shines.

When sudden, from the tier most high,
A voice is heard by all to cry :
" See there, see there, Timotheus !
Behold the Cranes of Ibycus ! "

The Heavens become as black as night,
  And o'er the theatre they see,
Far over-head, a dusky flight
  Of Cranes, approaching hastily.

" Of Ibycus ! "—That name so blést
With new-born sorrow fills each breast.
As waves on waves in ocean rise,
From mouth to mouth it swiftly flies :
" Of Ibycus, whom we lament ?
  Who fell beneath the murderer's hand ?
What mean those words that from him went ?
  What means this Cranes' advancing
      band ? "

And louder still become the cries,
And soon this thought foreboding flies
Through ev'ry heart, with speed of light—
" Observe in this the Furies' might !
The poet's manes are now appeas'd :
  The murderer seeks his own arrest !
Let him who spoke the word be seiz'd,
  And him to whom it was address'd ! "

That word he had no sooner spoke,
Than he its sound would fain revoke ;
In vain ! his mouth, with terror pale,
Tells of his guilt the fearful tale.
Before the Judge they drag them now,
  The scene becomes the tribunal ;
Their crimes the villains both avow,
  When 'neath the vengeance-stroke they
      fall.

HERO AND LEANDER.

Seest thou yonder castles grey,
Glitt'ring in the sun's bright ray,
  That arise on either side,
Where the Hellespont impels
Through the rocky Dardanelles
  Ceaselessly his angry tide?
Hear'st thou yonder billows roar,
  As against the cliffs they break?
Asia they from Europe tore—
  Love alone they ne'er could shake.

Hero and Leander's hearts
With his fierce but pleasing smarts
  Cupid's might immortal mov'd.
Hero rivall'd Hebe's grace,
While Leander, in the chase,
  O'er the mountains boldly rov'd.
But, ere long, parental wrath
  Sever'd the united pair,
And the fruit by love brought forth
  Hung in mournful peril there.

See, on Sestos' rocky tower
'Gainst whose base with ceaseless power
  Hellespont's wild waters foam,
Sits the maid, in sorrow lost,
Looking tow'rd Abydos' coast,
  Where the lov'd one has his home.
Ah, to that far-distant strand
  Bridge there was not to convey,—
Not a bark was near at hand,
  Yet true love soon found the way.

In the labyrinthine maze
Love a certain clue can raise,
  E'en the foolish makes he wise,—

Makes the savage monster bow,—
To the adamantine plough
  Yokes the steers with flaming eyes.
Styx, whose waters nine-times flow,
  Cannot bar his daring course;
For from Pluto's house of woe
  Orpheus' bride he tore by force.

Even through the boiling tide
He Leander's mind supplied
  With deep longing's glowing spark.
When grew pale the glitt'ring day,
Took the swimmer bold his way
  O'er the Pontine ocean dark;
Cleft the waves with mighty power,
  Striving for yon strand so dear,
Where, uprais'd on lofty tower,
  Shone the torch's radiance clear.

Circled in her loving arms,
Soon the glad Leander warms
  From the weary journey past,
And receives the godlike prize
That in her embraces lies
  As his bright reward at last;
Till Aurora once·again
  Wakes him from his vision blest,—
He must tempt the briny main,
  Driven from love's gentle breast.

Thirty suns had sped like this
In the joys of stolen bliss
  Swiftly o'er the happy pair,
As a bridal night of love,
Worthy e'en the Gods above,
  Ever young and ever fair.

Rapture true he ne'er can know,
 Who with daring hand has never
Pluck'd the Heavenly fruits that grow
 On the brink of Hell's dark river.

Hesper and Aurora bright
Each, in turns, put forth their light,
 Yet the happy ones saw not
How the leaves began to fall,—
How from Northern icy hall
 Winter fierce approach'd the spot.
Joyfully they saw each day
 More and more its span reduce;
For the night's now-lengthen'd sway,
 In their madness, bless'd they Zeus.

Nicely-balanced, day and night,
Held the scales of Heaven aright,—
 From the tower, with pensive eye,
Gaz'd the gentle maid alone
On the coursers of the sun,
 Hastening downwards through the sky.
Still and calm the ocean lay,
 Like a pure, unsullied glass,—
Not a zephyr sought, in play,
 O'er the crystal flood to pass.

Dolphin-shoals, in joyous motion
Through the clear and silv'ry ocean,
 Wanton'd its cool waves among;
And, in darkly-vestur'd train,
From the bosom of the main
 Tethys' varied band upsprung.
None but they e'er saw reveal'd
 Those fond lovers' blest delight:
But their silent lips were seal'd
 Evermore by Hecate's might.

Gladly on the smiling sea
Gaz'd she, and caressingly
   To the element exclaim'd :
" Lovely God, canst thou deceive ?
Ne'er the traitor I'll believe,
   Who thee false and faithless nam'd.
Treach'rous is the human race,
   Cruel is my father's heart ;
Thou art mild and full of grace,
   And art mov'd by love's soft smart.

" In these desert walls of stone
I had mourn'd in grief alone,
   Pin'd in sorrow without end,
If thou, on thy crested ridge,
Aided by no bark, no bridge,
   Hadst not hither borne my friend.
Dreaded though thy depths may be,
   Fierce the fury of thy wave,
Love can ever soften thee.
   Thou art vanquish'd by the brave.

" For the mighty dart of Love
E'en the Ocean God could move,
   When the golden ram of yore,
Helle, cloth'd in beauty bright,
With her brother in her flight,
   Over thy deep billows bore—
Sudden, vanquish'd by her charms,
   Starting from the whirlpool black,
Thou didst bear her in thine arms
   To thy realms from off his back.

" As a Goddess,—happy lot !—
In the deep and wat'ry grot,
   Evermore she now resides ;
Hapless lovers' cares dispels,
All thy raging passions quells,
   Into port the sailor guides.

Beauteous Helle, Goddess fair,
 Blessed one, to thee I pray :
Safely trusting to thy care,
 Hither bring my love to-day ! "

Dark the waters soon became,
And she wav'd the torch's flame
 From the lofty balcony,
That the wanderer belov'd,
As across the deep he rov'd,
 Might the trusty signal see.
Howling blast approach'd from far,
 Gloomier still the billows curl'd,
Quench'd was ev'ry glimm'ring star,
 And the storm its might unfurl'd.

Over Pontus' boundless plain
Night now spreads, while heavy rain
 Pours in torrents from each cloud ;
Lightning quivers through the air,
While from out its rocky lair
 Bursts the tempest fierce and loud.
In the waters, as they yell,
 Fearful chasms are expos'd ;
Gaping, like the jaws of Hell
 Are the ocean-depths disclos'd.

" Woe, oh, woe ! " she weeping cries ;
" Mighty Zeus, regard my sighs !
 Ah, how rash the boon I crav'd !
If the Gods gave ear to me,
If within the treach'rous sea,
 He the raging storm has brav'd !
Ev'ry bird that loves the tide
 Homeward swiftly wings its way
Ev'ry ship, in tempest tried,
 Refuge seeks in shelt'ring bay.

"Doubtless, ah! the dauntless one
Has his daring task begun,
  Urg'd by the great Deity;
When departing, he his troth
Pledg'd with Love's most sacred oath;
  Death alone can set him free.
He, alas, this very hour,
  Wrestles with the tempest's gloom;
And the madden'd billows' power
  Bears him downwards to their womb.

" Pontus false!—thy seeming calm
Serv'd suspicion to disarm;
  Thou wert like a spotless glass;
Basely smooth thy waters lay,
That they might my love betray
  Into thy false realms to pass.
In thy middle current now,
  Where no hopes of refuge lie,
On the hapless victim thou
  Let'st thy fearful terrors fly!"

Fiercer grows the tempest's might,
Leaping up to mountain-height
  Swells the sea,—the billows roar
'Gainst the cliffs with fury mad;
E'en the ship with oak beclad
  Breaks to pieces on the shore.
And the wind puts out the blaze
  That had serv'd to light the track;
Terror round the landing plays,
  Terror in the waters black.

Venus she implores to chain
The tempestuous hurricane,
  And the angry waves to bind;
And a steer with golden horn
Vows the maid, by anguish torn,
  As a victim to each wind.

Ev'ry Goddess of the deep,
  Ev'ry heavenly Deity,
She implores to lull to sleep
  With smooth oil the raging sea.

"To my mournful cry attend!
Blest Leucothĕa, ascend
  Hither from thy sea-green bower!
Thou who ofttimes com'st to save
When the fury of the wave
  Threats the sailor to devour!
O'er him cast thy sacred veil,
  Which, with its mysterious charm,
E'en when floods his life assail,
  Guards its wearer from all harm!"

And the wild winds cease to blow,
Brightly through the Heavens now go
  Eos' coursers, mounting high;
Gently in its wonted bed
Flows the ocean, smoothly spread,
  Sweetly smile both sea and sky.
Softly now the billows stray
  O'er the peaceful, rock-bound strand,
And, in calm and eddying play,
  Waft a lifeless corpse to land.

Ah, 'tis he who, even now,
Keeps in death his solemn vow!
  In an instant knows she him;
Yet she utters not a sigh,—
Not a tear escapes her eye,
  Cold and rigid is each limb.
Sadly looks she on the light,
  Sadly on the desert deep;
And unearthly flushes bright
  O'er her pallid features creep.

"Dreaded Gods, I own your force!
Fearfully, without remorse,
  Ye have urg'd your rights divine.
Though my race is early run,
Yet I happiness have known,
  And a blissful lot was mine.
Living, in thy temple, I
  As a priestess deck'd my brow,
And a joyful victim die,
  Mighty Venus, for thee now!"

And, with garments flutt'ring round,
From the tower, with madden'd bound,
  Plung'd she in the distant wave.
High the God through his domain
Bears those hallow'd corpses twain,—
  He himself becomes their grave;
And, rejoicing in his prize,
  Gladly on his way he goes,—
From his urn, that never dries,
  Pours his stream, that ceaseless flows.

CASSANDRA.

Mirth the halls of Troy was filling,
  Ere its lofty ramparts fell;
From the golden lute so thrilling
  Hymns of joy were heard to swell.
From the sad and tearful slaughter
  All had laid their arms aside,
For Pelides Priam's daughter
  Claim'd then as his own fair bride.

Laurel branches with them bearing,
  Troop on troop in bright array
To the temples were repairing,
  Owning Thymbrius' sov'reign sway.

Through the streets, with frantic measure,
　　Danced the bacchanal mad round,
And, amid the radiant pleasure,
　　Only *one* sad breast was found.

Joyless in the midst of gladness,
　　None to heed her, none to love,
Roam'd Cassandra, plung'd in sadness,
　　To Apollo's laurel grove.
To its dark and deep recesses
　　Swift the sorrowing priestess hied,
And from off her flowing tresses
　　Tore the sacred band, and cried :

"All around with joy is beaming,
　　Ev'ry heart is happy now, .
And my sire is fondly dreaming,
　　Wreath'd with flowers my sister's brow.
I alone am doom'd to wailing,
　　That sweet vision flies from me ;
In my mind, these walls assailing,
　　Fierce destruction I can see.

" Though a torch I see all-glowing,
　　Yet 'tis not in Hymen's hand ;
Smoke across the skies is blowing,
　　Yet 'tis from no votive brand.
Yonder see I feasts entrancing,
　　But, in my prophetic soul,
Hear I now the God advancing,
　　Who will steep in tears the bowl !

" And they blame my lamentation,
　　And they laugh my grief to scorn ;
To the haunts of desolation
　　I must bear my woes forlorn.
All who happy are, now shun me,
　　And my tears with laughter see ;
Heavy lies thy hand upon me,
　　Cruel Pythian Deity !

"Thy divine decrees foretelling,
    Wherefore hast thou thrown me here,
Where the ever-blind are dwelling,
    With a mind, alas, too clear?
Wherefore hast thou power thus given,
    What must needs occur to know?
Wrought must be the will of Heaven—
    Onward come the hour of woe!

"When impending fate strikes terror,
    Why remove the covering?
Life we have alone in error,
    Knowledge with it death must bring.
Take away this prescience tearful,
    Take this sight of woe from me:
Of thy truths, alas! how fearful
    'Tis the mouth-piece frail to be!

"Veil my mind once more in slumbers,
    Let me heedlessly rejoice;
Never have I sung glad numbers
    Since I've been thy chosen voice.
Knowledge of the future giving,
    Thou hast stol'n the present day,
Stol'n the moment's joyous living,—
    Take thy false gift, then, away!

"Ne'er with bridal train around me,
    Have I wreath'd my radiant brow,
Since to serve thy fane I bound me—
    Bound me with a solemn vow.
Evermore in grief I languish—
    All my youth in tears was spent;
And, with thoughts of bitter anguish
    My too-feeling heart is rent.

"Joyously my friends are playing,
    All around are blest and glad,
In the paths of pleasure straying,—
    My poor heart alone is sad.

Spring in vain unfolds each treasure,
  Filling all the earth with bliss;
Who in life can e'er take pleasure,
  When is seen its dark abyss?

" With her heart in vision burning,
  Truly blest is Polyxene,
As a bride to clasp him yearning,
  Him, the noblest, best Hellene!
And her breast with rapture swelling,
  All its bliss can scarcely know;
E'en the Gods in heavenly dwelling
  Envying not, when dreaming so.

" He to whom *my* heart is plighted
  Stood before my ravish'd eye,
And his look, by passion lighted,
  Tow'rd me turn'd imploringly.
With the lov'd one, oh, how gladly
  Homeward would I take my flight!
But a Stygian shadow sadly
  Steps between us ev'ry night.

" Cruel Proserpine is sending
  All her spectres pale to me;
Ever on my steps attending
  Those dread shadowy forms I see.
Though I seek, in mirth and laughter,
  Refuge from that ghastly train,
Still I see them hast'ning after,—
  Ne'er shall I know joy again.

" And I see the death-steel glancing,
  And the eye of murder glare;
On, with hasty strides advancing,
  Terror haunts me ev'rywhere.
Vain I seek alleviation;—
  Knowing, seeing, suff'ring all,
I must wait the consummation,
  In a foreign land must fall."

While her solemn words are ringing,
    Hark! a dull and wailing tone
From the temple's gate upspringing,—
    Dead lies Thetis' mighty son!
Eris shakes her snake-locks hated,
    Swiftly flies each Deity,
And o'er Ilion's walls ill-fated
    Thunder-Clouds loom heavily!

THE HOSTAGE.

A BALLAD.

To the tyrant Dionys Mœros once hied,—
    A dagger his mantle contain'd;
    They seize him, and soon he is chain'd.
"What sought'st thou to do with the dirk by thy
        side?"—
And Mœros with gloomy fury replied:
    " The town from the Tyrant to free!"—
    " The cross thy reward then shall be."

" I am," said the other, " prepar'd to die,
    Nor seek for permission to live;
    Yet, prithee, this one favour give:
A respite I ask till three days have gone by,
While the marriage-knot of my sister I tie;
    I'll leave thee my friend as my bail,—
    Thou canst kill him instead, if I fail."

The monarch then smil'd with a malice-fraught sneer,
    And after a pause answer'd he:
    " Three days I will give unto thee;
But know! if the end of that time shall appear,
And thou shalt not then have surrender'd thee here,
    Thy friend in thy place must then bleed,
    And thou, in return, shalt be freed."

And he went to his friend, and he said : " The king
      vows
    That I on the cross must atone
    For the impious thing I have done ;
And yet he a respite of three days allows,
Till I my sister have join'd to her spouse ;
    As bail to the king then remain,
    Till I'm back here to loose thee again !"

In silence embrac'd him his friend dear and true,
    Resign'd to the Sovereign's power ;
    The other went off the same hour :
And ere the third morning had dawn'd on the view,
His sister he join'd to her spouse, and then flew
    With anxious concern tow'rd his home,
    That true to his time he might come.

Soon the rain in torrents begins to pour,
    The springs down the mountain's side race,
    The brook and the stream swell apace,
And he comes with his pilgrim's staff to the shore,
When the whirlpool tears down the bridge with wild
      roar,
    And the waves, with a thundering crash,
    To atoms the vaulted arch dash.

And he wanders along the bank in despair,
    But far as he casts round his eyes,
    And far as re-echo his cries,
No friendly bark pushing off he sees there,
By whose aid to the wish'd for land to repair,
    None coming its pilot to be,—
    And the torrent now swells to a sea.

Then he sinks on the shore, and he weeps, and he prays
    With hands rais'd on high unto Zeus :
    " The torrent's wild force, oh reduce !
The hours haste on, and the mid-day rays
Of the sun now fall, and if quench'd is their blaze
    Before at the town I can be,
    My friend must then perish for me."

Yet the stream into greater fury now wakes,
    And billows on billows dash high,
    And hours on hours fleet by.
Then driven by anguish, courage he takes,
And leaps in the flood as it madly breaks,
    And the torrent he cleaves with strong limb,
    And a God has compassion on him.

And he gains the shore, and then onwards he speeds,
    And the God who has sav'd him he blesses;
    When out of the wood's dark recesses
A band of robbers sudden proceeds,
And menaces death, and his progress impedes,
    Obstructing the wanderer's course,
    And wielding the club with wild force.

" What would ye ?" all pallid with terror cries he,
    " Save my life, I have no other thing,
    And *that* I must give to the king !"
And the club from the next he tears hastily :
" For the sake of my friend, here's mercy for thee !"
    And three, with invincible might,
    He slays, and the rest take to flight.

And the sun pours down his hot beams on the land,
    And, worn by the toil he had pass'd,
    His knees sink beneath him at last.
"Oh! am I then sav'd from the spoiler's fierce hand,
And brought safe o'er the flood to the holy strand,
    That I here my last moments may see,
    While the friend that I love dies for me ?"

And hark! close at hand, with a purling sound,
    Comes a gush, and as silver it glistens;
    And he pauses, and anxiously listens:
And lo ! from the cliffs, with a rapid bound,
A murmuring fountain leaps down to the ground,
    And stooping to earth in glad mood,
    He laves his hot limbs in the flood.

And through the green foliage shines now the sun,
   And the giant-like shade of each tree
   On the glittering mead pictures he;
And he sees two travellers moving on,—
With hurried footstep seeks past them to run,
   When thus he o'erhears their discourse:
   "Ere this he is nail'd to the cross!"

And anguish gives wings to his hastening feet,
   That, goaded by care, seem to fly;
   Soon Syracuse bursts on his eye,
And its battlements glow in the sunset sweet,
And its glances ere long Philostratus meet,
   The steward of his household so true,—
   But he shudders his master to view.

"Back! Back! to rescue thy friend 'tis too late;
   Thyself, then, to save, hasten thou:
   For *he* suffers death even now.
From hour to hour, with confidence great,
For thy return he ceas'd not to wait;
   His courage and faith were not torn
   By the Tyrant's contemptuous scorn."

"And if 'tis too late, and I cannot, then, now
   Arrive to receive his last breath,
   I'll hasten to join him in death.
Ne'er the bloodthirsty Tyrant to boast I'll allow
That the friend to the friend has broken his vow;
   When *two* victims have bitten the dust,
   In Love and in Faith let him trust!"

And the sun sinks to rest, and he reaches the gate,
   And the cross he sees rais'd from the ground!
   While the wondering crowd stand around.
They are hoisting his friend on the rope to his fate,
When through the dense concourse he pushes him
     straight;
   "Now, Hangman!" he cries, " strangle me!
   For the one whom he bail'd,—I am he!"

Astonishment seizes on all that stand by,
    While fondly embrace the glad twain,
    And weep with mix'd rapture and pain;
And a tear is seen glist'ing in every eye,—
To the king with the wondrous story they fly,
    And he, mov'd by a merciful thought,
    To the foot of his throne has them brought.

And on them in wonderment long gazes he,
    Then speaks: " Ye the victory have won,
    And conquer'd my heart for your own.
That faith is no empty vision, I see,
So suffer me, too, your companion to be;
    And let my entreaty be heard,
    To form in your friendship the third !"

THE DIVER.

A BALLAD.

" What knight or what vassal will be so bold
    As to plunge in the gulf below?
See ! I hurl in its depths a goblet of gold,
    Already the waters over it flow.
The man who can bring back the goblet to me,
May keep it henceforward,—his own it shall be."

Thus speaks the King, and he hurls from the height
    Of the cliffs that, rugged and steep,
Hang over the boundless sea, with strong might,
    The goblet afar in the bellowing deep.
" And who'll be so daring,—I ask it once more,—
As to plunge in these billows that wildly roar ?

And the vassals and knights of high degree
 Hear his words, but silent remain.
They cast their eyes on the raging sea,
 And none will attempt the goblet to gain.
And a third time the question is ask'd by the King:
" Is there none that will dare in the gulf now to
  spring ?"

Yet all as before in silence stand,
 When a page, with a modest pride,
Steps out of the timorous squirely band,
 And his girdle and mantle soon throws aside,
And all the knights, and the ladies too,
The noble stripling with wonderment view.

And when he draws nigh to the rocky brow,
 And looks in the gulf so black,
The waters that she had swallow'd but now,
 The howling Charybdis is giving back ;
And, with the distant thunder's dull sound,
From her gloomy womb they all-foaming rebound.

And it boils and it roars, and it hisses and seethes,
 As when water and fire first blend ;
To the sky spurts the foam in steam-laden wreaths,
 And wave presses hard upon wave without end.
And the ocean will never exhausted be,
As if striving to bring forth another sea.

But at length the wild tumult seems pacified,
 And blackly amid the white swell
A gaping chasm its jaws opens wide,
 As if leading down to the depths of Hell :
And the howling billows are seen by each eye
Down the whirling funnel all madly to fly.

Then quickly, before the breakers rebound,
  The stripling commends him to Heaven,
And—a scream of horror is heard around,—
    And now by the whirlpool away he is driven,
And secretly over the swimmer brave
Close the jaws, and he vanishes 'neath the dark wave.

O'er the watery gulf, dread silence now lies,
  But the deep sends up a dull yell,
And from mouth to mouth thus trembling it flies:
  " Courageous stripling, oh, fare thee well! "
And duller and duller the howls recommence,
While they pause in anxious and fearful suspense.

" If even thy crown in the gulf thou shouldst fling,
  And shouldst say, ' He who brings it to me
Shall wear it henceforward, and be the king,'
    Thou couldst tempt me not e'en with that precious
        fee ;
What under the howling deep is conceal'd
To no happy living soul is reveal'd."

Full many a ship, by the whirlpool held fast,
  Shoots straightway beneath the mad wave,
And, dash'd to pieces, the hull and the mast
    Emerge from the all-devouring grave,—
And the roaring approaches still nearer and nearer,
Like the howl of the tempest, still clearer and clearer.

And it boils and it roars, and it hisses and seethes,
  As when water and fire first blend ;
To the sky spurts the foam in steam-laden wreaths,
    And wave presses hard upon wave without end.
And, with the distant thunder's dull sound
From the ocean-womb they all-bellowing bound.

M 2

And lo! from the darkly flowing tide
  Comes a vision white as a swan,
And an arm and a glistening neck are descried,
  With might and with active zeal steering on:
And 'tis *he*, and behold! his left hand on high
Waves the goblet, while beaming with joy is his eye.

Then breathes he deeply, then breathes he long,
  And blesses the light of the day;
While gladly exclaim to each other the throng:
  " He lives! he is here! He is *not* the sea's prey!
From the tomb, from the eddying waters' control,
The brave one has rescued his living soul!"

And he comes, and they joyously round him stand;
  At the feet of the monarch he falls,—
The goblet he, kneeling, puts in his hand,
  And the King to his beauteous daughter calls,
Who fills it with sparkling wine to the brim;
The youth turns to the monarch, and speaks thus to
    him :—

" Long life to the King! Let all those be glad
  Who breathe in the light of the sky!
For below all is fearful, of moment sad;
  Let not man to tempt the immortals e'er try,
Let him never desire the thing to see
That with terror and night they veil graciously.

" I was torn below with the speed of light,
  When out of a cavern of rock
Rush'd tow'rds me a spring with furious might;
  I was seiz'd by the twofold torrent's wild shock,
And like a top, with a whirl and a bound,
Despite all resistance, was whirl'd around.

" Then God pointed out,—for to Him I cried
In that terrible moment of need,—
A craggy reef in the gulf's dark side;
  I seiz'd it in haste, and from death was then freed.

And there, on sharp corals, was hanging the cup,—
The fathomless pit had else swallowed it up.

" For under me lay it, still mountain-deep,
   In a darkness of purple-tinged dye,
And though to the ear all might seem then asleep
   With shuddering awe 'twas seen by the eye
How the salamanders' and dragons' dread forms
Fill'd those terrible jaws of hell with their swarms.

" There crowded, in union fearful and black,
   In a horrible mass entwin'd,
The rock-fish, the ray with the thorny back,
   And the hammer-fish's mis-shapen kind,
And the shark, the hyena dread of the sea,
With his angry teeth, grinn'd fiercely on me.

" There hung I, by fulness of terror possess'd,
   Where all human aid was unknown,
Amongst phantoms, the only sensitive breast,
   In that fearful solitude all alone,
Where the voice of mankind could not reach to mine
     ear,
'Mid the monsters foul of that wilderness drear.

" Thus shudd'ring methought—when a Something
     crawl'd near,
   And a hundred limbs it out-flung,
And at me it snapp'd ;—in my mortal fear,
   I left hold of the coral to which I had clung ;
Then the whirlpool seiz'd on me with madden'd roar,
Yet 'twas well, for it brought me to light once
     more."

The story, in wonderment hears the King,
   And he says, " The cup is thine own,
And I purpose also to give thee this ring,
   Adorn'd with a costly, a priceless stone,
If thou'lt try once again, and bring word to me
What thou saw'st in the nethermost depths of the
     sea."

His daughter hears this with emotions soft,
   And with flattering accent prays she:
" That fearful sport, father, attempt not too oft!
   What none other would dare, he hath ventur'd for
      thee;
If thy heart's wild longings thou canst not tame,
Let the knights, if they can, put the squire to shame."

The King then seizes the goblet in haste,
   In the gulf he hurls it with might:
" When the goblet once more in my hands thou hast
      placed,
   Thou shalt rank at my court as the noblest knight,
And her as a bride thou shalt clasp e'en to-day,
Who for thee with tender compassion doth pray."

Then a force, as from Heaven, descends on him there,
   And lightning gleams in his eye,
And blushes he sees on her features so fair,
   And he sees her turn pale, and swooning lie;
Then eager the precious guerdon to win,
For life or for death, lo! he plunges him in!

The breakers they hear, and the breakers return,
   Proclaim'd by a thundering sound;
They bend o'er the gulf with glances that yearn,
   And the waters are pouring in fast around;
Though upwards and downwards they rush and they
      rave,
The youth is brought back by no kindly wave.

THE KNIGHT OF TOGGENBURG.

A BALLAD.

" I can love thee well, believe me,
    As a sister true ;
Other love, Sir Knight, would grieve me,
    Sore my heart would rue.
Calmly would I see thee going,
    Calmly, too, appear ;
For those tears in silence flowing
    Find no answer here."

Thus she speaks,—he hears her sadly,—
    How his heartstrings bleed !—
In his arms he clasps her madly,
    Then he mounts his steed.
From the Switzer land collects he
    All his warriors brave ;—
Cross on breast, their course directs he
    To the Holy Grave.

In triumphant march advancing,
    Onward moves the host,
While their morion plumes are dancing
    Where the foes are most.
Mortal terror strikes the Paynim
    At the chieftain's name ;
But the knight's sad thoughts enchain him,—
    Grief consumes his frame.

Twelve long months, with courage daring,
    Peace he strives to find ;
Then at last, of rest despairing,
    Leaves the host behind ;

Sees a ship, whose sails are swelling,
    Lie on Joppa's strand;
Ships him homeward for *her* dwelling,
    In his own lov'd land.

Now behold the pilgrim weary
    At her castle gate!
But, alas! these accents dreary
    Seal his mournful fate :—
"She thou seek'st, her troth hath plighted
    To all-gracious Heaven ;
To her God she was united
    Yesterday at even !"

To his father's home for ever
    Bids he now adieu ;
Sees no more his arms and beaver,
    Nor his steed so true.
Then descends he, sadly, slowly,—
    None suspect the sight,—
For a garb of penance lowly
    Wears the noble knight.

Soon he now, the tempest braving,
    Builds a humble shed,
Where, o'er lime-trees darkly waving,
    Peeps the convent's head.
From the orb of day's first gleaming,
    Till his race has run,
Hope in ev'ry feature beaming,
    There he sits alone.

Tow'rd the convent straining ever
    His unwearied eyes,—
From her casement looking never
    Till it open flies,
Till the lov'd one, soft advancing,
    Shows her gentle face,
O'er the vale her sweet eye glancing,
    Full of angel-grace.

Then he seeks his bed of rushes,
    Still'd all grief and pain,
Slumbering calm, till morning's blushes
    Waken life again.
Days and years fleet on, yet never
    Breathes he plaint or sighs,
On her casement gazing ever,
    Till it open flies,

Till the lov'd one, soft advancing,
    Shows her gentle face,
O'er the vale her sweet eye glancing,
    Full of angel-grace.
But, at length, the morn returning
    Finds him dead and chill,—
Pale and wan, his gaze, with yearning,
    Seeks her casement still!

THE FIGHT WITH THE DRAGON.

WHY run the crowd?   What means the throng
That rushes fast the streets along?
Can Rhodes a prey to flames, then, be?
In crowds they gather hastily,
And, on his steed, a noble knight
Amid the rabble, meets my sight;
Behind him—prodigy unknown!—
A monster fierce they're drawing on;
A dragon seems it by its shape,
    With wide and crocodile-like jaw,
And on the knight and dragon gape,
In turns, the people, fill'd with awe.

And thousand voices shout with glee:—
" The fiery dragon come and see,
Who hind and flock tore limb from limb!—
The hero see, who vanquish'd him!

Full many a one before him went,
To dare the fearful combat bent,
But none return'd home from the fight;
Honour ye, then, the noble knight!"
And tow'rd the convent move they all,
    While met in hasty council there
The brave knights of the Hospital,
    St. John the Baptist's Order, were.

Up to the noble Master sped
The youth, with firm but modest tread;
The people follow'd with wild shout,
And stood the landing place about,
While thus outspoke that Daring One:—
" My knightly duty I have done.
The dragon that laid waste the land
Has fallen 'neath my conquering hand.
The way is to the wanderer free,
    The shepherd o'er the plains may rove;
Across the mountains joyfully
    The pilgrim to the shrine may move."

But sternly look'd the prince, and said:
" The hero's part thou well hast play'd;
By courage is the true knight known,—
A dauntless spirit thou hast shown.
Yet speak!   What duty first should he
Regard, who would Christ's champion be,
Who wears the emblem of the Cross?"—
And all turn'd pale at his discourse.
Yet he replied, with noble grace,
    While blushingly he bent him low:
" That he deserves so proud a place
    Obedience best of all can show."

" My son," the Master answering spoke,
" Thy daring act this duty broke.
The conflict that the law forbade
Thou hast with impious mind essay'd."—

"Lord, judge when all to thee is known,"
The other spake, in steadfast tone,—
"For I the law's commands and will
Purpos'd with honour to fulfil.
I went not out with heedless thought,
    Hoping the monster dread to find;
To conquer in the fight I sought
    By cunning, and a prudent mind.

"Five of our noble Order, then
(Our faith could boast no better men),
Had by their daring lost their life,
When thou forbadest us the strife.
And yet my heart I felt a prey
To gloom, and panted for the fray;
Ay, even in the stilly night,
In vision gasp'd I in the fight;
And when the glimm'ring morning came,
    And of fresh troubles knowledge gave,
A raging grief consum'd my frame,
    And I resolv'd the thing to brave.

"And to myself I thus began:
'What is't adorns the youth, the man?
What actions of the heroes bold,
Of whom in ancient song we're told,
Blind heathendom rais'd up on high
To godlike fame and dignity?
The world, by deeds known far and wide,
From monsters fierce they purified;
The lion in the fight they met,
    And wrestled with the Minotaur,
Unhappy victims free to set,
    And were not sparing of their gore.

"'Are none but Saracens to feel
The prowess of the Christian steel?
False idols only shall he brave?
His mission is the world to save;

To free it, by his sturdy arm,
From ev'ry hurt, from ev'ry harm;
Yet wisdom must his courage bend,
And cunning must with strength contend.'
Thus spake I oft, and went alone
    The monster's traces to espy;
When on my mind a bright light shone,—
    'I have it!' was my joyful cry.

" To thee I went, and thus I spake:
' My homeward journey I would take.'
Thou, lord, didst grant my prayer to me,—
Then safely traversed I the sea;
And, when I reach'd my native strand,
I caus'd a skilful artist's hand
To make a dragon's image, true
To *his* that now so well I knew.
On feet of measure short was plac'd
    Its lengthy body's heavy load;
A scaly coat of mail embrac'd
    The back, on which it fiercely show'd.

" Its stretching neck appear'd to swell,
And, ghastly as a gate of hell,
Its fearful jaws were open wide,
As if to seize the prey it tried;
And in its black mouth, rang'd about,
Its teeth in prickly rows stood out;
Its tongue was like a sharp-edged sword,
And lightning from its small eyes pour'd;
A serpent's tail of many a fold
    Ended its body's monstrous span,
And round itself with fierceness roll'd,
    So as to clasp both steed and man.

" I form'd the whole to nature true,
In skin of grey and hideous hue;
Part dragon it appear'd, part snake,
Engender'd in the poisonous lake.

And, when the figure was complete,
A pair of dogs I chose me, fleet,
Of mighty strength, of nimble pace,
Inur'd the savage boar to chase;
The dragon, then, I made them bait,
 Inflaming them to fury dread,
With their sharp teeth to seize it straight,
 And with my voice their motions led.

" And, where the belly's tender skin
Allow'd the tooth to enter in,
I taught them how to seize it there,
And, with their fangs, the part to tear.
I mounted, then, my Arab steed,
The offspring of a noble breed;
My hand a dart on high held forth,
And, when I had inflam'd his wrath,
I stuck my sharp spurs in his side,
 And urg'd him on as quick as thought,
And hurl'd my dart in circles wide,
 As if to pierce the beast I sought.

" And though my steed rear'd high in pain,
And champ'd and foam'd beneath the rein,
And though the dogs howl'd fearfully,
Till they were calm'd ne'er rested I.
This plan I ceaselessly pursued,
Till thrice the moon had been renew'd;
And when they had been duly taught,
In swift ships here I had them brought;
And since my foot these shores has press'd,
 Flown has three mornings' narrow span;
I scarce allow'd my limbs to rest
 Ere I the mighty task began.

" For hotly was my bosom stirr'd
When of the land's fresh grief I heard;
Shepherds of late had been his prey,
When in the marsh they went astray.

I form'd my plans then hastily,—
My heart was all that counsell'd me.
My squires instructing to proceed,
I sprang upon my well-train'd steed,
And, follow'd by my noble pair
    Of dogs, by secret pathways rode,
Where not an eye could witness bear,
    To find the monster's fell abode.

" Thou, lord, must know the chapel well,
Pitch'd on a rocky pinnacle,
That overlooks the distant isle;
A daring mind 'twas rais'd the pile.
Though humble, mean, and small it shows,
Its walls a miracle enclose,—
The Virgin and her Infant Son,
Vow'd by the Three Kings of Cologne.
By three times thirty steps is led
    The pilgrim to the giddy height;
Yet, when he gains it with bold tread,
    He's quicken'd by his Saviour's sight.

" Deep in the rock to which it clings,
A cavern dark its arms outflings,
Moist with the neighbouring moorland's dew,
Where heaven's bright rays can ne'er pierce thro'.
There dwelt the monster, there he lay,
His spoil awaiting, night and day;
Like the hell-dragon, thus he kept
Watch near the shrine, and never slept;
And if a hapless pilgrim chanced
    To enter on that fatal way,
From out his ambush quick advanced
    The foe, and seiz'd him as his prey.

" I mounted now the rocky height,
Ere I commenced the fearful fight.
There knelt I to the Infant Lord,
And pardon for my sins implor'd.

Then in the holy fane I placed
My shining armour round my waist,
My right hand grasp'd my javelin,—
The fight then went I to begin;
Instructions gave my squires among,
    Commanding them to tarry there;
Then on my steed I nimbly sprung,
    And gave my spirit to God's care.

"Soon as I reach'd the level plain,
My dogs found out the scent amain;
My frighten'd horse soon rear'd on high,—
His fear I could not pacify,
For, coil'd up in a circle, lo!
There lay the fierce and hideous foe,
Sunning himself upon the ground.
Straight at him rush'd each nimble hound;
Yet thence they turn'd, dismay'd and fast,
    When he his gaping jaws op'd wide,
Vomited forth his poisonous blast,
    And like the howling jackal cried.

" But soon their courage I restor'd;
They seiz'd with rage the foe abhorr'd,
While I against the beast's loins threw
My spear with sturdy arm and true:
But, powerless as a bulrush frail,
It bounded from his coat of mail;
And ere I could repeat the throw,
My horse reel'd wildly to and fro
Before his basilisk-like look,
    And at his poison-teeming breath,—
Sprang backward, and with terror shook.
    While I seem'd doom'd to certain death.

" Then from my steed I nimbly sprung,
My sharp-edg'd sword with vigour swung;
Yet all in vain my strokes I plied,—
I could not pierce his rock-like hide.

His tail with fury lashing round,
Sudden he bore me to the ground;
His jaws then opening fearfully,
With angry teeth he struck at me;
But now my dogs, with wrath new-born,
　　Rush'd on his belly with fierce bite,
So that, by dreadful anguish torn,
　　He howling stood before my sight.

" And ere he from their teeth was free,
I rais'd myself up hastily,
The weak place of the foe explor'd,
And in his entrails plunged my sword,
Sinking it even to the hilt;
Black-gushing forth, his blood was spilt.
Down sank he, burying in his fall
Me with his body's giant ball,
So that my senses quickly fled;
　　And when I woke with strength renew'd,
The dragon in his blood lay dead,
　　While, round me group'd, my squires all
　　　stood."

The joyous shouts, so long suppress'd,
Now burst from ev'ry hearer's breast,
Soon as the knight these words had spoken;
And ten times 'gainst the high vault broken,
The sound of mingled voices rang
Re-echoing back with hollow clang.
The Order's sons demand, in haste,
That with a crown his brow be graced,
And gratefully in triumph now
　　The mob the youth would bear along—
When, lo! the Master knit his brow,
　　And called for silence 'mongst the throng.

And said, " The dragon that this land
Laid waste, thou slew'st with daring hand;

" Although the people's idol thou,
The Order's foe I deem thee now.
Thy breast has to a fiend more base
Than e'en this dragon given place.
The serpent that the heart most stings,
And hatred and destruction brings,
That spirit is, which stubborn lies,
    And impiously casts off the rein,
Despising order's sacred ties;
    'Tis *that* destroys the world amain.

" The Mameluke makes of courage boast,
Obedience decks the Christian most;
For where our great and blessèd Lord
As a mere servant walk'd abroad,
The Fathers, on that holy ground,
This famous Order chose to found,
That arduous duty to fulfil
To overcome one's own self-will!
'Twas idle glory mov'd thee there:
    So take thee hence from out my sight!
For who the Lord's yoke cannot bear,
    To wear his cross can have no right."

A furious shout now raise the crowd,
The place is fill'd with outcries loud;
The Brethren all for pardon cry;
The youth in silence droops his eye—
Mutely his garment from him throws,
Kisses the Master's hand, and—goes.
But he pursues him with his gaze,
Recalls him lovingly, and says:
" Let me embrace thee now, my son!
    The harder fight is gain'd by thee.
Take, then, this cross—the guerdon won
    By self-subdued humility."

N

FRIDOLIN;

OR,

THE WALK TO THE IRON FOUNDRY.

A GENTLE page was Fridolin,
    And he his mistress dear,
Savern's fair Countess, honour'd in
    All truth and godly fear.
She was so meek, and, ah! so good!
Yet each wish of her wayward mood,
    He would have studied to fulfil,
    To please his God, with earnest will.

From the first hour when daylight shone
    Till rang the vesper-chime,
He liv'd but for her will alone,
    And deem'd e'en *that* scarce time.
And if she said, " Less anxious be!"
His eye then glisten'd tearfully,
    Thinking that he in duty fail'd,
    And so before no toil he quail'd.

And so, before her serving train,
    The Countess lov'd to raise him;
While her fair mouth, in endless strain,
    Was ever wont to praise him.
She never held him as her slave,
Her heart a child's-rights to him gave;
    Her clear eye hung in fond delight
    Upon his well-form'd features bright.

Soon in the huntsman Robert's breast
    Was poisonous anger fir'd;
His black soul, long by lust possess'd,
    With malice was inspir'd;

He sought the Count, whom, quick in deed,
A traitor might with ease mislead,
   As once from hunting home they rode,
   And in his heart suspicion sow'd.

" Happy art thou, great Count, in truth,"
   Thus cunningly he spoke ;
" For ne'er mistrust's envenom'd tooth
   Thy golden slumbers broke ;
A noble wife thy love rewards,
And modesty her person guards.
   The Tempter will be able ne'er
   Her true fidelity to snare."

A gloomy scowl the Count's eye fill'd :
   " What's this thou say'st to me ?
Shall I on woman's virtue build,
   Inconstant as the sea ?
The flatterer's mouth with ease may lure ;
My trust is placed on ground more sure.
   No one, methinks, dare ever burn
   To tempt the wife of Count Savern."

The other spoke : " Thou sayest it well ;
   The fool deserves thy scorn
Who ventures on such thoughts to dwell,
   A mere retainer born,—
Who to the lady he obeys
Fears not his wishes' lust to raise."—
   " What ! " tremblingly the Count began,
   " Dost speak, then, of a living man ? "—

" Is, then, the thing, to all reveal'd,
   Hid from my master's view ?
Yet, since with care from thee conceal'd,
   I'd fain conceal it too "—

N 2

"Speak quickly, villain! speak or die!"
Exclaim'd the other fearfully.
　"Who dares to look on Cunigond?"
　"'Tis the fair page that is so fond."

"He's not ill-shap'd in form, I wot,"
　He craftily went on;
The Count meanwhile felt cold and hot,
　By turns in ev'ry bone.
"Is't possible thou seest not, sir,
How he has eyes for none but her?—
　At table ne'er attends to thee,
　But sighs behind her ceaselessly?

"Behold the rhymes that from him came
　His passion to confess"—
"Confess!"—"And for an answering flame,—
　The impious knave!—to press.
My gracious lady, soft and meek,
Through pity, doubtless, fear'd to speak;
　That it has 'scap'd me, sore I rue;
　What, lord, canst thou to help it do?"

Into the neighbouring wood then rode
　The Count, inflam'd with wrath,
Where, in his iron-foundry, glow'd
　The ore, and bubbled forth.
The workmen here, with busy hand,
The fire both late and early fann'd.
　The sparks fly out, the bellows ply,
　As if the rock to liquefy.

The fire and water's might twofold
　Are here united found;
The mill-wheel, by the flood seiz'd hold,
　Is whirling round and round;
The works are clatt'ring night and day,
With measur'd stroke the hammers play,
　And, yielding to the mighty blows,
　The very iron plastic grows.

'Then to two workmen beckons he,
    And speaks thus in his ire:
" The first who's hither sent by me
    Thus of ye to inquire:
' Have ye obey'd my lord's word well ? '
Him cast ye into yonder hell,
    That into ashes he may fly,
And ne'er again torment mine eye!"

Th' inhuman pair were overjoy'd,
    With devilish glee possess'd:
For as the iron, feeling void,
    Their heart was in their breast.
And brisker with the bellows' blast,
The foundry's womb now heat they fast,
    And with a murderous mind prepare
    To offer up the victim there.

Then Robert to his comrade spake,
    With false hypocrisy:
" Up, comrade, up! no tarrying make!
    Our lord has need of thee."
The lord to Fridolin then said:
" The pathway tow'rd the foundry tread,
    And of the workmen there inquire,
    If they have done their lord's desire."

The other answer'd, " Be it so ! "
    But o'er him came this thought,
When he was all-prepar'd to go,
    " Will *she* command me aught ? "
So to the Countess straight he went:
" I'm to the iron-foundry sent;
    Then say, can I do aught for thee ?
    For thou 'tis who commandest me."

To this the Lady of Savern
    Replied in gentle tone:
" To hear the holy mass I yearn,
    For sick now lies my son ;

So go, my child, and when thou'rt there,
Utter for me a humble prayer,
  And of thy sins think ruefully,
  That grace may also fall on me."

And in this welcome duty glad,
  He quickly left the place ;
But ere the village bounds he had
  Attain'd with rapid pace,
The sound of bells struck on his ear,
From the high belfry ringing clear,
  And ev'ry sinner, mercy-sent,
  Inviting to the sacrament.

" Never from praising God refrain
  Where'er by thee He's found ! "
He spoke, and stepp'd into the fane,
  But there he heard no sound ;
For 'twas the harvest time, and now
Glow'd in the fields the reaper's brow ;
  No choristers were gather'd there,
  The duties of the mass to share.

The matter paus'd he not to weigh,
  But took the sexton's part ;
" That thing," he said, " makes no delay
  Which heav'nward guides the heart."
Upon the priest, with helping hand,
He placed the stole and sacred band,
  The vessels he prepar'd beside,
  That for the mass were sanctified.

And when his duties here were o'er,
  Holding the mass-book, he,
Minist'ring to the priest, before
  The altar bow'd his knee,
And knelt him left, and knelt him right,
While not a look escap'd his sight,
  And when the holy SANCTUS came,
  The bell thrice rang he at the name.

And when the priest, bow'd humbly too,
  In hand uplifted high,
Facing the altar, show'd to view
  The Present Deity,
The sacristan proclaim'd it well,
Sounding the clearly-tinkling bell,
    While all knelt down, and beat the breast,
    And with a cross the Host confess'd.

The rites thus serv'd he, leaving none,
  With quick and ready wit;
Each thing that in God's house is done,
  He also practis'd it.
Unweariedly he labour'd thus,
Till the Vobiscum Dominus,
    When tow'rd the people turn'd the priest,
    Bless'd them,—and so the service ceas'd.

Then he dispos'd each thing again,
  In fair and due array;
First purified the holy fane,
  And then he went his way,
And gladly, with a mind at rest,
On to the iron-foundry press'd,
    Saying the while, complete to be,
    Twelve paternosters silently.

And when he saw the furnace smoke,
  And saw the workmen stand,
" Have ye, ye fellows," thus he spoke,
  " Obey'd the Count's command?"
Grinning they ope the orifice,
And point into the fell abyss:
    " He's car'd for—all is at an end!
    The Count his servants will commend."

The answer to his lord he brought,
  Returning hastily,
Who, when his form his notice caught,
  Could scarcely trust his eye:

" Unhappy one ! whence comest thou ? "—
" Back from the foundry "—" Strange, I vow !
  Hast in thy journey, then, delay'd ? "—
  " 'Twas only, lord, till I had pray'd.

" For when I from thy presence went
  (Oh pardon me !), to-day,
As duty bid, my steps I bent
  To her whom I obey.
She told me, lord, the mass to hear,
I gladly to her wish gave ear,
  And told four rosaries at the shrine,
  For her salvation and for thine."

In wonder deep the Count now fell,
  And, shudd'ring, thus spake he :
" And, at the foundry, quickly tell,
  What answer gave they thee ? "
" Obscure the words they answer'd in,—
Showing the furnace with a grin :
  ' He's car'd for—all is at an end !
  The Count his servants will commend.' "

" And Robert ? " interrupted he,
  While deadly pale he stood,—
" Did he not, then, fall in with thee ?
  I sent him to the wood."—
" Lord, neither in the wood nor field
Was trace of Robert's foot reveal'd."—
  " Then," cried the Count, with awe-struck
      mien,
  " Great God in heav'n his judge hath been ! "

With kindness he before ne'er prov'd,
  He led him by the hand
Up to the Countess,—deeply mov'd, --
  Who nought could understand.

" This child, let him be dear to thee,
No angel is so pure as he !
　　Though *we* may have been counsell'd ill,
　　God and His hosts watch o'er him still."

THE COUNT OF HAPSBURG.*

A BALLAD.

At Aix-la-Chapelle, in imperial array,
　　In its halls renown'd in old story,
At the coronation banquet so gay
　　King Rudolf was sitting in glory.
The meats were serv'd up by the Palsgrave of Rhine,
The Bohemian pour'd out the bright sparkling wine,
　　And all the Electors, the seven,
Stood waiting around the world-governing One,
As the chorus of stars encircle the sun,
　　That honour might duly be given.

And the people the lofty balcony round
　　In a throng exulting were filling ;
While loudly were blending the trumpets' glad sound,
　　And the multitude's voices so thrilling ;
For the monarchless period, with horror rife,
Has ended now, after long baneful strife,
　　And the earth had a lord to possess her.
No longer rul'd blindly the iron-bound spear,
And the weak and the peaceful no longer need fear
　　Being crush'd by the cruel oppressor.

And the emperor speaks with a smile in his eye,
　　While the golden goblet he seizes :
" With this banquet in glory none other can vie,
　　And my regal heart well it pleases ;

* The somewhat irregular metre of the original has been preserved in this ballad, as in other poems ; although the perfect
anapæstic metre is perhaps more familiar to the English ear.

Yet the minstrel, the bringer of joy, is not here,
Whose melodious strains to my heart are so dear,
    And whose words heav'nly wisdom inspire;
Since the days of my youth it hath been my delight,
And that which I ever have lov'd as a knight,
    As a monarch I also require."

And behold! 'mongst the princes who stand round the
       throne
    Steps the bard, in his robe long and streaming,
While, bleach'd by the years that have over him flown,
    His silver locks brightly are gleaming;
"Sweet harmony sleeps in the golden strings,
The minstrel of true love reward ever sings,
    And adores what to virtue has tended—
What the bosom may wish, what the senses hold
       dear;
But say, what is worthy the Emperor's ear
    At this, of all feasts the most splendid?"

"No restraint would I place on the minstrel's own
       choice,"
    Speaks the monarch, a smile on each feature;
"He obeys the swift hour's imperious voice,
    Of a far greater lord is the creature.
For, as through the air the storm-wind on-speeds,—
One knows not from whence its wild roaring
       proceeds—
    As the spring from hid sources up-leaping,
So the lay of the bard from the inner heart breaks—
While the might of sensations unknown it awakes,
    That within us were wondrously sleeping."

Then the bard swept the chords with a finger of
       might,
    Evoking their magical sighing:
"To the chase once rode forth a valorous knight,
    In pursuit of the antelope flying.

His hunting-spear bearing, there came in his train
His squire; and when o'er a wide-spreading plain
    On his stately steed he was riding,
He heard in the distance a bell tinkling clear,
And a priest, with the Host, he saw soon drawing near,
    While before him the sexton was striding.

" And low to the earth the Count then inclin'd,
    Bared his head in humble submission,
To honour, with trusting and Christian-like mind,
    What had sav'd the whole world from perdition.
But a brook o'er the plain was pursuing its course,
That, swell'd by the mountain stream's headlong
      force,
    Barr'd the wanderer's steps with its current;
So the priest on one side the blest sacrament put,
And his sandal with nimbleness drew from his foot,
    That he safely might pass through the torrent.

" ' What wouldst thou?' the Count to him thus began,
    His wondering look tow'rd him turning:
' My journey is, lord, to a dying man,
    Who for heavenly diet is yearning;
But when to the bridge o'er the brook I came nigh,
In the whirl of the stream, as it madly rush'd by
    With furious might, 'twas uprooted.
And so, that the sick the salvation may find
That he pants for, I hasten with resolute mind
    To wade through the waters bare-footed.'

" Then the Count made him mount on his stately steed,
    And the reins to his hands he confided,
That he duly might comfort the sick in his need,
    And that each holy rite be provided.
And himself, on the back of the steed of his squire,
Went after the chase to his heart's full desire,

While the priest on his journey was speeding :
And the following morning, with thankful look,
'To the Count once again his charger he took,
    Its bridle with modesty leading.

" ' God forbid that in chase or in battle,' then cried
    The Count with humility lowly,
' The steed I henceforward should dare to bestride
    That hath borne my Creator so holy !
And if, as a guerdon, he may not be thine,
He devoted shall be to the service divine,
    Proclaiming *His* infinite merit,
From whom I each honour and earthly good
Have received in fee, and my body and blood,
    And my breath, and my life, and my spirit.'

" ' Then may God, the sure rock, whom no time can e'er
      move,
    And who lists to the weak's supplication,
For the honour thou pay'st Him, permit thee to prove
    Honour *here*, and *hereafter* salvation !
Thou'rt a powerful Count, and thy knightly command
Hath blazon'd thy fame thro' the Switzer's broad land ;
    Thou art blest with six daughters admir'd ;
May they each in thy house introduce a bright crown,
Filling ages unborn with their glorious renown'—
    Thus exclaim'd he in accents inspir'd."

And the Emperor sat there all-thoughtfully,
    While the dream of the past stood before him ;
And when on the minstrel he turn'd his eye,
    His words' hidden meaning stole o'er him ;
For seeing the traits of the priest there reveal'd,
In the folds of his purple-dyed robe he conceal'd
    His tears as they swiftly cours'd down.
And all on the Emperor wond'ringly gaz'd,
And the blest dispensations of Providence prais'd,
    For the Count and the Caesar were one.

THE GLOVE.

A TALE.

Before his lion-court,
Impatient for the sport,
  King Francis sat one day;
The peers of his realm sat around,
And in balcony high from the ground
  Sat the ladies in beauteous array.

And when with his finger he beckon'd,
The gate open'd wide in a second,—
And in, with deliberate tread,
Enters a lion dread,
And looks around
Yet utters no sound;
Then long he yawns
  And shakes his mane,
And, stretching each limb,
  Down lies he again.

Again signs the king,—
  The next gate open flies,
And, lo! with wild spring,
  A tiger out hies.
When the lion he sees, loudly roars he about,
And a terrible circle his tail traces out.
Protruding his tongue, past the lion he walks,
And, snarling with rage, round him warily stalks:
Then, growling anew,
On one side lies down too.

Again signs the king,—
  And two gates open fly,
And, lo! with one spring,
  Two leopards out hie.
On the tiger they rush, for the fight nothing loth,
But he with his paws seizes hold of them both.
And the lion, with roaring, gets up,—then all's still;
The fierce beasts stalk around, madly thirsting to kill.

From the balcony rais'd high above
A fair hand lets fall now a glove
Into the lists, where 'tis seen
The lion and tiger between.

To the knight, Sir Delorges, in tone of jest,
   Then speaks young Cunigund fair;
"Sir Knight, if the love that thou feel'st in thy breast
  Is as warm as thou'rt wont at each moment to
     swear,
  Pick up, I pray thee, the glove that lies there!"

And the knight, in a moment, with dauntless tread,
   Jumps into the lists, nor seeks to linger,
And, from out the midst of those monsters dread,
   Picks up the glove with a daring finger.

And the knights and ladies of high degree
With wonder and horror the action see.
While he quietly brings in his hand the glove.
   The praise of his courage each mouth employs;
Meanwhile, with a tender look of love,
   The promise to him of coming joys,
Fair Cunigund welcomes him back to his place.
But he threw the glove point-blank in her face:
"Lady, no thanks from thee I'll receive!"
And that selfsame hour he took his leave.

THE VEILED STATUE AT SAIS.

A youth, impell'd by burning thirst for knowledge
To roam to Saïs, in fair Egypt's land,
The priesthood's secret learning to explore,
Had pass'd thro' many a grade with eager haste,
And still was hurrying on with fond impatience.
Scarce could the Hierophant impose a rein

Upon his headlong efforts.   "What avails
A part without the whole ?" the youth exclaim'd ;
" Can there be here a lesser or a greater ?
The truth thou speak'st of, like mere earthly dross,
Is't but a sum that can be held by man
In larger or in smaller quantity ?
Surely 'tis changeless, indivisible ;
Deprive a harmony of but one note,
Deprive the rainbow of one single colour,
And all that will remain is nought, so long
As that one colour, that one note, is wanting."

While thus they converse held, they chanced to stand
Within the precincts of a lonely temple,
Where a veil'd statue of gigantic size
The youth's attention caught.   In wonderment
He turn'd him tow'rd his guide, and ask'd him, saying,
" What form is that conceal'd beneath yon veil ?"
" Truth !" was the answer. " What !" the young man cried,
" When I am striving after Truth alone,
Seek'st thou to hide that very Truth from me ?"

    " The Godhead's self alone can answer thee,"
Replied the Hierophant.   " ' Let no rash mortal
Disturb this veil,' said he, ' till rais'd by me ;
For he who dares with sacrilegious hand
To move the sacred mystic covering,
He '—said the Godhead—"   " Well ?"— " ' will *see*
    the Truth.' "
" Strangely oracular, indeed ! And thou
Hast never ventur'd, then, to raise the veil ?"
" I ? Truly not ! I never even felt
The least desire."—" Is't possible ? If I
Were sever'd from the Truth by nothing else
Than this thin gauze—"   " And a divine decree,"
His guide broke in.   " Far heavier than thou think'st
Is this thin gauze, my son.   Light to thy hand
It may be—but most weighty to thy conscience."

The youth now sought his home, absorb'd in
        thought;
His burning wish to solve the mystery
Banish'd all sleep; upon his couch he lay,
Tossing his fev'rish limbs.   When midnight came,
He rose, and tow'rd the temple timidly,
Led by a mighty impulse, bent his way.
The walls he scal'd, and soon one active spring
Landed the daring boy beneath the dome.

Behold him now, in utter solitude,
Welcom'd by nought save fearful, deathlike silence,—
A silence which the echo of his steps
Alone disturbs, as through the vaults he paces.
Piercing an opening in the cupola,
The moon cast down her pale and silv'ry beams,
And, awful as a present deity,
Glitt'ring amid the darkness of the pile,
In its long veil conceal'd, the statue stands.

With hesitating step, he now draws near-
His impious hand would fain remove the veil—
Sudden a burning chill assails his bones,
And then an unseen arm repulses him.
"Unhappy one, what wouldst thou do?"   Thus cries
A faithful voice within his trembling breast.
"Wouldst thou profanely violate the All-Holy?"—
"'Tis true the oracle declar'd, 'Let none
Venture to raise the veil till rais'd by me.'
But did the oracle itself not add,
That he who did so would behold the Truth?
Whate'er is hid behind, I'll raise the veil."
And then he shouted: "Yes! I will behold it!"
                        "Behold it!"
Repeats in mocking tone the distant echo.

He speaks, and, with the word, lifts up the veil.
Would you inquire what form there met his eye ?
I know not,—but, when day appear'd, the priests
Found him extended senseless, pale as death,
Before the pedestal of Isis' statue.
What had been seen and heard by him when there,
He never would disclose, but from that hour
His happiness in life had fled for ever,
And his deep sorrow soon conducted him
To an untimely grave. " Woe to that man,"
He, warning, said to ev'ry questioner,
" Woe to that man who wins the Truth by guilt,
For Truth so gain'd will ne'er reward its owner."

THE DIVISION OF THE EARTH.

" TAKE the world !" Zeus exclaim'd from his throne
        in the skies
    To the children of man—" take the world I now
        give ;
It shall ever remain as your heirloom and prize.
    So divide it as brothers, and happily live."

Then all who had hands sought their share to obtain,
    The young and the agèd made haste to appear ;
The husbandman seiz'd on the fruits of the plain,
    The youth thro' the forest pursued the fleet deer.

The merchant took all that his warehouse could hold,
    The abbot selected the last year's best wine,
The king barr'd the bridges,—the highways controll'd,
    And said, " Now remember, the tithes shall be
        mine !"

But when the division long settled had been,
  The poet drew nigh from a far distant land;
But alas! not a remnant was now to be seen,
  Each thing on the earth own'd a master's command.

" Alas! shall then I, of thy sons the most true,—
  Shall I, 'mongst them all, be forgotten alone ?"
Thus loudly he cried in his anguish, and threw
  Himself in despair before Jupiter's throne.

" If thou in the region of dreams didst delay,
  Complain not of me," the Immortal replied;
" When the world was apportion'd, where then wert
      thou, pray ?"
  " I was," said the poet, " I was—by thy side !

" Mine eye was then fix'd on thy features so bright,
  Mine ear was entranced by thy harmony's power;
Oh, pardon the spirit that, aw'd by thy light,
  All things of the earth could forget in that hour !"

" What to do ?" Zeus exclaim'd,—" for the world has
      been given ;
  The harvest, the market, the chase, are not free ;
But if thou with me wilt abide in my heaven,
  Whenever thou com'st, 'twill be open to thee !"

THE UNKNOWN MAIDEN.

In a deep vale, 'mongst simple swains,
  Appear'd with each returning spring,
Soon as the lark began his strains,
  A maid, of beauty ravishing.

That vale was not her native-place,
  And where she came from, none could tell ;
Yet of her steps was left no trace
  Soon as the maiden said farewell.

Each heart was glad when she was seen,
  With nobler aspirations fir'd ;
And yet her grace, her lofty mien
  With silent awe each breast inspir'd.

She with her brought both flowers and fruit,
  But ripen'd in far distant plains,
Where warmer far the sunbeams shoot,
  Where a more bounteous nature reigns.

Her gifts among them all she shar'd,—
  To some gave fruit, gave flowers to some ;
The youth, the old man silver-hair'd,
  Alike rewarded sought their home.

To her was welcome every guest;
  Yet if approach'd a loving pair,
To them she ever gave her best,
  The flowers her store contain'd most fair.

THE IDEAL AND LIFE.

Smooth, and ever-clear, and crystal-bright,
Flows existence, zephyr-light,
  In Olympus, where the blest recline.
Moons revolve, and ages pass away ;
Changelessly 'mid ever-rife decay
  Bloom the roses of their youth divine.
Man has but a sad choice left him now,
  Sensual bliss and soul-repose-between ;
But, upon the great Celestial's brow,
  Wedded is their lustre seen.

Wouldst thou here be like a deity,
In the realm of death be free,
  Never seek to pluck its garden's fruit!
On its beauty thou may'st feast thine eye;
Soon wild longing's impulses will fly,
  And enjoyment's transient bliss pollute.
E'en the Styx, that nine times flows around,
  Ceres' child's return could not delay;
But she grasp'd the apple,—and was bound
  Evermore by Orcus' sway.

Bodies only yonder powers can bind
By whom gloomy fate is twin'd;
  But, set free from each restraint of time,
Blissful Nature's playmate, FORM, so bright,
Roams for ever o'er the plains of light,
  'Mongst the Deities, herself sublime.
Wouldst thou on her pinions soar on high,
  Far away each earthly sorrow throw!
To the ideal realm for refuge fly
  From this narrow life below!

Free from earthly stain, and ever young,
Blest Perfection's rays among,
  There humanity's fair form is view'd,
As life's silent phantoms brightly gleam
While they wander near the Stygian stream,
  Or, as in the heav'nly fields they stood,
Ere the great Immortal went its way
  Down to the sarcophagus so drear.
If in life the conflict-scales still sway
  Doubtfully, the triumph's *here.*

Not to free the weary limbs from strife,
Not to give the faint new life,
  Blooms the fragrant wreath of victory.
Tho' thy nerves may rest, yet, fierce and strong,
In its stream life bears thee still along,
  In its whirling dance Time hurries thee.

But should courage' daring wing not brook
   Sad confinement's painful sense to bear,
Then the soaring Aim with joy may look
   Down from Beauty's hill so fair.

If 'tis good to govern and defend,
Wrestlers bravely to contend
   On the path of fortune or renown,—
Then let boldness wreak itself in force,
And the chariots on the dust-strown course
   Blend together, as they thunder down.
Courage only here the prize can find
   Of the victor, in the Hippodrome,—
'Tis the strong alone who Fate can bind
   When the weak are overcome.

But although, when rocks its bed enclose,
Wildly foaming on it flows,
   Softly, smoothly runs life's gentle stream
Over Beauty's silent shadow-land,
While, upon its silvery waters' strand,
   Hesper and Aurora paint each beam.
Melted into soft and mutual love,
   Blended in the happy bond of grace,
Fiery impulses here cease to move,
   And the foe has fled the place.

If to animate what erst was dead,
If with matter now to wed,
   Active genius kindles into flame,
Let then industry strain ev'ry nerve,
Let the thought's courageous wrestling serve
   E'en the hostile element to tame.
Truth's deep-buried spring can only flow
   To the steadfast will, that wearies ne'er ;
Only to the chisel's heavy blow
   Yields the brittle marble e'er.

Piercing even into Beauty's sphere,
In the dust still lingers here
  Gravitation, with the world it sways:
Not from out the mass, with labour wrung,
Light and graceful, as from nothing sprung,
  Stands the image to the ravish'd gaze.
Mute is ev'ry struggle, ev'ry doubt,
  In the certain glow of victory;
While each witness hence is driven out
  Of frail man's necessity.

When thou seest the mighty precept placed
In Humanity's sad waste,
  Or when to the Holy, guilt draws nigh,
Then thy virtue well may pallid be
In the rays of truth,—despondingly
  From the Ideal shamefaced action fly.
Nought created e'er surmounted this,
  Not a bark, no bridge's span can bear
Safely o'er that terrible abyss,
  And no anchor catches there.

But, by fleeing from the sense confin'd
To the freedom of the mind,
  Ev'ry dream of fear thou'lt find thence flown,
And the endless depth itself will fill;
If thou tak'st the Godhead in thy will,
  'Twill soar upwards from its earthly throne.
Servile minds alone, that scorn its sway,
  Are subdued by precept's rigid rod;
With the man's resistance dies away
  E'en the glory of the God.

When thou art weigh'd down by human care,
When the son of Priam there
  Strives against the snakes with speechless pain,
Then let man revolt! Then let his cry
To the canopy of heav'n mount high,—
  Let thy feeling heart be rent in twain!

Let the radiant cheek of joy turn pale,
  Nature's fearful voice triumphant be,
And let holy sympathy prevail
  O'er thine immortality!

But in yonder blissful realms afar,
Where the forms unsullied are,
  Sorrow's mournful tempests cease to rave.
There reflection cannot pierce the soul,
Tears of anguish there no longer roll,
  Nought remains but mind's resistance brave.
Beauteous e'en as Iris' colour'd bow
  On the thunder-cloud's soft vaporous dew,
Glimm'ring through the dusky veil of woe
  There is seen Rest's radiant blue.

Great Alcides erst in endless strife
Trod the weary path of life,
  Humbled e'en the coward's slave to be,—
Hugg'd the lion, and the hydra fought;
Into Charon's bark, he, dreading nought,
  Plunged alive, that he his friend might free.
All the heavy loads that earth brings forth,
  On the shoulders of the hated one,
By the Goddess are heap'd up in wrath,
  Till at length his race is run.

Till the god soars hence like some bright flame,
Casting off his earthly frame,
  And the æther's balmy incense drinks.
In his new unwonted pinions glad,
Upward flies he, and the vision sad
  Life had fashion'd, sinks, and sinks, and sinks.
Harmony, that of Olympus speaks,
  Hails the blest one where Kronion lives,
And the Goddess with the rosy cheeks
  Smilingly the chalice gives.

PARABLES AND RIDDLES.

I.

A BRIDGE of pearls its form uprears
   High o'er a grey and misty sea;
E'en in a moment it appears,
   And rises upwards giddily.

Beneath its arch can find a road
   The loftiest vessel's mast most high,
Itself hath never borne a load,
   And seems, when thou draw'st near, to fly.

It comes first with the stream, and goes
   Soon as the wat'ry flood is dried.
Where may be found this bridge, disclose,
   And who its beauteous form supplied!

II.

It bears thee many a mile away,
   And yet its place it changes ne'er;
It has no pinions to display,
   And yet conducts thee through the air.

It is the bark of swiftest motion
   That every weary wanderer bore;
With speed of thought the greatest ocean
   It carries thee in safety o'er;
   One moment wafts thee to the shore.

III.

Upon a spacious meadow play
   Thousands of sheep, of silv'ry hue;
And as we see them move to-day,
   The man most aged saw them too.

They ne'er grow old, and, from a rill
    That never dries, their life is drawn ;
A shepherd watches o'er them still,
    With curv'd and beauteous silver horn.

He drives them out through gates of gold,
    And ev'ry night their number counts ;
Yet ne'er has lost, of all his fold,
    One lamb, though oft that path he mounts.

A hound attends him faithfully,
    A nimble ram precedes the way ;
Canst thou point out that flock to me,
    And who the shepherd, canst thou say ?

IV.

There stands a dwelling, vast and tall,
    On unseen columns fair ;
No wanderer treads or leaves its hall,
    And none can linger there.

Its wondrous structure first was plann'd
    With art no mortal knows ;
It lights the lamps with its own hand
    'Mongst which it brightly glows.

It has a roof, as crystal bright,
Form'd of one gem of dazzling light ;
    Yet mortal eye has ne'er
    Seen Him who placed it there.

V.

Within a well two buckets lie,
    One mounts, and one descends ;
When one is full, and rises high,
    The other downward wends.

They wander ever to and fro—
Now empty are, now overflow.
If to the mouth thou liftest *this*,
That hangs within the dark abyss.
In the same moment they can ne'er
Refresh thee with their treasures fair.

VI.

Know'st thou the form on tender ground?
  It gives itself its glow, its light;
And though each moment changing found,
  Is ever whole and ever bright.
In narrow compass 'tis confin'd,
  Within the smallest frame it lies;
Yet all things great that move thy mind,
  That form alone to thee supplies.

And canst thou, too, the crystal name?
  No gem can equal it in worth;
It gleams, yet kindles ne'er to flame,
  It sucks in even all the earth.
Within its bright and wondrous ring
  Is pictur'd forth the glow of heaven,
And yet it mirrors back each thing
  Far fairer than to it 'twas given.

VII.

For ages an edifice here has been found,
  It is not a dwelling, it is not a fane;
A horseman for hundreds of days may ride round,
  Yet the end of his journey he ne'er can attain.

Full many a century o'er it has pass'd,
  The might of the storm and of time it defies;
'Neath the rainbow of Heaven stands free to the
    last,—
  In the ocean it dips, and soars up to the skies.

It was not vain glory that bade its erection,
It serves as a refuge, a shield, a protection ;
Its like on the earth never yet has been known
And yet by man's hand it is fashion'd alone.

VIII.

Amongst all serpents there is one,
  Born of no earthly breed ;
In fury wild it stands alone,
  And in its matchless speed.

With fearful voice and headlong force
  It rushes on its prey,
And sweeps the rider and his horse
  In one fell swoop away.

The highest point it loves to gain ;
  And neither bar nor lock
Its fiery onslaught can restrain ;
  And arms—invite its shock.

It tears in twain like tender grass,
  The strongest forest-tree ;
It grinds to dust the harden'd brass,
  Though stout and firm it be.

And yet this beast, that none can tame,
  Its threat ne'er twice fulfils ;
It dies in its self-kindled flame,
  And dies e'en when it kills.

IX.

We children six our being had
  From a most strange and wondrous pair,—
Our mother ever grave and sad,
  Our father ever free from care.

Our virtues we from both receive,—
　Meekness from *her*, from *him* our light;
And so in endless youth we weave
　Round thee a circling figure bright.

We ever shun the caverns black,
　And revel in the glowing day;
'Tis we who light the world's dark track,
　With our life's clear and magic ray.

Spring's joyful harbingers are we,
　And her inspiring strains we swell;
And so the house of death we flee,
　For life alone must round us dwell.

Without us is no perfect bliss,
　When man is glad, we, too, attend,
And when a monarch worshipp'd is,
　To him our majesty we lend.

x.

What is the thing esteem'd by few?
　The monarch's hand it decks with pride,
Yet it is made to injure too,
　And to the sword is most allied.

No blood it sheds, yet many a wound
　Inflicts,—gives wealth, yet takes from none;
Has vanquish'd e'en the earth's wide round,
　And makes life's current smoothly run.

The greatest kingdoms it has fram'd,
　The oldest cities rear'd from dust,
Yet war's fierce torch has ne'er inflam'd;
　Happy are they who in it trust!

XI.

I live within a dwelling of stone,
   There buried in slumber I dally;
Yet, arm'd with a weapon of iron alone,
   The foe to encounter I sally.
At first I'm invisible, feeble, and mean,
   And o'er me thy breath has dominion;
I'm easily drown'd in a rain-drop e'en,
   Yet in victory waxes my pinion.
When my sister, all-powerful, gives me her hand,
To the terrible lord of the world I expand.

XII.

Upon a disk my course I trace,
   There restlessly for ever flit;
Small is the circuit I embrace,
   Two hands suffice to cover it.
Yet ere that field I traverse, I
   Full many a thousand mile must go,
E'en though with tempest-speed I fly,
   Swifter than arrow from a bow.

XIII.

A bird it is, whose rapid motion
   With eagle's flight divides the air;
A fish it is, and parts the ocean,
   That bore a greater monster ne'er;
An elephant it is, whose rider
   On his broad back a tower has put:
'Tis like the reptile base, the spider,
   Whenever it extends its foot;
And when, with iron tooth projecting,
   It seeks its own life-blood to drain,
On footing firm, itself erecting,
   It braves the raging hurricane.

THE WALK.*

Hail to thee, mountain belov'd, with thy glittering purple-
      dyed summit!
Hail to thee also, fair sun, looking so lovingly on!
Thee, too, I hail, thou smiling plain, and ye murmuring
      lindens,
  Ay, and the chorus so glad, cradled on yonder high
      boughs;
Thee, too, peaceable azure, in infinite measure extending
  Round the dusky-hued mount, over the forest so
      green,—
Round about me, who now from my chamber's confine-
      ment escaping,
  And from vain frivolous talk, gladly seek refuge with
      thee.
Through me to quicken me runs the balsamic stream of
      thy breezes,
  While the energetical light freshens the gaze as it
      thirsts.
Bright o'er the blooming meadow the changeable colours
      are gleaming,
  But the strife, full of charms, in its own grace melts
      away.
Freely the plain receives me, with carpet far away
      reaching,
  Over its friendly green wanders the pathway along.
Round me is humming the busy bee, and with pinion
      uncertain
  Hovers the butterfly gay over the trefoil's red flow'r.
Fiercely the darts of the sun fall on me,—the zephyr is
      silent,
  Only the song of the lark echoes athwart the clear
      air.

* In this, as in all the rest of Schiller's Elegiacs, the original
metre has been retained. (See *Preface*.)

Now from the neighbouring copse comes a roar, and the
    tops of the alders
  Bend low down,—in the wind dances the silvery
    grass;
Night ambrosial circles me round; in the coolness so
    fragrant
  Greets me a beauteous roof, form'd by the beeches'
    sweet shade.
In the depths of the wood the landscape suddenly leaves
    me,
  And a serpentine path guides up my footsteps on
    high.
Only by stealth can the light through the leafy trellis of
    branches
  Sparingly pierce, and the blue smilingly peeps through
    the boughs.
But in a moment the veil is rent, and the opening
    forest
  Suddenly gives back the day's glittering brightness
    to me!
Boundlessly seems the distance before my gaze to be
    stretching,
  And in a purple-tinged hill terminates sweetly the
    world.

Deep at the foot of the mountain, that under me falls
    away steeply,
  Wanders the greenish-hued stream, looking like glass
    as it flows.
Endlessly under me see I the Æther, and endlessly o'er
    me,—
  Giddily look I above, shudd'ringly look I below.
But between the infinite height and the infinite
    hollow
  Safely the wanderer moves over a well-guarded path.
Smilingly past me are flying the banks all-teeming with
    riches,
  And the valley so bright boasts of its industry glad.

See how yonder hedgerows that sever the farmer's pos·
　　sessions
　Have by Demeter been work'd into the tapestried
　　plain!
Kindly decree of the law, of the Deity mortal-sus-
　　taining,
　Since from the brazen world Love vanish'd for ever
　　away.
But in freer windings the measur'd pastures are tra-
　　vers'd
　(Now swallow'd up in the wood, now climbing up to
　　the hills)
By a glimmering streak, the highway that knits lands
　　together;
　Over the smooth-flowing stream, quietly glide on the
　　rafts.

Ofttimes resound the bells of the flocks in the fields that
　　seem living,
　And the shepherd's lone song wakens the echo
　　again.
Joyous villages crown the stream, in the copse others
　　vanish,
　While from the back of the mount, others plunge wildly
　　below.
Man still lives with the land in neighbourly friendship
　　united,
　And round his sheltering roof calmly repose still his
　　fields;
Trustingly climbs the vine high over the low-reaching
　　window,
　While round the cottage the tree circles its far·stretching
　　boughs.
Happy race of the plain! Not yet awaken'd to free-
　　dom,
　Thou and thy pastures with joy share in the limited
　　law;

Bounded thy wishes all are by the harvest's peaceable
    circuit,
  And thy lifetime is spent e'en as the task of the
    day!

But what suddenly hides the beauteous view? A strange
    spirit
  Over the still-stranger plain spreads itself quickly
    afar—
Coyly separates now, what scarce had lovingly mingled,
  And 'tis the like that alone joins itself on to the
    like.
Orders I see depicted; the haughty tribes of the
    poplars
  Marshall'd in regular pomp, stately and beauteous
    appear.
All gives token of rule and choice, and all has its
    meaning,—
  'Tis this uniform plan points out the Ruler to me.
Brightly the glittering domes in far-away distance pro-
    claim him.
  Out of the kernel of rocks rises the city's high
    wall.
Into the desert without, the Fauns of the forest are
    driven,
  But by devotion is lent life more sublime to the
    stone.
Man is brought into nearer union with man, and around
    him
  Closer, more actively wakes, swifter moves *in* him the
    world.
See! the emulous forces in fiery conflict are kindled,
  Much they effect when they strive, more they effect
    when they join.
Thousands of hands by *one* spirit are mov'd, yet in thou-
    sands of bosoms
  Beats one heart all alone, by but one feeling in-
    spir'd—

Beats for their native land, and glows for their ancestors'
    precepts;
    Here on the well-belov'd spot, rest now their time-
        honour'd bones.

Down from the heavens descends the blessèd troop of
    Immortals,
    In the bright circle divine making their festal
        abode;
Granting glorious gifts, they appear: and first of all,
    Ceres
    Offers the gift of the plough, Hermes the anchor brings
        next,
Bacchus the grape, and Minerva the verdant olive-tree's
    branches,
    Even his charger of war brings there Poseidon as
        well.
Mother Cybele yokes to the pole of her chariot the
    lions,
    And through the wide-open door comes as a citizen
        in.
Sacred stones! 'Tis from ye that proceed Humanity's
    founders,
    Morals and arts ye sent forth, e'en to the ocean's far
        isles.
'Twas at these friendly gates that the law was spoken by
    sages;
    In their Penates' defence, heroes rush'd out to the
        fray.
On the high walls appear'd the mothers, embracing their
    infants,
    Looking after the march, till in the distance 'twas
        lost.
Then in prayer they threw themselves down at the
    Deities' altars,
    Praying for triumph and fame, praying for your safe
        return.

Honour and triumph were yours, but nought return'd save
    your glory,
  And by a heart-touching stone, told are your valorous
    deeds.
"Traveller! when thou com'st to Sparta, proclaim to the
    people
  That thou hast seen us lie here, as by the law we were
    bid."
Slumber calmly, ye lov'd ones! for sprinkled o'er by your
    life-blood,
  Flourish the olive-trees there, joyously sprouts the
    good seed.
In its possessions exulting, industry gladly is kindled,
  And from the sedge of the stream smilingly signs the
    blue God.
Crushingly falls the axe on the tree, the Dryad sighs
    sadly;
  Down from the crest of the mount plunges the thunder-
    ing load.
Wing'd by the lever, the stone from the rocky crevice is
    loosen'd;
  Into the mountain's abyss boldly the miner de-
    scends.
Mulciber's anvil resounds with the measur'd stroke of the
    hammer;
  Under the fist's nervous blow, spurt out the sparks of
    the steel.
Brilliantly twines the golden flax round the swift-whirling
    spindles,
  Through the strings of the yarn whizzes the shuttle
    away.

Far in the roads the pilot calls, and the vessels are
    waiting,
  That to the foreigner's land carry the produce of
    home;
Others gladly approach with the treasures of far-distant
    regions,

High on the mast's lofty head flutters the garland of
    mirth.
See how yon markets, those centres of life and of glad-
    ness, are swarming!
  Strange confusion of tongues sounds in the wondering
    ear.
On to the pile the wealth of the earth is heap'd by the
    merchant,
  All that the sun's scorching rays bring forth on Africa's
    soil,
All that Arabia prepares, that the uttermost Thule
    produces,
  High with heart-gladdening stores fills Amalthēa her
    horn.
Fortune wedded to Talent gives birth there to children
    immortal,
  Suckled in Liberty's arms, flourish the Arts there of
    joy.
With the image of life the eyes by the sculptor are
    ravish'd,
  And by the chisel inspir'd, speaks e'en the sensitive
    stone.
Skies artificial repose on slender Ionian columns,
  And a Pantheon includes all that Olympus contains.
Light as the rainbow's spring through the air, as the dart
    from the bowstring,
  Leaps the yoke of the bridge over the boisterous
    stream.

But in his silent chamber the thoughtful sage is pro-
    jecting
  Magical circles, and steals e'en on the spirit that
    forms,
Proves the force of matter, the hatreds and loves of the
    magnet,
  Follows the tune through the air, follows through
    æther the ray,

Seeks the familiar law in chance's miracles dreaded,
 Looks for the ne'er-changing pole in the phenomena's
  flight.
Bodies and voices are lent by writing to thought ever
  silent,
 Over the centuries' stream bears it the eloquent
  page.
Then to the wondering gaze dissolves the cloud of the
  fancy,
 And the vain phantoms of night yield to the dawning
  of day.
Man now breaks through his fetters, the happy One!
  Oh, let him never
  Break from the bridle of shame, when from fear's
  fetters he breaks!
Freedom! is Reason's cry,—ay, Freedom! The wild
  raging passions
 Eagerly cast off the bonds nature divine had im-
  pos'd.

Ah! in the tempest the anchors break loose, that warn-
  ingly held him
 On to the shore, and the stream tears him along in
  its flood,—
Into infinity whirls him,—the coasts soon vanish before
  him,
 High on the mountainous waves rocks all-dismasted
  the bark;
Under the clouds are hid the stedfast stars of the
  chariot,
 Nought now remains,—in the breast even the God goes
  astray.
Truth disappears from language, from life all faith and
  all honour
 Vanish, and even the oath is but a lie on the lips.
Into the heart's most trusty bond, and into love's
  secrets,

Presses the sycophant base, tearing the friend from the
    friend.
Treason on Innocence leers, with looks that seek to
    devour,
    And the fell slanderer's tooth kills with its poisonous
      bite.
In the dishonoured bosom, thought is now venal, and
    love, too,
    Scatters abroad to the winds, feelings once God-like
      and free.
All thy holy symbols, O Truth, Deceit has adopted,
    And has e'en dar'd to pollute Nature's own voices so
      fair,
That the craving heart in the tumult of gladness dis-
    covers ;
    True sensations are now mute and can scarcely be
      heard.
Justice boasts at the tribune, and Harmony vaunts in the
    cottage,
    While the ghost of the law stands at the throne of the
      king.
Years together, ay, centuries long, may the mummy
    continue,
    And the deception endure, aping the fulness of life.
Until Nature awakes, and with hands all-brazen and
    heavy
    'Gainst the hollow-form'd pile Time and Necessity
      strikes.
Like a tigress, who, bursting the massive grating of
    iron,
    Of her Numidian wood suddenly, fearfully thinks,—
So with the fury of crime and anguish, humanity
    rises
    Hoping nature, long-lost, in the town's ashes to
      find.
Oh then open, ye walls, and set the captive at free-
    dom !

To the long desolate plains let him in safety re-
    turn!

But where am I? The path is now hid, declivities
    rugged
  Bar, with their wide-yawning gulfs, progress before
    and behind.
Now far behind me is left the gardens' and hedges' sure
    escort,
  Every trace of man's hand also remains far behind.
Only the matter I see pil'd up, whence life has its
    issue,
  And the raw mass of basalt waits for a fashioning
    hand.
Down through its channel of rock the torrent roaringly
    rushes,
  Angrily forcing a path under the roots of the trees.
All is here wild and fearfully desolate. Nought but the
    eagle
  Hangs in the lone realms of air, knitting the world to
    the clouds.
Not one zephyr on soaring pinion conveys to my
    hearing
  Echoes, however remote, marking man's pleasures and
    pains.
Am I in truth, then, alone? Within thine arms, on thy
    bosom,
  Nature, I lie once again!—Ah, and 'twas only a
    dream
That assail'd me with horrors so fearful; with life's
    dreaded phantom,
  And with the down-rushing vale, vanish'd the gloomy
    one too.
Purer my life I receive again from thine altar un-
    sullied,—
  Purer receive the bright glow felt by my youth's hope-
    ful days.

Ever the will is changing its aim and its rule, while for
    ever,
  In a still varying form, actions revolve round them-
    selves.
But in enduring youth, in beauty ever renewing,
  Kindly Nature, with grace, thou dost revere the old
    law!
Ever the same, for the man in thy faithful hands thou
    preservest
  That which the child in its sport, that which the youth
    lent to thee;
At the same breast thou dost suckle the ceaselessly-vary-
    ing ages;
  Under the same azure vault, over the same verdant
    earth,
Races, near and remote, in harmony wander together,—
  See, even Homer's own sun looks on *us*, too, with a
    smile!

THE SONG OF THE BELL.

VIVOS VOCO.   MORTUOS PLANGO.   FULGURA FRANGO.

    WALL'D securely in the ground,
      Stands the mould of well-bak'd clay:
    Comrades, at your task be found!
      We must cast the Bell to-day!
        From the burning brow
        Sweat must run, I trow,
    Would we have our work commended—
    Blessings must be heaven-descended.

    A solemn word may well befit
      The task we solemnly prepare;
    When goodly converse hallows it,
      The labour flows on gladly there.

Let us observe with careful eyes
  What thro' deficient strength escapes;
The thoughtless man we must despise,
  Who disregards the thing he shapes.
This forms a man's chief attribute,
  And Reason is to him assign'd,
That what his hand may execute,
  Within his heart, too, he should find.

Heap ye up the pinewood first,
  Yet full dry it needs must be,
That the smother'd flame may burst
    Fiercely through the cavity!
      Let the copper brew!
      Quick the tin add too,
That the tough bell-metal may
Fuse there in the proper way!

The Bell that in the dam's deep hole
  Our hands with help of fire prepare,
From the high belfry-tower will toll,
  And witness of us loudly bear.
'Twill there endure till distant days,
  On many an ear its sounds will dwell,
Sad wailings with the mourner raise,—
  The chorus of devotion swell.
Whatever changeful fate may bring
  To be man's portion here below,
Against its metal crown will ring,
  And through the nations echoing go.

Bubbles white I see ascend;
  Good! the heap dissolves at last;
Let the potash with it blend,
  Urging on the fusion fast.
    Foam and bubble-free
    Must the mixture be,
That from metal void of stain
Pure and full may rise the strain.

For in a song with gladness rife
  The cherish'd child it loves to greet,
When first he treads the path of life,
  Wrapt in the arms of slumbers sweet ;
His coming fate of joy or gloom
Lies buried in the future's womb ;
The tender cares that mothers prove
His golden morning guard with love :
  The years with arrowy swiftness fleet.
The proud boy bids the maid adieu,
  And into life with wildness flies,
The world on pilgrim's-staff roams through,—
  Then as a stranger homeward hies ;
And gracefully, in beauty's pride,
  Like to some heav'nly image fair,
Her modest cheeks with blushes dyed,
  He sees the maiden standing there.
A nameless yearning now appears
  And fills his heart ; alone he strays,
His eyes are ever moist with tears,
  He shuns his brothers' noisy plays ;
Her steps he blushingly pursues,
  And by her greeting is made blest,
Gathers the flow'rs of fairest hues,
  With which to deck his true love's breast.
Oh, tender yearning, blissful hope,
  Thou golden time of love's young day !
Heav'n seems before the eye to ope,
  The heart in rapture melts away.
Oh may it ever verdant prove,
That radiant time of early love !

Dusky-hued becomes each pipe !
  Let me plunge this rod in here :
All for casting will be ripe
  When we see it glaz'd appear.
        Comrades, stand ye by !
        Now the mixture try,

If the brittle will combine
With the soft—propitious sign!

For there is heard a joyous sound
Where sternness is with softness bound,
  Where joins the gentle with the strong.
Who binds himself for ever, he
Should prove if heart and heart agree!
  The dream is short, repentance long.

Through the bride's fair locks so dear
  Twines the virgin chaplet bright,
When the church-bells, ringing clear,
  To the joyous feast invite.
Ah! life's happiest festival
  Needs must end life's happy May;
With the veil and girdle, all
  Those sweet visions fade away.

Though passion may fly,
  Yet love must remain;
Though the flow'ret may die,
  Yet the fruit scents the plain.
Man must gird for his race
  Thro' the stern paths of life,
  Midst turmoil and strife,
  Must plant and must form,
  Gain by cunning or storm;
  Must wager and dare,
  Would he reach fortune e'er.
Then wealth without ending upon him soon pours,
His granaries all overflow with rich stores;
The room is enlarged, and his house grows apace;
  And o'er it is ruling
  The housewife so modest,
  His children's dear mother;
  And wisely she governs
  The circle of home.

The maidens she trains,
And the boys she restrains,
Keeps plying for ever
Her hands that flag never,
And wealth helps to raise
With her orderly ways,
The sweet-scented presses with treasures piles
        high,
Bids the thread round the fast-whirling spindle
        to fly;
The cleanly and bright-polish'd chest she heaps
        full
With the flax white as snow, and the glistening
        wool;
All glitter and splendour ordains for the best,
And takes no rest.

And the father, with rapturous gaze,
  From the far-seeing roof of his dwelling,*
All his blossoming riches surveys;
Sees each projecting pillar and post,
Sees his barns, that of wealth seem to boast;
Sees each storehouse, by blessings down-borne,
And the billow-like waving corn,—
Cries with exulting face:
" Firm as the earth's firm base,
'Gainst all misfortune's powers
Proudly my house now towers! "—
But with mighty destiny
Union sure there ne'er can be;
Woe advances rapidly.

Let the casting be begun!
  Traced already is the breach;
Yet before we let it run,
  Heaven's protecting aid beseech!

* There is no rhyme to this line in the original.

Let the plug now fly!
May God's help be nigh!
In the mould all-smoking rush
Fire-brown billows with fierce gush.

Beneficent the might of flame,
When 'tis by man watch'd o'er, made tame;
For to this heav'nly power he owes,
All his creative genius knows;
Yet terrible that power will be,
When from its fetters it breaks free,
Treads its own path with passion wild,
As nature's free and reckless child.
Woe, if it casts off its chains,
   And, without resistance, growing,
Through the crowded streets and lanes
   Spreads the blaze, all fiercely glowing!
For the elements still hate
All that mortal hands create.
From the clouds all blessings rill,
'Tis the clouds that rain distil;
From the clouds, with quivering beams,
Lightning gleams.
From yon tower the wailing sound
Spreads the fire alarm around!
Blood-red, lo!
   Are the skies!
But 'tis not the day's clear glow!
   Smoke up-flies!
      Loud the shout
      Round about!
High the fiery column glows,
Through the streets' far-stretching rows
On with lightning speed it goes.
Hot, as from an oven's womb,
Burns the air, while beams consume,
Windows rattle, pillars fall,
Children wail and mothers call.

Beasts are groaning,
Underneath the ruins moaning;
All their safety seek in flight,
Day-clear lighted is the night.
Through the hands' extended chain
Flies the bucket on amain;
Floods of water high are thrown;
Howling comes the tempest on,
Roaring in the flames' pursuit.
Crackling on the wither'd fruit
Falls it,—on the granary,
On the rafters' timber dry,
And, as if earth's heavy weight
  Seeking in its flight to bear,
Mounts it, as a giant great,
  Wildly thro' the realms of air.
Man now loses hope at length,
Yielding to immortal strength;
Idly, and with wond'ring gaze,
All the wreck he now surveys.

Burnt to ashes is the stead,
Now the wildstorm's rugged bed.
In the empty window-panes
Shudd'ring horror now remains,
And the clouds of heaven above
Peep in, as they onward move.

Upon the grave where buried lies
His earthly wealth, his longing eyes
The man one ling'ring moment throws,
Then, as a pilgrim, gladly goes.
Whate'er the fierce flames may destroy,
  One consolation sweet is left;
His lov'd ones' heads he counts,—and, Joy!—
  He is not e'en of one bereft!

In the earth it now has pour'd,
  And the mould has fill'd aright;
Skill and labour to reward,
  Will it beauteous come to light?
    If the mould should crack?
    If the casting lack?
While we hope, e'en now, alas,
Mischief may have come to pass!

To the dark womb of holy earth
  We trust what issues from our hand,
  As trusts the sower to the land
His seed, in hope 'twill have its birth
  To bless us, true to Heaven's command.
Seed still more precious in the womb
  Of earth we trusting hide, and wait
In hope that even from the tomb
  'Twill blossom to a happier fate.

Sad and heavy from the dome
Hark! the Bell's death-wailings come.
Solemnly the strains, with sorrow fraught,
On her way a pilgrim now escort.

For a mother tolls the Bell!
For a fond wife sounds the knell!
Death, regardless of her charms,
Tears her from her husband's arms,
From her children tears her too,
Offspring of affection true,
Whom she cherish'd with the love
None but mothers e'er can prove.
All the ties their hearts uniting
  Are dissolv'd for evermore;
She whose smile that home was lighting
  Wanders on oblivion's shore.
Who will now avert each danger?
  Who will now each care dispel?
In her seat will sit a stranger—
  She can never love so well!

Till the Bell has cool'd aright,
   Let the arduous labour rest;
As the bird midst foliage bright
   Flutters, each may thus be blest.
         When the daylight wanes,
         Free from duty's chains
Workmen hear the vesper chime;
Masters have for rest no time.

Gladly hies the wanderer fast,
   Through the forest-glades so deep,
Tow'rd his own lov'd cot at last.
   Bleating homeward go the sheep;
Broad-brow'd, smooth-skinn'd cattle, all
Bellowing come, and fill each stall.
Home returns the heavy wain,
Stagg'ring 'neath its load of grain.
Many-hued, the garlands lie
On the sheaves, while gladly fly
To the dance the reaper-boys,—
Hush'd each street and market noise,
Round the candle's social light
All the household now unite.
Creakingly the town-gates close,
Darkness its black mantle throws
O'er the earth; but yet the night,
   Though it fills the bad with awe,
Gives the townsman no affright,
For he trusts the wakeful law.

Holy Order, blessing-rife,
Heaven's own child, by whom in life
Equals joyously are bound,
And whose task 'tis towns to found,—
Who the wand'ring savage led
From the plains he us'd to tread,

Enter'd the rude huts of men,
Softening their wild habits then,
And who wove that dearest band,—
Love for home and fatherland!

Thousand busy hands are plying,
  Into loving union thrown,
And, in fiery motion vieing,
  All the forces here are known.
Under freedom's shelter holy
  Man and master now unite,
Love their stations, high or lowly,
  And defy the scorner's might.
Blessings are our labour's guerdon,
  Work adorns the townsman most;
Honour is a king's chief burden,
  We in hands industrious boast.

  Peace all-lovely!
  Blissful concord!
  Linger, linger
  Kindly over this our town!
May we ne'er the sad day witness
When the hordes of cruel warriors
Wildly tread this silent valley;
When the heavens,
That the eve's bright colours blending
  Softly gild,
With the light of flames ascending,
  From the burning towns are fill'd!

Let us now the mould destroy,
  Well it has fulfill'd its part,
That the beauteous shape with joy
  May inspire both eye and heart.
    Wield the hammer, wield,
    Till the mantle yield!
Would we raise the Bell on high,
Must the mould to atoms fly.

The founder may destroy the mould
  With cunning hand, if time it be;
But woe, if, raging uncontroll'd,
  The glowing bronze itself should free!
Blind-raging, like the crashing thunder,
It bursts its tenement asunder,
And, as from open jaws of hell,
Around it spews destruction fell.
Where forces rule with senseless might,
No structure there can come to light;
When mobs themselves for freedom strive,
True happiness can never thrive.

Woe, when within a city's walls,
  Where firebrands secretly are pil'd,
The people, bursting from their thralls,
  Tread their own path with fury wild!
Sedition then the Bell surrounds,
  And bids it yield a howling tone;
And, meant for none but peaceful sounds.
  The signal to the fray spurs on.

" Freedom ! Equality !" they shout:
  The peaceful townsman grasps his arms.
Mobs stand the streets and halls about,
  The place with bands of murderers swarms.
Into hyenas women grow,
  From horrors their amusement draw;
The heart, still quivering, of the foe
  With panther's teeth they fiercely gnaw.
All that is holy is effaced,
  Rent are the bonds of modesty;
The good is by the bad replaced,
  And crime from all restraint is free.
Death-fraught the tiger's tooth appears,
  To wake the lion madness seems;
Yet the most fearful of all fears
  Is man obeying his wild dreams.

Woe be to him who, to the blind,
    The heav'nly torch of light conveys!
It throws no radiance on *his* mind,
    But land and town in ashes lays.*

God hath hearken'd to my vow!
    See, how like a star of gold
Peels the metal kernel now,
    Smooth and glistening from the mould!
        E'en from crown to base
        Sunlike gleams its face,
While the scutcheons, fairly plann'd,
Praise the skilful artist's hand.

Now let us gather round the frame!
    The ring let ev'ry workman swell,
    That we may consecrate the Bell!
Concordia be henceforth its name,
Assembling all the loving throng
In harmony and union strong!

And *this* be the vocation fit
For which the founder fashion'd it!
High, high above earth's life, earth's labour,
    E'en to the heav'ns' blue vault to soar,
To hover as the thunder's neighbour,
    The very firmament explore;
To be a voice as from above,
    Like yonder stars so bright and clear,
That praise their Maker as they move
    And usher in the circling year.
Tun'd be its metal mouth alone
    To things eternal and sublime,
And, as the swift-wing'd hours speed on,
    May it record the flight of time!

* The first French Revolution is alluded to in the preceding
lines.

Its tongue to Fate it well may lend;
  Heartless itself, and feeling nought,
May with its warning notes attend
  On human life, with change so fraught.
And, as the strains die on the ear
  That it peals forth with tuneful might,
So let it teach that nought lasts here,
  That all things earthly take their flight!

Now then, with the rope so strong,
  From the vault the Bell upweigh,
That it gains the realms of song,
  And the heav'nly light of day!
    All hands nimbly ply!
    Now it mounts on high!
To this city Joy reveals,—
Peace be the first strain it peals!

THE POWER OF SONG.

The foaming stream from out the rock
  With thunder roar begins to rush,—
The oak falls prostrate at the shock,
  And mountain-wrecks attend the gush.
With rapturous awe, in wonder lost,
  The wanderer hearkens to the sound;
From cliff to cliff he hears it toss'd,
  Yet knows not whither it is bound:
'Tis thus that song's bright waters pour
From sources never known before.

In union with those dreaded ones
  That spin life's thread all-silently,—
Who can resist the singer's tones?
  Who from his magic set him free?

With wand like that the Gods bestow,
  He guides the heaving bosom's chords,
He steeps it in the realms below,
  He bears it, wondering, heavenwards,
And rocks it, 'twixt the grave and gay,
On Feeling's scales that trembling sway.

As when, before the startled eyes
  Of some glad throng, mysteriously,
With giant-step, in spirit-guise,
  Appears a wondrous Deity,
Then bows each greatness of the earth
  Before the stranger, heaven-born,
Mute are the thoughtless sounds of mirth,
  While from each face the mask is torn,
And from the truth's triumphant might
Each work of falsehood takes to flight:

So, from each idle burden free,
  When summon'd by the voice of song,
Man soars to spirit-dignity,
  Receiving force divinely strong:
Among the Gods is now his home,
  Nought earthly ventures to approach—
All other powers must now be dumb,
  No fate can on his realms encroach;
Care's gloomy wrinkles disappear,
Whilst Music's charms still linger here.

As, after long and hopeless yearning,
  And separation's bitter smart,
A child, with tears repentant burning,
  Clings fondly to his mother's heart—
So to his youthful happy dwelling,
  To rapture pure and free from stain,
All strange and false conceits expelling,
  Song guides the wanderer back again,
In faithful Nature's loving arm.
From chilling precepts to grow warm.

THE PRAISE OF WOMAN.

ALL honour to women!—they soften and leaven
The cares of the world with the roses of Heaven—
　The ravishing fetters of love they entwine ;
Their charms from the world's eye modestly veiling,
They foster and nourish, with care never failing,
　The fire eternal of feelings divine.

　　Man's wild force, in constant motion,
　　　Spurns the bounds by truth assign'd :
　　And, on passion's stormy ocean,
　　　To and fro is toss'd his mind.
　　Peace his bosom visits never,
　　　As he heaps up scheme on scheme,
　　And through space pursues for ever
　　　Each vain phantom of his dream.

But with her sweet look, so soft and enchaining,
Woman, the fugitive gently restraining,
　Summons him back to the regions of earth ;
The daughter of Nature, with meekness unshaken,
The home of her mother has never forsaken—
　Has ever been true to the place of her birth.

　　Man, the torrent sternly breasting,
　　　Spends his days in ceaseless strife ;
　　Never pausing, never resting,
　　　Wild he treads the paths of life.
　　All his plans to ruin bringing,
　　　Ne'er his changing wish grows cold,
　　When destroy'd, again up-springing,
　　　Like the Hydra's heads of old.

But in a gentler sphere passing her hours,
Woman plucks ever the moment's sweet flowers,

Lovingly tends them with fostering care;
Freer than man, though less wide her dominion,
Soaring above him on wisdom's bright pinion,
   Glitt'ring in poesy's circle so fair.

   Selfishness and pride combining,
      Man's cold bosom ne'er can prove,
   Round a fond heart fondly twining,
      All the heav'nly bliss of love.
   Soul communion never feeling,
      Tears to him no balm impart,
   Life's hard conflicts only steeling
      Sterner still his rugged heart.

But as when softly to Zephyr replying,
Æolus' harp gently breathes forth its sighing,
   The soft soul of woman its sighs breathes forth
      too ;
At the sad tale of misery tenderly grieving,
See we her bosom with sympathy heaving,
   Her melting eye sparkling with heavenly dew.

   Man, imperious, stern, insulting,
      Knows no law save that of might;
   Scythians wave their swords exulting—
      Persians tremble in affright.
   Furious passions raging wildly
      Fiercely struggle day by day;
   And, where Charis govern'd mildly,
      Eris now asserts her sway.

But, with her eloquence winning, yet yielding,
Woman, the sceptre of love gently wielding,
   Quenches the smouldering embers of strife;
Each ling'ring emotion of hatred effaces,
Compels the late foes to unite their embraces,
   Rivets the transient pleasures of life.

HOPE.

Of better and brighter days to come
  Man is talking and dreaming ever;
To gain a happy, a golden home,
  His efforts he ceases never;
The world decays, and again revives,
But man for improvement ever strives.

'Tis Hope first shows him the light of day,
  Through infancy hovers before him,
Enchants him in youth with her magic ray,
  Survives, when the grave closes o'er him;
For when in the tomb ends his weary race,
E'en there still see we her smiling face!

'Tis no vain flattering vision of youth,
  On the fool's dull brain descending;
To the heart it ever proclaims this glad truth:
  Tow'rd a happier life we are tending;
And the promise the voice within us hath spoken
Shall ne'er to the hoping soul be broken.

THE GERMAN MUSE.

No Augustan century,
No propitious Medici
  Smil'd on German art when young;
Glory nourish'd not her powers,
She unfolded not her flowers
  Princes' fav'ring rays among.

From the mighty Fred'rick's throne
Germany's most glorious son,—

Went she forth, defenceless, spurn'd;
Proudly Germans may repeat,
While their hearts more gladly beat,—
  They themselves their crown have earn'd.

Therefore mounts with nobler pride,
Therefore with a fuller tide
  Pours the stream of German bards;—
With his own abundance swells,—
From the inmost bosom wells,—
  Chains of method disregards.

THE SOWER.

See! with a heart full of hope, to the earth golden
    seed thou entrustest,
  And with joy in the Spring, waitest to see it
    appear.
Art thou mindful to strew in the furrows of Time
    worthy actions,
  Which for Eternity bloom, calmly by wisdom's
    hand sown?

THE MERCHANT.

Whither is sailing the Ship? It bears the people of
    Sidon
  From the cold realms of the North, bringing the
    amber and tin.
Bear it up gently, O Neptune! and peacefully rock
    it, ye zephyrs!—
  Let it in sheltering bay find the refreshment it
    needs!

'Tis to you, ye Gods, that the Merchant belongs. Seeking riches,
    Goes he,—yet to his ship that which is good ever clings.

ODYSSEUS.

Seeking to find his home, Odysseus crosses each water;
    Through Charybdis so dread; ay, and through Scylla's wild yells,
Through the alarms of the raging sea, the alarms of the land too,—
    E'en to the kingdom of Hell leads him his wandering course.
And at length, as he sleeps, to Ithaca's coast Fate conducts him;
    There he awakes, and, with grief, knows not his fatherland now.

CARTHAGE.

Oh thou degenerate child of the great and glorious mother,
    Who with the Romans' strong might couplest the Tyrians' deceit!
But *those* ever govern'd with vigour the earth they had conquer'd,—
    These instructed the world that they with cunning had won.
Say! what renown does history grant thee? Thou, Roman-like, gainedst
    That with the steel, which with gold, Tyrian-like, then thou didst rule!

Nobly, in truth, ye are cloth'd by the Cross's equip-
     ment so dreaded,
  When ye, the lions in fight, Accon and Rhodus
       protect,—
When through the Syrian deserts ye guide the
     sorrowing pilgrim,
  And, with the Cherubin's sword, stand o'er the
     Saviour's blest tomb.
But a glory still nobler surrounds ye,—the garb of
     the nurser,
  When ye, the lions in fight, sons of the race so
     renown'd,
Serve at the bed of the sick, refreshment prepare for
     the thirsty,—
  When ye perform the mean rites Christian-like
     mercy enjoins.
Glorious Faith of the Cross ! thou only in *one* wreath
     unitest
  Those two flourishing palms, Meekness and Valour,
     at once !

GERMAN FAITH.*

Once for the sceptre of Germany, fought with
     Bavarian Louis
  Fred'rick of Hapsburg descent, both being call'd
     to the throne.
But the envious fortune of war deliver'd the
     Austrian
  Into the hands of the foe, who overcame him
     in fight.

---

* For this interesting story, see Cox's ' House of Austria,' vol. i.,
pp. 87-98 (Bohn's Standard Library).

With the throne he purchas'd his freedom, pledging
    his honour
      For the victor to draw 'gainst his own people his
        sword;
But what he vow'd when in chains, when free he
    could not accomplish,
      So, of his own free accord, put on his fetters
        again.
Deeply mov'd, his foe embraced him,—and from
    thenceforward
      As a friend with a friend, pledg'd they the cup at
        the feast;
Arm-in-arm, the princes on *one* couch slumber'd
    together,
      While a still bloodier hate sever'd the nations apart.
'Gainst the army of Fred'rick, Louis now went, and
    behind him
      Left the foe he had fought, over Bavaria to watch.
" Ay, it is true! 'Tis really true! I have it in
    writing!"
      Thus did the Pontifex cry, when he first heard of
        the news.

COLUMBUS.

On, thou sailor undaunted! Though shallow witlings
    deride thee,
      And though the steersman his hand carelessly
        drops from the helm.
On, still on, tow'rd the West! 'Tis there that the
    coast will first greet thee,
      For to thy reason it lies clear and distinct even
        now.
Trust to the guiding God, and follow the world's
    silent ocean!
      And though as yet never seen, lo! it ascends from
        the flood!

With the intellect Nature standeth in union eternal:
  And what is promis'd by one, that will the other
    fulfil.

POMPEII AND HERCULANEUM.

WHAT strange wonder is this? Our prayer to thee
    was for water,
  Earth! What is this that thou now send'st from
    thy womb in reply?
In the abyss is there life? Or hidden under the lava
  Dwelleth some race now unknown? Does what
    hath fled e'er return?
Greeks and Romans, oh come! Oh, see the ancient
    Pompeii
  Here is discover'd again,—Hercules' town is
    rebuilt!

Gable on gable arises, the roomy portico opens
  Wide its halls, so make haste,—haste ye to fill it
    with life!
Open, too, stands the spacious theatre, let, then, the
    people,
  Like a resistless flood, pour through its sevenfold
    mouths!
Mimes, where are ye? Advance! Let Atrides
    finish the rites now
  He had begun,—let the dread chorus Orestes
    pursue!
Whither leads yon triumphal arch? Perceive ye the
    forum?
  What are those figures that sit on the Curulian
    chair?
Lictors! precede with your fasces,—and let the
    Prætor in judgment

Sit,—let the witness come forth ! let the accuser
      appear !
Cleanly streets spread around, and with a loftier
      pavement
   Does the contracted path wind close to the houses'
      long row ;
While, to protect them, the roofs protrude,—and the
      handsome apartments
   Round the now desolate court peacefully, fondly
      are ranged.
Hasten to open the shops, and the gateways that
      long have been chok'd up,
   And let the bright light of day fall on the desolate
      night !
See how around the edge extend the benches so
      graceful,
   And how the floor rises up, glitt'ring with many-
      hued stone !
Freshly still shines the wall with colours burning and
      glowing !
   Where is the artist ?   His brush he has but now
      laid aside.
Teeming with swelling fruits, and flowers dispos'd in
      fair order,
   Chases the brilliant festoon ravishing images there.
Here, with a basket full-laden, a Cupid gaily is
      dancing,
   Genie industrious *there* tread out the purple-dyed
      wine.
High there the Bacchanal dances and here she calmly
      is sleeping,
   While the listening Faun has not yet sated his
      eyes ;
Here she puts to flight the swift-footed Centaur,
      suspended
   On *one* knee, and, the while, goads with the
      Thyrsus his steps.

Boys, why tarry ye? Quick! The beauteous vessels
    still stand there;
  Hasten, ye maidens, and pour into the Etrurian jar!
Does not the tripod stand here, on sphinxes graceful
    and wingèd?
  Stir up the fire, ye slaves! Haste to make ready
    the hearth!
Go and buy; Here is money that's coined by Titus
    the Mighty;
  Still are the scales lying here; not e'en one weight
    has been lost.
Place the burning lights in the branches so gracefully
    fashion'd,
  And with the bright-shining oil see that the lamp
    is supplied!
What does this casket contain? Oh, see what the
    bridegroom has sent thee!
  Maiden! 'Tis buckles of gold; glittering gems
    for thy dress.
Lead the bride to the odorous bath,—here still are
    the unguents;
  Paints, too, are still lying here, filling the hollow-
    shap'd vase.

But where tarry the men? the elders? In noble
    museum
  Still lies a heap of strange rolls, treasures of infinite
    worth!
Styles, too, are here, and tablets of wax, all ready for
    writing;
  Nothing is lost, for, with faith, earth has protected
    the whole.
E'en the Penates are present, and all the glorious
    Immortals
  Meet here again, and of all, none, save the priests,
    are not here.
Hermes, whose feet are grac'd with wings, his
    Caduceus is waving,

And from the grasp of his hand victory lightly
  escapes.
Still are the altars standing here,—oh come, then,
  and kindle—
Long hath the God been away,—kindle the incense
  to Him !

THE ILIAD.

Tear for ever the garland of Homer, and number
  the fathers
  Of the immortal work, that through all time will
    survive !
Yet it has but *one* mother, and bears that mother's
  own features,
  'Tis *thy* features it bears,—Nature,—thy features
    eterne !

ZEUS TO HERCULES.*

'Twas not by means of my nectar, that thou hast
  made thee immortal ;
  Nought but thine own godlike strength conquer'd
    that nectar for thee.

THE ANTIQUE TO THE NORTHERN WANDERER.

Thou hast cross'd over torrents, and swum through
  wide-spreading oceans,—
  Over the chain of the Alps dizzily bore thee the
    bridge,

* It is curious to see how often Schiller mixes up the Greek and
Latin Deities. In *Semele*, for instance, he uses *Zeus* and *Jupiter*
indiscriminately.

That thou might'st see me from near, and learn to
    value my beauty,
    Which the voice of renown spreads through the
        wondering world.
And now before me thou standest,—canst touch my
    altar so holy,—
    But art thou nearer to me, or am I nearer to
        thee ?

THE BARDS OF OLDEN TIME.

SAY, where is now that glorious race, where now are
    the singers
    Who, with the accents of life, listening nations
        enthrall'd,
Sung down from heaven the gods, and sung mankind
    up to heaven,
    And who the spirit bore up high on the pinions of
        song ?
Ah! the singers still live; the actions only are
    wanting,
    And to awake the glad harp, only a welcoming
        ear.
Happy bards of a happy world! Your life-teeming
    accents
    Flew round from mouth unto mouth, gladdening
        every race.
With the devotion with which the Gods were receiv'd,
    each one welcom'd
    That which the genius for him, plastic and
        breathing, then form'd.
With the glow of the song were inflam'd the listener's
    senses,
    And with the listener's sense, nourish'd the singer
        the glow—

R

Nourish'd and cleans'd it,—fortunate one! for whom
    in the voices
  Of the people still clear echoed the soul of the
    song,
And to whom from without appear'd, in life, the
    great Godhead,
  Whom the bard of *these* days scarcely can feel in
    his breast.

THE ANTIQUES AT PARIS.

THAT which Grecian art created,
Let the Frank, with joy elated,
  Bear to Seine's triumphant strand,
And in his museums glorious
Show the trophies all-victorious
  To his wond'ring fatherland.

They to him are silent ever,
Into life's fresh circle never
  From their pedestals come down.
He alone e'er holds the muses
Through whose breast their power diffuses,—
  To the Vandal they're but stone!

THEKLA.

A SPIRIT-VOICE.

WHITHER was it that my spirit wended
  When from thee my fleeting shadow mov'd?
Is not now each earthly conflict ended?
  Say,—have I not liv'd,—have I not lov'd?

Art thou for the nightingales inquiring
  Who entranc'd thee in the early year
With their melody so joy-inspiring?
  Only whilst they lov'd, they linger'd here.

Is the lost one lost to me for ever?
  Trust me, with him joyfully I stray
There, where nought united souls can sever,
  And where ev'ry tear is wiped away.

And thou, too, wilt find us in yon heaven,
  When thy love with our love can compare;
There my father dwells, his sins forgiven,—
  Murder foul can never reach him there.

And he feels that him no vision cheated
  When he gaz'd upon the stars on high;[*]
For, as each one metes, to him 'tis meted;
  Who believes it, hath the Holy nigh.

Faith is kept in those blest regions yonder
  With the feelings true that ne'er decay.
Venture thou to dream, then, and to wander:
  Noblest thoughts oft lie in childlike play.

THE MAID OF ORLEANS.

Humanity's bright image to impair,
  Scorn laid thee prostrate in the deepest dust;
Wit wages ceaseless war on all that's fair,—
  In Angel and in God it puts no trust;
The bosom's treasures it would make its prey,—
Besieges Fancy,—dims e'en Faith's pure ray.

* See 'Piccolomini,' act ii. scene 6; and 'The Death of Wallenstein,' act v. scene 3.

Yet, issuing like thyself from humble line,
    Like thee a gentle shepherdess is she—
Sweet Poesy affords her rights divine,
    And to the stars eternal soars with thee.
Around thy brow a glory she hath thrown;
The heart 'twas form'd thee,—ever thou'lt live on !

The world delights whate'er is bright to stain,
    And in the dust to lay the glorious low;
Yet fear not! noble bosoms still remain,
    That for the Lofty, for the Radiant glow.
Let Momus serve to fill the booth with mirth;
A nobler mind loves forms of nobler worth.

NÆNIA.

Even the Beauteous must die! This vanquishes
    Men and Immortals ;
  But of the Stygian God moves not the bosom of
    steel.
Once and once only could Love prevail on the Ruler
    of Shadows,
  And on the threshold e'en then, sternly his gift he
    recall'd.
Venus could never heal the wounds of the beauteous
    stripling,
  That the terrible boar made in his delicate skin ;
Nor could his mother immortal preserve the hero so
    godlike,
  When, at the west gate of Troy, falling, his fate he
    fulfill'd.
But she arose from the ocean with all the daughters
    of Nereus,
  And o'er her glorified son rais'd the loud accents
    of woe.

See! where all the gods and goddesses yonder are
      weeping,
  That the Beauteous must fade, and that the Perfect
      must die.
Even a woe-song to be in the mouth of the lov'd ones
      is glorious,
  For what is vulgar descends mutely to Orcus'
      dark shades.

THE PLAYING CHILD.

PLAY, fair child, in thy mother's lap! In that island
      so holy,
  Withering grief cannot come, desolate care not
      approach.
O'er the abyss the arms of thy mother lovingly hold
      thee.
  Into the watery grave smilest thou guilelessly
      down.
Play, sweet innocent, still! Arcadia yet dwells around
      thee,
  Nature, as yet unrestrain'd, follows the impulse of
      joy.
Still does luxuriant vigour raise up its barriers
      poetic,—
  Duty and object as yet guide not thy tractable soul.
Play, then! for soon will labour approach thee,
      haggard and solemn,
  And even duty's command, pleasure and mind
      disobey.

THE SEXES.

See in the tender child two beauteous flow'rets
 united!
  Maiden and youth are both now hid in the bud
   from the eye.
Gently loosens the band, the natures with softness
 are parted,
  And from the modest-fac'd shame, severs the fiery
   might.
Suffer the boy to play, with raging passions to bluster!
  Sated vigour alone turns into beauty again.
From the bud begins the twofold flow'ret to issue,—
  Both are precious, but yet, neither thy yearning
   heart calms.
Ravishing fulness swells the blooming limbs of the
 maiden,
  But, like her girdle, her pride watches with care
   o'er her charms.
Shy as the trembling roe, whom the hunter pursues
 through the forest,
  Flies she from man as a foe,—hates him, because
   she loves not.
Boldly and proudly looks the youth from beneath
 his dark eyebrow,
  And, girded up for the fight, strains to the utmost
   his nerves.
Far, in the turmoil of spears, and on the race-course
 so dusty,
  Hurries him fame's craving thirst, bears him his
   boisterous mind.
Now, great Nature, protect thy work! What seeks
 itself ever,
  Flies, if thou rivet it not, ever in anger apart.
Mighty one! thou already art there; from the wildest
 of conflicts
  Thou dost call forth into life harmony's concord
   divine.

Sudden is hush'd the sound of the chase; the day's
    busy echo
  Dies on the ear, and the stars gently sink down to
    their rest.
Sighing whispers the reed,—soft-murmuring glides on
    the streamlet,
  And her melodious song Philomel trills through
    the grove.
What is it forces a sigh from the heaving breast of
    the maiden?
  Youth, what is it that bids tears to mount up to
    thine eye?
Ah! she seeks in vain for a *something* all-gently to
    cling to,
  And the o'er ripe fruit bends to the ground with
    its weight.
Restlessly-striving, the youth in his self-lighted flame
    is consuming;
  Ah! o'er that fierce-burning glow breathes not a
    softening wind.
See, at length they meet,—'tis Cupid has brought
    them together,
  And to the deity wing'd, victory wing'd soon
    succeeds.
Love divine, 'tis thou that joinest mortality's flowers!
  Parted for ever, by thee are they for evermore
    link'd!

THE POWER OF WOMAN.

Mighty art thou, because of the peaceful charms of
    thy presence;
  That which the silent does not, never the boastful
    can do.

Vigour in man I expect, the law in its honours main-
    taining,
  But, through the graces alone, woman e'er rules or
    should rule.
Many, indeed, have rul'd through the might of the
    spirit and action,
  But then, thou noblest of crowns, they were deficient
    in thee.
No real queen exists but the womanly beauty of
    woman ;
  Where it appears, it must rule ; ruling because it
    appears !

THE DANCE.

See, how like billows the couples with hovering
    motion are whirling!
  Scarce does the swift-wingèd foot seem to alight
    on the earth.
See I fugitive shadows set free from the weight of
    the body ?
  Weave, in the light of the moon, elves their ethereal
    dance ?
As when, rock'd by the zephyr, the weightless vapour
    flies upwards,
  As on the silvery flood lightly is balanc'd the bark,
So on the tuneful billows of Time is the docile foot
    moving ;
  Murmuring tones from the chords wafting the
    body through air.
Now, as if seeking with might to burst through the
    dance's strong fetters,
  There, where the throng is most dense, boldly a
    couple whirl round.
Quickly before them arises a path, disappearing
    behind them ;
  As with a magical hand, opens and closes the way.

See! now they vanish from sight; in wild entangle-
      ment blended,
  Falls the edifice proud, built of this movable world.
No, there it rises again exulting, the knot is
      unravell'd ;
  While the old rule is restor'd, with but a new form
      of charm.
Ever demolish'd, the whirling creation renews itself
      ever,
  And, by a law that is mute, each transformation is
      led.
Say, how is it that, ever renew'd the figures are
      hov'ring,
  While repose is not found, save in the changeable
      form ?
How is each one at freedom to follow the will of his
      bosom,
  And to find out the sole path, as he pursues his
      swift course ?
Wouldst thou know how it is ? 'Tis Harmony's
      powerful godhead,
  Changing the boisterous leap into the sociable
      dance,
That, like Nemesis, links to the golden bridle of
      rhythm
  Every violent lust, taming each thing that was wild.
Is't then in vain that the universe breathes its har-
      monious numbers ?
  Does not the music divine bear thee away in its
      stream ?
Feelest thou not the inspiriting time that all creatures
      are beating ?
  Not the swift-whirling dance that through the wide
      realms of space
Brandishes glittering suns, in paths intertwining with
      boldness ?
  Honouring Measure in sport, thou dost avoid it in
      deed.

FORTUNE.

Blest is the man whom the merciful gods, ere he
    came into being,
  Cherish'd, and whom, as a child, Venus then rock'd
    in her arms;
And whose eyes by Phœbus, whose lips by Hermes
    were open'd,
  And on whose forehead great Zeus stamp'd the
    impression of might!
Truly, a glorious lot is his,—ay! e'en a divine one,
  For, ere the contest begins, wreath'd with a crown
    is his brow;
Ere he has liv'd it, the fulness of life as his portion
    is meted,
  Ere he has labour endur'd, he has to Charis attain'd.
Great I must call the man, who, his own creator and
    sculptor,
  Vanquishes even the Fates, by his strong virtue
    alone;
Fortune, alas! he ne'er can o'ercome, and what
    Charis refuses
  Grudgingly, ne'er can he reach, strive with what
    courage he may.
Thou canst defend thee with resolute will from what
    is unworthy;
  All that is noble the gods freely send down from
    above.
As thou art lov'd by the lov'd one, so fall the gifts
    granted by Heaven;
  Yonder, in Jupiter's realm, Favour is lord, as in
    Love's.
Gods by affections are govern'd—the curly locks of
    green childhood
  Love they full well, for the glad ever by rapture
    are led.

'Tis not they who can see that are ever made blest by
    their presence,—
  No one save he who is blind views their bright
    glory reveal'd.
Gladly they choose for themselves simplicity's inno-
    cent spirit,
  And in the vessel so meek, that which is godlike
    enclose.
All unforeseen they come, deceiving each proud ex-
    pectation,
  No anathema's might forces the free ones from
    high.
Down to the man whom he loves, the Father of men
    and immortals
  Bids his eagle descend, bearing him then to the
    skies.
'Mongst the multitude ever pursues he his self-will'd
    researches,
  And, when well-pleas'd with a head, round it he
    wreathes with kind hand
Now the laurel, and now the fillet dominion-
    bestowing,—
  Favouring fortune alone e'er can the god himself
    crown.

Phœbus, the Pythian victor, precedes the happy one's
    footsteps,
  And the subduer of hearts, Amor, the sweet-smiling
    god.
Neptune makes level the ocean before him, the keel
    of the vessel
  Glides softly on, as it bears Cæsar and Cæsar's
    great fate.
Down at his feet sinks the roaring lion, the blustering
    dolphin
  Mounts from the deep, and his back offers with
    meekness to Him.

Envy the happy one not, if an easy triumph the
    Immortals
  Grant him, or if from the fight Venus her darling
    preserves.
Him whom that smiling one rescues, the favour'd
    of Heaven, I envy,
  Not the man o'er whose eyes she a dark covering
    throws.
Should Achilles be reckon'd less glorious, in that
    Hephæstus
  Fashion'd his buckler himself, fashion'd his terrible
    sword,
In that around him when dying the whole of Olympus
    was gather'd?
  Great was his glory, in truth, in that the gods lov'd
    him well;
In that they honour'd his wrath, and to give renown
    to their fav'rite,
  Hurlèd the best of the Greeks down to the darkness
    of hell.

Envy not beauty because she shines like the lily's
    sweet calyx
  Owing to Venus's gift, void of all merit herself.
Let her the happy one be; if thou seest her, thou,
    then, art the blest one!
  As without merit she shines, so thou art joy'd by
    her charms.
Be thou glad that the gift of song descends from the
    heavens,
  And that thou hear'st from the bard what he has
    learn'd from the muse!
Since by the god he's inspir'd, a god he becomes to
    the hearer;
  Since he the happy one is, thou canst the blissful
    one be.

In the busy market let Themis appear with her
    balance,
  Let the reward mete itself, strictly proportion'd to
    toil ;
Only a god can tinge the cheeks of a mortal with
    rapture,—
  Where no miracle is, there can no blest one be
    found.
All that is human must first be born, must grow, and
    must ripen,
  And from shape on to shape, fashioning Time leads
    it on ;
But thou seest not the blissful, the beautiful, come
    into being,
  Since the beginning of time, perfect they ever have
    been.
Every Venus of earth, like the first one of heaven.
    arises
  Only an ill-defin'd form, out of the infinite sea ;
But, like the first Minerva, proceeds, with the ægis
    provided,
  Every lightning-like thought out of the thunderer's
    brain.

GENIUS.

"Do I believe," sayest thou, "what the masters of
    wisdom would teach me,
  And what their followers' band boldly and readily
    swear ?
Cannot I ever attain to true peace, excepting through
    knowledge,
  Or is the system upheld only by fortune and law ?

Must I distrust the gently-warning impulse, the
    precept
    That thou, Nature, thyself hast in my bosom im-
      press'd,
Till the schools have affix'd to the writ eternal their
    signet,
    Till a mere formula's chain binds down the fugitive
      soul?
Answer me, then! for thou hast down into these
    deeps e'en descended,—
    Out of the mouldering grave thou didst uninjur'd
      return.
Is't to thee known what within the tomb of obscure
    works is hidden,
    Whether, yon mummies amid, life's consolations
      can dwell?
Must I travel the darksome road? The thought
    makes me tremble;
    Yet I *will* travel that road, if 'tis to truth and to
      right."—

Friend, hast thou heard of the golden age? Full
    many a story
    Poets have sung in its praise, simply and touchingly
      sung—
Of the time when the holy still wander'd over life's
    pathways,—
    When with a maidenly shame ev'ry sensation was
      veil'd,—
When the mighty law that governs the sun in his
    orbit,
    And that, conceal'd in the bud, teaches the point
      how to move,
When necessity's silent law, the steadfast, the change-
    less,
    Stirr'd up billows more free, e'en in the bosom of
      man,—

When the sense, unerring, and true as the hand of the
    dial,
  Pointed only to truth, only to what was eterne ?—

Then no profane one was seen, then no Initiate was
    met with,
  And what as living was felt, was not then sought
    'mongst the dead ;
Equally clear to every breast was the precept eternal,
  Equally hidden the source whence it to gladden us
    sprang ;
But that happy period has vanish'd ! And self-will'd
    presumption
  Nature's godlike repose now has for ever destroy'd.
Feelings polluted the voice of the deities echo no
    longer,
  In the dishonourèd breast now is the oracle
    dumb.
Save in the silenter self, the listening soul cannot
    find it,
  There does the mystical word watch o'er the
    meaning divine ;
There does the searcher conjure it, descending with
    bosom unsullied ;
  There does the nature long-lost give him back
    wisdom again.
If thou, happy one, never hast lost the angel that
    guards thee,
  Forfeited never the kind warnings that instinct
    holds forth ;
If in thy modest eye the truth is still purely depicted ;
  If in thine innocent breast clearly still echoes its
    call ;
If in thy tranquil mind the struggles of doubt still
    are silent,
  If they will surely remain silent for ever, as now ;

If by the conflict of feelings a judge will ne'er be
    required ;
  If in its malice thy heart dims not the reason so
    clear,
Oh, then, go thy way in all thy innocence precious!
  Knowledge can teach thee in nought; thou canst
    instruct *her* in much !
Yonder law, that with brazen staff is directing the
    struggling,
  Nought is to thee. What thou dost, what thou
    may'st will, is thy law,
And to every race a godlike authority issues.
  What thou with holy hand form'st, what thou with
    holy mouth speak'st,
Will with omnipotent power impel the wondering
    senses ;
  Thou but observ'st not the God ruling within thine
    own breast,
Not the might of the signet that bows all spirits
    before thee ;
  Simple and silent thou go'st through the wide world
    thou hast won.

THE PHILOSOPHICAL EGOTIST.

Hast thou e'er watch'd the infant, who, feeling not
    yet the affection
  Wherewith he's cradled and warm'd, tosses in sleep
    in the arm,
Till as a youth he awakes, obeying the impulse of
    passion,
And till his conscience's light, dawning, first shows
    him the world ?

Hast thou e'er watch'd the mother, procuring sweet rest
    for her darling
  At the expense of her own,—tending the babe as it
    dreams,—
With her own life supporting and feeding the flame as
    it trembles,—
  And in her own care itself, meeting that care's own
    reward ?
And great Nature thou slanderest, who, now child, and
    now mother,
  Now receives and now gives, but through necessity
    lasts?
Self-sufficient, wilt thou from the beauteous link disen-
    chain thee,
  Which, in an intimate bond, creature to creature
    unites?
Frail one ! wilt thou stand, then, alone, in thee only
    relying,
  When by the forces' exchange even the Infinite
    stands ?

THE WORDS OF FAITH.

THREE words of mighty moment I'll name,
  From mouth unto mouth they fly ever,
Yet the heart can alone their great value proclaim,
  For their source from without rises never.
No virtue, no merit, man's footsteps e'er guides,
When in those three words he no longer confides,

For LIBERTY, man is created,—*is* free,
  Though fetters around him be chinking ;
Let the cry of the mob never terrify thee,
  Nor the scorn of the doltard unthinking !
Fear not the bold slave when he breaks from his
    chains,
Nor the man who in freedom enduring remains !

And VIRTUE is more than a mere empty sound,
　His practice through life man may make it;
And though oft, ere he yet the divine one has found,
　He may stumble, he still may o'ertake it.
And that which the wise in his wisdom ne'er knew,
Can be done by the mind that is childlike and true.

And a GOD, too, there is, with a purpose sublime,
　Though frail may be reason's dominion;
High over the regions of space and of time
　The noblest of thoughts waves its pinion;
And tho' all things in ceaseless succession may roll,
Yet constant for ever remains a calm soul.

Preserve, then, the three mighty words I have nam'd;
　From mouth unto mouth spread them ever,
By thy heart will their infinite worth be proclaim'd,
　Though their source from without rises never.
Forget not that virtue man's footsteps still guides,
While in those three words he with firmness confides.

THE WORDS OF ERROR.

IN the mouth of the good and the noble are found
　Three words of an import momentous;
Yet vain is their echo and empty their sound,
　They ne'er can console or content us.
The fruit that life yields is but lost to mankind,
As long as he seeks these vain shadows to find.

As long as he trusts in the golden age,
　Where the right and the good conquer ever,—
The right and the good an eternal strife wage,
　And the foe will succumb to them never,—
Unless in the air thou canst crush him to death,
For contact with earth but restores his lost breath.

As long as he trusts that fortune's rays
   With the noble can ever be blended—
She follows the bad with loving gaze;
   For the good is the earth not intended.
A stranger he is, and his fate is to roam,
And seek an enduring, a ne'er changing home.

As long as he trusts that the truth will e'er stand
   Reveal'd to the reason unstable—
Her veil can be rais'd by no mortal hand;
   But to guess and suppose, we are able.
In a word of mere sound thou enchainest the soul;
But the free one defies e'en the tempest's control.

From that error, then, Spirit of Light, set thee
    free,—
   In thy breast be a true faith victorious!
What no ear could e'er hear, what no eye could e'er
    see,
   Remains still the truthful, the glorious!
It is not *without*, for the fool seeks it there;
Within thee it flourishes, constant and fair.

PROVERBS OF CONFUCIUS.

I.

THREEFOLD is the march of TIME:
   While the future slow advances,
   Like a dart the present glances,
Silent stands the past sublime.

No impatience e'er can speed him
   On his course, if he delay;
No alarm, no doubts impede him
   If he keep his onward way;
No regrets, no magic numbers
Wake the tranc'd one from his slumbers.

Wouldst thou wisely, and with pleasure,
Pass the days of life's short measure,
From the slow one counsel take,
But a tool of him ne'er make;
Ne'er as friend the swift one know,
Nor the constant one as foe!

II.

Threefold is the form of SPACE:
Length, with ever restless motion,
Seeks eternity's wide ocean;
Breadth with boundless sway extends;
Depth to unknown realms descends.

All as types to thee are given:
Thou must onward strive for heaven,
Never still or weary be
Wouldst thou perfect glory see;
Far must thy researches go
Wouldst thou learn the world to know;
Thou must tempt the dark abyss
Wouldst thou prove what *Being* is.

Nought but firmness gains the prize,—
Nought but fulness makes us wise,—
Buried deep, truth ever lies!

LIGHT AND WARMTH.

THE world, a man of noble mind
    With glad reliance enters;
Around him spread, he hopes to find
    What in his bosom centres;
And dedicates, with ardour warm,
To truth's good cause his trusty arm.

That all is mean and small, ere long
   Experience shows him ever;
Himself to guard amid the throng
   Is now his sole endeavour.
His heart, in calm and proud repose,
Soon e'en to love begins to close.

Alas! truth's clear and brilliant rays
   Are not for ever glowing;
How blest is he whose heart ne'er pays
   For gift from knowledge flowing!
So thou the worldling's gaze shouldst bind
To the enthusiast's steadfast mind!

BREADTH AND DEPTH.

FULL many in the world we find
   To whom nothing seems e'er a mystery;
And when aught pleases or charms the mind,
   They're able to give all its history.
To hear them speak, one could ne'er have denied
That they had won the long-wished-for bride.

In silence, however, they quit the earth,
   Their life leaves behind it no traces:—
Let him who to something that's great would give
     birth,—
   To something that time ne'er effaces,—
With patience collect, and unweariedly,
In the smallest point, boundless energy.

The stalk the region around it fills
   With branches luxuriant and slender;
The foliage glitters, and balms distils,
   But fruit it can never engender.
The kernel alone, in its narrow space,
The pride of the forest, the tree, can embrace.

THE GUIDES OF LIFE.*

Two kinds of *genie* there are, through life's mazy path-
    ways to guide thee;
  Happy art thou if they stand, join'd into one by thy
    side!
One with his gladdening sport beguileth thy tedious
    journey,—
  Duty and fate become light, when thou'rt upheld by
    his arm.
Laughing and talking the while, he on to the chasm
    conducts thee,
  Where, on eternity's sea, trembling mortality
    stands.
There does the Other receive thee, with solemn resolve
    and in silence,
  And with his giant-like arm bears thee across the
    abyss.
Ne'er to one only devote thee! Thine honour ne'er think
    of confiding
  Into the hands of the first, nor to the other thy
    bliss!

ARCHIMEDES AND THE STUDENT.

To Archimedes once came a youth, who for knowledge
    was thirsting,
  Saying, "Initiate me into the science divine,
Which for my country has borne forth fruit of such
    wonderful value,
  And which the walls of the town 'gainst the Sambuca †
    protects."

* Originally entitled 'The Beautiful and the Sublime.'
† The name of a machine used in sieges, employed by Marcellus
against Syracuse.

"Call'st thou the science divine?   It *is* so," the wise man
    responded;
"But it was so, my son, ere it avail'd for the town.
Wouldst thou have fruit from her only, e'en mortals with
    that can provide thee;
Wouldst thou the goddess obtain, seek not the woman
    in Her!"

HUMAN KNOWLEDGE.

SINCE thou readest in her what thou thyself hast there
    written,
    And, to gladden the eye, placest her wonders in
        groups;—
Since o'er her boundless expanses thy cords to extend
    thou art able,
    Thou dost think that thy mind wonderful Nature can
    grasp.

Thus the astronomer draws his figures over the
    heavens,
    So that he may with more ease traverse the infinite
        space,
Knitting together e'en suns that by Sirius-distance are
    parted,
    Making them join in the swan and in the horns of the
    bull.
But because the firmament shows him its glorious
    surface,
    Can he the spheres' mystic dance therefore decipher
    aright?

THE TWO PATHS OF VIRTUE.

Two are the pathways by which mankind can to virtue
    mount upward;
    If thou shouldst find the one barr'd, open the other
        will lie.
'Tis by exertion the Happy obtain her, the Suffering by
    patience.
    Blest is the man whose kind fate guides him along
        upon both!

HONOURS.

As the column of light in the waves of the brook is
    reflected,
    Bright as from its own glow, flameth the border with
        gold;
But by the stream are the waves hurried on,—through the
    glittering pathway
    Each thrusts the other along, swift, as the former, to
        fly,—
So is a mortal that perishes lighted by splendour of
    honours,—
    Not himself, but the place, through which he wandereth,
        shines.

ZENITH AND NADIR.

Wheresoever thou wand'rest in space, thy Zenith and
    Nadir
    Unto the heavens knit thee, unto the axis of
        earth.
Howsoever thou actest, let heaven be mov'd by thy
    purpose,
    Let the aim of thy deeds traverse the axis of
        earth!

DEPARTURE FROM LIFE.

Two are the roads that before thee lie open from life to
    conduct thee;
To the Ideal one leads thee, the other to Death.
See that while yet thou art free, on the first thou com-
    mencest thy journey,
Ere by the merciless Fates on to the other thou'rt
    led!

THE CHILD IN THE CRADLE.

Happy infant! to thee an infinite space is the cradle.
    When to man's age thou shalt come, narrow thou'lt
    think the wide world!

THE IMMUTABLE.

Time incessantly hasteneth on—he seeks for perfec-
    tion.
    If thou art true, thou canst cast fetters eternal on
    him.

THEOPHANIA.

When the happy appear, I forget the Gods in the
    heavens;
    But before me they stand, when I the suffering see.

THE HIGHEST.

Seek'st thou the Highest, the Greatest? In that the
    plant can instruct thee;
    What it unwittingly is, be thou of thine own free
    will!

IMMORTALITY.

Dread'st thou the aspect of Death! Thou wishest to
  live on for ever?
  Live in the Whole, and when long thou shalt have
  gone, 'twill remain!

VOTIVE TABLETS.

That which I learn'd from the Deity,—that which
  through lifetime hath help'd me,
  Meekly and gratefully now, here I suspend in his
  shrine.

DIFFERENT DESTINIES.

Millions busily toil, that the human race may con-
  tinue;
  But by only a few is propagated our kind.
Thousands of seeds by the autumn are scatter'd, yet fruit
  is engender'd
  Only by few, for the most back to the element go.
But if one only can blossom, *that* one is able to scatter
  Even a bright living world, fill'd with creations
  eterne.

THE ANIMATING PRINCIPLE.

Nowhere in the organic or sensitive world ever
  kindles
  Novelty, save in the flow'r, noblest creation of
  life.

TWO DESCRIPTIONS OF ACTION.

Do what is good, and Humanity's godlike plant thou wilt
  nourish;
  Plan what is fair, and thou'lt strew seeds of the godlike around.

DIFFERENCE OF STATION.

EVEN the moral world its nobility boasts—vulgar
  natures
  Reckon by that which they *do;* noble, by that which
  they *are.*

WORTH AND THE WORTHY.

IF thou anything *hast,* let me have it,—I'll pay what is
  proper;
  If thou anything *art,* let us our spirits exchange.

THE MORAL FORCE.

IF thou *feel'st* not the beautiful, still thou with reason
  canst *will* it;
  And as a spirit canst do, that which as man thou canst
  not.

PARTICIPATION.

E'EN by the hand of the wicked can truth be working with
  vigour;
  But the vessel is fill'd by what is beauteous
  alone.

TO   *

TELL me all that thou knowest, and I will thankfully
  hear it!
  But wouldst thou give me *thyself,*—let me, my friend,
  be excus'd!

TO   *   *

WOULDST thou teach me the truth? Don't take the
  trouble! I wish not,
  Through thee, the thing to observe,—but to see *thee*
  through the thing.

TO　*　*　*

THEE would I choose as my teacher and friend. Thy living example
　Teaches me,—thy teaching word wakens my heart unto life.

THE PRESENT GENERATION.

WAS it always as now? This race I truly can't fathom.
　Nothing is young but old age; youth, alas! only is old.

TO THE MUSE.

WHAT I had been without thee, I know not—yet, to my sorrow,
　See I what, without *thee*, hundreds and thousands now are.

THE LEARNED WORKMAN.

NE'ER does he taste the fruit of the tree that he rais'd with such trouble;
　Nothing but taste e'er enjoys that which by learning is rear'd.

THE DUTY OF ALL.

EVER strive for the whole; and if no whole thou canst make thee,
　Join, then, thyself to some whole, as a subservient limb!

A PROBLEM.

LET none resemble another; let each resemble the highest!
　How can that happen? let each be all complete in itself.

THE PECULIAR IDEAL.

What thou thinkest, belongs to all; what thou feel'st,
    is thine only.
    Wouldst thou make him thine own, feel thou the God
        whom thou think'st!

TO MYSTICS.

That is the only true secret, which in the presence of all
    men
    Lies, and surrounds thee for aye, but which is witness'd
        by none.

THE KEY.

Wouldst thou know thyself, observe the actions of
    others.
    Wouldst thou other men know, look thou within thine
        own heart.

THE OBSERVER.

Stern as my conscience, thou seest the points wherein
    I'm deficient;
    Therefore I've always lov'd thee, as my own conscience
        I've lov'd.

WISDOM AND PRUDENCE.

Wouldst thou, my friend, mount up to the highest
    summit of wisdom,
    Be not deterr'd by the fear, prudence thy course may
        deride:
That short-sighted one sees but the bank that from thee
    is flying,
    Not the one which ere long thou wilt attain with bold
        flight.

THE AGREEMENT.

Both of us seek for truth—in the world without thou
    dost seek it,
  I in the bosom within; both of us therefore
    succeed.
If the eye be healthy, it sees from without the
    Creator;
  And if the heart, then within doubtless it mirrors the
    world.

POLITICAL PRECEPT.

All that thou doest is right; but, friend, don't carry this
    precept
  On too far,—be content, all that is right to effect.
It is enough to true zeal, if what is existing be perfect;
  False zeal always would find finish'd perfection at
    once.

MAJESTAS POPULI.

Majesty of the nature of man! In crowds shall I seek
    thee?
  'Tis with only a few that thou hast made thine
    abode.
Only a few ever count; the rest are but blanks of no
    value,
  And the prizes are hid 'neath the vain stir that they
    make.

TO A WORLD-REFORMER.

" I have sacrific'd all," thou sayest, " that Man I might
    succour;
  Vain the attempt; my reward was persecution and
    hate."
Shall I tell thee, my friend, how I to humour him
    manage?
  Trust the proverb! I ne'er have been deceiv'd by it
    yet.

Thou canst not sufficiently prize Humanity's value;
   Let it be coin'd in deed as it exists in thy breast.
E'en to the man whom thou chancest to meet in life's
     narrow pathway,
   If he should ask it of thee, hold forth a succouring
     hand.
But for rain and for dew, for the general welfare of
     mortals,
   Leave thou Heaven to care, friend, as before, so e'en
     now.

MY ANTIPATHY.

I HAVE a heartfelt aversion for crime,—a twofold aver-
     sion,
   Since 'tis the reason why man prates about virtue so
     much.
" What! thou hatest, then, virtue?"—I would that by all
     it were practis'd,
   So that, God willing, no man ever need speak of it
     more.

TO ASTRONOMERS.

PRATE not to me so much of suns and of nebulous
     bodies ;
   Think ye nature but great, in that she gives thee to
     count?
Though your object may be the sublimest that space
     holds within it,
   Yet, my good friends, the sublime dwells not in
     regions of space.

ASTRONOMICAL WRITINGS.

OH, how infinite, how unspeakably great, are the
     heavens !
   Yet by frivolity's hand downwards the heavens are
     pull'd!

THE BEST STATE.

" How can I know the best state?" In the way that thou
   know'st the best woman ;
   Namely, my friend, that the world ever is silent of
   both.

MY FAITH.

WHICH religion do I acknowledge? None that thou
   namest.
   " None that I name? And why so?"—Why, for religion's own sake!

INSIDE AND OUTSIDE.

" GOD alone sees the heart "—and therefore, since he
   alone sees it,
   Be it our care that we, too, something that's worthy
   may see.

FRIEND AND FOE.

DEARLY I love a friend; yet a foe I may turn to my
   profit ;
   Friends show me that which I *can :* foes teach me that
   which I *should.*

LIGHT AND COLOUR.

THOU that art ever the same, with the Changeless One
   take up thy dwelling !
   Colour, thou changeable one, kindly descend upon
   man !

BEAUTEOUS INDIVIDUALITY.

THOU in truth shouldst be one, yet not with the whole
   shouldst thou be so.
   'Tis through the reason thou'rt one,—art so with *it*
   through the heart.

Voice of the whole is thy reason, but thou thine own
    heart must be ever;
If in thy heart reason dwells evermore, happy art
    thou.

VARIETY.

Many are good and wise; yet all for one only reckon,
    For 'tis conception, alas, rules them, and not a fond
    heart.
Sad is the sway of conception,—from thousandfold varying
    figures,
    Needy and empty but *one* it is e'er able to bring.
But where creative beauty is ruling, there life and
    enjoyment
    Dwell; to the ne'er-changing One, thousands of new
    forms she gives.

THE THREE AGES OF NATURE.

Life she receiv'd from fable; the schools deprived her of
    being,
    Life creative again she has from reason receiv'd.

GENIUS.

Understanding, indeed, can repeat what already ex-
    isted,—
    That which Nature has built, after her she, too, can
    build.
Over Nature can Reason build, but in vacancy only:
    But thou, Genius, alone, Nature *in* Nature canst
    form.

THE IMITATOR.

Good from the good,—to the reason this is not hard of
    conception;
    But the genius has pow'r good from the bad to
    evoke.

'Tis the conceiv'd alone, that thou, Imitator, canst
    practise;
  Food the conceiv'd never is, save to the mind that
    conceives.

GENIALITY.

How does the genius make itself known? In the way that
    in nature
  Shows the Creator Himself,—e'en in the infinite
    whole.
Clear is the æther, and yet of depth that ne'er can be
    fathom'd;
  Seen by the eye, it remains evermore clos'd to the
    sense.

THE INQUIRERS..

Men now seek to explore each thing from within and
    without too;
  How canst thou make thy escape, Truth, from their
    eager pursuit?
That they may catch thee, with nets and poles extended
    they seek thee;
  But with a spirit-like tread, glidest thou out of the
    throng.

THE DIFFICULT UNION.

Why are taste and genius so seldom met with united?
  Taste of strength is afraid,—genius despises the rein.

CORRECTNESS.

Free from blemish to be, is the lowest of steps, and the
    highest;
  Weakness and greatness alone ever arrive at this
    point.

THE LAW OF NATURE.

It has ever been so, my friend, and will ever remain so:
    Weakness has rules for itself,—vigour is crown'd
        with success.

CHOICE.

If thou canst not give pleasure to all by thy deeds and
        thy knowledge,
    Give it then, unto the few; many to please is but vain.

SCIENCE OF MUSIC.

Let the creative art breathe life, and the bard furnish
        spirit;
    But the soul is express'd by Polyhymnia alone.

LANGUAGE.

Why can the living spirit be never seen by the spirit?
    Soon as the soul 'gins to speak, then can the soul
        speak no more!

TO THE POET.

Let thy speech be to thee what the body is to the
        loving;
    Beings it only can part,—beings it only can join.

THE MASTER.

Other masters one always can tell by the words that
        they utter;
    That which he wisely omits, shows me the master
        of style.

THE GIRDLE.

APHRODITE preserves her beauty conceal'd by her girdle;
    That which lends her her charms, is what she covers—
        her shame.

THE DILETTANTE.

MERELY because thou hast made a good verse in a
    language poetic,
    One which composes for thee, thou art a poet,
        forsooth !

THE BABBLER OF ART.

DOST thou desire the good in Art? Of the good art thou
    worthy,
    Which by a ne'er ceasing war 'gainst thee thyself is
        produced ?

THE PHILOSOPHIES.

WHICH among the philosophies will be enduring? I
    know not.
But that philosophy's self ever may last, is my hope.

THE FAVOUR OF THE MUSES.

FAME with the vulgar expires; but, Muse immortal, thou
    bearest
    Those whom thou lov'st, who love thee, into
        Mnemosyne's arms.

HOMER'S HEAD AS A SEAL.

TRUSTY old Homer! to thee I confide the secret so
    tender ;
    For the raptures of love none but the bard should e'er
    know.

THE BEST STATE-CONSTITUTION.

I can recognise only as such, the one that enables
   Each to think what is right,—but that he thinks so,
      cares not.

TO LAWGIVERS.

Ever take it for granted, that man collectively wishes
   That which is right; but take care, never to think
      so of one!

THE HONOURABLE.

Ever honour the whole; individuals only I honour;
   In individuals I always discover the whole.

FALSE IMPULSE TO STUDY.

Oh, how many new foes against truth! My very soul
      bleedeth
   When I behold the owl-race now bursting forth to
      the light.

THE FOUNTAIN OF SECOND YOUTH.

Trust me, 'tis not a mere tale,—the fountain of youth
      really runneth,
   Runneth for ever. Thou ask'st, Where? In the poet's
      sweet art!

THE CIRCLE OF NATURE.

ALL, thou gentle one, lies embrac'd in thy kingdom; the
    greybeard
  Back to the days of his youth, childish and childlike,
    returns.

THE GENIUS WITH THE INVERTED TORCH.

LOVELY he looks, 'tis true, with the light of his torch now
    extinguish'd;
  But remember that death is not æsthetic, my friends!

THE VIRTUE OF WOMAN.

MAN of virtue has need;—into life with boldness he
    plunges,
  Ent'ring with fortune more sure into the hazardous
    strife;
But to woman *one* virtue suffices; it ever is shining
  Lovingly forth to the heart: so let it shine to the
    eye!

THE FAIREST APPARITION.

IF thou never hast gazed upon beauty in moments of
    sorrow,
  Thou canst with truth never boast that thou true
    beauty hast seen
If thou never hast gazed upon gladness in beauteous
    features,
  Thou canst with truth never boast that thou true
    gladness hast seen.

THE FORUM OF WOMAN.

WOMAN, never judge man by his individual actions;
But upon man, as a whole, pass thy decisive decree.

FEMALE JUDGMENT.

MAN frames his judgment on reason; but woman on love
founds her verdict;
If her judgment loves not, woman already has
judg'd.

THE IDEAL OF WOMAN.

TO AMANDA.

WOMAN in everything yields to man; but in that which is
highest,
Even the manliest man yields to the woman most
weak.
But that highest,—what is it? The gentle radiance of
triumph
As in thy brow upon me, beauteous Amanda, it
beams.
When o'er the bright shining disk the clouds of affliction
are fleeting,
Fairer the image appears, seen through the vapour of
gold.
Man may think himself free! thou *art* so,—for thou never
knowest
What is the meaning of choice,—know'st not necessity's
name.
That which thou givest, thou always giv'st wholly; but
one art thou ever,
Even thy tenderest sound is thine harmonious self.
Youth everlasting dwells here, with fulness that never is
exhausted,
And with the flower at once pluck'st thou the ripe
golden fruit.

EXPECTATION AND FULFILMENT.

Into life's ocean the youth with a thousand masts
    daringly launches;
Mute, in a boat sav'd from wreck, enters the greybeard
    the port.

THE COMMON FATE.

See how we hate, how we quarrel, how thought and how
    feeling divide us!
But thy locks, friend, like mine, meanwhile are
    bleachening fast.

HUMAN ACTION.

Where the pathway begins, eternity seems to lie open,
    Yet at the narrowest point even the wisest man stops.

THE FATHER.

Work as much as thou wilt, alone thou'lt be standing for
    ever,
Till by nature thou'rt join'd forcibly on to the Whole.

LOVE AND DESIRE.

Rightly said, Schlosser! Man loves what he has; what
    he has not, desireth;
None but the wealthy minds love; poor minds desire
    alone.

GOODNESS AND GREATNESS.

Only two virtues exist. Oh, would they were ever united !
  Ever the good with the great, ever the great with the
    good !

THE IMPULSES.

Fear with his iron staff may urge the slave onward for
    ever ;
  Rapture, do thou lead me on ever in roseate chains !

NATURALISTS AND TRANSCENDENTAL
PHILOSOPHERS.

Enmity be between ye ! Your union too soon is
    cemented ;
  Ye will but learn to know truth, when ye divide in
    the search.

GERMAN GENIUS.

Strive, O German, for Roman-like strength and for
    Grecian-like beauty !
  Thou art successful in both ; ne'er has the Gaul had
    success.

TRIFLES.

THE EPIC HEXAMETER.

Giddily onward it bears thee with resistless impetuous
    billows ;
  Nought but the ocean and air seest thou before or
    behind.

THE DISTICH.

In the Hexameter rises the fountain's watery column,
  In the Pentameter sweet falling in melody down.

THE EIGHT-LINE STANZA.

Stanza, by love thou'rt created,—by love all-tender and
      yearning ;
  Thrice dost thou bashfully fly ; thrice dost with long-
      ing return.

THE OBELISK.

On a pedestal lofty the sculptor in triumph has rais'd
      me.
  "Stand thou," spake he,—and I stand proudly and
      joyfully here.

THE TRIUMPHAL ARCH.

"Fear not," the builder exclaim'd, "the rainbow that
      stands in the heavens ;
  "I will extend thee, like it, into infinity far !"

THE BEAUTIFUL BRIDGE.

Under me, over me, hasten the waters, the chariots ; my
      builder
  Kindly has suffer'd e'en me, over myself, too, to go !

THE GATE.

Let the gate open stand, to allure the savage to precepts ;
  Let it the citizen lead into free nature with joy.

ST. PETER'S.

If thou seekest to find Immensity here, thou'rt mis-
      taken ;
  For my greatness is meant greater to make thee thyself !

GERMANY AND HER PRINCES.

Thou hast produced mighty monarchs, of whom thou art
    not unworthy,
  For the obedient alone make him who governs them
    great.
But, O Germany, try if thou for thy rulers canst make it
  Harder as kings to be great,—easier, though, to be men !

TO PROSELYTISERS.

" Give me only a fragment of earth beyond the earth's
    limits,"—
  So the godlike man said,—" and I will move it with
    ease."
Only give me permission to leave myself for one
    moment,
  And without any delay I will engage to be yours.

THE CONNECTING MEDIUM.

How does nature proceed to unite the high and the
    lowly
  In mankind ? She commands vanity 'tween them to
    stand !

THE MOMENT.

Doubtless an epoch important has with the century
    risen ;
  But the moment, so great, finds but a race of small
    worth.

GERMAN COMEDY.

Fools we may have in plenty, and simpletons, too, by
    the dozen ;
  But for comedy these never make use of themselves.

BOOKSELLER'S ANNOUNCEMENT.

NOUGHT is for man so important as rightly to know his
    own purpose;
For but twelve groschen hard cash, 'tis to be bought at
    my shop!

DANGEROUS CONSEQUENCES.

DEEPER and bolder truths be careful, my friends, of
    avowing;
For as soon as ye do, all the world on ye will fall.

GREEKISM.

SCARCE has the fever so chilly of Gallomania departed,
    When a more burning attack in Grecomania breaks
    out.
Greekism,—what did it mean?—'Twas harmony, reason,
    and clearness!
    Patience, good gentlemen, pray, ere ye of Greekism
    speak!
'Tis for an excellent cause ye are fighting, and all that
    I ask for
Is that with reason it ne'er may be. a laughing-stock
    made.

THE SUNDAY CHILDREN.

YEARS has the master been lab'ring, but always without
    satisfaction;
To an ingenious race, 'twould be in vision conferr'd.
What they yesterday learnt, to-day they fain would be
    teaching:
Small compassion, alas, is by those gentlemen shown!

THE PHILOSOPHERS.

PUPIL.

I AM rejoic'd, worthy sirs, to find you *in pleno* assembled ;
    For I have come down below, seeking the *one* needful
      thing.

ARISTOTLE.

Quick to the point, my good friend ! For the *Jena*
    Gazette comes to hand here,
    Even in hell,—so we know all that is passing above.

PUPIL.

So much the better ! So give me (I will not depart
    hence without it)
    Some good principle now,—one that will always
      avail !

FIRST PHILOSOPHER.

Cogito, ergo sum. I have thought, and therefore existence !
    If the first be but true, then is the second one sure.

PUPIL.

As I think, I exist. 'Tis good ! But who always is
    thinking ?'
    Oft I've existed e'en when I have been thinking of
      nought.

SECOND PHILOSOPHER.

Since there are things that exist, a thing of all things
    there must needs be ;
    In the thing of all things dabble we, just as we
      are.

THIRD PHILOSOPHER.

Just the reverse say I. Besides myself there is
    nothing ;
Ev'rything else that there is, is but a bubble to me.

FOURTH PHILOSOPHER.

Two kinds of things I allow to exist,—the world and the
    spirit ;
Nought of others I know ; even these signify one.

FIFTH PHILOSOPHER.

I know nought of the thing, and know still less of the
    spirit ;
Both but appear unto me ; yet no appearance they are.

SIXTH PHILOSOPHER.

I am I, and settle myself,—and if I then settle
    Nothing to be, well and good—there's a nonentity
    form'd.

SEVENTH PHILOSOPHER.

There is conception at least ! A thing conceiv'd there is,
    therefore ;
And a conceiver as well,—which, with conception,
    make three.

PUPIL.

All this nonsense, good sirs, won't answer my purpose a
    tittle :
I a real principle need,—one by which something is
    fix'd.

EIGHTH PHILOSOPHER.

Nothing is now to be found in the theoretical province ;
  Practical principles hold, such as : thou canst, for thou
    shouldst.

PUPIL.

If I but thought so ! When people know no more sen-
    sible answer,
  Into the conscience at once plunge they with desperate
    haste.

DAVID HUME.

Don't converse with those fellows ! That Kant has turn'd
    them all crazy ;
  Speak to me, for in hell I am the same that I was.

LAW POINT.

I have made use of my nose for years together to smell
    with ;
  Have I a right to my nose that can be legally prov'd ?

PUFFENDORF.

Truly a delicate point !   Yet the first possession
    appeareth
  In thy favour to tell ; therefore make use of it still !

SCRUPLE OF CONSCIENCE.

Willingly serve I my friends ; but, alas, I do it with
    pleasure ;
  Therefore I often am vex'd, that no true virtue I have.

DECISION.

As there is no other means, thou hadst better begin to
    despise them ;
  And with aversion, then, do that which thy duty
    commands.

G. G.

Each one, when seen by himself, is passably wise and
    judicious;
When they *in corpore* are, nought but a blockhead is
    seen.

THE HOMERIDES.

Who is the bard of the Iliad among you? For since he
    likes puddings,
    Heyne begs he'll accept these that from Göttingen
    come.
"Give them to *me!* The kings' quarrel I sang!"—
    " I the fight near the vessels!"—
    " Hand *me* the puddings! I sang what upon Ida took
    place!"
Gently! Don't tear me to pieces! The puddings will
    not be sufficient;
    He by whom they are sent destin'd them only for
    one.

THE MORAL POET.

Man is in truth a poor creature,—I know it,—and fain
    would forget it;
    Therefore (how sorry I am!) came I, alas, unto
    thee!

THE DANAIDES.

Into the sieve we've been pouring for years,—o'er the
    stone we've been brooding;
    But the stone never warms,—nor does the sieve ever
    fill.

THE SUBLIME SUBJECT.

'Tis thy Muse's delight to sing God's pity to mortals ;
But, that they pitiful are,—is it a matter for song ?

THE ARTIFICE.

Wouldst thou give pleasure at once to the children of
 earth and the righteous ?
Draw the image of lust—adding the devil as well !

JEREMIADS.

All, both in prose and in verse, in Germany fast is
 decaying ;
 Far behind us, alas, lieth the golden age now !
For by philosophers spoil'd is our language—our logic
 by poets,
 And no more common sense governs our passage
 through life.
From the æsthetic, to which she belongs, now virtue is
 driven,
 And into politics forced, where she's a troublesome
 guest.
Where are we hastening now ? If natural, dull we are
 voted,
 And if we put on constraint, then the world calls us
 absurd.
Oh, thou joyous artlessness 'mongst the poor maidens of
 Leipzig,
 Witty simplicity come,—come, then, to glad us
 again !
Comedy, oh repeat thy weekly visits so precious,
 Sigismund, lover so sweet,—Mascarill, valet jocose !
Tragedy, full of salt and pungency epigrammatic,—
 And thou, minuet-step of our old buskin preserv'd !

Philosophic romance, thou mannikin waiting with
    patience,
  When, 'gainst the pruner's attack, nature defendeth
    herself!
Ancient prose, oh return,—so nobly and boldly ex-
    pressing
  All that thou think'st and hast thought,—and what
    the reader thinks too!
All, both in prose and in verse, in Germany fast is
    decaying;
  Far behind us, alas, lieth the golden age now!

KNOWLEDGE.

Knowledge to one is a goddess both heav'nly and high,—
    to another
  Only an excellent cow, yielding the butter he wants.

KANT AND HIS COMMENTATORS.

See how a single rich man gives a living to numbers
    of beggars!
  'Tis when sovereigns build, carters are kept in
    employ.

SHAKESPEAR'S GHOST.

A PARODY.

I, too, at length discern'd great Hercules' energy
    mighty,—
  Saw his shade. He himself was not, alas, to be seen.

Round him were heard, like the screaming of birds, the
      screams of tragedians,
  And, with the baying of dogs, bark'd dramaturgists
      around.
There stood the giant in all his terrors; his bow was
      extended,
  And the bolt, fix'd on the string, steadily aim'd at the
      heart.
" What still hardier action, Unhappy One, dost thou now
      venture,
  Thus to descend to the grave of the departed souls
      here ?"—
" 'Tis to see Tiresias I come, to ask of the prophet
  Where I the buskin of old, that now has vanish'd, may
      find ?"
" If they believe not in Nature, nor in the old Grecian,
      but vainly
  Wilt thou convey up from hence that dramaturgy
      to them."
" Oh, as for Nature, once more to tread our stage she has
      ventur'd,
  Ay, and stark-naked besides, so that each rib we can
      count."
" What ? Is the buskin of old to be seen in truth on
      your stage, then,
  Which even I came to fetch, out of mid-Tartarus'
      gloom ?"—
" There is now no more of that tragic bustle, for scarcely
  Once in a year on the boards moves thy great soul,
      harness clad."
" Doubtless 'tis well ! Philosophy now has refin'd your
      sensations,
  And from the humour so bright, fly the affections so
      black."—
" Ay, there is nothing that beats a jest that is stolid and
      barren,
  But then e'en sorrow can please, if 'tis sufficiently
      moist."

u 2

" But do ye also exhibit the graceful dance of Thalia,
    Join'd to the solemn step with which Melpomene
        moves ?"—
" Neither ! For nought we love but what is Christian
        and moral ;
    And what is popular too, homely, domestic, and
        plain."
" What ? Does no Cæsar, does no Achilles, appear on
        your stage now,
    Not an Andromache e'en, not an Orestes, my
        friend ?"
" No ! there is nought to be seen there but parsons, and
        syndics of commerce,
    Secretaries perchance, ensigns and majors of horse."
" But, my good friend, pray tell me, what can such people
        e'er meet with
    That can be truly call'd great ?—what that is great can
        they do ?"—
" What ? Why they form cabals, they lend upon mortgage,
        they pocket
    Silver spoons, and fear not e'en in the stocks to be
        placed."
" Whence do ye, then, derive the destiny, great and
        gigantic,
    Which raises man up on high, e'en when it grinds him
        to dust ?"—
" All mere nonsense ! Ourselves, our worthy acquaintances
        also,
    And our sorrows and wants, seek we and find we, too,
        here."
"But all this ye possess at home both apter and
        better,—
    Wherefore, then, fly from yourselves, if 'tis yourselves
        that ye seek ?"
" Be not offended, great hero, for *that* is a different
        question ;
    Ever is destiny blind,—ever is righteous the bard."

"Then one meets on your stage your own contemptible
　　nature,
　　While 'tis in vain one seeks there nature enduring and
　　　great?"
"There the poet is host, and act the fifth is the
　　reck'ning;
　　And, when crime becomes sick, virtue sits down to the
　　　feast!"

THE RIVERS.

RHINE.

True, as becometh a Switzer, I watch over Germany's
　　borders;
　　But the light-footed Gaul jumps o'er the suffering
　　stream.

RHINE AND MOSELLE.

Many a year have I clasp'd in my arms the Lorrainian
　　maiden;
　　But our union as yet ne'er has been blest with a son.

DANUBE IN ——

Round me are dwelling the falcon-ey'd race, the Phæacian
　　people;
　　Sunday with them never ends; ceaselessly moves round
　　the spit.

MAIN.

Ay, it is true that my castles are crumbling; yet, to my
　　comfort,
　　Have I for centuries past seen my old race still
　　endure.

SAALE.

Short is my course, during which I salute many princes
    and nations;
  Yet the princes are good—ay! and the nations are free.

ILM.

Poor are my banks, it is true; but yet my soft-flowing
    waters
  Many immortal lays hear, borne by the current along.

PLEISSE.

Flat is my shore and shallow my current; alas, all my
    writers,
  Both in prose and in verse, drink far too deep of its
    stream!

ELBE.

All ye others speak only a jargon; 'mongst Germany's
    rivers
  None speak German but me; I but in Misnia alone.

SPREE.

Ramler once gave me language,—my Cæsar a subject;
    and therefore
  I had my mouth then stuff'd full; but I've been silent
    since that.

WESER.

Nothing, alas, can be said about me; I really can't
    furnish
  Matter enough to the Muse e'en for an epigram small.

MINERAL WATERS AT ———.

Singular country! what excellent taste in its fountains
    and rivers!
In its people alone none have I ever yet found!

PEGNITZ.

I for a long time have been a hypochondriacal subject;
    I but flow on because it has my habit been long.

THE ——— RIVERS.

We would gladly remain in the lands that own ——— as
    their masters;
Soft their yoke ever is, and all their burdens are light.

SALZACH.

I, to salt the archbishopric, come from Juvavia's
    mountains;
Then to Bavaria turn, where they have great need
    of salt!

THE ANONYMOUS RIVER.

Lenten food for the pious bishop's table to furnish,
    By my Creator I'm pour'd over the famishing land.

LES FLEUVES INDISCRETS.

Pray be silent, ye rivers! One sees ye have no more
    discretion
Than, in a case we could name, Diderot's favourites had.

THE METAPHYSICIAN.

" How far beneath me seems the earthly ball !
   The pigmy race below I scarce can see ;
How does my art, the noblest art of all,
   Bear me close up to heaven's bright canopy !"
So cries the slater from his tower's high top,
   And so the little would-be-mighty man,
Hans Metaphysicus, from out his critic-shop.
   Explain, thou little would-be mighty man !
The tower from which thy looks the world survey,
Whereof,—whereon is it erected, pray ?
How didst thou mount it ?   Of what use to thee
Its naked heights, save o'er the vale to see ?

THE PHILOSOPHERS.

The principle by which each thing
   Tow'rd strength and shape first tended,—
The pulley whereon Zeus the ring
Of earth, that loosely us'd to swing,
   With cautiousness suspended,—
He is a clever man, I vow,
Who its real name can tell me now,
Unless to help him I consent—
'Tis : ten and twelve are different !

   Fire burns,—'tis chilly when it snows,
   Man always is two-footed,—
The sun across the heavens goes,—
This, he who nought of logic knows
   Finds to his reason suited.
Yet he who metaphysics learns,
Knows that nought freezes when it burns,—
Knows that what's wet is never dry,—
And that what's bright attracts the eye.

Old Homer sings his noble lays,
  The hero goes through dangers ;
The brave man duty's call obeys,
And did so, even in the days
  When sages yet were strangers—
But heart and genius now have taught
What Locke and what Descartes ne'er thought ;
By them immediately is shown
That which is possible alone.

In life, avails the right of force.
  The bold the timid worries ;
Who rules not, is a slave of course,
Without design each thing across
  Earth's stage for ever hurries.
Yet what would happen if the plan
Which guides the world now first began,
Within the moral system lies
Disclos'd with clearness to our eyes.

" When man would seek his destiny,
  Man's help must then be given ;
Save for the whole, ne'er labours he,—
Of many drops is form'd the sea,—
  By water mills are driven ;
Therefore the wolf's wild species flies,—
Knit are the state's enduring ties."
Thus Puffendorf and Feder, each
Is *ex cathedrâ* wont to teach.

Yet if what such professors say,
  Each brain to enter durst not,
Nature exerts her mother-sway,
Provides that ne'er the chain gives way,
  And that the ripe fruits burst not.
Meanwhile, until earth's structure vast
Philosophy can bind at last,
'Tis *she* that bids its pinion move,
By means of hunger and of love !

PEGASUS IN HARNESS.

ONCE to a horse-fair,—it may perhaps have been
Where other things are bought and sold,—I mean
At the Haymarket,—there the muses' horse
A hungry poet brought—to sell, of course.

The hippogriff neigh'd shrilly, loudly,
And rear'd upon his hind-legs proudly;
In utter wonderment each stood and cried:
"The noble regal beast!   But, woe betide!
Two hideous wings his slender form deface,
The finest team he else would not disgrace."—
"The breed," said they, "is doubtless rare,
But who would travel through the air?"—
Not one of them would risk his gold.
At length a farmer grew more bold:
"As for his wings, I of no use should find them,
But then how easy 'tis to clip or bind them!
The horse for drawing may be useful found,—
So, friend, I don't mind giving twenty pound!"
The other, glad to sell his merchandise,
Cried, "Done!"—And Hans rode off upon his prize.

The noble creature was, ere long, put-to,
    But scarcely felt the unaccustom'd load,
Than, panting to soar upwards, off he flew,
And, fill'd with honest anger, overthrew
    The cart where an abyss just met the road.
"Ho! ho!" thought Hans: "No cart to this mad
        beast
I'll trust.   Experience makes one wise at least.
To drive the coach to-morrow now my course is,
    And he as leader in the team shall go.
The lively fellow'll save me full two horses;
    As years pass on, he'll doubtless tamer grow."

All went on well at first.   The nimble steed
His partners rous'd,—like lightning was their speed.
What happen'd next?   Tow'rd heaven was turn'd his
      eye,—
Unus'd across the solid ground to fly,
He quitted soon the safe and beaten course,
And true to nature's strong resistless force,
Ran over bog and moor, o'er hedge, and pasture
      till'd ;
An equal madness soon the other horses fill'd,—
No reins could hold them in, no help was near,
Till,—only picture the poor travellers' fear !—
The coach, well shaken, and completely wreck'd,
Upon a hill's steep top at length was check'd.

"If this is always sure to be the case,"
Hans cried, and cut a very sorry face,
" He'll never do to draw a coach or waggon ;
Let's see if we can't tame the fiery dragon
By means of heavy work and little food."
And so the plan was tried.—But what ensued ?
The handsome beast, before three days had past,
Wasted to nothing.   " Stay ! I see at last ! "
Cried Hans.   " Be quick, you fellows ! yoke him now
With my most sturdy ox before the plough."

No sooner said than done.   In union queer
Together yok'd were soon wing'd horse and steer.
The griffin pranc'd with rage, and his remaining might
Exerted to resume his old-accustom'd flight.
'Twas all in vain—his partner stepp'd with circumspec-
      tion,
And Phœbus' haughty steed must follow *his* direction ;
Until at last, by long resistance spent,
   When strength his limbs no longer was controlling,
The noble creature, with affliction bent,
Fell to the ground, and in the dust lay rolling.

"Accursèd beast!" at length with fury mad
  Hans shouted, while he soundly plied the lash,—
"Even for ploughing, then, thou art too bad!—
  That fellow was a rogue to sell such trash!"

Ere yet his heavy blows had ceas'd to fly,
A brisk and merry youth by chance came by.
A lute was tinkling in his hand,
  And through his light and flowing hair
Was twin'd with grace a golden band.
  "Whither, my friend, with that strange pair?"
From far he to the peasant cried.
"A bird and ox to *one* rope tied—
Was such a team e'er heard of, pray?
Thy horse's worth I'd fain essay;
Just for one moment lend him me,—
Observe, and thou shalt wonders see!"

The hippogriff was loosen'd from the plough,
Upon his back the smiling youth leap'd now;
No sooner did the creature understand
That he was guided by a master-hand,
Than 'gainst his bit he champ'd, and upward soar'd,
While lightning from his flaming eyes outpour'd.
No longer the same being, royally
A spirit, ay, a god, ascended he,
Spread in a moment to the stormy wind
His noble wings, and left the earth behind,
And, ere the eye could follow him,
Had vanish'd in the heavens dim.

———

THE PUPPET-SHOW OF LIFE.

Thou'rt welcome in my box to peep!
Life's puppet-show, the world in little,
Thou'lt see depicted to a tittle,—
  But pray at some small distance keep!

'Tis by the torch of love alone,
By Cupid's taper, it is shown.

See, not a moment void the stage is!
   The child in arms at first they bring,—
The boy then skips,—the youth now storms and
     rages,—
   The man contends, and ventures everything!

   Each one attempts success to find,
Yet narrow is the race-course ever;
The chariot rolls, the axles quiver,
   The hero presses on, the coward stays behind,
The proud man falls with mirth-inspiring fall,
The wise man overtakes them all!

Thou seest fair woman at the barrier stand,
With beauteous hands, with smiling eyes,
To glad the victor with his prize.

TO A YOUNG FRIEND,

ON HIS DEVOTING HIMSELF TO PHILOSOPHY.

MANY an arduous trial the Grecian youth had to suffer
   Ere th' Eleusinian house welcom'd him under its roof.
Art thou ripe and prepar'd, the holy temple to enter,
   Where her mysterious lore Pallas Athene pre-
     serves?
Know'st thou what there 'tis awaits thee? How dear thy
   purchase may cost thee?
   That with a gift that is sure, one that is *not*, thou must
     buy?

Feelest thou strength enough to fight that sternest of
   conflicts
  Where the reason and heart, mind and the thought
    disagree?.
Courage enough with doubt's undying hydra to
   wrestle,
  And to contend like a man 'gainst the dread foe in
    thyself?
With an eye that is sound, with a heart of innocence
   sacred,
  Then to unmask the deceit veil'd in the garments of
    truth?
Fly, if thou canst not depend on the guide within thine
   own bosom,
  Fly from the treacherous brink, ere thou art chok'd in
    the gulf!
Many have sought for light, and only plung'd into
   darkness;
  'Tis but in twilight alone infancy wanders secure!

THE POETRY OF LIFE.

" Oh, who would feed on dreams for ever fleeing,
That with a borrow'd lustre clothe the being,
Deceiving hope with a possession vain?
The truth uncover'd I would see remain.
Though with my dream should vanish all my heaven,
Though the free spirit to whose wings 'twas given
To scale the Possible's unbounded realm,
The present with strong chains should overwhelm :
'Twould teach itself then to obey;
  'Twould find, then, duty's sacred call,
  And that of need, most stern of all,
The more subservient to its sway.
He who would 'scape the gentle rule of truth,
Can he endure necessity forsooth?"

My rigid friend, thus dost thou cry and see
  From 'neath experience's safe portal,
Looking with scorn on what but *seems* to be.
  Soon flies the loving band immortal,
Stricken with terror by thy solemn word;—
The dancing hours stand still, no muse's strains are
      heard,—
The sister-deities, with beauteous hair,
Take up their garlands now in mute despair,—
Apollo breaks his lyre of gold,
  His wondrous staff breaks Hermes too,
While from life's features wan and cold
  Falls the dream's veil of rosy hue.
The world a tomb is,—Venus' son
  The magic band tears from his eyes,—
His mother in the godlike one
  Sees now the mortal,—trembles, flies.
Age steals on beauty's youthful form,
Upon thy lips no more is warm
The kiss of love,—and ere thy joy has pass'd,
Into a lifeless stone thou'rt changed at last.

TO GOETHE,

ON HIS PRODUCING VOLTAIRE'S 'MAHOMET' ON THE
STAGE.

THOU, by whom, freed from rules constrain'd and
      wrong,
  On truth and nature once again we're plac'd,—
Who, in the cradle e'en a hero strong,
  Stiflest the serpents round our genius lac'd,—
Thou whom the godlike science has so long
  With her unsullied sacred fillet grac'd,—
Dost thou on ruin'd altars sacrifice
To that false muse whom we no longer prize?

This theatre belongs to native art,
   No foreign idols worshipp'd here are seen ;
A laurel we can show, with joyous. heart,
   That on the German Pindus has grown green :
The sciences' most holy, hidden part
   The German genius dares to enter e'en,
And, following the Briton and the Greek,
A nobler glory now attempts to seek.

For *yonder*, where slaves kneel, and despots hold
   The reins,—where spurious greatness lifts its head,
Art has no power the noble there to mould,
   'Tis by no Louis that its seed is spread ;
From its own fulness it must needs unfold,
   By earthly majesty 'tis never fed ;
'Tis with truth only it can e'er unite,
Its glow free spirits only e'er can light.

'Tis not to bind us in a worn-out chain
   Thou dost this play of olden time recall,—
'Tis not to seek to lead us back again
   To days when thoughtless childhood rul'd o'er all.
It were, in truth, an idle risk and vain
   Into the moving wheel of time to fall ;
The wingèd hours for ever bear it on,
The new arrives, and, lo ! the old has gone.

The narrow theatre is now more wide,
   Into its space a universe now steals ;
In pompous words no longer is our pride,
   Nature we love when she her form reveals ;
Fashion's false rules no more are deified ;
   And as a man the hero acts and feels.
'Tis passion makes the notes of freedom sound,
And 'tis in truth the beautiful is found.

Weak is the frame of Thespis' chariot fair,
   Resembling much the bark of Acheron,
That carries nought but shades and forms of air ;
   And if rude life should venture to press on,
The fragile bark its weight no more can bear,
   For fleeting spirits it can hold alone.
Appearance ne'er can reach reality,—
If nature be victorious, art must fly.

For on the stage's boarded scaffold here
   A world ideal opens to our eyes,
Nothing is true and genuine save—a tear ;
   Emotion on no dream of sense relics.
The real Melpomene is still sincere,
   Nought as a fable merely she supplies—
By truth profound to charm us is her care ;
The false one, truth pretends, but to ensnare.

Now from the scene, Art threatens to retire,
   Her kingdom wild maintains still Phantasy ;
The stage she like the world would set on fire,
   The meanest and the noblest mingles she.
The Frank alone 'tis Art can now inspire,
   And yet her archetype can his ne'er be ;
In bounds unchangeable confining her,
He holds her fast, and vainly would she stir.

The stage to him is pure and undefil'd ;
   Chas'd from the regions that to her belong
Are Nature's tones, so careless and so wild,
   To him e'en language rises into song ;
A realm harmonious 'tis, of beauty mild,
   Where limb unites to limb in order strong.
The whole into a solemn temple blends,
And 'tis the dance that grace to motion lends.

x

And yet the Frank must not be made our guide,
　　For in his art no living spirit reigns;
The boasting gestures of a spurious pride
　　That mind which only loves the true disdains.
To nobler ends alone be it applied,
　　Returning, like some soul's long-vanish'd manes,
To render the oft-sullied stage once more
A throne befitting the great muse of yore.

NUPTIAL ODE.*

Fair bride, attended by our blessing,
Glad Hymen's flowery path 'gin pressing!
　　We witness'd with enraptur'd eye
The graces of thy soul unfolding,
Thy youthful charms their beauty moulding
　　To blossom for love's ecstasy.
A happy fate now hovers round thee,
　　And friendship yields without a smart
To that sweet god whose might hath bound thee;—
　　He needs must have, he *hath* thy heart!

To duties dear, to troubles tender,
Thy youthful breast must now surrender,
　　Thy garland's summons must obey.
Each toying infantine sensation,
Each fleeting sport of youth's creation,
　　For evermore hath pass'd away;
And Hymen's sacred bond now chaineth
　　Where soft and flutt'ring Love was shrin'd;
Yet for a heart, where beauty reigneth,
　　Of flowers alone that bond is twin'd.

　* Addressed in the original to Mdlle. Slevoigt, on her marriage
to Dr. Sturm.

The secret that can keep for ever
In verdant links, that nought can sever,
   The bridal garland, wouldst thou find?
'Tis purity the heart pervading,
The blossoms of a grace unfading,
   And yet with modest shame combin'd,
Which, like the sun's reflection glowing,
Makes every heart throb blissfully;—
'Tis looks with mildness overflowing,
   And self-maintaining dignity!

GRECIAN GENIUS.

TO MEYER IN ITALY.

SPEECHLESS to thousands of others, who with deaf hearts
    would consult him,
Talketh the spirit to thee, who art his kinsman and
    friend.

VERSES WRITTEN IN THE ALBUM OF A FRIEND.

(HERR VON MECHELN OF BASLE.)

NATURE in charms is exhaustless, in beauty ever
    reviving;
And, like nature, fair art is inexhaustible too.
Hail, thou honour'd old man! for *both* in thy heart thou
    preservest
Living sensations, and thus ne'er ending youth is thy
    lot!

VERSES WRITTEN IN THE FOLIO ALBUM OF
A LEARNED FRIEND.

Once wisdom dwelt in tomes of ponderous size,
  While friendship from a pocket-book would talk;
But now that knowledge in small compass lies,
  And floats in almanacs, as light as cork,
Courageous man, thou dost not hesitate
To open for thy friends this house so great!
Hast thou no fear, I seriously would ask,
That thou may'st thus their patience overtask?

THE PRESENT.

Ring and staff, oh to me on a Rhenish flask ye are
    welcome!
  Him a true shepherd I call, who thus gives drink to
    his sheep.
Draught thrice blest! It is by the Muse I have won
    thee,—the Muse, too,
  Sends thee,—and even the Church places upon thee her
    seal.

WILLIAM TELL.*

When hostile elements with rage resound,
  And fury blindly fans war's lurid flame,—
When in the strife of party quarrel drown'd,
  The voice of justice no regard can claim,—
When crime is free, and impious hands are found
  The sacred to pollute, devoid of shame,
And loose the anchor which the State maintains,—
No subject *there* we find for joyous strains.

* These verses were sent by Schiller to the then Electoral High
Chancellor, with a copy of his 'William Tell.'

But when a nation, that its flocks still feeds
  With calm content, nor other's wealth desires,
Throws off the cruel yoke 'neath which it bleeds,
  Yet, e'en in wrath, humanity admires,—
And, e'en in triumph, moderation heeds,—
  That is immortal, and our song requires.
To show thee such an image now is mine;
Thou know'st it well, for all that's great is thine!

TO THE HEREDITARY PRINCE OF WEIMAR,
ON HIS PROCEEDING TO PARIS.

(SUNG IN A CIRCLE OF FRIENDS.)

WITH one last bumper let us hail
  The wanderer belov'd,
Who takes his leave of this still vale
  Wherein in youth he rov'd.

From loving arms, from native home,
  He tears himself away,
To yonder city proud to roam,
  That makes whole lands its prey.

Dissension flies, all tempests end,
  And chain'd is strife abhorr'd;
We in the crater may descend
  From whence the lava pour'd.

A gracious fate conduct thee through
  Life's wild and mazy track!
A bosom nature gave thee true,—
  A bosom true bring back!

Thou'lt visit lands that war's wild train
　　Had crush'd with careless heed ;
Now smiling Peace salutes the plain,
　　And strews the golden seed.

The hoary Father Rhine thou'lt greet,
　　Who thy forefather* blest
Will think of, whilst his waters fleet
　　In ocean's bed to rest.

Do homage to the hero's manes,
　　And offer to the Rhine,
The German frontier who maintains,
　　His own-created wine,—

So that thy country's soul thy guide
　　May be, when thou hast cross'd
On the frail bark to yonder side,
　　Where German faith is lost !

THE COMMENCEMENT OF THE NEW CENTURY.

TO ——

WHERE will a place of refuge, noble friend,
　　For peace and freedom ever open lie !
The century in tempests had its end,
　　The new one now begins with murder's cry.

Each land-connecting bond is torn away,
　　Each ancient custom hastens to decline ;
Not e'en the ocean can war's tumult stay.
　　Not e'en the Nile-god, not the hoary Rhine.

* Duke Bernard of Weimar, one of the heroes of the Thirty
Years' War.

Two mighty nations strive, with hostile power,
    For undivided mastery of the world;
And, by them, each land's freedom to devour,
    The trident brandish'd is—the lightning hurl'd.

Each country must to them its gold afford,
    And, Brennus-like, upon the fatal day,
The Frank now throws his heavy iron sword,
    The even scales of justice to o'erweigh.

His merchant-fleets the Briton greedily
    Extends, like Polyp-limbs, on ev'ry side;
And the domain of Amphitrité free
    As if his home it were, would fain bestride.

E'en to the south pole's dim, remotest star,
    His restless course moves onward, unrestrain'd;
Each isle he tracks,—each coast, however far,
    But Paradise alone he ne'er has gain'd!

Although thine eye may ev'ry map explore,
    Vainly thou'lt seek to find that blissful place,
Where freedom's garden smiles for evermore,
    And where in youth still blooms the human race.

Before thy gaze the world extended lies,
    The very shipping it can scarce embrace;
And yet upon her back, of boundless size,
    E'en for ten happy men there is not space!

Into thy bosom's holy, silent cells,
    Thou needs must fly from life's tumultuous throng!
Freedom but in the realm of vision dwells,
    And beauty bears no blossoms but in song.

FAREWELL TO THE READER.

A MAIDEN blush o'er ev'ry feature straying,
  The Muse her gentle harp now lays down here,
And stands before thee, for thy judgment praying,—
  She waits with reverence, but not with fear;
Her last farewell for *his* kind smile delaying.
  Whom splendour dazzles not, who holds truth dear.
The hand of him alone whose soaring spirit
Worships the Beautiful, can crown her merit.

These simple lays are only heard resounding,
  While feeling hearts are gladden'd by their tone,
With brighter phantasies their path surrounding,
  To nobler aims their footsteps guiding on.
Yet coming ages ne'er will hear them sounding,
  They live but for the present hour alone;
The passing moment call'd them into being,
And, as the hours dance on, they, too, are fleeing.

The spring returns, and nature then awaking,
  Bursts into life across the smiling plain;
Each shrub its perfume through the air is shaking,
  And heaven is fill'd with one sweet choral strain;
While young and old, their secret haunts forsaking,
  With raptur'd eye and ear rejoice again.
The spring then flies,—to seed return the flowers,
And nought remains to mark the vanish'd hours.

SUPPRESSED POEMS.

MOST high and mighty Czar of all flesh, ceaseless reducer of empires, unfathomable glutton in the whole realms of nature.

With the most profound flesh-creeping I take the liberty of kissing the rattling leg-bones of your voracious Majesty, and humbly laying this little book at your dried-up feet. My predecessors have always been accustomed, as if on purpose to annoy you, to transport their goods and chattels to the archives of eternity, directly under your nose, forgetting that, by so doing, they only made your mouth water the more, for the proverb: *Stolen bread tastes sweetest*, is applicable even to you. No! I prefer to dedicate this work to you, feeling assured that you will—throw it aside.

But, joking apart! methinks we two know each other better than by mere hearsay. Enrolled in the order of Æsculapius, the first-born of Pandora's box, as old as the fall of man, I have stood at your altar,—have sworn undying hatred to your hereditary foe Nature, as the son of Hamilcar to the seven hills of Rome,—have sworn to besiege her with a whole army of medicines,—to throw up barricades round the obstinate soul,—to drive from the field the insolents who cut down your fees and cripple your finances,—and on the Archæan battle-plain to plant your midnight standard.—In return (for one good turn deserves another), you must prepare for me the precious TALISMAN, which can save me from the gallows and the wheel uninjured, and with a whole skin—

Jusque datum sceleri.

Come then! act the generous Mæcenas; for observe, I should be sorry to fare like my foolhardy colleagues and cousins, who, armed with stiletto and pocket-pistol, hold their court in gloomy ravines, or mix in the subterranean laboratory the wondrous polychrest, which, when taken with proper zeal, tickles our political noses, either too little or too much, with throne vacancies or state-fevers.— D'Amiens and Ravaillac!—Ho, ho, ho!—'Tis a good thing for straight limbs!

Perhaps you have been whetting your teeth at Easter and Michaelmas?—the great book-epidemic times at Leipzig and Frankfort! Hurrah for the waste-paper!— 'twill make a royal feast. Your nimble brokers, Gluttony and Lust, bring you whole cargoes from the fair of life.— Even Ambition, your grandpapa—War, Famine, Fire, and Plague, your mighty huntsmen, have provided you with many a jovial man-chase.—Avarice and Covetous-ness, your sturdy butlers, drink to your health whole towns floating in the bubbling cup of the world-ocean.—I know a kitchen in Europe where the rarest dishes have been served up in your honour with festive pomp.—And yet—who has ever known you to be satisfied, or to com-plain of indigestion?—Your digestive faculties are of iron; your entrails fathomless!

Pooh—I had many other things to say to you, but I am in a hurry to be off.—You are an ugly brother-in-law —go!—I hear you are calculating on living to see a general collation, where great and small, globes and lexicons, philosophies and knick-knacks, will fly into your jaws—a good appetite to you, should it come to that.—Yet, ravenous wolf that you are! take care that you don't over-eat yourself, and have to disgorge to a hair all that you have swallowed, as a certain Athenian (no particular friend of yours, by-the-bye) has prophesied.

PREFACE.

Tobolsko, the 2nd February.

Tum primum radiis gelidi incaluere Triones.

FLOWERS in Siberia? —— Behind this lies a piece of knavery, or the sun must make face against midnight.— And yet—if ye were to exert yourselves! 'Tis really so; we have been hunting sables long enough; let us for once in a way try our luck with flowers. Have not enough Europeans come to us step-sons of the sun, and waded through our hundred-years' snow, to pluck a modest flower? Shame upon our ancestors—we'll gather them ourselves, and frank a whole basketful to Europe.— Do not crush them, ye children of a milder heaven!

But to be serious.—To remove the iron weight of prejudice that broods heavily over the north, requires a stronger lever than the enthusiasm of a few individuals, and a firmer Hypomochlion than the shoulders of two or three patriots. Yet if this Anthology reconciles you squeamish Europeans to us snow-men as little as—let's suppose the case—our 'Muses' Almanac,' * which we— let's again suppose the case—might have written, it will at least have the merit of helping its companions through

---

* This was the title of the publication in which many of the finest of Schiller's 'Poems of the Third Period' originally appeared.

the whole of Germany to give the last neck-stab to expiring taste, as we people of Tobolsko like to word it.

If your Homers talk in their sleep, and your Herculeses kill flies with their clubs,—if every one who knows how to give vent to his portion of sorrow in dreary Alexandrines, interprets that as a call to Helicon, shall we Northerns be blamed for tinkling the Muses' lyre?—Your matadors claim to have coined silver, when they have stamped their effigy on wretched pewter;—and at Tobolsko, coiners are hanged. 'Tis true that you may often find paper-money amongst us instead of Russian roubles, but war and hard times are an excuse for anything.

Go forth, then, Siberian Anthology!—Go!—thou wilt make many a coxcomb happy, wilt be placed by him on the toilet-table of his sweetheart, and in reward wilt obtain her alabaster, lily-white hand for his tender kiss.—Go!—thou wilt fill up many a weary gulf of *ennui* in assemblies and city-visits, and, may be, relieve a *Circassienne*, who has confessed herself weary amidst a shower of calumnies.—Go!—thou wilt be consulted in the kitchens of many critics; they will fly thy light, and, like the screech-owl, retreat into thy shadow.—Ho, ho, ho!—Already I hear the ear-cracking howls in the inhospitable forest, and anxiously conceal myself in my sable.

THE JOURNALISTS AND MINOS.

I CHANCED the other eve,—
    But *how* I ne'er will tell,—
The paper to receive
    That's publish'd down in hell.

In general, one may guess,
    I little care to see
This free-corps of the press
    Got up so easily;

But suddenly my eyes
    A side-note chanced to meet,
And fancy my surprise
    At reading in the sheet :—

" For twenty weary springs "—
    (The post from Erebus,
Remark me, always brings
    Unpleasant news to us)—

" Through want of water, we
    Have well-nigh lost our breath;
In great perplexity
    Hell came and ask'd for Death :

" ' They can wade through the Styx,
    Catch crabs in Lethe's flood;
Old Charon's in a fix,
    His boat lies in the mud.

" ' The dead leap over there,
    The young and old as well;
The boatman gets no fare,
    And loudly curses Hell.'

"King Minos bade his spies
    In all directions go;
The devils needs must rise,
    And bring him news below.

"Hurrah! The secret's told!
    They've caught the robber's nest!
A merry feast let's hold!
    Come, Hell, and join the rest!

"An authors' countless band,
    Stalk'd round Cocytus' brink,
Each bearing in his hand
    A glass for holding ink.

"And into casks they drew
    The water, strange to say,
As boys suck sweet wine through
    An elder-reed in play.

"Quick! o'er them cast the net,
    Ere they have time to flee!
Warm welcome ye will get,
    So come to Sans-souci!

"Smelt by the king ere long,
    He sharpen'd up his tooth,
And thus address'd the throng
    (Full angrily, in truth):

"'The robbers is't we see?
    What trade? What land, perchance?'—
'GERMAN NEWS-WRITERS WE!'—
    'Enough to make us dance!

"'A wish I long have known
    To bid ye stop and dine,
Ere ye by Death were mown,
    That brother-in-law of mine.

"'Yet now by Styx I swear,
    Whose flood ye would imbibe,
That torments and despair
    Shall fill your vermin-tribe!

"'The pitcher seeks the well,
    Till broken 'tis one day;
They who for ink would smell,
    The penalty must pay.

"'So seize them by their thumbs,
    And loosen straight my beast
E'en now he licks his gums,
    Impatient for the feast.'—

"How quiver'd ev'ry limb
    Beneath the bull-dog's jaws!
Their honours baited him,
    And he allow'd no pause.

"Convulsively they swear,
    Still writhe the rabble rout,
Engaged with anxious care
    In pumping Lethe out."

Ye Christians, good and meek,
    This vision bear in mind;
If journalists ye seek,
    Attempt their thumbs to find.

Defects they often hide,
    As folks whose hairs are gone
We see with wigs supplied:
    Probatum!   I have done!

BACCHUS IN THE PILLORY.

Twirl him! twirl him! blind and dumb,
    Deaf and dumb,
  Twirl the carle so troublesome!
Sprigs of fashion by the dozen
Thou dost bring to book, good cousin.
  Cousin, thou art not in clover;
Many a head that's fill'd with smoke
Thou hast twirl'd and well-nigh broke,
Many a clever one perplex'd,
Many a stomach sorely vex'd,
  Turning it completely over;
Many a hat put on awry,
Many a lamb chas'd cruelly,
Made streets, houses, edges, trees,
Dance around us fools with ease.
  Therefore thou art not in clover,
Therefore thou, like other folk,
Hast thy head fill'd full of smoke,
Therefore thou, too, art perplex'd,
And thy stomach's sorely vex'd,
  For 'tis turn'd completely over;
  Therefore thou art not in clover.

Twirl him! twirl him! blind and dumb,
    Deaf and dumb,
  Twirl the carle so troublesome!
Seest thou how our tongues and wits
Thou hast shiver'd into bits—
  Seest thou this, licentious wight?
How we're fasten'd to a string,
Whirl'd around in giddy ring,
Making all like night appear,
Filling with strange sounds our ear?
  Learn it in the stocks aright!

When our ears wild noises shook,
On the sky we cast no look,
Neither stock nor stone review'd,
But were punish'd as we stood.
   Seest thou now, licentious wight?
That, to us, yon flaring sun
Is the Heidelbergers' tun;
Castles, mountains, trees and towers,
Seem like chopin-cups of ours.
   Learn'st thou now, licentious wight?
   Learn it in the stocks aright!

Twirl him! twirl him! blind and dumb,
   Deaf and dumb,
   Twirl the carle so troublesome!
Kinsman, once so full of glee,
Kinsman, where's thy drollery,
   Where thy tricks, thou cunning one?
All thy tricks are spent and past,
To the devil gone at last!
Like a silly fop thou'lt prate,
Like a washerwoman rate.
   Thou art but a simpleton.
Now thou may'st—more shame to thee —
Run away, because of me;
Cupid, that young rogue, may glory,
Learning wisdom from thy story.
   Haste, thou sluggard, hence to flee!
As from glass is cut our wit,
So, like lightning, 'twill be split;
If thou won't be chas'd away,
Let each folly also stay!
   Seest my meaning?   Think of me!
   Idle one, away with thee!

SPINOSA.

A MIGHTY oak here ruin'd lies,
Its top was wont to kiss the skies,
 Why is it now o'erthrown?—
The peasants needed, so they said,
Its wood, wherewith to build a shed,
 And so they've cut it down.

EPITAPH.

HERE lies a man cut off by Fate
 Too soon for all good men;
For sextons he died late—too late
 For those who wield the pen.

TO THE FATES.

NOT in the crowd of masqueraders gay,
 Where coxcombs' wit with wondrous splendour
  flares,
And, easier than the Indian's net the prey,
 The virtue of young beauties snares;—

Not at the toilet-table of the fair,
 Where vanity, as if before an idol, bows,
And often breathes a warmer prayer
 Than when to Heaven it pays its vows;

And not behind the curtain's cunning veil,
 Where the world's eye is hid by cheating night,
And glowing flames the hearts assail,
 That seem'd but chilly in the light,—

Where wisdom we surprise with shame-dyed lip,
  While Phœbus' rays she boldly drinks,
Where men, like thievish children, nectar sip,
  And from the spheres e'en Plato sinks—

To ye—to ye, O lonely sister-band,
  Daughters of Destiny, ascend,
When o'er the lyre all-gently sweeps my hand,
  These strains, where bliss and sadness blend.

You only has no sonnet ever woo'd,
  To win *your* gold no usurer e'er sigh'd,
No coxcomb e'er with plaints *your* steps pursued,
  For *you*, Arcadian shepherd ne'er has died.

Your gentle fingers ye for ever ply,
  Life's nervous thread with care to twist,
Till sound the clanging shears, and fruitlessly
  The tender web would then resist.

Since thou my thread of life hast kindly spun,
  Thy hand, O Clotho, I now kiss!
Since thou hast spar'd that life, whilst scarce begun,
  Receive this nosegay, Lachesis!

Full often thorns upon the thread,
  But oft'ner roses, thou hast strung;
For thorns and roses there outspread,
  Clotho, to thee this lay be sung!

Oft did tempestuous passions rise,
  And threat to break the thread by force;
Oft projects of gigantic size
  Have check'd its free, unfetter'd course.

Oft, in sweet hours of heav'nly bliss,
  Too fine appear'd the thread to me;
Still oft'ner, when near sorrow's dark abyss,
  Too firm its fabric seem'd to be.

Clotho, for this and other lies,
   Thy pardon I with tears implore;
Henceforth I'll take whatever prize
   Sage Clotho gives, and asks no more.

But never let the shears cut off a rose—
   Only the thorns,—yet as thou will'st!
Let, if thou will'st, the death-shears, sharply close,
   If thou this single prayer fulfill'st!

Oh, goddess! when, enchain'd to Laura's breath,
   My spirit from its shell breaks free,
Betraying when, upon the gates of death,
   My youthful life hangs giddily,

Let to infinity the thread extend,
   'Twill wander through the realms of bliss,—
Then, goddess, let thy cruel shears descend!
   Then let them fall, O Lachesis!

KLOPSTOCK AND WIELAND.

(WHEN THEIR MINIATURES WERE HANGING SIDE BY SIDE.)

In truth, when I have cross'd dark Lethe's river,
The man upon the right I'll love for ever,
   For 'twas *he* first that wrote for me.
For all the world the left man wrote, full clearly,
And so we all should love him dearly;
   Come, left man! I must needs kiss thee!

DIALOGUE.

A. HARK, neighbour, for one moment stay !—
   Herr Doctor Scalpel, so they say,
     Has got off safe and sound;
     At Paris I your uncle found
     Fast to a horse's crupper bound,—
   Yet Scalpel made a king his prey.
B. Oh, dear me, no!   A real misnomer!
   The fact is, *he* has his diploma;
     The other one has *not*.
A. Eh!   What?   Has a diploma?
     In Suabia may such things be got?

THE PARALLEL.

HER likeness Madame Ramler bids me find ;
   I try to think in vain, to *whom* or *how ;*
Beneath the moon there's nothing of the kind.—
   I'll show she's like the moon, I vow!

The moon—she rouges, steals the sun's bright light,
   By eating stolen bread her living gets,—
Is also wont to paint her cheeks at night,
   While, with untiring ardour, she coquets.

The moon—for this may Herod give her thanks !—
   Reserves her best till night may have return'd ;
Our lady swallows up by day the francs
   That she at night-time may have earn'd.

The moon first swells, and then is once more lean,
   As surely as the month comes round ;
With Madame Ramler 'tis the same, I ween—
   But *she* to need more time is found !

The moon to love her silver-horns is said,
　But makes a sorry show;
She likes them on her husband's head,—
　She's right to have it so!

THE MUSES' REVENGE.

AN ANECDOTE OF HELICON.

Once the Nine all weeping came
　To the God of Song:
"Oh, papa!" they there exclaim—
　"Hear our tale of wrong!

"Young ink-lickers swarm about
　Our dear Helicon;
There they fight, manœuvre, shout,
　Even to thy throne.

"On their steeds they gallop hard
　To the spring to drink,
Each one calls himself a bard—
　Minstrels—only think!

"There they—how the thing to name?
　Would our persons treat—
This, without a blush of shame,
　We can ne'er repeat;

"One, in front of all, then cries:
　'I the army lead!'
Both his fists he wildly plies,
　Like a bear indeed!

" Others wakes he in a trice
    With his whistlings rude;
But none follow, though he twice
    Has those sounds renew'd.

" He'll return, he threats, ere long,
    And he'll come no doubt!
Father, friend to lyric song,
    Please to show him out!—"

Father Phœbus laughing hears
    The complaint they've brought;
" Don't be frighten'd, pray, my dears,
    We'll soon cut them short!

" One must hasten to hell-fire,
    Go, Melpomene!
Let a Fury borrow lyre,
    Notes, and dress, of thee.

" Let her meet, in this array,
    One of these vile crews,
As though she had lost her way,
    Soon as night ensues.

" Then with kisses dark, I trust,
    They'll the dear child greet,
Satisfying their wild lust
    Just as it is meet!"—

Said and done!—The one from hell
    Soon was dress'd aright.
Scarcely had the prey, they tell,
    Caught the fellows' sight,

Than, as kites a pigeon follow,
    They attack'd her straight—
Part, not *all*, though, I can swallow
    Of what folks relate.

If fair boys were 'mongst the band,
  How came they to be—
This I cannot understand,—
  In such company ?

*   *   *   *

The goddess a miscarriage had, good lack !
And was deliver'd of an—Almanack !

EPITAPH

ON A CERTAIN PHYSIOGNOMIST.

ON ev'ry nose he rightly read
What intellects were in the head :
  And yet—that he was not the one
  By whom God meant it to be done,
This on his *own* he never read.

THE HYPOCHONDRIACAL PLUTO.

A ROMANCE.

BOOK I.

THE sullen mayor who reigns in hell,
  By mortals Pluto hight,
Who thrashes all his subjects well,
Both morn and eve, as stories tell,
  And rules the realms of night,
All pleasure lost in cursing once,
All joy in flogging, for the nonce.

The sedentary life he led
  Upon his brazen chair
Made his hind-quarters very red,
While pricks, as from a nettle-bed,
  He felt both here and there :
A burning sun, too, chanc'd to shine,
And boil'd down all his blood to brine.

'Tis true he drank full many a draught
  Of Phlegethon's black flood;
By cupping, leeches, doctors' craft,
And venesection, fore and aft,
  They took from him much blood.
Full many a clyster was applied,
And purging, too, was also tried.

His doctor, vers'd in sciences,
  With wig beneath his hat,
Argued and show'd with wondrous ease,
From Celsus and Hippocrates,
  When he in judgment sat,—
"Right worshipful the mayor of hell,
The liver's wrong, I see full well."—

"He's but a booby," Pluto said,
  "With all his trash and pills!
A man like me—pray where's his head?
A young man yet—his wits have fled!
  While youth my veins yet fills!
Unless electuaries he'll bring,
Full in his face my club I'll fling!"

Or right or wrong,—'twas a hard case
  To weather such a trial;
(Poor men, who lose a king's good grace!)
He's straight saluted in the face
  By ev'ry splint and phial.—
He very wisely made no fuss;
This hint he learnt of Cerberus.

"Go! fetch the barber of the skies,
  Apollo, to me soon!"
An airy courier straightway flies
Upon his beast, and onward hies,
  And skims past poles and moon;
As he went off, the clock struck four,
At five his charger reached the door.

Just then Apollo happen'd—"Heigh-ho!
　　A sonnet to have made?"
Oh, dear me, no!—upon Miss Io
(Such is the tale I heard from Clio)
　　The midwife to have play'd.
The boy, as if stamp'd out of wax,
Might Zeus as father fairly tax.

He read the letter half asleep,
　　Then started in dismay:
"The road is long, and hell is deep,
Your rocks I know are rough and steep . . .
　　Yet like a king he'll pay!"
He dons his cap of mist and furs,
Then through the air the charger spurs.

With locks all frizzled *à la mode*,
　　And ruffles smooth and nice,
In gala dress, that brightly glow'd
(A gift Aurora had bestow'd),
　　With watch-chains of high price,
With toes turn'd out, and *chapeau bas*,—
He stood before hell's mighty czar.

BOOK II.

The grumbler, in his usual tone,
　　Receiv'd him with a curse:
"To Pomerania straight begone!
Ugh! how he smells of eau de Cologne!
　　Why, brimstone isn't worse.
He'd best be off to heaven again,
Or he'll infect hell's wide domain."

The god of pills, in sore surprise,
　　A spring then backwards took . . .
"Is this his highness' usual guise?
'Tis in the brain, I see, that lies
　　The mischief—what a look!

See how his eyes in frenzy roll!
The case is bad, upon my soul!

" A journey to Elysium
    Th' infectus would dissolve,
Making the saps less tough become,
As through the capitolium
    And stomach they revolve.
Provisionally be it so :
    Let's start, then—but incognito !"—

" Ay, worthy sir, No doubt well meant!
    If, in these regions hazy,
As with you folk, so charg'd with scent,
You dapper ones, who heaven frequent,
    'Twere proper to be lazy,
If hell a master needed not,
Why, then I'd follow on the spot!

" Ha! if the cat once turn'd her back,
    Pray where would be the mice ?
They'd sally forth from ev'ry crack,
My very mufti would attack,
    Spoil all things in a trice!
Oddsbodikins ! 'tis pretty cool !
I'll let him see I'm no such fool !

" A pleasant uproar happen'd erst,
    When they assail'd my tower !
No fault of mine 'twas, at the worst,
That from their desks and chains to burst
    Philosophers had power.
What, has there e'er escaped a poet ?
Help, heaven ! what misery to know it !

" When days are long, folks talk more stuff!
    Upon your seats, no doubt,
With all your cards and music rough,
And scribblings too, 'tis hard enough
    The moments to eke out.

Idleness, like a flea, will gnaw
On velvet cushions,—as on straw.

"My brother no attempt omits
   To drive away ennui;
His lightning round about him flits,
The target with his storms he hits
   (Those howls prove *that* to me),
Till Rhea's trembling shoulders ache,
And force me e'en for hell to quake.

"Were I grandfather Cœlus, though,
   You wouldn't soon escape!
Into my belly straight you'd go,
And in your swaddling-clothes cry 'oh!'
   And through five windows gape!
First o'er my stream you'd have to come.
And then, perhaps, to Elysium!—

"Your steed you mounted, I dare say,
   In hopes to catch a goose;
If it is worth the trouble, pray
Tell what you've heard from me to-day,
   At shaving-time, to Zeus.
Just leave him, then, to swallow it;
I don't care what he thinks, a bit!

"You'd better now go homeward straight!
   Your servant! there's the door!
For all your pains—one moment wait!
I'll give you—liberal is the rate—
   A piece of ruby-ore.
In heaven such things are rarities;
   We use them for base purposes."—

BOOK III.

The god at once, then, said farewell,
  At small politeness striving;
When, sudden through the crowds of hell
A flying courier rush'd pell-mell,
  From Tellus' bounds arriving.
" Monarch ! a doctor follows me !
Behold this wondrous prodigy !"

" Place for the doctor !" each one said—
  He comes with spurs and whip,
To ev'ry one he nods his head,
As if he had been born and bred
  In Tartarus,—the rip !
As jaunty, fearless, full of νοῦς
As Britons in the Lower House.

" Good morrow, worthy sirs !—Ahem !
  I'm glad to see that here
(Where all they of Prometheus' stem
Must come, whene'er the Fates condemn)
  One meets with such good cheer !
Why for Elysium care a rush ?
I'd rather see hell's fountains gush !"—

" Stop ! stop ! his impudence, I vow,
  Its due reward shall meet ;
By Charles's Wain, I swear it now !
He must—no questions I'll allow,—
  Prescribe me a receipt.
All hell is mine, I'm Pluto hight !
Make haste to bring your wares to light !"

The doctor, with a knowing look,
  The swarthy king survey'd ;
He neither felt his pulse, nor took
The usual steps,—(see Galen's book),—
  No difference 'twould have made
As piercing as electric fire
He ey'd him to his heart's desire.

"Monarch! I'll tell thee in a trice
    The thing that's needed here;
Though desperate may seem the advice,—
The case itself is very nice—
    And children dragons fear.
Devil must devil eat!—no more!—
Either a wife,—or hellebore!

" Whether she scold, or sportive play
    ('Tween these, no medium's known),
She'll drive the incubus away
That has assail'd thee many a day
    Upon thine iron throne.
She'll make the nimble spirits fleet
Up tow'rds the head, down tow'rds the feet."

Long may the doctor honour'd be
    Who let this saying fall!
He ought to have his effigy
By Phidias sculptur'd, so that he
    May be discern'd by all ;
A monument for ever thriving,
Boerhaave, Hippocrates, surviving!

   *   *   *   *

ACTÆON.

THY wife is destin'd to deceive thee !
She'll seek another's arms, and leave thee,
    And horns upon thy head will shortly sprout !
How dreadful, that, when bathing, thou shouldst see
        me
    (No æther-bath can wash the stigma out),
And then, in perfect innocence, shouldst flee me !

TRUST IN IMMORTALITY.

THE dead has risen here, to live thro' endless ages ;
This I with firmness trust and know.
I was first led to *guess* it by the sages,
The knaves convince me that 'tis *really* so.

REPROACH—TO LAURA.

MAIDEN, stay !—oh, whither wouldst thou go ?
Do I still or pride or grandeur show ?
    Maiden, was it right ?
Thou the giant mad'st a dwarf once more,
Scatter'dst far the mountains that of yore
    Climb'd to glory's sunny height.

Thou hast doom'd my flow'rets to decay,
All the phantoms bright hast blown away,
    Whose sweet follies form'd the hero's trust ;
All my plans that proudly rais'd their head
Thou dost, with thy gentle zephyr-tread,
    Prostrate, laughing, in the dust.

To the godhead, eagle-like, I flew,—
Smiling, fortune's juggling wheel to view,
    Careless wheresoe'er her ball might fly ;
Hov'ring far beyond Cocytus' wave,
Death and life receiving like a slave—
    Life and death from out one beaming eye !

Like the victors, who, with thunder-lance,
On the iron plain of glory dance,
    Starting from their mistress' breast,—
From Aurora's rosy bed upsprings
God's bright sun, to roam o'er towns of kings,
    And to make the young world blest !

Z

Tow'rd the hero doth this heart still strain?
Drink I, eagle, still the fiery rain
    Of thine eye, that burneth to destroy?
In the glances that destructive gleam,
Laura's LOVE I see with sweetness beam,—
    Weep to see it—like a boy!

My repose, like yonder image bright,
Dancing in the waters—cloudless, light,
    Maiden, hath been slain by thee!
On the dizzy height now totter I—
Laura—if from me—my Laura fly!
    Oh, the thought to madness hurries me!

Gladly shout the revellers as they quaff,
Raptures in the leaf-crown'd goblet laugh,
    Jests within the golden wine have birth.
Since the maiden hath enslav'd my mind,
I have left each youthful sport behind,
    Friendless roam I o'er the earth.

Hear I still bright glory's thunder-tone?
Doth the laurel still allure me on?
    Doth thy lyre, Apollo Cynthius?
In my breast no echoes now arise,
Ev'ry shame-fac'd muse in sorrow flies,—
    And thou, too, Apollo Cynthius?

Shall I still be, as a woman, tame?
Do my pulses, at my country's name,
    Proudly burst their prison-thralls?
Would I boast the eagle's soaring wing?
Do I long with Roman blood to spring,
    When my Hermann calls?

Oh, how sweet the eye's wild gaze divine!
Sweet to quaff the incense at that shrine!

Prouder, bolder, swells the breast.—
That which once set ev'ry sense on fire,
That which once could ev'ry nerve inspire,
    Scarce a half-smile now hath power to wrest!

That Orion might receive my fame,
On the time-flood's heaving waves my name
    Rock'd in glory in the mighty tide;
So that Kronos' dreaded scythe was shiver'd,
When against my monument it quiver'd,
    Tow'ring tow'rd the firmament in pride.

Smil'st thou?—No? To me nought's perish'd now!
Star and laurel I'll to fools allow,
    To the dead their marble cell;—
Love hath granted *all* as my reward,
High o'er man 'twere easy to have soar'd,
    So I love him well!

THE SIMPLE PEASANT.*

MATTHEW.

Gossip, you'll like to hear, no doubt!
A learned work has just come out—
Messias is the name 'twill bear;
The man has travell'd through the air,
And on the sun beplaster'd roads
Has lost shoe-leather by whole loads,—
Has seen the heavens lie open wide,
And hell has travers'd with whole hide.
The thought has just occurr'd to me
That one so skill'd as he must be
May tell us how our flax and wheat arise.
    What say you?—Shall I try to ascertain?

* A pointless satire upon Klopstock and his *Messias*.

LUKE.

You fool, to think that any one so wise
　About mere flax and corn would rack his brain.

THE MESSIAD.

RELIGION 'twas produced this poem's fire;
Perverted also?—prithee, don't inquire!

MAN'S DIGNITY.

I AM a man!—Let ev'ry one
　Who is a man too, spring
With joy beneath God's shining sun,
　And leap on high, and sing!

To God's own image fair on earth
　Its stamp I've power to show;
Down to the front, where heaven has birth,
　With boldness I dare go.

'Tis well that I both dare and can!
　When I a maiden see,
A voice exclaims: thou art a man!
　I kiss her tenderly.

And redder then the maiden grows,
　Her bodice seems too tight—
That I'm a man the maiden knows,
　Her bodice therefore's tight.

Will she, perchance, for pity cry,
　If unawares she's caught?
She finds that I'm a man—then, why
　By her is pity sought?

I am a man; and if alone
  She sees me drawing near,
I make the emperor's daughter run,
  Though ragged I appear.

This golden watchword wins the smile
  Of many a princess fair;
They call—ye'd best look out the while,
  Ye gold-laced fellows there!

That I'm a man, is fully shown
  Whene'er my lyre I sweep;
It thunders out a glorious tone—
  It otherwise would creep.

The spirit that my veins now hold,
  My manhood calls its brother!
And both command, like lions bold,
  And fondly greet each other.

From out this same creative flood
  From which we men have birth,
Both godlike strength and genius bud,
  And ev'ry thing of worth.

My talisman all tyrants hates,
  And strikes them to the ground;
Or guides us gladly through life's gates
  To where the dead are found.

E'en Pompey, at Pharsalia's fight,
  My talisman o'erthrew;
On German sand it hurl'd with might
  Rome's sensual children too.

Didst see the Roman, proud and stern,
  Sitting on Afric's shore?
His eyes like Hecla seem to burn,
  And fiery flames outpour.

Then comes a frank and merry knave,
  And spreads it through the land:
"Tell them that thou on Carthage' grave
  Hast seen great Marius stand!"

Thus speaks the son of Rome with pride,
  Still mighty in his fall;
He is a man, and nought beside, —
  Before him tremble all.

His grandsons afterwards began
  Their portions to o'erthrow,
And thought it well that ev'ry man
  Should learn with grace to crow.

For shame, for shame,—once more for
    shame!
  The wretched ones!—they've even
Squander'd the tokens of their fame,
  The choicest gifts of Heaven.

God's counterfeit has sinfully
  Disgrac'd his form divine,
And in his vile humanity
  Has wallow'd like the swine.

The face of earth each vainly treads,
  Like gourds, that boys in sport
Have hollow'd out to human heads,
  With skulls, whose brains are—nought!

Like wine that by a chemist's art
  Is through retorts refin'd,
Their spirits to the deuce depart,
  The phlegma's left behind.

From ev'ry woman's face they fly,
  Its very aspect dread,—
And if they dar'd—and could not—why,
  'Twere better they were dead.

*   *   *   *

They shun all worthies when they can,
  Grief at their joy they prove—
The man who cannot make a man,
  A man can never love!

The world I proudly wander o'er,
  And plume myself and sing:
I am a man!—Whoe'er is more?
  Then leap on high and spring!

HYMN TO THE ETERNAL.

'Twixt the heavens and earth, high in the airy ocean,
In the tempest's cradle I'm borne with a rocking motion;
    Clouds are tow'ring,
    Storms beneath me are low'ring,
Giddily all the wonders I see,
And, O Eternal, I think of Thee!

All Thy terrible pomp, lend to the Finite now,
Mighty Nature! Oh, of Infinity, thou
    Giant daughter!
    Mirror God, as in water!
Tempest, oh, let thine organ-peal
God to the reasoning worm reveal!

Hark! it peals—how the rocks quiver beneath its growls!
Zebaoth's glorious name, wildly the hurricane howls!
    Graving the while
    With the lightning's style:
"Creatures, do ye acknowledge Me?"—
Spare us, Lord! We acknowledge Thee!

THOUGHTS ON THE 1st OCTOBER, 1781.

WHAT mean the joyous sounds from yonder vine-clad
    height?
    What the exulting Evoë?*
Why glows the cheek? Whom is't that I, with pinions
    light,
    Swinging the lofty Thyrsus see?

Is it the Genius whom the gladsome throng obeys?
    Do I his numerous train descry?
In plenty's teeming horn the gifts of Heaven he sways,
    And reels from very ecstasy!—

See how the golden grape in glorious beauty shines,
    Kiss'd by the earliest morning-beams!
The shadow of yon bow'r, how lovingly it signs,
    As it with countless blessings teams!

Ha! glad October, thou art welcome unto me!—
    October's first-born, welcome thou!
Thanks of a purer kind, than all who worship thee,
    More heartfelt thanks I'm bringing now!

For thou to me the one whom I have lov'd so well,
    And love with fondness to the grave,
Who merits in my heart for evermore to dwell,—
    The best of friends in Rieger † gave.

'Tis true thy breath doth rock the leaves upon the trees,
    And sadly make their charms decay;
Gently they fall:—and swift, as morning phantasies
    With those who waken, fly away.

---

* Schiller, who is not very particular about the quantities of classical names, gives this word with the *o* long—which is, of course, the correct quantity—in *The Gods of Greece* (see page 73).

† A well-known General, who died in 1783.

'Tis true that on thy track the fleecy spoiler hastes,
    Who makes all nature's chords resound
With discord dull, and turns the plains and groves to
    wastes,
    So that they sadly mourn around.

See how the gloomy forms of years, as on they roll,
    Each joyous banquet overthrows,
When, in uplifted hand, from out the foaming bowl,
    Joy's noble purple brightly flows!

See how they disappear, when friends sweet converse hold,
    And loving wander arm-in-arm ;
And, to revenge themselves on winter's north wind cold,
    Upon each other's breasts grow warm!

And when Spring's children smile upon us once again,
    When all the youthful splendour bright,
When each melodious note of each sweet rapturous strain
    Awakens with it each delight :

How joyous then the stream that our whole soul per-
    vades !
    What life from out our glances pours !
Sweet Philomela's song, resounding through the glades,
    Ourselves, our youthful strength restores !

Oh, may this whisper breathe—(let Rieger bear in
    mind
    The storm by which in age we're bent!)—
His guardian angel, when the evening star so kind
    Gleams softly from the firmament!

In silence be he led to yonder thund'ring height,
  And guided be his eye, that he,
In valley and on plain, may see his friends aright,
  And that, with growing ecstasy,

On yonder holy spot, when he their number tells,
  He may experience friendship's bliss,
Now first unveil'd, until with pride his bosom swells,
  Conscious that all their love is his.

Then will the distant voice be loudly heard to say :
  " And G—, too, is a friend of thine !
When silv'ry locks no more around his temples play,
  G— still will be a friend of thine !

" E'en yonder "—and now in his eye the crystal tear
  Will gleam—" e'en yonder he will love !
Love *thee* too, when his heart, in yonder spring-like
    sphere,
  Link'd on to thine, can rapture prove ! "

THE WIRTEMBERGER.

THE name of Wirtemberg they hold
To come from *Wirth am Berg*,* I'm told.
A Wirtemberger who ne'er drinks
No Wirtemberger is, methinks!

* The Landlord on the Mountain.

THE PLAGUE.

A PHANTASY.

PLAGUE's contagious murderous breath
   God's strong might with terror reveals,
As through the dreary valley of death
   With its brotherhood fell it steals!

Fearfully throbs the anguish-struck heart,
   Horribly quivers each nerve in the frame;
   Frenzy's wild laughs the torment proclaim,
Howling convulsions disclose the fierce smart.

Fierce delirium writhes upon the bed—
Poisonous mists hang o'er the cities dead;
   Men all haggard, pale, and wan,
   To the shadow-realm press on.
Death lies brooding in the humid air,
Plague, in dark graves, piles up treasures fair,
   And its voice exultingly raises.
Funeral silence—churchyard calm,
Rapture change to dread alarm.—
   Thus the plague GOD wildly praises!

THE MOLE.

HUSBAND.

THE boy's my very image! See!
   Even the scars my small-pox left me!

WIFE.

I can believe it easily:
   They once of all my senses reft me.

MONUMENT OF MOOR THE ROBBER.*

'Tis ended!
Welcome! 'tis ended!
Oh thou sinner majestic,
All thy terrible part is now play'd!

Noble abas'd one!
Thou, of thy race beginner and ender!
Wondrous son of her fearfulest humour,
Mother Nature's blunder sublime!

Through cloud-cover'd night a radiant gleam!
Hark how behind him the portals are closing!
Night's gloomy jaws veil him darkly in shade!
Nations are trembling,
At his destructive splendour afraid!
Thou art welcome!   'Tis ended!
Oh thou sinner majestic,
All thy terrible part is now play'd!

Crumble,—decay
In the cradle of wide-open heaven!
Terrible sight to each sinner that breathes,
When the hot thirst for glory
Raises its barriers OVER AGAINST THE DREAD THRONE!
See! to eternity shame has consign'd thee!
To the bright stars of fame
Thou hast clamber'd aloft, on the shoulders of shame!
Yet time will come when shame will crumble beneath
thee,
When admiration at length will be thine!

* See the play of *The Robbers.*

With moist eye, by thy sepulchre dreaded,
    Man has pass'd onward—
Rejoice in the tears that man sheddeth,
    Oh thou soul of the judg'd!
With moist eye, by thy sepulchre dreaded,
    Lately a maiden pass'd onward,
    Hearing the fearful announcement
Told of thy deeds by the herald of marble;
And the maiden—rejoice thee! rejoice thee!
    Sought not to dry up her tears.
Far away I stood as the pearls were falling,
    And I shouted: Amalia!

    Oh, ye youths! Oh, ye youths!
With the dangerous lightning of Genius
    Learn to play with more caution!
Wildly his bit champs the charger of Phœbus;
    Though, 'neath the reins of his master,
More gently he rocks Earth and Heaven,
    Rein'd by a child's hand, he kindles
Earth and Heaven in blazing destruction!
    Obstinate Phaëton perish'd,
    Buried beneath the sad wreck.

    Child of the heavenly Genius!
    Glowing bosom all panting for action!
    Art thou charm'd by the tale of my robber
Glowing like thine was his bosom, and panting for
    action!
He, like thee, was the child of the heavenly Genius.
    But thou smilest and go'st—
    Thy gaze flies through the realms of the world's long
    story,
    Moor the robber it finds not there—
    Stay, thou youth, and smile not!
    Still survive all his sins and his shame—
Robber Moor liveth—in all but name.

QUIRL.

You tell me that you feel surprise
Because Quirl's paper's grown in size;
And yet they're crying through the street
That there's a rise in bread and meat.

THE BAD MONARCHS.*

EARTHLY gods—my lyre shall win your praise,
Though but wont its gentle sounds to raise
    When the joyous feast the people throng;
Softly, at your pompous-sounding names,
Shyly round your greatness' purple flames,
    Trembles now my song.

Answer! shall I strike the golden string,
When, borne on by exultation's wing,
    O'er the battle-field your chariots trail?
When ye, from the iron grasp set free,
For your mistress' soft arms, joyously
    Change your pond'rous mail?—

Shall my daring hymn, ye gods, resound,
While the golden splendour gleams around,
    Where, by mystic darkness overcome,
With the thunderbolt your spleen may play,
Or in crime humanity array,
    Till—the grave is dumb?

* Written in consequence of the ill-treatment Schiller experienced at the hands of the Grand Duke Charles of Wirtemberg.

Say! shall peace 'neath crowns be now my theme?
Shall I boast, ye princes, that ye *dream?*—
    While the worm the monarch's heart may tear,
Golden sleep twines round the Moor by stealth,
As he, at the palace, guards the wealth,
    Guards—but covets ne'er.

Show how kings and galley-slaves, my Muse,
Lovingly one single pillow use,—
    How their lightnings flatter, when suppress'd,
When their humours have no power to harm,
When their mimic Minotaurs are calm,
    And—the lions rest!

Up, thou Hecate! with thy magic seal
Make the barr'd-up grave its wealth reveal,—
    Hark! its doors like thunder open spring!
When death's dismal blast is heard to sigh,
And the hair on end stands fearfully,
    Princes' bliss I sing!

Do I here the strand, the coast, detect
Where your wishes' haughty fleet was wreck'd,—
    Where was stay'd your greatness' proud career?
That they ne'er with glory may grow warm,
Night, with black and terror-spreading arm,
    Forges monarchs here.

On the death-chest sadly gleams the crown,
With its heavy load of pearls weigh'd down,
    And the sceptre, needed now no more.
In what splendour is the mould array'd!
Yet but worms are with the body paid,
    That—the world watch'd o'er.

Haughty plants within that humble bed!
See how death their pomp decay'd and fled
    With unblushing ribaldry besets!

They who rul'd o'er north and east and west
Suffer now his ev'ry nauseous jest,
          And—no sultan threats?

Leap for joy, ye stubborn dumb, to-day,
And your heavy slumber shake away!
          From the battle, victory upsprings!
Hearken to the trump's exulting song!
Ye are worshipp'd by the shouting throng!—
          Rouse ye, then, ye kings!

Seven sleepers!—to the clarion hark!
How it rings, and how the fierce dogs bark!
          Shots from out a thousand barrels whizz;
Eager steeds are neighing for the wood,—
Soon the bristly boar rolls in his blood,—
          Yours the triumph is!

But what now?—Are even princes dumb?
Tow'rd me scornful echoes ninefold come,
          Stealing through the vault's terrific gloom—
Sleep assails the page by slow degrees,
And Madonna gives to you the keys
          Of—her sleeping-room.

Not an answer—hush'd and still is all—
Does the veil, then, e'en on monarchs fall,
          Which enshrouds their humble flatt'rers' glance?
And ye ask for worship in the dust,
Since the blind jade, Fate, a world has thrust
          In your purse, perchance?

And ye clatter, giant puppet-troops,
Marshall'd in your proudly childish groups,
          Like the juggler on the opera scene?—
Though the sound may please the vulgar ear,
Yet the skilful, fill'd with sadness, jeer
          Powers so great, but mean.

*   *   *   *

Let your tow'ring shame be hid from sight
In the garment of a sovereign's right,
 From the ambush of the throne outspring !
Tremble, though, before the voice of song :
Through the purple, vengeance will, ere long,
 Strike down e'en a king !

THE PEASANTS.*

Look outside, good friend, I pray !
 Two whole mortal hours
Dogs and I've out here to-day
 Waited, by the powers !

Rain comes down as from a spout,
Doomsday-storms rage round about,
 Dripping are my hose ;
Drench'd are coat and mantle too,
Coat and mantle, both just new,
 Wretched plight, Heav'n knows !
Pretty stir's abroad to-day ;
Look outside, good friend, I pray !

Ay, the devil ! look outside !
 Out is blown my lamp,—
Gloom and night the heavens now hide,
 Moon and stars decamp.
Stumbling over stock and stone,
 Jerkin, coat, I've torn, ochone !
 Let me pity beg !
Hedges, bushes, all around,
Here a ditch, and there a mound,
 Breaking arm and leg.

* Written in the Suabian dialect.

2 A

Gloom and night the heavens now hide!
Ay, the devil! look outside!

Ay, the deuce, then look outside!
   Listen to my prayer!
Praying, singing, I have tried,
   Wouldst thou have me swear?
I shall be a steaming mass,
Freeze to rock and stone, alas!
   If I don't remove.
All this, love, I owe to thee,
   Winter-bumps thou'lt make for me,
   Thou confounded love!
Cold and gloom spread far and wide!
Ay, the deuce! then look outside!

Thousand thunders! what's this now
   From the window shoots?
Oh, thou witch! 'Tis dirt, I vow,
   That my head salutes!
Rain, frost, hunger, tempests wild,
Bear I for the devil's child,
   Now I'm vex'd full sore.
Worse and worse 'tis! I'll begone.
Pray be quick, thou Evil One!
   I'll remain no more.
Pretty tumult there's outside!
   Fare thee well—I'll homeward stride.

THE SATYR AND MY MUSE.

An aged satyr sought
   Around my Muse to pass,
Attempting to pay court,
   And eyed her fondly through his glass.

By Phœbus' golden torch,
    By Luna's pallid light,
Around her temple's porch
    Crept the unhappy sharp-ear'd wight;

And warbled many a lay,
    Her beauty's praise to sing,
And fiercely scrap'd away
    On his discordant fiddle-string.

With tears, too, swell'd his eyes,
    As large as nuts, or larger;
He gasp'd forth heavy sighs,
    Like music from Silenus' charger.

The Muse sat still, and play'd
    Within her grotto fair,
And peevishly survey'd
    Signor Adonis Goatsfoot there.

" Who ever would kiss thee,
    Thou ugly, dirty dunce?
Wouldst thou a gallant be,
    As Midas was Apollo once?

"Speak out, old hornèd boor!
    What charms canst thou display?
Thou'rt swarthy as a Moor,
    And shaggy as a beast of prey.

" I'm by a bard ador'd
    In far Teutonia's land;
To him, who strikes the chord,
    I'm link'd in firm and loving band."

She spoke, and straightway fled
    The spoiler,—he pursued her,
And, by his passion led,
    Soon caught her, shouted, and thus
        woo'd her:

2 A 2

" Thou prudish one, stay, stay !
    And hearken unto me !
Thy poet, I dare say,
    Repents the pledge he gave to thee.

" Behold this pretty thing,—
    No merit would I claim,—
Its weight I often fling
    On many a clown's back, to his shame.

" His sharpness it increases,
    And spices his discourse,
Instilling learned theses,
    When mounted on his hobby-horse.

" The best of songs are known,
    Thanks to this heavy whip ;
Yet fool's blood 'tis alone
    We see beneath its lashes drip.

" This lash, then, shall be his,
    If thou'lt give me a smack ;
Then thou may'st hasten, miss,
    Upon thy German sweetheart's track."

The Muse, with purpose sly,
    Ere long agreed to yield—
The satyr said good bye,
    And now the lash *I* wield !

And I won't drop it here,
    Believe in what I say !
The kisses of one's dear
    One does not lightly throw away.

They kindle raptures sweet,
    But fools ne'er know their flame !
The gentle Muse will kneel at honour's feet,
    But cudgels those who mar her fame.

THE WINTER NIGHT.

Farewell! the beauteous sun is sinking fast,
    The moon lifts up her head ;
Farewell! mute night o'er earth's wide round at last
    Her darksome raven-wing has spread.

Across the wintry plain no echoes float,
    Save, from the rock's deep womb,
The murmuring streamlet, and the screech-owl's note,
    Arising from the forest's gloom.

The fish repose within the watery deeps,
    The snail draws in his head ;
The dog beneath the table calmly sleeps,
    My wife is slumb'ring in her bed.

A hearty welcome to ye, brethren mine !
    Friends of my life's young spring !
Perchance around a flask of Rhenish wine
    Ye're gather'd now, in joyous ring.

The brimming goblet's bright and purple beams
    Mirror the world with joy,
And pleasure from the golden grape-juice gleams—
    Pleasure untainted by alloy.

Conceal'd behind departed years, your eyes
    Find roses now alone ;
And, as the summer tempest quickly flies,
    Your heavy sorrows, too, are flown.

From childish sports, to e'en the doctor's hood,
    The book of life ye thumb,
And reckon o'er, in light and joyous mood,
    Your toils in the Gymnasium ;

Ye count the oaths that Terence—may he ne'er,
    Though buried, calmly slumber!—
Caus'd you, despite Minelli's notes, to swear,—
    Count your wry faces without number.

How, when the dread examinations came,
    The boy with terror shook!
How, when the rector had pronounc'd his name,
    The sweat stream'd down upon his book!

   *   *   *   *

All this is now involv'd in mist for ever,
    The boy is now a man,
And Frederick, wiser grown, discloses never
    What little Fritz once lov'd to plan.

At length—a doctor one's declar'd to be,—
    A regimental one!
And then,—and not too soon,—discover we
    That plans soap-bubbles are alone.*

Blow on! blow on! and let the bubbles rise,
    If but this heart remain!
And if a German laurel as the prize
    Of song, 'tis given me to gain!

---

* An allusion to the appointment of regimental surgeon, con-
ferred upon Schiller by the Grand Duke Charles in 1780, when he
was 21 years of age.

APPENDIX:

CONTAINING

TRANSLATIONS OF THE VARIOUS POEMS, ETC.,

COMPRISED IN

SCHILLER'S DRAMATIC WORKS.

APPENDIX.

THE following variations appear in the first two verses of
Hector's Farewell (see page 1), as given in *The Robbers,*
act ii. scene 2.

ANDROMACHE.

WILT thou, Hector, leave me?—leave me weeping,
Where Achilles' murderous blade is heaping
   Bloody off'rings on Patroclus' grave?
Who, alas, will teach thine infant truly
Spears to hurl, the gods to honour duly,
   When thou'rt buried 'neath dark Xanthus' wave?

HECTOR.

Dearest wife, go,—fetch my death-spear glancing,
Let me join the battle-dance entrancing,
   For my shoulders bear the weight of Troy!
Heaven will be our Astyanax' protector!
Falling as his country's saviour, Hector
   Soon will greet thee in the realms of joy.

THE following additional verse is found in *Amalia's Song*
(see page 2), as sung in *The Robbers,* act iii. scene 1.
It is introduced between the first and second verses, as
they appear in the Poems.

HIS embrace—what madd'ning rapture bound us!—
   Bosom throbb'd 'gainst bosom with wild might;
Mouth and ear were chain'd—night reign'd around us —
   And the spirit wing'd tow'rd heaven its flight.

From *The Robbers*, act iv. scene 5.

CHORUS OF ROBBERS.

WHAT so good for banishing sorrow
    As women, theft, and bloody affray?
We must dance in the air to-morrow,
    Therefore let's be right merry to-day!

A free and jovial life we've led,
    Ever since we began it.
Beneath the tree we make our bed,
We ply our task when the storm's o'erhead,
    And deem the moon our planet.
The fellow we swear by is Mercury,
A capital hand at our trade is he.

To-day we become the guests of a priest,
    A rich farmer to-morrow must feed us;
And as for the future, we care not the least,
    But leave it to Heaven to heed us.

And when our throats with a vintage rare
    We've long enough been supplying,
Fresh courage and strength we drink in there,
And with the Evil One friendship swear,
    Who down in hell is frying.

The groans o'er fathers reft of breath,
The sorrowing mothers' cry of death,
Deserted brides' sad sobs and tears,
Are sweetest music to our ears.

Ha! when under the axe each one quivering lies,
When they bellow like calves, and fall round us
        like flies,
    Nought gives such pleasure to our sight,
    It fills our ears with wild delight.

And when arrives the fatal day
    The devil straight may fetch us !
Our fee we get without delay—
    They instantly Jack-Ketch us.
One draught upon the road of liquor bright and clear,
And hip ! hip ! hip ! hurrah ! we're seen no longer here !

From *The Robbers*, act iv. scene 5.

MOOR'S SONG.

BRUTUS.

Ye are welcome, peaceful realms of light !
    Oh, receive Rome's last-surviving son !
From Philippi, from the murderous fight,
    Come I now, my race of sorrow run.—
Cassius, where art thou ?—Rome overthrown !
    All my brethren's loving band destroy'd !
Safety find I at death's door alone,
    And the world to Brutus is a void !

CÆSAR.

Who now, with the ne'er-subdued-one's tread,
    Hither from yon rocks makes haste to come ? —
Ha ! if by no vision I'm misled,
    'Tis the footstep of a child of Rome.—
Son of Tiber—whence dost thou appear ?
    Stands the seven-hill'd city as of yore ?
Oft her orphan'd lot awakes my tear,
    For, alas, her Cæsar is no more !

BRUTUS.

Ha! thou with the three-and-twenty wounds!
   Who hath, dead one, summon'd thee to light?
Back to gaping Orcus' fearful bounds,
   Haughty mourner! Triumph not to-night!
On Philippi's iron altar, lo!
   Reeks now Freedom's final victim's blood;
Rome o'er Brutus' bier feels her death-throe,—
   He seeks Minos.—Back to thy dark flood!

CÆSAR.

Oh, the death-stroke Brutus' sword then hurl'd!
   Thou, too—Brutus—thou? Could this thing be?
Son!—It was thy father!—Son! The world
   Would have fallen heritage to thee!
Go—'mongst Romans thou art deem'd immortal,
   For thy steel hath pierc'd thy father's breast.
Go—and shout it even to yon portal:
" Brutus is 'mongst Romans deem'd immortal,
   For his steel hath pierc'd his father's breast."
Go—thou know'st now what on Lethe's strand
Made me as a prisoner stand.——
Now, grim steersman, push thy bark from land!

BRUTUS.

Father, stay!—In all earth's realms so fair,
   It hath been my lot to know but one,
Who with mighty Cæsar could compare;
   And of yore thou calledst *him* thy son.
None but Cæsar could a Rome o'erthrow,
   Brutus only made great Cæsar fear;
Where lives Brutus, Cæsar's blood must flow;
   If thy path lies *yonder*, mine is *here*.

From *Wallenstein's Camp*, scene 7.

RECRUIT'S SONG.

How sweet the wild sound
　Of drum and of fife!
To roam o'er earth's round,
　Lead a wandering life,
With a steed train'd aright,
And bold for the fight,
With a sword by the side,
To rove far and wide,—
Quick, nimble, and free
As the finch that we see
On bushes and trees,
Or braving the breeze,—
Huzza, then! the Friedlander's banner for me!

From *Wallenstein's Camp*, scene the last.

SECOND CUIRASSIER *sings*.

Up, up, my brave comrades! to horse! to horse!
　Let us haste to the field and to freedom!
To the field, for 'tis *there* that is prov'd our hearts' force,
　'Tis *there* that in earnest we need 'em!
None other can *there* our places supply,
Each must stand alone,—on himself must rely.

CHORUS.

None other can there our places supply,
Each must stand alone,—on himself must rely.

DRAGOON.

Now freedom appears from the world to have flown,
  None but lords and their vassals one traces ;
While falsehood and cunning are ruling alone
  O'er the living cowardly races.
The man who can look upon death without fear—
The soldier,—is now the sole freeman left here.

CHORUS.

The man who can look upon death without fear—
The soldier,—is now the sole freeman left here.

FIRST YAGER.

The cares of this life, he casts them away,
  Untroubled by fear or by sorrow ;
He rides to his fate with a countenance gay,
  And finds it to-day or to-morrow ;
And if 'tis to-morrow, to-day we'll employ
To drink full deep of the goblet of joy,

CHORUS.

And if 'tis to-morrow, to-day we'll employ
To drink full deep of the goblet of joy.
          [*They re-fill their glasses, and drink.*

CAVALRY SERGEANT.

The skies o'er him shower his lot fill'd with mirth,
  He gains, without toil, its full measure ;
The peasant, who grubs in the womb of the earth,
  Believes that he'll find there the treasure.
Through lifetime he shovels and digs like a slave,
And digs—till at length he has dug his own grave.

CHORUS.

Through lifetime he shovels and digs like a slave,
And digs—till at length he has dug his own grave.

FIRST YAGER.

The horseman, as well as his swift-footed beast,
   Are guests by whom all are affrighted.
When glimmer the lamps at the wedding feast,
   In the banquet he joins uninvited;
He woos not long, and with gold he ne'er buys,
But carries by storm love's blissful prize.

CHORUS.

He woos not long, and with gold he ne'er buys,
But carries by storm love's blissful prize.

SECOND CUIRASSIER.

Why weeps the maiden? Why sorrows she so?
   Let me hence, let me hence, girl, I pray thee!
The soldier on earth no sure quarters can know;
   With *true* love he ne'er can repay thee.
Fate hurries him onward with fury blind,
His peace he never can leave behind.

CHORUS.

Fate hurries him onward with fury blind,
His peace he never can leave behind.

FIRST YAGER.

*(Taking his two neighbours by the hand. The rest do
the same, forming a large semicircle.)*

Away, then, my comrades, our chargers let's mount!
   In the battle the bosom bounds lightly!
Youth boils, and life's goblet still foams at the fount,
   Away! while the spirit glows brightly!
Unless ye have courage your life to stake,
That life ye never your own can make!

CHORUS.

Unless ye have courage your life to stake,
That life ye never your own can make!

From *William Tell*, act i. scene 1.

SCENE—*The high rocky shore of the Lake of Lucerne, opposite
Schwytz.*

*The Lake forms an inlet in the land; a cottage is near the shore;
a Fisher-boy is rowing in a boat. Beyond the Lake are seen the
green pastures, the villages, and farms of Schwytz, glowing in the
sunshine. On the left of the spectator are the peaks of the Hacken,
enveloped in clouds; on his right, in the distance, are seen the
glaciers. Before the curtain rises, the RANZ DES VACHES and
the musical sound of the cattle-bells are heard, and continue also
for some time after the scene opens.*

FISHER-BOY (*sings in his boat*).

AIR—*Ranz des Vaches.*

BRIGHT smiles the lake, as it woos to its deep,—
A boy on its margin of green lies asleep;
 Then hears he a strain,
  Like the flute's gentle note,
 Sweet as voices of angels
  In Eden that float.
And when he awakens, with ecstasy blest,
The waters are playing all over his breast.
 From the depths calls a voice:
  " Dearest child, with me go!
 I lure down the sleeper,
  I draw him below."

HERDSMAN (*on the mountain*).

AIR—*Variation of the Ranz des Vaches.*

Ye meadows, farewell!
  Ye pastures so glowing!
  The herdsman is going,
For summer has fled!
We depart to the mountain; we'll come back again,
When the cuckoo is calling,—when wakens the strain,—
When the earth is trick'd out with her flowers so gay,
When the stream sparkles bright in the sweet month of
  May.
      Ye meadows, farewell!
        Ye pastures so glowing!
        The herdsman is going,
      For summer has fled!

CHAMOIS-HUNTER (*appearing on the top of a rock*).

AIR—*Second Variation of the Ranz des Vaches.*

O'er the heights growls the thunder, while quivers the
  bridge,
Yet no fear feels the hunter, though dizzy the ridge;
      He strides on undaunted,
        O'er plains icy-bound,
      Where spring never blossoms,
        Nor verdure is found;
And, a broad sea of mist lying under his feet,
Man's dwellings his vision no longer can greet:
      The world he but views
        When the clouds broken are,—
      With its pastures so green,
        Through the vapour afar.

From *William Tell*, act iii. scene 1.

Walter *sings.*

Bow and arrow bearing,
  Over hills and streams
Moves the hunter daring,
  Soon as daylight gleams.

As all flying creatures
  Own the eagle's sway,
So the hunter, nature's
  Mounts and crags obey.

Over space he reigneth,
  And he makes his prize
All his bolt attaineth,
  All that creeps or flies.

From *William Tell*, act iv. scene 3.

CHORUS OF BROTHERS OF MERCY.

DEATH comes to man with hasty stride,
  No respite is to him e'er given ;
He's stricken down in manhood's pride,
  E'en in mid race from earth he's driven.
Prepar'd, or not, to go from here,
Before his Judge he must appear !

From *Turandot*, act ii. scene 4.

RIDDLE.

THE tree whereon decay
  All those from mortals sprung,—
Full old, and yet whose spray
  Is ever green and young;
To catch the light, it rolls
  Each leaf upon one side;
The other, black as coals,
  The sun has ne'er descried.

It places on new rings
  As often as it blows;
The age, too, of all things
  To mortal gaze it shows.
Upon its bark so green
  A name oft meets the eye,
Yet 'tis no longer seen,
  When it grows old and dry.
This tree—what can it mean?
  I wait for thy reply.*

From *Mary Stuart*, act iii. scene 1.

SCENE—*A Park.* MARY *advances hastily from behind some trees.*
HANNAH KENNEDY *follows her slowly.*

MARY.

LET me my newly-won liberty taste!
  Let me rejoice as a child once again!
And as on pinions, with airy foot haste
  Over the tapestried green of the plain!

* The year.

Have I escap'd from my prison so drear?
　Shall I no more in my sad dungeon pine?
Let me in long and in thirsty draughts here
　Drink in the breezes, so free, so divine!

*　　　*　　　*　　　*

Thanks, thanks, ye trees, in smiling verdure dress'd,
　In that ye veil my prison-walls from sight!
I'll dream that I am free and blest:
　Why should I waken from a dream so bright?
Do not the spacious heavens encompass me?
Behold! my gaze, unshackled, free,
　Pierces with joy the trackless realms of light!
There, where the grey-ting'd hills of mist project,
　My kingdom's boundaries begin;
Yon clouds, that tow'rd the south their course direct,
　France's far-distant ocean seek to win.

Swift-flying clouds, hardy sailors through air!
Mortal hath roam'd with ye, sail'd with ye, ne'er!
Greetings of love to my youthful home bear!
I am a prisoner, I am in chains,
Ah, not a herald, save *ye*, now remains!
Free through the air hath your path ever been,
Ye are not subject to England's proud queen!

*　　　*　　　*　　　*

Yonder's a fisherman trimming his boat.
　E'en that frail skiff from all danger might tear me,
　And to the dwellings of friends it might bear me.
Scarcely his earnings can keep life afloat.
Richly with treasures his lap I'd heap over,—
　Oh! what a draught should reward him to-day!
Fortune held fast in his nets he'd discover,
　If in his bark he would take me away!

*　　　*　　　*　　　*

Hear'st thou the horn of the hunter resound,
  Wak'ning the echo through forest and plain?
Ah, on my spirited courser to bound!
  Once more to join in the mirth-stirring train!
  Hark! how the dearly-lov'd tones come again!
Blissful, yet sad, the remembrance they wake;
  Oft have they fallen with joy on mine ear,
  When in the highlands the bugle rang clear,
Rousing the chase over mountain and brake.

From *The Maid of Orleans*, Prologue, scene 4.

JOAN OF ARC (*soliloquizing*).

FAREWELL, ye mountains, and ye pastures dear,
  Ye still and happy valleys, fare ye well!
No longer may Joan's footsteps linger here,
  Joan bids ye now a long, a last farewell!
Ye meadows that I water'd, and each bush
Set by my hands, ne'er may your verdure fail!
Farewell, ye grots, ye springs that cooling gush!
  Thou echo, blissful voice of this sweet vale,
So wont to give me back an answering strain,—
Joan must depart, and ne'er return again!

Ye haunts of all my silent joys of old,
  I leave ye now behind for evermore!
Disperse, ye lambs, far o'er the trackless wold!
  She now hath gone who tended you of yore!
I must away to guard *another* fold,
  On yonder field of danger, stain'd with gore.
Thus am I bidden by a spirit's tone:
'Tis no vain earthly longing drives me on.

For He who erst to Moses on the height
  Of Horeb, in the fiery bush came down,
And bade him stand in haughty Pharaoh's sight,—
  He who made choice of Jesse's pious son,
The shepherd, as His champion in the fight,—
  He who to shepherds grace hath ever shown,—
He thus address'd me from this lofty tree :
" Go hence ! On earth my witness thou shalt be !

" In rugged brass, then, clothe thy members now,
  In steel thy gentle bosom must be dress'd !
No mortal love thy heart must e'er allow,
  With earthly passion's sinful flame possess'd.
Ne'er will the bridal wreath adorn thy brow,
  No darling infant blossom on thy breast ;
Yet thou with warlike honours shalt be laden,
Raising thee high above each earthly maiden.

" For when the bravest in the fight despair,
  When France appears to wait her final blow,
Then thou my holy Oriflamme must bear ;
  And, as the ripen'd corn the reapers mow,
Hew down the conqueror as he triumphs there ;
  His fortune's wheel thou thus wilt overthrow,
To France's hero-sons salvation bring,
Deliver Rheims once more, and crown thy king !"

The Lord hath promis'd to send down a sign :
  A helmet He hath sent, it comes from *Him*,—
His sword endows mine arm with strength divine,
  I feel the courage of the cherubim ;
To join the battle-turmoil how I pine !
  A raging tempest thrills through ev'ry limb ;
The summons to the field bursts on mine ear,
My charger paws the ground, the trump rings clear.

From *The Maid of Orleans*, act iv. scene 1.

SCENE—*A hall prepared for a festival.*

*The pillars are covered with festoons of flowers; flutes and hautboys
are heard behind the scene.*

JOAN OF ARC (*soliloquizing*).

EACH weapon rests, war's tumults cease to sound,
  While dance and song succeed the bloody fray;
Through ev'ry street the merry footsteps bound,
  Altar and church are clad in bright array,
And gates of branches green arise around,
  Over the columns twine the garlands gay;
Rheims cannot hold the ever-swelling train
That seeks the nation-festival to gain.

All with *one* joyous feeling are elate,
  One single thought is thrilling ev'ry breast;
What, until now, was sever'd by fierce hate,
  Is by the general rapture truly bless'd.
By each who call'd this land his parent-state,
  The name of Frenchman proudly is confess'd;
The glory is reviv'd of olden days,
And to her regal son France homage pays.

Yet *I* who have achiev'd this work of pride,
  I cannot share the rapture felt by all;
My heart is chang'd, my heart is turn'd aside,
  It shuns the splendour of this festival;
'Tis in the British camp it seeks to hide,—
  'Tis on the foe my yearning glances fall;
And from the joyous circle I must steal,
My bosom's crime o'erpowering to conceal.

  Who? I? What! in my bosom chaste
    Can mortal's image have a seat?
  This heart, by heav'nly glory graced,—
    Dares it with earthly love to beat?

The saviour of my country, I,— '
The champion of the Lord Most High,
Own for my country's foe a flame—
To the chaste sun my guilt proclaim,
And not be crush'd beneath my shame?

*(The music behind the scene changes into a soft, melting
melody.)*

Woe! oh woe! what strains enthralling!
    How bewildering to mine ear!
Each *his* voice belov'd recalling,
    Charming up *his* image dear!

Would that battle-tempests bound me!
Would that spears were whizzing round me
    In the hotly-raging strife!
    Could my courage find fresh life!

How those tones, those voices blest
    Coil around my bosom burning!
All the strength within my breast
    Melting into tender yearning,
    Into tears of sadness turning!
      *   *   *   *

*(The flutes are again heard—she falls into a silent
melancholy.)*

Gentle crook! oh that I never
    For the sword had barter'd thee!
Sacred oak! why didst thou ever
    From thy branches speak to me?
Would that Thou to me in splendour,
    Queen of heav'n, hadst ne'er come down!
Take—all claim I must surrender,—
    Take, oh take away thy crown!

Ah, I open saw yon heaven,
    Saw the features of the blest!
Yet to earth my hopes are riven,
    In the skies they ne'er can rest!
Wherefore make me ply with ardour
    This vocation, terror-fraught?
Would this heart were render'd harder
    That by heaven to *feel* was taught!

To proclaim Thy might sublime
Those select, who, free from crime,
In Thy lasting mansions stand;
Send Thou forth Thy spirit-band,
The Immortal, and the Pure,
Feelingless, from tears secure!
Never choose a maiden fair,
Shepherdess' weak spirit ne'er!

Kings' dissensions wherefore dread I,
    Why the fortune of the fight?
Guilelessly my lambs once fed I
    On the silent mountain-height.
Yet Thou into life didst bear me,
    To the halls where monarchs throne,
In the toils of guilt to snare me—
    Ah, the choice was not mine own!

THE END.

LONDON: PRINTED BY WILLIAM CLOWES AND SONS, STAMFORD STREET
AND CHARING CROSS.